BEYOND BEYOND

BEYOND BEYOND

A Lute Bapcat Mystery

JOSEPH HEYWOOD

LYONS
PRESS

Guiford, Connecticut

An imprint of The Rowman & Littlefield Publishing Group, Inc.
4501 Forbes Blvd., Ste. 200
Lanham, MD 20706
www.rowman.com

Distributed by NATIONAL BOOK NETWORK

Maps by The Rowman & Littlefield Publishing Group, Inc.

British Library Cataloguing in Publication Information available

Library of Congress Control Number: 2020942495

ISBN 978-1-4930-5115-1 (cloth : alk. paper)
ISBN 978-1-4930-5116-8 (electronic)

∞™ The paper used in this publication meets the minimum requirements of American National Standard for Information Sciences—Permanence of Paper for Printed Library Materials, ANSI/ NISO Z39.48-1992.

For all who've been patiently asking for more of Lute,
Zakov, and the hard times they lived through.

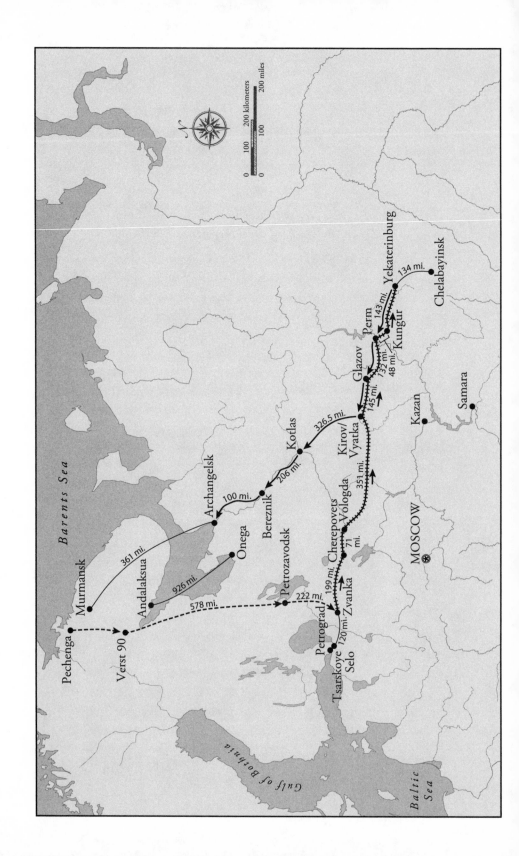

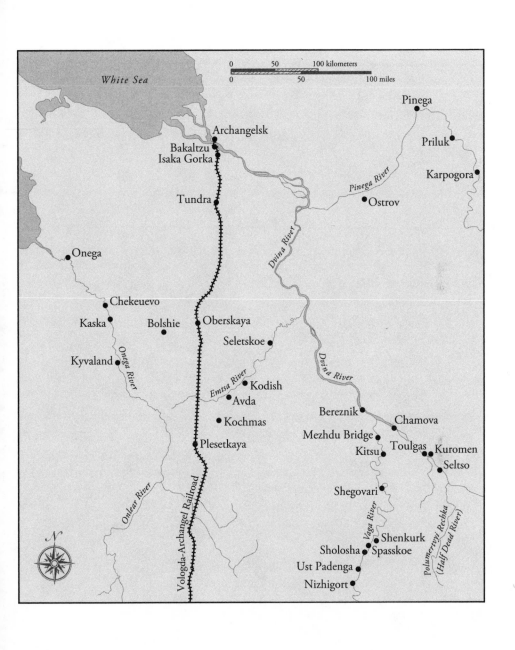

Part I: Beyond

So many things are lost and have disappeared. We think we know the past. We don't know the past. We know pieces of the past.

—*Stephen Greenblatt, quoted in* The Wall Street Journal

Late Fall, 1917. Washington Street Railroad Station, Marquette, Michigan

Roosevelt frowned. "Serving one's country isn't
complicated. You do it or you don't."

Lute Bapcat couldn't remember the last time he'd gone to Marquette for anything other than State business, or without his partner, Pinkhus Sergeyevich Zakov, but this was the case today. Bapcat found his mind on Nelson Blackfish, his new partner—six-foot-seven, a graduate of Carlyle College, which Blackfish claimed was an Indian school in Pennsylvania. The full-blooded Ojibwa had degrees in biology and botany and had appeared unannounced and unintroduced one day at the State cabin in Bumbletown. This was a month after Zakov went missing. The Russian had been there one day and gone the next, no good-byes, no explanations, nothing, just gone. Over their five-year partnership the Russian had been friend, roommate in the house the State rented for them, game warden partner, and, when Lute could face it, his first and best male friend.

But Zakov had fallen off the Earth, and Nellie Blackfish had shown up and gradually worked his way into game warden status. Like Zakov, the giant Ojibwa could survive in the wilderness and all weather conditions with no more than a knife for a tool and the clothes on his back.

Neither the Russian nor the Indian were with him today. Marquette sat on Lake Superior and was fetchingly beautiful, but the main language one heard was English, and Lute Bapcat felt more comfortable back in Red Jacket, where he never knew what language might come flying his way. Was this State business? No clue. All he knew for sure was that Colonel Theodore Roosevelt, leader of the Rough Riders and former president of the United States, wanted to see him and Jordy Klubishar.

The boy would soon be eighteen and had it in his head to volunteer for the army to go to France, and Bapcat wanted desperately to change the boy's mind. Not that he objected to service—he didn't—but Jordy was smart and ought to better himself before he went off to serve his country. His longtime girlfriend Jaquelle Frei believed this even more strongly than he. What he knew for certain was that war was not a lark for any man.

There was a civilian guard on the caboose platform of Roosevelt's personal train. Lute Bapcat climbed the metal steps and handed the man the letter, asking for the meeting.

"Cap'n Tope," Bapcat said, recognizing the old Rough Riders officer.

Tope said, "Got to say you look a lot more fit than the rest of our Cuba mob. The Colonel's inside. He's been real anxious to see you."

The man looked past Bapcat at his hulking shadow.

Bapcat said, "Jordy Klubishar. My ward."

The captain showed them into a mahogany-paneled car where Theodore Roosevelt sat squinting and scowling behind an immense shiny wooden desk. The former president looked up, grinning with gapped teeth, and, with some obvious effort, got to his feet.

"Corporal!"

The last time he'd seen Roosevelt, the Colonel had helped recruit him to Michigan's force of deputy game, fish, and forestry wardens. Later, Bapcat had recruited Zakov.

The Colonel looked good. The man rarely changed.

"Colonel."

All Rough Riders were expected to address Roosevelt as Colonel, rather than Mr. President.

"I take it that strapping young lad behind you is your ward, Jordy Klubishar?"

"Yessir, that's him." *How does he know about Jordy? Why does he know? Why does he want both of us here?* He didn't have a good feeling about this whole thing, and he hadn't bothered to let Jaquelle know. Usually he told her everything.

Roosevelt shook Jordy's hand and admired his size.

"You're a stout lad," the Colonel told the boy. "Big, strong, and fit. Good for you, young man. Enlisted yet?"

Jordy glanced nervously at Bapcat. "No, sir, but I mean to serve my country in France."

"Hmm," Roosevelt said. "Training at Fort Custer in Battle Creek?"

"I believe so," Jordy said. "Yes, sir."

Roosevelt looked at Bapcat. "You're in favor of him enlisting, Corporal?"

Why were they discussing this? "It's complicated."

Roosevelt frowned. "Serving one's country isn't complicated. You do it or you don't."

"We . . . my . . ." How did he describe his relationship with Jaquelle Frei, his girlfriend? It was more than boyfriend–girlfriend, but less than married. Even so, the courts had granted them joint custody of Jordy as their ward.

"We think he'd better serve his country by going to college and becoming a teacher."

The Colonel said, "We, meaning you and Miss Jaquelle Frei, the boy's other guardian?"

How did he know her name? What's going on here?

"Yessir," he managed.

"Teaching is a noble goal," Roosevelt said, "but citizens ought to serve their nation *before* they pursue personal goals. You afraid for the boy, Corporal?"

His fear wasn't theoretical. He had been to war, seen how random death could happen—as in the enemies he had shot. They would be alive one second and dead the next, with no clue it was even coming. He nodded rather than answered out loud, and Roosevelt nodded back at him. He understood, too.

"I hope to sign up next week," Jordy offered, but neither of the older men paid any attention.

Roosevelt grinned and motioned for his visitors to be seated in plush, blue wingback chairs in front of the former president's shiny desk.

"Let's get to business, men; there's no time for shallow talk when a war is on. Lute, the United States is asking you to serve our nation again."

A familiar road. He had served with Roosevelt in Cuba, and as a boy, had worked on the Colonel's ranch. There was hardly any light in the railcar, which made Roosevelt's habitual squint look even more severe.

"Hell, I'm no spring chicken, Colonel. Cuba was one thing; France—well, I don't know."

The Colonel looked like he was ready for a scrap.

"Nonsense, Corporal, you're still a young man, and fit as can be. I envy you."

"Not sure I'm up to another war, Colonel."

Roosevelt glared at him. "Haven't you ever missed our war, Lute? The fighting, the fear, the anger, the camaraderie?"

"Never," Bapcat said.

Roosevelt tugged at the tips of his mustache.

"Lute, the United States wants you to go to Russia. Your mission there is to find the Tsar of Russia and his family, find out if they are alive, and if so, where they are."

Bapcat scoured his memory.

"I thought the newspapers said that tsar fellow up and quit," Bapcat said, trying to recall what he had read, which he rarely was able to do for news outside that of local towns and counties.

He remembered Zakov describing the tsars as "God on Earth" to Russians, that the Tsar and the government he appointed decided what was legal and who would live and who would die. Absolute power, Zakov insisted, and with such unlimited power what was legal today might very well be illegal tomorrow, "capricious at best." Zakov—a small man with black hair and a neatly trimmed mustache that swept past the corners of his severe mouth—rarely talked about the country where he had been born, but when he did, his comments tended to be upsetting and disturbing. "Lute, Russians are immersed from birth in the ambiguous, unexplained, and imponderable," he had said. The game wardens' young friend George Gipp had asked if the Russians believed in God, and Zakov had told the boy, "Only if He believes in them, and so far there's no evidence to support such a conclusion." Bapcat had laughed at this. Zakov's mind was one of a kind, and he missed his friend. Not that he wouldn't give him a kick in the pants for disappearing, but done was done.

"Abdicated," Jordy inserted, breaking his reverie.

Roosevelt nodded supportively. "He did abdicate, and at exactly the wrong time," he said. "The truth is, Tsar Nicholas's quitting could cost the Allies the war against Germany. The Tsar panicked, as he always does, when lots of his troops refused to report to the war, and rather than solving the problem, and leading, the man walked away from everything. He always makes the selfish decision, that one." Shaking his head, Roosevelt continued. "His departure has created a vacuum in leadership, and now the Bolsheviks are fighting the former regime's supporters for control of the country. It's an unimaginable mess, is what it is. The Brits, French, and we Americans have been keeping the Russians in the war with supplies, weapons, ammo, gold, virtually all their war materiel, and the point has come for us to do something to protect the massive supplies and our investment. We send it in through the Northern Russian ports of Murmansk and Archangelsk, and into the Russian Far East, through the Pacific port of Vladivostok. We and the British are about to put troops into both locations to secure our investment and make sure the Tsar's enemies don't steal everything. We're not going to war with the Russians—though damned if my gut doesn't tell me that's what we ought to do, and the sooner the better. For now, our fellows are going there as allies who are concerned and trying to protect our mutual interests, which is diplomatic gibberish that people can interpret any way they please."

Bapcat looked at Jordy, then Roosevelt. "When do you want me to leave?"

"Not just you, Corporal; young Klubishar, too. And I want you on the move today, tomorrow, yesterday, the sooner the better. We've got to get you there with great dispatch."

Bapcat was flabbergasted. "You want *both* of us to go to Russia? Jordy's never been trained. And we have things to do back in the Keweenaw, people, things I have to take care of before I can head off to war."

"Yes, both of you," Roosevelt said. "Young Klubishar speaks Croatian, Russian, and Czech. He will be an important asset to the mission."

"He's had no military training, Colonel," Bapcat said. What was Roosevelt thinking? The boy was still wet behind the ears.

"You're not going there to fight a war. You two are going there to find out what happened to the Tsar. Think of it as information-gathering, a G-2 assignment."

G-2 was army talk for intelligence work; he remembered this aspect from Cuba, when information often ranged from flat wrong to incomplete to wholly inadequate.

"Information-gathering in uniform?" Bapcat asked.

"No," Roosevelt said. "Not in uniform. You'll be more like tourists with notebooks."

Bapcat kept looking at Jordy, felt his head beginning to throb. He didn't want to offend the former president. "Jordy's not trained as a soldier, sir."

"We've covered this, Lute. The boy's fluent in Croatian, his native language, and Russian and Czech, as well. These are the tools we're mainly interested in, and he's obviously fit, which is important in Russia. Life outside Russian cities is very, very difficult and socially backwards. Bit like these parts, some might say."

The Upper Peninsula, like Russia? Bapcat blinked, trying to sort out his thoughts. Mind roiling with questions, he managed, "Colonel, if we are supposed to discover this Tsar fellow's fate, we'll need to be invisible, and that would mean civilian clothes, and as few people as possible knowing we're there. It also means that whoever does this thing needs to speak Russian like a native, and that ain't me, sir. Like you said, Jordy can maybe make out all right in the lingo, but I don't know but a word or two. Hell, Colonel, I can hardly manage English—you know that."

Roosevelt flashed one of his toothy grins.

"You seem to be handling it quite nicely at the moment, Corporal. Don't sell yourself short. I don't, and besides, you won't be going alone. Don't worry, we have a man who will be with you, and it will be fine. You'll meet him soon." Roosevelt chewed his bottom lip. "To make sure we understand each other: We—that is, the raw United States of America, our country—is *not* at war with Russia, the country, or the Russian people."

Bapcat reacted immediately. "What the heck does *that* mean, Colonel? Won't the Russians know we're in their country? Even if we're not at war with them, they still ought to know, right? Have they given us permission to snoop around?"

The former president's voice was leaden. "They know we're sending troops. General William Graves will lead that effort and be in charge of uniformed troops in Russia, but you and Jordy and your escort, absolutely not. Your effort will be known officially as Operation Odysseus. You know the story, Corporal?"

Lute didn't, but Jordy chimed in. "Sir, he's the hero of *The Odyssey*. He went on the road and after twenty years finally made it back home to Ithaca, and when he got there he refused to tell the story of what happened to him until he had 'paid off his debt to sleep.'"

Roosevelt grinned. "Bravo! Cracking good performance, young fellow. Odysseus was a remarkable character who met every challenge thrown at him, and, most importantly, he never gave up."

How did this relate to them? "We're *already* home," Bapcat pointed out. "Sir." He had a tendency to look at stories and facts with surgically literal eyes. "I think we should both just stay put, especially Jordy."

Roosevelt smiled. "Young Klubishar there will be a good addition to Operation Odysseus. Would you rather have him with Black Jack Pershing in the trenches of France?"

"*I'd* rather go to France," Jordy offered, but the two men ignored him.

Lute thought for a moment and nodded. "I ain't so sure about that, nor this Russia thing, neither. I don't think he's old enough to be a soldier anywhere."

"How about what I think?" Jordy whined.

Bapcat said, "I guess my biggest concern is about going anywhere outside America, either of us. I sort of saw Cuba, and the truth is, that sashay was enough for me, Colonel."

Jordy said, "Do I get to have a say in this? I want to enlist, and my Michigan outfit will be going to France. I want to go and fight with them. It's my duty. The recruiter promised me that our outfit would go directly to France after training."

The former leader of the Rough Riders said, "Duty to country means many things, my boy. Anyone can go to war, but few are called to a secret mission in a foreign land." Roosevelt shook his head again, adding, "Not sure how or if Graves wants to manage you fellas. I'm thinking maybe you'll need to be totally independent of him and his operations. I think you might travel with his HQ staff up to a point, then separate from them once you're all in Russia, but these aren't my decisions to make. The man you'll be with will manage all of these details."

Roosevelt stared at the corporal who had led his personal bodyguard in battle.

"Until you get to Russia, your escort will make all decisions and arrangements for the mission. Once the three of you are inside Russia, you'll have a say in what your plans and actions will be, Corporal. And by the way, you are to be sworn into the army today by me, with the rank of captain. Jordy will be inducted with the rank of sergeant."

"I'd prefer to earn my stripes, sir," the boy said.

"Very commendable, and to your credit, young man, but there's no doubt in my mind that you will earn your stripes, and more," the former president said quietly.

"Ignore him," Bapcat told Roosevelt. "Sir, this whole thing sounds crazier than crazy."

"Not in the least, Lute. The Russian Tsar is a weak, petty, and pathetic man, but as God determines at times, he has the power to make things happen. Not the way we'd do it perhaps, but the Russians have their own ways. We need to convince Nicky that the world needs Russia to stay in the fight, and ask him what we can do to help him make that happen again."

"You *know* the man?" Bapcat asked. Nicky was what Zakov called the tsar. They had been boyhood friends.

Roosevelt nodded. "Met him once, and didn't at all care for the man."

"When does this thing happen?" Lute asked his former commander.

"Now, from here. You'll travel on my express back to the East Coast, meet Graves when his team embarks from New York City. There will no doubt be a stop in England along the way, but your escort will fill you in on all the details."

"What about clothes and gear?" Jordy asked.

"Everything you need will be provided," Roosevelt said. "Uniforms for travel, clothing and gear for the field, all of it."

"When?" Bapcat pressed.

"You'll be told later. Now, raise your right hands and let's get on with this."

"Any idea where this Tsar fellow might be?" Bapcat asked.

Roosevelt sighed and half shrugged. "There are copious theories. You'll meet with G-2 before you leave the States. Could be he's in Moscow, or he could be anywhere east or north of there. We know for sure that he and the Romanov family are no longer in Petrograd, or anywhere near there, and that rumors are rife and varied on what's happened to them. We've had men searching all around the region, with no success. The Romanovs have disappeared. Russia is a big country, which makes it easy enough to do."

Bapcat's mind was growling and churning. *There are already men on the ground, and still he wants* us *to go? This made even less sense.*

"How far *is* this Moscow place from where we'll be?" Bapcat asked.

"A far piece. The plan, I believe, is for you to enter Russia near Murmansk, which is close to Finland."

Bapcat said, "I don't even know where Finland is, Colonel, and I never heard of no Murmansk. See, I'm not the man for this job."

Roosevelt grimaced. "No one said this will be easy, and it won't be. You want out, just say. I would never send a man who doesn't want to go. This is a job for volunteers."

Jordy said, "I'll volunteer."

Roosevelt's eyes were locked on his former corporal, who also ignored the boy.

"Who would you send if not us?" Bapcat asked.

"I'm not sure, but I know we'd find someone. This whole notion, by the way, the whole plan of sending our people in, belongs to someone else, not me. Lute, I'm here strictly in the role of messenger and facilitator. Were it up to me, I'd lead you fellows."

"You support this plan, sir?" Bapcat asked.

"It's certainly strategically sound, and of the utmost importance to the war's outcome—in fact, to the future of America, and the world—but part of me wonders if it also might be tactical suicide."

"How will we communicate while we're ashore?" Bapcat asked.

"You won't," Roosevelt said. "You'll be all by your lonesome."

"What soldier isn't?" Bapcat quipped, and Roosevelt brayed.

The former president stared at Jordy. "Can you handle yourself, Sergeant?"

"He shoots as well as me," Bapcat said before Jordy could answer. "And he's been running his own traplines since he was twelve. Jordy is good in the woods, and he's fearless and got uncommon good sense." Good in the woods was the highest compliment a Northerner could bestow on another man.

"You going with him or not?" the twenty-sixth president of the United States asked.

Bapcat looked at Jordy and his pleading eyes and thought, Better he's with me than with some unknown and green leader in the trenches in France.

"Yessir, I guess I accept."

Was this a mistake? He couldn't let Jordy go alone. No way. Given the situation, there was only one right choice.

"Then let's get you fellows sworn in."

Minutes later, ceremony done, Bapcat held captain's trax in his hand, and Jordy, stiff embroidered stripes for his sleeve.

Roosevelt sighed. "Edith and I lost our son Kermit in France." The Colonel's pain seemed deep and fresh. "Kermit could handle himself, too, for a while. He shot down one German before they got him on another day."

Roosevelt stood and saluted the two men. "You undertake a sacred mission for the future of your country, men. I know you will serve your country well. Captain Bapcat, talk to Captain Tope; he'll show you to your compartment and start making arrangements for those things you need. I will release the train to take you to Houghton, where you will take care of your personal business as quickly as possible and then head for where Captain Tope tells you. We have a telegrapher on board, and I'll notify General Graves that Operation Odysseus is activated. Your escort will instruct you from that point forward.

"Good luck, men. Wish I could go with you. Damn, how I wish that."

Bapcat flinched. It was rare for the Colonel to use a swear word, even in the heat of battle.

The former president's final words to them before leaving were, "Your Russian colleague, Zakov; where is he these days?"

Bapcat knew he was uneducated, but he was a good listener. *Where* is the Russian-born game warden, not *how* is he?

"Zakov left us a year ago come April. With us one day, gone the next, and no explanation." The leaving still frosted him. "Why do you ask, sir?"

"I see," was all the former president had to say as he exited the car, leaving his personal train to Bapcat and Jordy.

Dammit—Roosevelt already knew Zakov was gone! Was Zakov somehow involved in this . . . business? That's the only thing that seemed to make any sense, but that alone didn't make any sense at all. There was something more to all this. The Colonel was tight-lipped on some things, typical army and government. It had disgusted him in Cuba, and still did.

Lute thought Roosevelt looked to be in no shape for the kind of vigorous activity he'd once relished. How old was he now, fifty-eight, fifty-nine? He looked older, and exhausted, his skin pale and sickly yellow instead of its customary rosy glow.

"Does this mean I'm officially sworn into the army now?" Jordy asked.

"It sure looks that way," Bapcat said.

"I was supposed to get sworn in next week before I left for Fort Custer. What about my basic training?" Jordy looked confused.

Bapcat suspected such training wouldn't give Jordy much he couldn't give him, or already had given him as he'd grown up, with a lot less stress and waste than army training, and told Jordy as much.

The boy nodded, and said, "So, you're a captain and I'm a sergeant? Really?"

"You raised your right hand and swore the oath."

"Three stripes, that's me?"

"No, you're you, and you just happen to be authorized to wear three stripes. They're a lot more difficult to live up to when they are sewn on your sleeve."

"You know, Lute, I'd rather have gotten sworn in with the fellas back in Houghton and Red Jacket."

"What you'd rather is of no interest or concern to the United States Army. What you want doesn't amount to a hill of beans."

"You don't understand, Lute. A girl was coming to my swearing-in."

"A girl?" Good grief.

"Genessy Calibressi," Jordy said.

"Enzo Calibressi's daughter?"

"What of it?"

"Calibressi's a Black Hand man. Some say he *is* the Black Hand."

"His daughter ain't, and she likes me a lot."

"And here I told Roosevelt you have uncommon common sense."

"She's real good-looking, Lute—an Italian beauty."

"*Stupido*," Bapcat snapped, shaking his head. Medals and a girl? God save us from the nonsense that drives young men.

2

Late Fall, 1917. Champion Grade,
Between Marquette and Houghton

"Trench warfare ain't an adventure, Jordy.
It's a slaughterhouse, and nothing more."

The train swayed under Lute Bapcat's feet as he soldiered down the aisle of Roosevelt's personal train, now temporarily his and Jordy's, Lute's mind awash with things they had to do quickly, most of all, how to break the news to Jaquelle Frei. He had no idea how she was going to react, but he guessed it would not be a happy occasion.

Lute was antsy. Summer now, and already too bloody hot. Why can't there be a place where it's brisk and cold most of the year? At least with some months that weren't winter, because unlike him, some people seemed to need that. Maybe some months without winter would be good for attitudes, but the blasted heat and custard-pudding air of summer were intolerable. He was made for winter, and so, too, was Jordy Klubishar.

With Zakov in the saddle as his partner before he had disappeared, they had been able to cover more than twice as much ground. When cases warranted special attention, they could double eyes and brains and look for opportunities to take them deeper into investigations. But Pinkhus Sergeyevich Zakov had literally disappeared almost eight months ago, in April 1917, saying nothing about where he was going, why, or even that he was leaving. It was damn inconsiderate, inconvenient, and not at all like the Zakov he'd thought he'd known. People could be so dang unpredictable.

Bapcat had a full plate, and now Roosevelt was sending him *and* Jordy to Russia? Good grief. The reality was that he missed his partner, both professionally and personally. Jordy Klubishar, who had adored the Russian and hung on his every word, was about to turn eighteen. He had grown into a handsome, self-assured, powerful man-boy.

Widow Frei insisted the boy's luster came from her education and social polish, and Lute wouldn't deny it. Jaquelle was a force in any life she got involved with, and she had taken Jordy under her wing and put him firmly on the right path. Early on, the boy had fought her, but Jaquelle was strong-willed and eventually wore him down, and he had surrendered to her rule.

Too many things to think about. Going to Russia? What about the state of Michigan? And telling Jaquelle? On top of that, the damn Ford wasn't working, and he was on foot most of the time, today leaving his big red mule, Joe, to a leisurely day in his field. What would happen to Joe? He couldn't just leave the animal. Most of the time he preferred to walk or ride Joe, but he had to admit that the Ford could cover certain ground more rapidly, and he begrudgingly granted some value to the dratted machine, which he was barely able to operate, and fix, not a whit.

Having finished his smoke on the caboose platform, Bapcat made his way forward through the dining car, to the car assigned to them. Sliding back the door, he was surprised to find Jordy entertaining a short and swarthy stranger, who oozed slowly to his feet.

"This here is Captain Lute Bapcat," Jordy Klubishar said to the man in the rumpled blue serge suit.

"Yes, Deputy Warden Bapcat," the man said. "I'm Major Raul Dodge, US Marine Corps."

"You're a long paddle from any marines up this way," Bapcat said, setting his .30-40 Krag-Jørgensen carbine on a table.

Dodge smirked. "I'm not a marine as you probably think of most marines. I have a somewhat different mission. By the way, young Klubishar here speaks excellent Russian and Czech. He and I have been talking in tongues."

"His name is Jordy," Lute corrected the major, who said nothing.

"He's as good in Russian as Zakov," Jordy offered to Lute.

"Zakov also talked to the boy in Russian. Or did." Bapcat said.

"May I ask where your partner is?"

"I still don't know who you are, Major."

Dodge seemed to ignore this, and asked, "Care to speculate on Zakov's whereabouts?"

Bapcat shook his head. "Ask all you want, Major, but I don't know. I don't have time to think about things over which I have no control. I adjust and adapt—that's all I can say for certain."

"A commendable attitude," Dodge said. "There any chow nearby?"

"I went through a dining car," Bapcat said. "How long have you been on this train?"

"Less time than you two," the man said. "Wonder why I'm here?"

How would he explain to this man that his mind didn't live on trivialities.

"I assume you'll tell us more when you're good and ready," Bapcat said, feeling unspecific bad vibrations about the man, and not sure why. Something about him grated.

"Your husband is in Russia," Dodge said.

Bapcat blinked. *Husband?* Zakov's in Russia? He stared at Dodge, who was smirking, looking very pleased with himself. "I know the wife-story tale, including your rocky courtship."

Damn you, Pinkhus Sergeyevich!

"An old, tired joke, better left asleep," Bapcat said. Zakov in Russia; how could that be? Why hadn't Roosevelt told him?

Strange circumstances, serendipity, and the state of Michigan had gotten a push by the former president of the United States to hire him as a game warden, and Zakov, a former fur-trapping competitor, had joined him not long thereafter. In forming their team, they had both resorted to kiddingly referring to each other as spouses. It was briefly, momentarily funny, but soon irritated him. Of course, Widow Frei thought it hilarious and flogged it incessantly. Good thing he didn't live with Jaquelle or see her all that often; otherwise, it might've become a sore point.

He'd seen her more often before he and Zakov had taken legal responsibility for Jordy and delivered him to Frei in Copper Harbor for schooling, which had been successful. Now the boy was about to graduate. He hadn't just scraped by, but had made a fine showing, excelling both in the classroom and on high school playing fields. These things Frei also took credit for, and he neither objected nor disputed her claims. What he *did* know was that Zakov had played a major role in getting the boy to embrace reading and in teaching him to speak and read languages other than English in a formal, organized way, rather than letting him pick it up ad hoc in the streets of Red Jacket and other parts of the Keweenaw Peninsula. Five years ago during the mine strike, when he'd first met Jordy, they had been reading on about the same low level, but Jordy had since left him far behind. Though he might not read as well as he'd like to, he knew that both he and Jordy Klubishar had come a long way.

"I take it Roosevelt swore you fellas in," the major said to them.

"Captain and sergeant," Jordy said, with a tinge of pride in his voice. "I still wish I was headed to France for an adventure, but at least I'll be with Lute, and that's good."

"Adventure in the army is a good way to get yourself dead," Lute Bapcat said. "Trench warfare ain't an adventure, Jordy. It's a slaughterhouse, and nothing more."

"Roel Renard came back from France with a chest full of medals," Jordy argued. "He volunteered in Canada, and fought with the Canucks."

Dodge interrupted. "Deputy Warden Bapcat is correct in his assessment. No war is an adventure, and no war is sought by sane men. Medals don't mean a damn thing. War's the last resort, and only men who've seen the elephant know that for sure."

"But you're a marine," Jordy pointed out. "A volunteer, right?"

Dodge turned to Bapcat. "What did Roosevelt tell you?"

"Can't say. I still don't know you from a mossy rock."

Dodge sighed. "Skepticism is good, but wasted here. He told you about Operation Odysseus, which is tasked with determining the fate of the Tsar and the Romanov family."

Should he acknowledge this? Dodge seemed legit, and there was no sense getting off on the wrong foot. "What is it you want, Major?"

"Wanted to meet the both of you, get a feel for what you fellas got down deep in your guts."

"Want to share your opinion?"

"You both seem to have what it takes, that's clear; that's what I had to know."

"Why?" Bapcat asked.

Jordy added, "Yeah, why?"

"We'll talk more later," Dodge said, getting up.

"Thought you were hungry," Bapcat pointed out.

"I am, but my taste doesn't run toward fancy train food, so I'll bid you lads adieu."

"Where are you headed?" Lute asked.

"Where the wind blows me, somewhere over the horizon—you know, the rambler's code. In my business it doesn't pay to light long in any one place, so I keep moving. I've seen what I came here to see, and that's good. I'll next see you lads in New York, or somewhere out that way."

"What the heck is going on, Lute?" Jordy asked after the major had disappeared.

"I wish I knew," Lute Bapcat said.

This mission . . . it had the smell of trouble, and more.

He'd not seen the Colonel in four years, and after seeing him in Marquette in 1913, had never expected to see him again—had no reason to see him. Zakov: First, Roosevelt had asked about him. Now Dodge says he's in Russia, and that's where we're going? These things had to be connected.

3

Late Fall, 1917. Bumbletown Hill, Allouez

"I swear, I cannot understand how a mere game warden can have the highfalutin comrades you have, Deputy Bapcat."

They rode the public electric train north from Houghton, and the whole way Bapcat felt increasingly queasy. Telling Jaquelle that he and Jordy were off to—where, for what? Could he actually tell her they were looking for Zakov or the Russian Tsar? Good grief.

Roosevelt had said emphatically that they wouldn't be fighting the Russians, but if armed American soldiers were going, anything could happen. Finding the Tsar seemed reasonable, but why not use men you already had on the ground over there? The Tsar had just quit, hadn't he? Wasn't that his own business? A tsar was like a king; who cared what the heck kings did? Why not just ask the Russians where their boss was? After all, he was their responsibility . . . wasn't he?

Jordy was busy with a beautiful young woman who had begun making eyes at him as soon as they boarded. Bapcat knew the woman, who worked professionally in an establishment called Willing's House outside Red Jacket. He doubted if she was eighteen. Maybe it was good they were headed to Russia.

When they dismounted from the electric at the Allouez stop, Jordy seemed quiet and lost in his own thoughts as they started on the mile-long steep uphill hike to their State cabin.

Jordy kept pace. "The president's train is actually waiting just for us?"

"You heard the man."

"Does that make us important people?" the boy asked.

Bapcat snickered. "Hardly. It means we've got to hurry and get done all the things we need to get done."

"Widow Frei won't be happy with either of us," Jordy said.

Bapcat had been thinking the same thing. Mostly she'd be unhappy with Jordy's decision to get involved and at him for allowing it. Not that he was pleased at how this had turned out so far. He wasn't, but no doubt Jordy would make a good soldier. As soon as the thought struck him, he told himself that he knew even the very best soldiers sometimes got killed or maimed. Captain and sergeant. Me, a captain? He shook his head. Got soldier-boy ranks, but are we to be fighting soldiers or something else? What other kind of soldier is there? A fighting soldier was the only kind he'd ever known or even heard of.

"What about the Ford?" Jordy asked. "Do we just leave it? That can't be good for a machine, can it?"

The Ford. Damn. Maybe the answer was to leave it for his supervisor, Horri Harju—let him deal with it. Did the State know anything about Zakov? He'd asked Harju about the Russian last year and gotten a blank look. Did Horri know what happened to Zakov? No way to know for sure.

Yes, Horri could take the Ford, but when? Harju was bound up the way all game wardens were, dealing with all kinds of problems and situations and trying to sort and prioritize them. Forget the dang Ford. Focus on Jaquelle. Right now, she's your priority, your real challenge, but Lute couldn't. He respected the Colonel too much.

"Dammit, Jordy, stop lollygagging and pick up the pace!"

The boy laughed. "Damn, Lute, we're running up the hill as it is."

Bapcat sped up even more and heard Jordy swear and run to catch up and settle in beside him.

And Dodge, who the hell is he, and what's his story? And Joe . . . so dang much to do and think about.

The game warden bumped open the door to the State-leased cabin to find himself eye to eye with Jaquelle Frei, her brown eyes the hue of sunlit fox fur.

She said, "Welcome home, boys, come right on in."

Bapcat couldn't quite suss out her tone. Tense and wired, for sure. She wasn't one to hide her emotions too deeply. Bapcat was taken off guard by the widow's presence and proximity.

"Something we should know?" he asked her, and she grabbed him and kissed him hard.

Especially disturbing behavior from her. She loathed public displays of affection or any sort of sentimental shows other than occasional anger. In private she was hopelessly affectionate and passionate, but not outside her fortress. As she was kissing him, he looked past her and got a glimpse of his friend, Dominick Vairo, and immediately broke off and pulled her to the side.

Not just Vairo from Red Jacket, but also Keweenaw County sheriff John Hepting from Eagle River, and Himself, Judge Patrick H. O'Brien, who lived in Laurium, as well as Nellie Blackfish, all friends and pals.

Opposite the men stood a woman with hair the color of corn and a perpetual frown that would freeze a wiggling puppy. She was called Sunbeam, and was Jaquelle's longtime chief bookkeeper and alleged best friend, though he could not remember ever seeing any evidence of fondness, much less friendship. As the wealthiest woman in Copper Country, Widow Frei had innumerable contacts and associates, but few intimates or friends.

"I swear," Frei said in her honeyed voice, "I cannot understand how a mere game warden can have the highfalutin comrades you have, Deputy Bapcat. Why, ex-president Theodore Roosevelt *himself* personally sent me a telegram and a letter informing me that you and Jordy have volunteered for military service in France and will soon be off to battle the bloody Hun. Said I should be proud of my men. I was under the impression that you had seen enough war, Lute—that Cuba was, and I am trying to recall the precise quote in this matter, 'More than plenty.' I do believe those were your exact words, sir."

Sir. Uh-oh. She was angry. Before he could react, she was back on the attack.

"It always knocks me off my stride how fast things happen with you, Deputy, you *and* yours. First, Pinkhus Sergeyevich disappears faster than an autumn rainbow, and now you *and* Jordy *volunteer* to go and serve our country?"

Assault launched, she continued. "Off to France it is, and not a word, not a peep. I am not the least bit surprised because you, sir, are the tightest-lipped individual I have ever had the pleasure, and displeasure—oh yes, displeasures aplenty, heaps of them—the most frustrating individual I have ever come to be associated with. Care to explain yourself, *sir*?"

"Which part?" Bapcat came back, which caused Dominick to snigger.

Frei wheeled and hissed, "You four *men* are no better than *him*."

"What's going on here?" Bapcat asked again, trying to regain some small measure of control.

She turned back to him, eyes fiery. "The judge is here to marry us. Dominick is your best man. Sunbeam will stand up for me, and John's a witness."

"Shouldn't there be two witnesses?" Bapcat ventured.

She fumed. "You live in the pages of *Tiffany's Criminal Law* and somehow this confers on you omniscience in all fields of law, sir?"

He held up his hands in surrender. "It was just a question."

"Fawn Bridderly will be here momentarily," Frei said, "our second witness." She wrinkled her nose at Bapcat and turned to Jordy, who now towered over her.

Fawn was a schoolteacher from Laurium, a sometime tagalong of Jaquelle's.

"You, young man," Frei said to Jordy Klubishar, "you are not yet eighteen and cannot enlist unless you have your guardian's permission—in writing. I remember no such documents, nor discussions of said interests, plans, or wants. Care to enlighten me?"

"Me and Lute talked," Jordy said sheepishly.

"Me and Lute *indeed*," she sputtered. "Me and Lute? Let me remind *both* of you that I, too, am your legal guardian."

"Yes, ma'am," Jordy said. "But it takes just one signature."

Frei sighed dramatically. "You know I would never stand in your way, Jordy."

"Yes, ma'am, I know, but Mr. Roosevelt swore us in on the spot."

"Did he . . . ?" she said, raising her left eyebrow, which meant she was scaldingly angry. It would remain elevated until her anger dissipated—at least, that's how it had been for the five years he had known her intimately.

"*Marry* us? Now who's not talking to whom?" he growled at her. She had been merciless in trying to polish his language skills, and Jordy's, and the who-versus-whom thing was one of her pets.

She suddenly pressed against her game warden and whispered, "We have been a family in every way but legally. I want us to marry, officially and legally. Mrs. Lute Bapcat. I *love* that name and title."

He grimaced. "It ain't no real name; it was made up by the orphanage, just nonsense—Lutheran Baptist Catholic—Lute Bapcat. I got no idea what my real name is, or if I even had one, or who my real people are. Nothing."

He felt her arm slide around his waist and hold him.

"I care not a whit about any of that, Mr. Bapcat. In case you haven't noticed, I am a lady of means, and if something were to befall me, I want you and Jordy to inherit everything. Patrick has looked over our circumstances and agrees. Don't you, Your Honor?"

"Yes, madam, absolutely," Judge O'Brien said, in pristinely formal English, instead of sliding into his ridiculous Irish-English.

"Lose your brogue?" Bapcat threw at the judge, who could slide into Irish as thick as molasses when the mood overcame him.

O'Brien grimaced and winked.

Jaquelle took away her arm and held a finger in the game warden's face.

"Yea or nay, Deputy Bapcat?"

"I aways thought the man was supposed to pop this particular question," he said, adding, "Yea, but I've got nothing to leave you."

"Do I get a say in this?" Jordy asked.

"*No!*" Bapcat and Frei barked in unison, and even Sunbeam cracked a faint smile.

"How long do we have?" Frei asked her man.

"There's a train waiting for us in Houghton."

"You can catch another train."

"This is Roosevelt's personal train."

"Why would he give his own train to the likes of you two? What's the dang hurry? There's thousands of boys headed to France, which can't make you two special to any but us assembled here in this room."

"This is how the Colonel wants it to be," Bapcat said.

"How the *Colonel*, wants it, eh?"

"Have you met anyone named Dodge—Major Dodge?" he asked her impulsively.

"No bells ring on that name. Why?"

"Just wondering. It's not important."

Fawn Bridderly arrived, apologizing, and Judge O'Brien said, "Shall we get this show moving?"

Which they did.

When it was over, congratulations offered, kisses, hugs, and handshakes exchanged, a small cake was unveiled and consumed quickly.

Frei took Jordy by the hand. "One more thing. Lute and I want to adopt you, change your name to ours. Got anything to say to that?"

"I got to call you Mother and Father?"

"If you don't, you'll get a thrashing," Frei said.

Bapcat grinned. Me, father? Amazing.

Paperwork on the adoption and name-change forms complete, the new Mrs. Lute Bapcat ushered everyone to the front door. As Lute and Jordy tried to leave, she grabbed Bapcat's arm and held him back.

"I got to see to Joe," he said.

"Joe's gone—been moved out to my place," Jaquelle Frei said. "Jordy, dear, go on ahead to Houghton and tell Roosevelt's pet train wranglers your father will be along presently."

Jordy didn't hurry, just stood there, waiting.

Bapcat stepped over to Nelson Blackfish. "Wish I didn't have to leave like this."

The Ojibwa looked smug. "Maybe you'll see your Russian friend."

Bapcat felt his heart jump. "What's that mean?"

The Indian crossed his arms, his face impassive.

Bapcat had a hunch, a wild hair. "You know Zakov, you sonuvagun!"

Not a question. Blackfish said. "He lectured at Carlyle on light cavalry tactics of Indian fighting units. He said they were world-class, tactically superb in all skills, but our strategy was doomed."

Bapcat knew there was more, and he could sense Jaquelle waiting impatiently.

"Doomed?"

Blackfish said, "When snow comes down at three inches an hour, there's no way to stop it with a shovel. You're going to be snowed in. The whites were snow, a human blizzard. Your Russian is a smart man, and he knows his business."

"What business would *that* be?" Bapcat asked in a whisper.

"Soldier business," Blackfish told him and tried to walk away, but Bapcat caught his arm and held him in place. "He did more than lecture."

Blackfish closed his eyes. "He stopped by the campus last April and asked me to come help you. Said you are the best at what you do, but you can't do everything alone."

Zakov.

Bapcat said, "You're a good man, Nellie. Thanks."

The Ojibwa said, "Horri Harju called me and asked me if I wanted to be sworn in, to cover your counties while you're gone."

How did Harju know he was going anywhere?

"And you told him?"

"Said, sure, I'll do it."

"What were you doing in Pennsylvania when Zakov came by last year?"

"Game warden," the towering Ojibwa said, deadpan.

Bapcat fought a laugh. Zakov, his sneaky, slippery partner.

As he turned back to his new wife, he realized all sorts of things had been going on around him, much of which he'd known nothing about, and now he was not certain how, or what, to feel.

Jordy finally spoke up.

"How long's 'presently,'" the boy asked, "in case the president's train guys press me?"

Jaquelle kissed Jordy. "That's about to be defined," she said, and closed the door in her newly adopted son's face.

When she turned to face her new husband, he saw that her left eyebrow was no longer elevated and she was hurriedly unbuttoning her dress.

4

Late Fall, 1917. Garland Hotel, New York City

"What do *you* think it means, Captain?"

They got off the train at Grand Central Station in New York City and were told by a captain at the army office in the station to report to the Garland Hotel on Third Avenue, where there were reservations in their names. All they had to do was identify themselves.

An hour after they had checked in, Major Raul Dodge sauntered in, wearing what looked like the same wrinkled blue serge he'd had on in Michigan.

"Newly minted, all sworn in, and married too," he said. "Quite a cascade of unexpected events. Congratulations. You're probably feeling a bit confused over all this business with Russia. Here's the scoop, men. Your friend Colonel Zakov was asked a year ago by America to go back to Russia and find and establish contact with the Tsar and his family."

Ah, Bapcat thought. "Did he?"

"Find them? Unknown," Dodge said to the newly commissioned captain. "See, he disappeared, and we thought he was lost in the fog of civil war, but we've recently gotten a message from him through the Swedish embassy. It says only 'Send wife and boy.'"

"That ain't very specific," Lute remarked.

"Presumably you know the man better than anyone," Dodge said. "Does it sound like him?"

Bapcat nodded. "It's him."

"Good. At least he is alive, which means theoretically that the mission remains alive. He's our key, but now we have to find him and get him out."

"What if he doesn't want out?" Bapcat asked. Pinkhus Sergeyevich was not one to abandon tasks he thought important.

"Of course we're not going to bring him out until we find the Tsar and complete the mission."

"You think this Tsar is alive?"

"We have to assume that unless we learn that he's dead. All we know with certainty is that he disappeared."

Jordy said, "That could mean dead."

Major Dodge nodded. "Could mean just that, but we don't know, and if he's dead, we'll need to confirm that."

Bapcat did not like talking to Jordy about so mature a subject—missing people, dead people. This was for adults, not kids.

Lute asked, "Where's General Graves?"

Dodge cleared his throat. "You know how the army is, Captain. The Colonel recruited you both for me, not for Graves, though the general is vaguely aware of the mission. Now that we're on our way and you're in the nation's omniscience, you will both report to me."

"Who recruited Zakov?" Bapcat asked.

"Decision above my pay grade," Dodge answered.

"The Colonel said I would be in charge after we arrive in Russia or would share the leadership."

"I heard him," Jordy chimed in.

Dodge seemed unimpressed. "I'm certain that will occur at some point, but this isn't Russia. We've a long journey ahead of us."

At some point? "What's that mean?" Bapcat asked.

The major said, "What do *you* think it means, Captain?"

Hearing his rank spoken aloud so casually set Bapcat back on his heels. He'd never been more than a corporal in Cuba, a lowly enlisted man; what did he know about being an officer?

"I don't know," Bapcat told Dodge.

"Me either. We'll both have to see how it works out."

"We three," Jordy said.

Bapcat smirked. The boy had grit, which was good; he just hoped Jordy's luck bank was full, too. He had a feeling they would all need luck to survive what lay ahead. He'd always had plenty of both grit and luck. Was there enough still to be drawn on?

Dodge turned the conversation right back to the Russian.

"Honestly, we don't know if Tsar Nicholas is dead, sick, or a political prisoner. All are possible, but there have been countless rumors, and no solid news of them in months. Rumors aren't evidence. Majority opinion favors the man's demise, but my gut can't go along with the majority. If anyone can find the missing tsar, it's Zakov. He once knew the man and was close to him. Zakov is the key, and you two will go with me to help find him. If he's dead, we'll need to find his body and make positive identification of the remains."

"I don't speak Russian," Bapcat said. "And I've already got a good job."

"Stop fighting the inevitable. You've taken the oath. You know how to find people and how to live in impossible conditions, much like those in Northern Russia. Meanwhile, I speak Russian and other languages, as does the sergeant."

"Well, I prefer game warden work, and you ought to be aware that most missing people I find are already dead."

"The point is that you do find them, and not *all* of them are dead, so don't sell yourself short. And keep this in mind: Roosevelt wants *you* on this mission. You could be critical to the success of Operation Odysseus."

"You're a marine and we're army. How does that work?"

"We're not so much soldiers as in the line of military attachés to diplomats."

"I don't even know what that means," Bapcat said.

"Nobody does," Dodge said. "Therein lies the beauty of linguistic ambiguity."

"How will Jordy and I make this work?" Bapcat asked, thinking of his handicaps and Roosevelt's leaving him with the impression that he would be in charge in Russia.

"You, Jordy, and me," Dodge said. "Three Musketeers."

"And Zakov."

"The Three Musketeers had a fourth as well."

Bapcat asked pointedly, "You got any notions where Zakov is?"

"Notions—some. Evidence, none, but there is a certain Englishman I need to talk to."

"An Englishman in England?"

"No, he's in Russia, and he's been there a long time. Once we're there and I can get better information, we can make more-intelligent calculations and investigate from there—refine our search as we go."

"Are the Russians going to let us run around looking for their tsar? And why can't *they* find him?"

"The Russians don't care where he is. In fact, most Russians are glad he quit the throne. They don't like the chaos in the country now, but at least the Tsar is no longer in the country's way."

"Who's this Englishman?" Bapcat asked.

"In good time. Now let's eat," Dodge said, picking up his huge grayish-brown leather rucksack wrapped with woven red cords.

Bapcat said, "You two go ahead; I need to sit alone for a while."

Jordy grunted. "Well, I have to eat."

Bapcat shook his head. Had he ever been that age?

Jordy stepped outside the room, but Dodge hung back in the doorway. The major had a slippery look to him—here, but not here, an insider playing outsider playing insider.

"Jaquelle Frei," Dodge said. "Certainly the richest woman in the Upper Peninsula, maybe in the entire Upper Midwest. Quite the catch for you, Captain; beautiful, and wealthy too. Came to it, I guess she could have the pick of the litter. What I don't get is, why *you*? That's not meant to degrade, but you, with hardly any education and rough as a cob, and her smart as the dickens, sophisticated, *and* hugely wealthy . . . it makes no sense."

"We've been friends a long time," Bapcat replied.

Dodge snarled. "Ah, friends, that certainly explains it," his tone clearly saying it didn't come close.

"My private life is none of your concern," Bapcat told the marine.

Dodge tilted his head thoughtfully. "You are mistaken, Captain. Everything about you and the boy is my business, as long as we're on a mission together."

"To find Zakov?" Bapcat asked. "How exactly do we go about that?"

Jordy had once shown Lute a map of Russia, which dwarfed the United States in size. It looked like it was half the world, west to east. How did a country like that even happen?

"No need for you to waste time worrying," Dodge said. "I have a plan."

"And if you aren't around?"

Dodge tilted his head in the opposite direction and waggled a finger.

"Valid point, Captain." But no answer followed. Instead, Dodge said, "Jaquelle Frei had her pretty paws into a lot of businesses, some thought to be on the shady side."

Shady side? "Mind your mouth, Dodge."

The major raised his hands.

Bapcat turned away from Dodge, deep in thought. Going to Russia to find Zakov, who went to Russia to find the Tsar and got lost or something? Now Zakov had asked for him and Jordy? What was the Russian asking for? And why were all of his internal alarms firing? He needed to start dealing with reality, whatever that was, and right now his mind was as blank as a summer bat cave.

A game warden lived (or could die) on initial impressions, first looks. It was hard to peg Dodge: loosey-tight, laid-back, but seemingly on his tiptoes, alert and distant, dweller in a world all his own, the sort who harbored grand plans so long as others did the dirty work. Maybe all right at first blush, but only time would tell.

You needed to know the people you go into battle with, which is why replacements rarely last long. They make mistakes in calculations about risks others had already rejiggered for themselves. Dodge had a sort of vague cloud around him which rendered his outline a bit fuzzy, made you want to hold back. It wasn't so much what the man said, but the pauses before he spoke, the things you suspected he wasn't saying.

Shady side to Jaquelle? No way.

5

Early Winter, 1918. East Fox Trotting, Surrey, England

"I've found that men who've killed other men in war can be relied upon."

The man was uncomfortably angular, seemingly chiseled by an inept sculptor in a form both rounded and sharp, the eyes slightly baggy but glowing with the secret intensity of a cougar hunting from a tree branch in the night. The figure behind the giant desk spoke with a mushy slight lisp which Bapcat could hardly follow, though the language was said to be English, and all the shiny men around the man at the desk spoke with the same unintelligible slurred pronunciation—something shared, then, a disease or fad, Bapcat couldn't make out which.

"Mr. Churchill," Major Dodge greeted the red-haired man behind the desk.

"Raul, so good of you to come by," Churchill said. He had the kind of vigorous pink complexion Roosevelt had once had. The man arched his head to see past the major, still in blue serge. "These are our lads, the erstwhile wife and boy?"

"Yessir, Captain Bapcat and Sergeant Klubishar."

Bapcat weighed calling Jordy by his new name, but decided it wasn't critical. They would fix this when their war was over and they were home. Churchill gave them both an icy stare, but fixed on Bapcat.

"You were a sniper with Roosevelt in Cuba?"

"Sharpshooter, sir."

"Yesh," Churchill sputtered. "Almighty ambiguity in word choice. Quite silly, I must say." Then, "I've corresponded with your colonel and former president, and we share certain views on action and inaction. I've found that men who've killed other men in war can be relied upon. You agree, Captain?"

"No opinion, sir," Bapcat said.

What the heck was this about, and who was this person? Dodge had told them nothing, just dragged them out into the country on a train and then walked them almost two miles to this great house on a hill with a pond in front and uniformed men everywhere.

Churchill emitted a soft growl. "Theodore said you run silent and deep, like a torpedo. I like that. You think the boy is equal to this, Captain?"

"Sir, I have no idea what *this* really is, *sir*."

Churchill looked like he had just sucked a fresh lemon. "You don't know the *mission*?" The Englishman looked daggers at Major Dodge.

Bapcat said, "Find Zakov, then the Tsar and his family. That's all I know."

The Englishman nodded. "You have the core of it, the nugget. The rest you'll have to improvise as you go, Captain. Hoist your sails, aim your bow into the political winds, and tack your way forward at an angle. You a sailor, perchance?"

"Never been fond of ships or the seas," Bapcat admitted.

"Pity," Churchill said. "The sea tends to expand a man's perspective, widen his horizons, sharpen his senses. There's been a great deal of unrest to the east toward the Urals," he continued. "We suspect our Russian will gravitate toward the trouble and strife. More likely to be decision-makers there, and information."

"You have information indicating this, or you know his history?" Bapcat asked.

"Neither; more my gut on what little I know about the man. Truth is, I can't believe we've heard from him after such a long silence. Could be a Bolshevik trick, a provocation. This Zakov is using great portions of the luck God allots some of us."

"Just the one message from the Swedes?" Dodge asked.

The Swedes contacted the Brits instead of the Americans?

Churchill said, "Yesh, the one only; their man who got the message was at the time in Vyatka. The Swedes were trying to decide if they should relocate their embassy from Petrograd to Moscow. We and the Americans have decided against Moscow for the moment, in favor of further north, in Archangelsk. Better we move operations north until Russia's internal situation is more thoroughly clarified. Early civil war, you see, every man against every man, sides in this game not so clearly writ. You'll need a Bible-thick program to know all the players—other than the major ones—and you are highly unlikely to see them in the flesh. Comrade Lenin and most Bolshevik leaders prefer intellectual leadership from the rear to active leadership from and at the front."

"Assets on the ground?" Dodge asked.

"Few," Churchill said.

"Bloody war's got us all as stretched as starving whales," Dodge said, with an inflection Bapcat could hear but not identify. "Odysseus will be operating quite blind over there. Everything prepared ahead of us?"

"To the extent possible and forseeable," the shiny Britisher said. "Like the mission namesake, adrift in the winds of chance, I should think. Let's hope you lads are not gone twenty years," Churchill added with a mischievous grin. "How long d'ye need here?"

"Not long. Some weapons training up north, I should think, but the sooner we're underway, the sooner we'll have an answer to our questions, sir."

"Quite," Churchill said again. "These Bolsheviks are mad dogs. Treat them accordingly."

"We're not at war with them," Dodge said. "Neither Britain, nor the United States."

Churchill grunted. "Balderdash. We just don't formally recognize we're in that stew yet. Best time to kill an opposing political movement is before it is fully formed and solidified."

Dodge silently acknowledged the Englishman's views, but no further words were exchanged, and Bapcat assumed the meeting was over. Why had they even met with this Churchill character?

Bapcat was about to turn to leave when Churchill said, "If you would be so kind, Major, I should like to reminisce with the captain about our mutual associate."

"Yessir, of course, sir," Dodge said, and nudged Jordy toward the door. "By your leave sir," and looked at Bapcat. "I won't be far." With that he took Jordy out of the room.

Churchill pushed a cigar at the American. "South African tobacco; nothing of the quality of Cubans, but it will smoke, wot."

Bapcat accepted and mirrored the Englishman's ritual in trimming the cigar for smoking, wetting tips and the whole rigmarole, and when his was ready, he accepted a light from Churchill's rock-steady hand.

The Englishman sucked in a lungful and funneled a smoke rope into the air.

"Known Major Dodge long?" he asked Bapcat.

"A month, but truthfully, I can't say I know him at all."

"Impressions?"

Why was the Englishman asking this? He still had no idea who this man was, his role in all of this, or even his relationship to the United States and the war.

"He seems competent," Bapcat ventured.

Churchill stared at him through goggle eyes and floating smoke.

"Competent indeed; no question, the man is a master of his trade."

"He's a marine," Bapcat offered.

"Is he now?" Churchill came back. "I'd forgotten that."

The Englishman had the sort of intensity and sharpness of eye that suggested to Bapcat he never forgot anything, major or minor.

"Familiar with the term 'cool heart,' Captain?"

Bapcat lurched when he heard the phrase. "Long time ago, sir."

"Theodore is my source," Churchill said. "Been chums for years. We regale each other with the most preposterous things. Theodore insists that true warriors have cool hearts, which let them channel their passions and do what must be done. You once had a mentor with an odd name, I seem to recall."

"Mentor, sir?"

"Teacher—informal teacher or a guide, if you will."

"All Things," Bapcat said.

"Sioux?"

"Northern Cheyenne."

"Harvard lad like Theodore, I understand."

"No idea, sir. I don't know Harvard except by name."

"This chap, All Things—that's his name, yes?"

"Yessir, All Things."

"He taught you. Theodore tells me he worked exclusively with you."

How did this Churchill know so much? All Things had been his nemesis for years, his teacher of life and everything connected to life. The Cheyenne carried a staff of musclewood, the gnarly blue beech that grew along trout streams in Michigan, and every time the boy made an error, the Indian struck him hard. No such wood grew in South Dakota, and it was painful. Every time the Indian took exception, he whacked the boy, hard whacks for major mistakes and almost imperceptible hits for minor miscues.

One day the Indian had drawn back to strike, stopped, laughed out loud, flipped the cudgel over to Bacat, and said, "I thought you erred, but after some reconsideration, I've decided the mistake is all mine."

Lute had tentatively taken hold of the heavy staff—recalling this now, he could still remember his confusion that day when All Things had urged, "Go ahead. I made the mistake, so it's up to you: small mistake, big mistake—your call, young man. Decide."

Bapcat had no idea what error or mistake the man was talking about, and after some moments of confusion and indecision, he had taken the cudgel firmly in two hands and struck the Cheyenne so hard it took him off his feet and raised a cloud of prairie dust. The old man lay in the dirt, laughing until he was crying, the tears making trails in the dust on his face, managing to get out, "You figure it out yet?"

He had. The whole thing was staged, and he'd no idea why, only that it was.

"You gave me the stick, Lute," the man yelped, still laughing. "Where'd such a little cuss as you get the strength to strike like that?"

Eventually All Things had gotten to his feet, but not without extending his hand to Lute.

"Help me up, son." Which the boy did, and All Things said, "Henceforth, it's up to you to decide what are your mistakes and to correct them yourself. My work is done here."

When Roosevelt next came to the ranch, All Things stayed only a couple of days. One morning Lute awoke and found that the man had cleared out of the bunkhouse, leaving only his belt knife and the musclewood staff. No note, just the two items, which Bapcat still had, the knife on a lanyard inside his shirt.

"Theodore insists nobody ever knocked his bloody red Indian off his feet before. Theodore loves to tell that story. All Things grew up on the ranch and Theodore sent him to Harvard. He planned to do the same for you, but Cuba came calling, and he decided soldiering was more to the point for you. 'Lute's got the cool heart,' Theodore insisted to me, 'none like him. Never panics, always sees what needs to be done, and takes care of it.' *Sangfroid*. Familiar with the word? It's from the French, and means cold blood. That's you, Captain. That Indian All Things also possessed the same trait, and it was he who told Roosevelt that you and he were of a kind, and rare birds.

"But that's not true, Captain. Major Dodge has the same qualities, and I'm telling you this for your own welfare. Dodge operates on several levels, simultaneously. Be sure you see all that's there at every moment you can, savvy?"

Bapcat didn't understand, but nodded. The red-haired Englishman was a passionate man with the most lively eyes he'd ever faced. "You're telling me to not trust the major?"

"No, not in so many words. I am telling you that Dodge plays several games of chess with different people simultaneously, and depending on which game you are in, the move you see may have one meaning for you and another for others."

This advice, if that's what it was, did not clarify anything. He was accustomed to a transparent command structure, not some sort of continual need to read stupid tea leaves.

"Why was the major selected for this job?" Bapcat asked the man.

Churchill paused, took a pull from his cigar, exhaled, said, "He's most qualified to operate in the milieu you and young Mr. Klubishar are about to be awash in. He is skilled at moving between disparate, warring factions."

"Why send an American rather than one of your countrymen?"

Churchill glowered. "Theodore told me you'd be direct. Who says Dodge is American?"

"You mean he's English?"

"I asked only who says he's American? I myself am half American, through my mother."

Bapcat rubbed his eyes, let the subject drop.

The two men had biscuits and tea and a whiskey, and Churchill told Bapcat the story Roosevelt had shared from when Lute had been one of his guides on a hunt. Roosevelt had killed an eight-hundred-pound grizzly with fur the color of sunbaked prairie grass. Roosevelt had killed the animal as it charged and it fell not ten feet from them. They'd sat side by side, staring wide-eyed at the animal's massive head.

"Thought sure you were going to have to shoot," Roosevelt told his boy guide.

"I did shoot," Lute told him.

"The dickens, you say," chirped the future president of the United States.

"Same time you shot," Lute added quietly.

Later they retrieved the slugs, finding them not an inch apart, and Roosevelt had shaken his head. "Had no idea, Lute. This bear's half yours."

"No, sir, I just made sure your shot was first off."

Churchill and Bapcat chattered more about hunting, the American West, Indians, ranch life, everything. The Englishman's curiosity seemed unquenchable.

Eventually a man in a Royal Army uniform knocked and came in, and Churchill took a last swig of whiskey and clamped the cigar between his teeth.

"Time for you to get on, dear boy. Regarding Dodge—remember, multiple simultaneous levels and *sangfroid*. Perhaps when you've completed your mission, we shall have another opportunity to chat. I certainly hope so. Theodore and I have the utmost confidence in you."

"Yessir, thank you, sir."

Dodge was in the corridor outside Churchill's office, talking to a Tommy who had a face covered with burn scars.

"Tea and crumpets?" Dodge greeted him.

"Tea, cigars, whiskies, and little cookies."

Dodge smiled. "Interesting bloke, Churchill. Indomitable. Seems to emerge unscathed from every scrape and disaster of his own making. Gallipoli," Dodge tacked on and shook his head.

Bapcat said only, "I have no idea who the man is, but he's a friend of my Colonel's."

"Britain's minister of munitions for the moment, but Churchill's a man for every moment of import."

"Meaning?"

"Meaning, anytime his country needs a man of action rather than a hand-wringing intellectual."

Dodge led them outside to a Royal Army sedan waiting with a driver and Jordy. When they climbed in, Dodge said only "Proceed as planned" to the driver, and they drove away.

Bapcat looked at Dodge. "We don't know anything about you personally. Married, family, nothing."

"Quite true," Dodge said, and nothing more as he stared straight ahead.

6

Winter, 1918. Royal Navy Anchorage,
Scapa Flow, Scotland

"What do you mean, *under* the ocean?"

They'd come north on a train with only a half-dozen cars, one of them reserved for special government passengers, and serviced by uniformed men and servants all spiffily shined and rigid as scabs. Bapcat wasn't sure if they were army or not. The average Englishman's understated reserve and slurred speech habits gave Bapcat the heebie-jeebies. He had a lot of questions for Dodge, who kept to his own space in the wagon.

It was dreary in Scotland, cold, drizzly, a yellow haze hanging over everything like a stubborn Keweenaw fog that resisted all winds and could hang on for days.

The train delivered them to a village station where a waiting truck took them on a fifteen-minute ride to a Spartanized barren military barracks built for a company or more, but was theirs alone.

"We'll be using 1891 Mosin–Nagant rifles, thirty-caliber. They'll deliver some to us later today for some practice. Good weapons, made in the United States for the Russians and now plentiful there, as is the ammo."

Bapcat closed his eyes. A new weapon? He had already unhappily left his beloved .30-40 Krag-Jørgensen with Jaquelle.

It was dark in the barracks, and Dodge showed no interest in lighting it.

Bapcat said, "That Churchill seems to have a real sharp edge to him."

"You can't begin to imagine *how* sharp," Dodge replied.

"We're American soldiers," Bapcat reminded the marine. "We report ultimately to our commander in chief, President Wilson."

"I suppose that's one way to look at it," Dodge said.

What other way was even possible? "We need a clear chain of command. We learned this in Cuba."

"We're on loan to the Brits for this venture. It was Churchill's idea, and he sold it to Roosevelt, who helped sell it to Pershing and Wilson."

"What about General Graves?"

"He's aware of the operation—in bold, broad strokes, no details. Our ultimate mission here is to keep Russia in the war against the Germans. Finding the Tsar is a huge step toward that strategic goal."

"How have the Russians done against the Germans?" Jordy asked. "There's never much about them in the papers."

"Not well," Dodge said, "which is beside the point. With the Russians in, the Germans are accumulating casualties in their effort to cause casualties among the Russians. Just as in France, it's a bloody mindless slugfest. The Russians and Germans bleed each other."

Bapcat did not like this picture. Dodge was too cavalier about casualties. Had he been in real combat? Claimed at one point that he'd been in France, but at the Front or in the rear echelon, as a spectator, along with other camp followers? He was still feeling reservations about this Dodge; not a good situation, given the circumstances they were bound for.

"Who *are* you?" Bapcat asked. "Have you ever been *in* a war?"

Dodge stared off in the distance, into a dark corner of the barracks.

"I've had more wars than women," the major said quietly.

"How'd you end up in the Marine Corps . . . ?"

"I tell people I'm Annapolis, Naval Academy, and that keeps them from asking too many questions. Actually, I have a degree in international relations from the University of Michigan in Ann Arbor. By saying Annapolis, I can hide in plain sight in the long line of middies. Nobody in the Marine Corps or navy would dare question or doubt an Annapolis man. In my work we have to be cats. We start off with nine lives on our first legend and keep shedding and discarding them as we go. I have some lives left. The thing is, I was very concerned when Zakov asked for you two and wasn't quite sure why he did."

Dodge looked Bapcat in the eye.

"But then I knew why, just moments after I met you both. You're the real deal, and the boy, if he lives, will be too. One look into your eyes and I was certain. You don't overthink and you don't overfeel. You live minute by minute, and I envy you that—the lack of ambition and not having much baggage, which lets you focus on right and wrong as if they were the only options in life."

Now what was Dodge rambling on about?

"Wilson, Pershing—they don't care about this except in the broadest strokes. Only Churchill had the foresight to send someone to Russia to make contact with the Tsar. Even though Tsar Nicholas is highly incompetent, millions would still kowtow to him, and if he wants Russia to stay in the war, he has ways to make that happen."

Bapcat switched directions. "Where's Vyatka?"

Jordy answered before Dodge could. "It's the start of the main rail route to Archangelsk."

Dodge smiled. "It's a place of immense strategic value. We'll be putting thousands of men into Archangelsk, and when the time comes for the main breakout offensive, Vyatka will be the key to controlling the Russian rail system, which in many ways is the country's technological spine."

"What breakout offensive?" Bapcat pressed.

Dodge look flustered, but only for a flash. Slip of words perhaps.

"Understand, we are not at war," Dodge said. "But invariably there will come a moment when we will have to decide whether we're in or out, and when that time arrives, we will drive south to link with the Czech Legion, which is supposed to be driving north and west from the Urals."

"War with the Russians would require a *casus belli*," Jordy said.

"Yes, exactly," Dodge said, "a cause for war."

Jordy had hated Latin and had fought it at the beginning. Jaquelle would be so proud of the boy.

"Where exactly are we?" Bapcat asked, "and why are we here?"

"This is one of the Royal Navy's major anchorages. We're in Scotland."

"We sail from here?"

"Not exactly. We depart from here."

"If not sailing, depart how?"

"Under the ocean."

"What do you mean, *under* the ocean?"

"Submarine."

"Under the water?" Jordy asked, with an eye on Lute, who was claustrophobic.

Dodge said, "Not the entire way—unless circumstances dictate. Submarines need air, like whales, and have to be on the surface to recharge generators and such."

"You've done this before?" Bapcat asked.

"It's rather peaceful, submerged versus surface running."

Peaceful. What did *peaceful* have to do with anything? Ships were far from peaceful. This was under the dang water—not something he had anticipated.

"Are others going by submarine, with us?"

"There will be just us in the submarine. The others will arrive in an armada of surface ships. The submarine will enable us to slip unnoticed into Russia, which will be to our advantage."

"How long, here to there?" Jordy asked.

"A week, I should think—certainly no longer than ten days. But the time en route depends on a lot of factors, not the least being the craft and the attitude of our skipper. Putting men ashore where we're going is dicey business. I look forward to having my boots back on the beach," Dodge said.

"Why Mosin–Nagant rifles, and not our own?" Bapcat wanted to know.

"Pragmatism. We've shipped millions of them to the Russians, with ammo, and they will be plentiful and available, which will make resupply simpler for us."

"You expect the Russians to hand over weapons and ammo to us?"

"I do," Dodge said.

The man was daft.

"We'll need some practice," the game warden advised the marine.

"That's why we're here. We have full use of the British rifle range."

"What about supplies and other support?" Bapcat asked. "We're only three—four, after we find Zakov."

"We'll sort of live off the land, and when we can't, the Russians should be willing and happy to help us," Dodge said, "so to speak. We'll start rifle practice this afternoon."

Living off the land Bapcat could understand. He had practiced this to one extent or another for most of his life, as had Jordy. But Russia? And a submarine? All he could do was shake his head.

"One more thing," Dodge said, as they walked to the rifle range later. "Your language inadequacy will not do; no sir, it will not do."

Bapcat said, "I'm not going to magically learn Russian in a few days." He doubted he could *ever* learn it.

"We'll take another tack," the major said.

"You mean I can talk English?" Bapcat came back.

"I mean, total silence. From this moment forward you are a mute—caused by a head injury. You can hear and understand, but you can't communicate except by gestures. You can't write or talk, and for some reason, you can't read Cyrillic, either."

"But ..." Bapcat said, and found the point of a dagger against his throat.

"Total silence—not a bloody peep. From this point on, you are mute, no matter what happens. If the time comes when I want you to speak, I will tell you so."

"I won't understand what's going on," Bapcat said.

As Dodge pressed on the knife and drew a drop of blood, Bapcat tried to resign himself to his new condition.

"Lute the mute," Jordy quipped, and his father cuffed him lightly on the side of his head. The boy only laughed, and said, "This is gonna be real interesting. He who rarely speaks is now not allowed to speak at all. Good luck with that, Pop."

Bapcat cuffed the boy again, this time with a little more force.

PART II: BEFORE BEYOND

All revolutions are bloody. The October Revolution
was bloodless, but it was only the beginning.

—*Dmitri Volkogonov*

7

Winter, 1918. Making Landfall,
North of Murmansk, Russia

"We are not yet at war with the bloody Ivans. Bear that in mind . . ."

The three men came ashore in a bulky rubber raft. They wore rubber suits over their clothing, and boots only marginally made for winter wear, much less winter warfare. It was late summer in England, but already looking and smelling like winter here, a black, gray, and green landscape tinged with white, yawing in front of them.

Through their weeklong voyage from Scotland, the British sailors of the tiny submarine, the HMS *G7*, had acted like the three passengers did not exist. The sub had no name, which in Bapcat's mind made it an orphan, like him.

Only the *G7*'s captain spoke to them, and it was he alone who oversaw their departure from the deck of the sub about a third of a mile offshore. The voyage from Scapa Flow to the Murmansk area had been just short of a living nightmare for Bapcat, whose claustrophobia was extreme the entire time they were submerged, which was about half the voyage. As soon as they were on deck he was ready to make for land, glad to be in a rocking, bouncing raft and paddling madly to ride the hard gray waves to shore. He'd rather die in a rough sea or on the rocks than sink in gray water, trapped in an iron coffin.

Dodge kept chanting "Paddle, paddle, paddle," all the way, and as they drew within a hundred yards of the shore, he shouted "You two, stop!" as he paddled furiously to turn them slightly left. Bapcat felt the nose of the raft swing, and then Dodge was yelping, "Paddle hard, paddle hard, paddle hard!" They did, and as the incoming waves drove them closer, Bapcat saw that they were heading for a place smoothed white with snow, a narrow spot between huge banks of shore rocks and ice. How the hell had Dodge navigated to this exact spot? It had been invisible from the submarine's deck. Had Dodge been here before?

Their landing site was relatively clear of boulders, but not free of rocks, and when they hit, all of them got thrown from the raft and slid spinning on their sides and backs like duckpins.

When he finally stopped sliding, Bapcat got to his feet and helped both Jordy and the major stand up. He looked around and noticed that ice and snow were starting to accumulate on the beach, and could see that in a short time their little landing space would be swallowed by ice. He'd seen this happen many times on Lake Superior as the huge lake changed shape all year long. One thing was clear from their landing: Dodge had steel nerves.

The major seemed lost in himself, as they stood, brushing snow off their rubber suits. They had small rubber duffels lashed to the raft. Bapcat used his knife to slash cords and toss bags to the other men, and then they turned their attention to deflating the raft and cutting the rubber into many pieces, which they pitched into the sea, knowing the tide would eventually carry it all away.

"Raft dismantled and discarded, evidence of our landing gone," Dodge said, "Let's go," and took off inland.

Jordy said, "Hernando Cortez," and Lute the mute shrugged and held out his hands in a silent question.

"Landed in Mexico and ordered his ships burned," the boy explained. "No direction but forward. That's us."

Bapcat cuffed the boy on the shoulder and pointed at Dodge's back as he loped farther away from the beach.

Thirty minutes later they were in a dense copse of mixed conifers and yellow and silver birch. All the groves they had seen on their way to this one looked like small islands in a snowy sea, under which Bapcat guessed there was soft sphagnum, which was akin to walking on sponge in the best of times. But now the footing was reasonable and Dodge seemed to know his way. Bapcat and Jordy followed. There was no conversation.

In the dark grove there was a pale gray stone shelter, which was invisible until you were right next to it. Made of stone, it had metal doors eight or nine feet above the ground. Bapcat saw holes in metal trim along the corners. Dodge put down his pack and took out a package and handed it to Jordy. He pushed the metal peg into one of the holes, tapped and twisted it into place.

"Once they're all in, they'll form a ladder," Dodge told the boy.

Bapcat again noticed the major's pack, which had woven red cords wound snakelike around it.

Jordy climbed up, putting all the posts in place as he went. When he came back down, Dodge gave him three keys. "There're three locks on the right door panel, which will swing left behind the other," Dodge said, handing Jordy another package, identical to the first. "Pegs for inside, same setup. Get them in and then we'll join you."

Jordy immediately ascended, opened the hatch, reached into the opening, and began installing posts. He disappeared, and twenty minutes later, reappeared at the opening, looked down, and said, "All set," dropping out of sight.

Bapcat and Dodge followed.

There was a smooth wooden pole in the wall beside the rung posts Jordy had installed, and Bapcat hung onto the pole to descend the narrow ladder posts, eventually reaching a flat, smooth surface. Dodge had his torch lit, but almost before Bapcat hit the floor, had two paraffin lamps going as well. Not great light because of their flickering, but it was enough.

Bapcat saw three wooden coffins in the middle of the floor, and wooden racks along two walls, no doubt rifles in oilskins and cases. He kept playing over and over in his mind what the Englishman Churchill had told them in England: "We are not yet at war with the bloody Ivans. Bear that in mind lest you start some bloody row that could flare quickly out of proportion."

The game warden was still shaky from the submarine. Having quit the mines because of claustrophobia, he had rarely felt it since, largely because he avoided situations where he might experience it. This time it had hit even before he went belowdecks in the *G7*, the sailors and officers saying nothing, simply pointing to a hatch and ladder as the *Odysseus* team brought their minimal belongings below to store them in a small area beside their own "stateroom," called that only because it was closed off with a canvas wall.

"They keep bodies in here until they can be buried at sea," Dodge told his team.

Bapcat shook his head. The submarine stank of sweat and oil and other smells Bapcat couldn't identify. He watched Jordy furtively checking out his new surroundings.

All the coffins in the cement building had triple locks, which Dodge opened. He then began pulling clothing out of the coffins and handing the items to his companions.

"Dress. It should all fit. A lot of trouble went into finding, making, and sizing all this."

So many questions. Bapcat kept cautioning himself to slow down, knowing full well that in time his mind would settle, as it always did, no matter the conditions. He'd learned long ago that his mind had its own stubborn streak. Besides, he was a voluntary mute, forbidden to speak.

They had not yet been to Murmansk, so he couldn't say from firsthand experience, but from the photos he had seen before boarding the sub, it looked to him like most (or all) of Murmansk was new, built of wood, not steel or stone. What was this place they had crawled into?

The twinge of claustrophobia he'd felt coming down the ladder had passed. It felt a bit like the sub, but this was on land, above land, which helped. Seven days and nights in the sub had taken him to his limits, but now he was out and, if the only option for getting home was by sub . . . well, he'd deal with that when the time came.

Each man dressed in one-piece long-handles, over which they pulled loose, oversize reindeer trousers and wool shirts under sheepskin jerkins. For outerwear they donned shiny reindeer parkas with fur linings and soft black fur hats of a quality that fascinated Bapcat. Sable? Their boots were reindeer-skin mukluks with thick felt linings that reached just above their knees, tied off at the instep and again under the knee. Very snug, very warm, he hoped not too much so, but he had worn felt-packs at times back home, and they were reliable. People who lived north put little stake in style or looks and everything into function and comfort. None of their clothing was made outside Russia. Dodge didn't volunteer where the clothing came from, other than to say it was all authentic, none of it new.

Why land here instead of Murmansk? The land at the beach and beyond looked similar to parts of the Upper Peninsula, impossible to cross easily in summer and more easily done on snow. Why this secrecy? Russia was an ally against the Germans, wasn't it? And why a British sub and not one of their own? Dodge is a US Marine. Churchill hadn't seemed to put a lot of trust in Dodge or his leadership. Something was being withheld, but Bapcat had no way of knowing what it was.

"Let's finish here," Dodge said, and guided them in assembling their kits, which they packed into a reindeer skin covered by oilcloth. They each had an extra shirt and long-handles and woolen socks, and not much more. Bapcat guessed right on the rifles, which they took out of their cases. They had been recently cleaned and oiled. Someone had been here before them, and not long ago, by the looks of them.

The rifles were Mosin-Nagants, and though they'd fired them at Scapa Flow and found them reliable and accurate, they were not an ideal choice. Made on contract by Remington Arms for the Russians, the rifles were too damn heavy, and worse, more than four feet long, an aspect Bapcat did not like after so many years with his Krag carbine. Five-round magazine, bolt-action, ladder sight. The ones they had shot at Scapa had been good weapons, accurate. He'd like to get some practice with his new weapon here.

He started to disassemble his weapon and clean it, but Dodge stopped him.

"What are you doing?"

"Cleaning my weapon."

"Mute, you dumb bastard, *mute*! Do you not hear me? The rifles are clean and ready to use."

Bapcat dead-eyed the major. Jerk. Was there never to be a time-out from the silliness?

"Slide your rifles in their scabbards and put them on your sled," Dodge instructed.

Each man had a sled with a four-foot-long-by-two-foot-deep wooden box on it for their gear. The sled and box seemed primitive;

perfectly workable for the backcountry, but what if they went into towns? Bapcat looked at the bayonet which had been stored in the rifle case. It was not knifelike. Rather, it was a crucifer with a clip—no carrying scabbard. Bapcat affixed his bayonet to the rifle and laughed out loud. The damn thing was almost eighteen inches long. He threw the bayonet aside, which earned a scowl from Dodge.

Jordy asked Dodge in a hushed tone, "What is this building, sir? It's in the middle of nowhere."

"Any of you know what this building is?" Dodge asked. "You're from snowy Michigan. How do you bury your dead in the winter?"

"We don't," Jordy said. "We keep them on ice in a beer warehouse until thaw and runoff is complete, and we've got softer ground."

"Same here. Every Russian village has a place like this for their winter dead. The high doors keep out wolves and carrion-eaters."

"You had equipment left here, with no guard?" Jordy asked.

"It's safe. Russians are superstitious. They think the devil hovers around the dead, and they wouldn't willingly come within a *verst* of this place. They call these places *Cherti dom*—devil's houses."

"*Verst?*" Jordy asked.

"A Russian measurement: point-six miles, thirty-five hundred meters—a little over one kilometer. Any more questions?" the major asked sarcastically.

Bapcat waved a hand.

Dodge sighed. "Jesus Pete, don't you get it? Not you—you're a mute. Good grief. Shut up, the both of you, and that's an order!"

Fool. What if a person did not believe in the devil, as he didn't? Or God, for that matter. Not a god with all the powers ascribed to Him by nuns and priests and parsons. Bapcat might be uneducated, but he was not simple, or stupid, or unfeeling. He understood odds—if not in the formal, learned way Jaquelle understood numbers, then from experience. He knew that misfortune landed so often on innocents that it had to be less than a shining light from a creator.

The three men had snowshoes with poles and flat-terrain Nordic snow skis, all of which he and Jordy and Zakov had used extensively over all kinds of Michigan terrain. Russia might not be familiar, but winter and cold were old chums, and foes. With all his winter traipsing as a trapper and game warden, he had learned important lessons. Wind is the ally of cold. Both are deadly enemies. Snow is soft, ice, hard, and traveling on ice is faster, smoother, and generally safer, if you knew where you were.

"*Odin brykat'sya pri banka,*" Zakov would always say before they launched into winter's fangs. *One kick at the cat,* which made no sense, but he had grown familiar with it. Russian was a language of spit-sopped mush-in-the-mouth, as pleasant as a cat hacking up a hairball.

The three moved their gear outside and removed the climbing posts, which Dodge stowed in his sled basket. Apparently whoever came here had his own keys and climbing posts, which meant more people knew about this than Dodge was admitting.

Their last act was to burn all their civilian clothes outside the building. This done, they got on their skis and adjusted the simple bindings. They got ready to move out, the major in front. Dodge looked back at them with a grin and said, "*Odin brykat'sya pri banka.*"

Bapcat answered, "One kick at the cat!"

A red-faced Dodge smacked his own leg with his sheepskin-lined choppers. "Mute, mute!"

Jordy howled with laughter as the trio surged forward into the snow.

Bapcat waited until Dodge had shushed ahead and looked at Jordy, took off his glove, made a fist, and pushed his thumb between his first and second fingers, a gesture of disrespect. He had no idea if the sign had a name, but he knew it was universal, or close to it. Jordy grinned.

Bapcat pulled his goggles into place and shushed after the major, who skied at a surprisingly robust pace. Their weird leader was breaking trail at a frenetic pace, at least for now. Had to give him that. Energy, like brains, was a gift you were born with.

8

Winter, 1918. South of Murmansk

"Are we skiing all the way to Zvanka?"

One of the supplies in their cache was *makhorka*, a bitter Russian tobacco, as coarse as last year's hay. In a previous and rare respite from skiing, Dodge had told them they were bound for Zvanka, which meant nothing to Bapcat. Dodge had leaned on a ski pole as he rolled a cigarette with the foul-smelling stuff, saying to Jordy, " I want you to listen carefully to me, Sergeant. You have not been trained in the ways of a soldier. I don't know what you know or what you don't know, and neither do you."

Dodge took a puff and went on. "There are almost no rules in the trenches in France, and here in Russia, there are no rules at all. This is chaos, totally uncharted, continuously changing territory. Our strategy is to get control. Our tactics? We charm and buffalo, or kill if we can't. There can be no hesitation, no timidity, no second-guessing me. When I give an order, do it. Captain Bapcat understands this because he's danced with the elephant—right, Captain?"

Lute nodded.

Dodge never took his eyes off Jordy. "Understand me now, son. Do as ordered, when ordered, no questions."

Jordy hunched his massive shoulders, and Lute knew a question was about to surface.

"What if I don't agree and can see a better way?" the boy asked.

Dodge stiffened. "You see a better way? You're eighteen, and by definition, you know less than nothing."

Jordy Klubishar retorted, "Well, *you* sure as heck can't know everything, Major. Nobody can, not even Lute and Zakov, and they know about all there is to know between the two of them."

"They have taken human lives under orders, and you have not," Dodge said with a growl.

Jordy came back, "Yessir, Major, sir. No rules. Do as I'm ordered. Ask no questions. Seems to me these are rules, and you just finished saying there ain't rules in Russia. Which is it?"

Bapcat expected an explosion, but Dodge only galumphed his annoyance, maybe even hinted at a little mirth. It was damn hard to read the man's stone face, and this left Lute feeling uncomfortable. His fast read on the man was that he seemed to know his business, and yet this mission was leaving him as unsure as his two charges. Beyond that, Dodge was unreadable.

Bapcat set his mind to changing this.

"Over here, Captain," Dodge said, and held out a leather bag. "You have permission to speak for the moment."

Bapcat looked inside the bag and then at the major. "Spring-loaded wrist knife?"

"Ever used one?"

"No. Some of our men had them in Cuba and they were lousy, springs undoing, or something. I prefer my own blade."

"These are improved models," the major said.

Bapcat shook his head and tapped the scabbard of his own knife. "This won't get hung up, and it doesn't need a spring to jump into my hand." He flipped the bag back to Dodge.

"The sergeant is untrained," the major said.

"By the army," Bapcat said. "But Zakov and I have been training him since he was twelve or thirteen. You can depend on him."

"Widow Frei helped, too," Jordy chimed in. "And my schoolteachers. You like books, Major?"

Dodge sighed. "Books are little help in a place like this."

"What *does* help here?" Jordy asked.

"Force, applied swiftly and mercilessly. It's what Russians understand and expect."

Bapcat said, "Zakov told us the peasants here are treated like animals."

"It's a matter of definition," the major said. "Some believe they *are* animals."

"People are people," Jordy offered. "We got all kinds back where we live."

Bapcat thought he detected impatience in Dodge, who said, "The people have been beaten down here, by the Tsar, and before that it was Napoleon, and before him, Ghengis Khan and his foul offspring." Dodge continued staring at Jordy. "All that has led to this mess we've landed in— if you take the long view. When the Tsar abdicated last year, a provisional government took his place, and elections were held, but the provisionals didn't have the organizational strength to govern, and the Bolsheviks, who got less than three in ten votes, pushed their way into power, which they now hold, albeit tenuously. There're Whites, those Royalists still loyal to the Tsar, wherever he is, some Cossacks similarly allied, and a huge force of Czechs loose in Russia and out to destroy the Bolos."

Dodge handed Bapcat and Jordy small red ribbons. "For your shapkas, or parka. The red signifies Bolo. Display it at all times unless I tell you otherwise."

"This is Bolshevik country?" Jordy asked.

"We will assume that until proven differently. Hope for the best, plan for the worst, the most basic pillar of planning."

Jordy frowned with intensity. "If we aren't at war with Russia and the Bolos are running the country, doesn't that mean we're not at war with them?"

"All here are enemies, even those I know and who purport to be my friends."

Bapcat tucked this into his memory. Dodge had contacts here, presumably local Russians, not Englishmen. As he had suspected from early on. Who were these people, and why did he have doubts about them?

"You don't paint a pretty picture," Jordy Klubishar said.

"It will get uglier and more confusing than you can imagine."

"How do we find Zakov?" Bapcat asked.

Dodge puffed out his cheeks. "I believe he followed the Tsar and his family. We know that the Tsar announced his abdication at his military

HQ in Mogilev, and from there joined his family at their estate, Tsarskoye Selo, which is near Petrograd and the Finnish border. I believe that the Tsar, his entire family, and their entourage were moved from Tsarskoye Selo to Tobolsk last July."

All Russian place-names sounded to Bapcat like belches and snarls in a catfight.

"And now?"

Dodge shrugged. "Tobolsk, perhaps, or not. We shall go and have a look. If the Tsar is anywhere near Tobolsk, rumors among the locals will help us to locate him. Absent official news, Russians rely on their own gossip and nosiness to keep track of events and people. The Bolos and many Russians loathe the Tsar, call him Nicholas the Bloody. There was a riot at his coronation party and more than a thousand citizens died. The Tsar hardly noticed. Tens of thousands have been killed in the German War, and he hardly noticed that. Human lives are nothing to the man. The Bolos's name for him is not undeserved."

This information matched much of what Zakov had told him. Bapcat wondered what the major's personal politics were. Did he favor a particular side?

"Are you sympathetic to the Bolos?" Bapcat asked.

Dodge didn't answer right away. "I understand them," he said after a long pause, a less than full response.

"How big is Tobolsk; how many people?" Jordy asked.

Dodge grinned, which left Bapcat shaking his head. Instead of answering Jordy, the major started talking.

"Anson Bertin Dodge was the Menne Professor of History at Columbia in New York City. I was born in St. Petersburg, but my parents were killed in a streetcar accident. The Dodges were my parents' American friends, and they adopted me. I graduated from Annapolis, and after that, the marines sent me to Colombia. I was an observer on the Russian side in the Sino-Japanese War in 1905, and since then, with one exception, I've been seconded to the State Department as a military attaché. I spent ten months at the Front in France with a French battalion, and saw that mess firsthand. I've been in and out of Russia ever since."

What prompted all of this unsolicited information? Bapcat wondered if Dodge knew Zakov from the war with the Japanese. Earlier Dodge had said he'd not gone to school at Annapolis, and in this latest version, he had? He'd said something about Georgetown, and now he was saying Columbia? Inconsistencies in stories were markers for game wardens, sudden outpourings of information, reason for suspicion. What was Dodge's game?

"You learned Russian as a kid?" Bapcat asked.

"The Dodges made sure I grew up multilingual. I have smatterings of many languages."

Bapcat thought about the contrast: one orphan adopted by college-educated parents, and the other, running away from a lousy orphanage to become a cowboy, ending up poorly schooled and barely competent in English. Luck and fate. Both had four letters, but they were far from the same thing.

"Where *is* this city we're looking for?" Jordy asked.

Dodge took a deep breath. "As I said, Russians are incorrigible gossips and rumormongers. Money is the fuel of the rich, but for the masses it is information with which their government is pathologically stingy. Doesn't matter which city. Someone will know where they are. The Tsar has traveled with a military escort of two hundred men, and the royal train is marked *Krasni Krest Missiya*."

"Red Cross," Jordy said, and the major smiled his approval.

"Very good, Sergeant, very good. When we are underway, you and I shall speak only Russian, even in private."

Bapcat said, "When Jordy asked which city, I think he meant the city where we'll find Zakov, and if you two nabobs speak only Russian when we're alone, I won't understand anything that's going on."

Dodge said. "You don't *need* to understand. Your only job is to intimidate. You are our muscle. If I touch the side of my head with either hand and point at someone, you immediately jump them and back them up, or knock them down, and do it without hesitation."

Why wasn't the man answering the question about Zakov? Was his Russian partner arrested or dead? If so, how had the Swedes gotten a message from him to pass west?

"If I do that, I won't know *why* I'm doing it," Bapcat said.

"This is Russia in total upheaval. It is not the muscle's job to know why, only what; understood, Captain?"

"Understood, Major."

He'd fight when circumstances called for it, but he wasn't accustomed to, or comfortable with, the idea of attacking, manhandling, and abusing people without good reason. He felt Jordy's hand on his back to reassure him. This almost brought a grin, adopted son soothing adopted father.

"How do we get to Tobolsk?" Jordy asked Dodge.

"We let the Bolos take us east by rail. As far as I know, they control nearly everything from here eastward, to the Urals, or they soon will. How long they can hold what they have remains a large question mark."

"Where do we catch the train to the east?" Bapcat asked.

"Zvanka," Dodge said. "And from there, to Vologda, where last I knew the American embassy was relocating to. I have reason to believe our people will soon shift north from there to Archangelsk, which is where many of our troops will be; if necessary, this location will make a diplomatic pullout easier."

This information sort of matched what Churchill had told him, but a diplomatic pullout? Wasn't that what you did when war was about to be declared?

Bapcat said, "The last you knew?"

"Russia is a giant vat of swirling *pertsovka*, vodka clouded with pepper. It is never clear."

Bapcat sensed the major was holding something back.

"You haven't answered about Zakov."

When Dodge still didn't answer, Jordy asked, "Are we skiing all the way to Zvanka?"

"Only to *verst* ninety," the major said, "and it will be a ride on rails from there."

"Why *verst* ninety?" Bapcat asked.

"To get us behind the Bolo front, where their security is little to nonexistent."

Bapcat wondered how the major knew that *verst* 90 was the demarcation.

"The Bolos that bad?" Jordy asked.

"Worse," Dodge said. "There is no way the Bolsheviks can prevail, except through divine improvidence, pure luck, or colossal accident."

"How far are we from this place?" Bapcat asked.

"I should think we'll be there late this afternoon."

Bapcat heard the word *should* more clearly than anything else in the statement.

Who the hell was this major? And why does Zakov want Jordy and me? Wife and boy? That Russian bastard. The thought made him smile. He'd missed his partner, his friend.

9

Winter, 1918. Verst 90

"Hereafter, you are *Muskul.* That is now your
name. *Muskul* means 'muscle.'"

The snow with its cardboard crust had new powder on it, two or three
inches, the air still as stone, the snow coming straight down. Dodge kept
a hard pace and they followed. Bapcat was glad that their leader at least
seemed to be physically fit. About Dodge's mental state, he still had some
doubts.

The three men kept a space of twenty to thirty feet between them, the
routine military interval in the event of an ambush or surprise. The falling
snow had a yellow-gray, smudgy color, which intrigued Bapcat. Usually
it had to land near towns and factories to take on such a color, but here it
fell already spoiled. How could that be? What was in the Russian sky that
was different from the air and sky in Michigan?

Dodge was a strong, confident skier, as was Jordy. Personally, he preferred the more-contemplative pace of snowshoes, which helped you see
more as you moved, but snowshoes were for much deeper snow, and skis
let them quickly cover miles.

Before his unexpected appointment as a state deputy fish and game
warden, Bapcat had worked an expansive trapline at the tip of the
Keweenaw. Over time he had discovered all the best routes to minimize
traversing the deepest snow, even the frequent and sudden dumps that
beset that wild country.

The three men skied for hours, stopping twice to make pots of tea loaded with sugar. Bapcat had no idea what lay ahead, and knew from experience to not allow his imagination to get carried away. His imagination's ability to conjure possibilities had always been both fertile and cumbersome, beginning in childhood in the orphanage; he'd had to teach himself that creative worrying did not help day-to-day comfort. All but the thickest orphans suffered similarly, but did not often talk about their fears to other inmates, which is how they thought of themselves. Bapcat saw himself as a flinty island among other flinty islands, and he had learned that "creative disaster" thinking always made the picture far more horrible than reality, which usually was ugly enough. For years he had constantly admonished himself to clear his mind at every opportunity and just let life happen, without trying to guess outcomes. It was never easy.

As a former military scout and sharpshooter, and later, as a game warden, he had forced himself to stay in the present as much as possible, and until actual contact, to think no more than a few seconds or minutes ahead, to keep focused on his immediate surroundings. Even with Zakov as his partner, Bapcat usually led their forays and patrols. Not leading this time was a huge adjustment, and uncomfortable in the early going, as he didn't feel the sort of illusion of control which usually pushed him along in normal circumstances (and even in those that were far from normal).

The game warden had become not so much comfortable as begrudgingly accepting of the major leading the operation, which hardly seemed an operation at this juncture. Russia was real enough in an unreal way, and he reserved complete support for the major. So far the man had given him no compelling reason to think or act otherwise. The mute role was annoying and stifling, but with his deficiency in languages, it seemed to be a reasonable if odd practical adaptation to a potentially difficult reality.

They were shushing along at a stiff pace when Dodge suddenly stopped before some silver birches, planted his sticks, and lit a cigarette with a shaky hand. Strange. Nerves? He needed to keep an eye on that.

Dodge said, "There are easy ways to enter a party uninvited and there are difficult and severe ways. Normally I let circumstances dictate, but in this situation we need to take as much control as we can grab. Most Bolos are hard men, but untrained in most things military, including security, at which they are pathetically shortsighted. We need to overwhelm and shock them, and capture control quickly."

Bapcat sensed the major was talking to himself as much as to them. Another sign of nerves? Was Dodge as confident and experienced as he liked to make out? Fear was a normal thing in normal men. How a man dealt with it, pushed it behind him and acted despite the fear—this was the real measure of courage. Maybe the cigarette and self-talk were Dodge's ways of coping. If so, although it could be disconcerting to those following him, Bapcat was willing to cut the man some slack, as long as he didn't falter when the moment came to take action.

Dodge looked over at Lute. "Do not answer out loud. Are you listening to me?"

Bapcat nodded.

"*Da*," Jordy chimed in. "*Vslushaksya.*"

"Good, you're both listening." Dodge took Bapcat's sleeve and blew smoke at him. "Hereafter, you are *Muskul*. That is now your name. *Muskul* means 'muscle.' When I say your name and point to a person, you will confront that person immediately. If they resist the slightest bit, I will take the next closest person and Jordy will wade in to support us by confronting who is left. No pistols or rifles; blades only. The first one is always the most difficult. When I call him out, *Muskul*, you stick him in the thigh and in the bicep, deep and hard! I will tell him that if he resists further, you will sever the arteries in his legs, and he will be irretrievably dead and facing the devil alone, because we are on a mission from Trotsky, and Trotsky has ordered the devil's cure for any and all who fail to assist us, or anyone who interferes with our official Bolshevik business. Russians are highly superstitious, the devil their worst nightmare. *Da, Muskul?*"

Bapcat nodded.

As a game warden, an unprovoked attack was neither lawful nor his way, but this was war, right? Or was it? This was not like his previous war, but was it a war nevertheless? In Cuba they understood when they could confront the enemy, but both Roosevelt and Churchill had told him America was not at war with Russia. Where was Dodge getting his rules of engagement from? No uniforms. Did that make them spies? A foreboding thought. The fate of spies was universally ugly and often immediate after a short interval of torture. Stabbing a man is certainly an aggressive act, but is it an act of war? Could a few men in the middle of nowhere cause a war to happen?

"The Bolos are six hundred to eight hundred yards ahead of us." Dodge announced. "I will lead us in and pull them toward me. Muskul, you are my right flank, one step behind me; Sergeant, to my left and one step back. Sergeant, your nom de guerre is *Molot*."

"'Hammer,'" Jordy muttered.

Bapcat could tell by the boy's voice that he was unhappy, but the reason eluded him, as it often did. He could no longer remember being eighteen, and even less of the times that came before that. Jordy was an enigma, self-contained yet emotionally needy, wanting approval. He was steady most of the time, but sometimes unpredictably erratic. Could only hope he was solid right now.

"Remember," Dodge whispered conspiratorially, "everything from here on in is a matter of life and death. You are in a time and place where individual lives have no value, and even less impact. Before Nicholas abdicated, the Romanovs ruled with an iron hand for four hundred years. It has always been bad for the common people, and yet, it is even worse now. Perhaps this will pass if and when one political faction gains control and stabilizes power. Or not."

Bapcat glanced at Jordy, who wore a passive mask, the same one he'd worn since he was twelve. *Sfinks mal'chik*, Zakov had called him at first; Sphinx Boy—always boiling inside, but accustomed to holding it all in, even when his old man was beating on him, which was not infrequently. Not that he wouldn't fight back when he'd had enough. It was no surprise he wanted to be a soldier.

—◦—

They stepped out of their skis, lashed them and the poles with elk sinew to their sled boxes, and set off toward the Russians in their mukluks.

Bapcat kept his eye on Dodge, watching for clues—but to what? Something . . . a waver, a halt, a stutter? Dodge surged forward with his jaw stuck out like the bow of an icebreaker.

Bapcat smelled the Russian campfire before he saw it. The fire, and the nasty black Russian tobacco.

The men they approached were not at all what Bapcat had imagined. He had expected soldiers. Instead, he found a half-dozen men in bulky greatcoats of different colors and a ridiculous mixture of clothing and bizarre weapons, including a woodsman's ax and a pike. Two of the men were holding squat, clear bottles, and he could smell some sort of strong alcohol mixed with tobacco. All six men wore dirty red armbands, and were smoking either cigarettes or clay pipes with long black stems and bowls.

Five of the men were quite short and slight, but one man was tall—not of the magnitude of his seven-foot-plus friend, the late Louie Moilanen of Hancock, but taller than his companions, and wide and bulky, hands the size of cheese wheels. Dodge, predictably, made straight for the giant and began snarling and barking in Russian.

"Muskul," he said, touching his head and pointing at the giant.

This was happening too fast, much faster than he'd anticipated. No time to collect his wits and unjumble his stomach, which always danced wildly before impending violence, but at least they had a plan, and he had no need to sort out alternatives, given that Dodge was in charge—for now. Chain of command was chain of command, but again, he thought, we are at war with Germany, not these people. So why am I attacking this man?

Bapcat ducked under the giant's long reach as the big man's arms arced toward him; he ducked the massive fists, pulled his knife, and, as he had learned from All Things, drove it straight forward into the man's right thigh, feeling the blade strike something hard as the man screamed like thunder. Before the tall man could gather his wits to do anything, Bapcat stabbed the knife into the man's left bicep, dropping the man to his knees, where he scrambled and screamed angrily, looking like a steer struck between the eyes in an abattoir chute.

One of the large man's comrades immediately began to fawn over Major Dodge, who hissed sharply at the man and slapped him aside. "Ostavlyatim, budet!"

Bapcat didn't know the words, but the tone and pitch seemed obvious.

The Russians seemed intimidated, and on his knees, the giant now looked pathetic.

That he had made an unprovoked attack on the man left Bapcat uneasy. The man stood out solely because of his size and had done nothing wrong or threatening.

What the hell were they doing? What was he doing? This whole thing made no sense. When they found Zakov, they would learn why. Zakov always thought things through and had sound reasons for his actions. There would be a good one for this extraordinary mission, even if he couldn't see it right now. (The Russian liked that word—extraordinary—used it in all sorts of situations. The first time Bapcat had heard it, he and Jaquelle had been making love for the first time. She had laid her arm over her forehead and whispered "Extraordinary," and she was still saying it five years later.)

Dodge pushed past the Russians, who didn't resist or block. The Russian guards got in front of them and tried to grab their equipment to help load it, but Dodge shouted *Skoi!* and slapped them away, and began loading his own gear. Bapcat and Jordy did the same.

Climbing onto the platform between the two passenger wagons, Dodge looked at the side toward the locomotive, where the engineer was motioning for him to move south. The locomotive belched steam and slowly began to lurch forward.

Bapcat looked around. The train consisted of a steam locomotive and coal car, two dark green passenger coaches, and a yellow caboose.

Bapcat and Jordy moved quickly into the first passenger coach, pushing and pulling their gear inside with them. Benches, not compartments, but comfortable enough. Small-gauge rails, small cars. No other passengers. Bapcat looked through small dirty windows and saw their sleds falling behind the moving train. From here on out, how would they carry their gear?

Bapcat found his knife hand twitching and said only, "Did that really happen?"

"Impressive and professionally done, Captain," Dodge said, beginning to shed his outer layer of snowy clothing, then, remembering his edict, "Silence! You're a mute!"

A knock on their door interrupted them.

Jordy, after a nod from the major, said, "*Nastat.*"

Two slightly built men in civilian clothes brought a polished samovar for tea, and Dodge waved them out with an irritated gesture.

"Sonuvabitch," Jordy whispered. "You *stabbed* that guy, Lute. *Twice.* Son . . . of . . . a . . . bitch."

Bapcat understood Jordy's astonishment, his son's first unvarnished look at the cold-blooded reality of war.

"You afraid?" the boy asked.

"Of course. Fear keeps us on our toes."

"I've never seen you afraid of nothing," Jordy said.

"Feeling and showing are different things."

The boy had a lot to learn. Bapcat had not expected to ever be in uniform again, but here they were, thousands of miles from home, and if technically not in uniform, they were legally in the army and on government business. Churchill said American troops were coming in behind them. Did anyone back home know American boys were in Russia? Would they even care?

Bapcat had been in Cuba, killing Spaniards, wading through the dead and dying while back home, people knew only what they read in newspapers, much of it inaccurate, or even downright lies written by unethical reporters. Nothing had changed these twenty years later, nothing except his age. He had been around Jordy's age when he'd ridden with Colonel Roosevelt and the Rough Riders.

"Taiga," Jordy said, pointing at the dark, snowy land passing by. "That's what the Russians call this kind of land."

"Looks like the Upper Peninsula," Lute said.

"This place have a name?" Jordy wanted to know.

"Dodge mentioned we were somewhere between Soroka and something called Povynets."

Jordy chuckled. "*Soroka* means 'magpie,' and Povynets means *visyachynet*—'no hanging.' So we are somewhere between a magpie and no hanging."

Good grief. Russians. He felt Zakov in everything around them.

Dodge eventually stripped off his parka. "The engineer says there's Spanish influenza everywhere. Russian soldiers caught it from the

Germans, and when Russian soldiers pulled out of the war and came back, they brought it with them. Now it's spreading across the Fatherland. Luck and constitution determine who lives and who dies."

"Same as war," Bapcat said. "What's next?"

"Zvanka."

"Zakov's there?"

"No," the major said. Then, "I don't know."

"It's south of us," Jordy contributed. He had studied maps during the sub's journey and now carried them in his head. "On Lake Onega."

If Zakov wasn't in this Zvanka place, where in the dickens was he?

"What's in Zvanka that concerns us?" Bapcat ventured.

"Railroads," Dodge answered.

"How far?" Bapcat wondered out loud.

"Distances in Russia are irrelevant. It takes as long as it takes to get anywhere, and weather and luck each play a role."

"Just like back home in the Keweenaw, eh," Jordy said, smiling at Bapcat.

Winter, 1918. Zvanka at Last

"Further west is a rotten corpse of Bolos, Whites, Old Believers, and only God knows who—or what—else."

How to describe the place? Bapcat asked himself. The great Chicago rail-yards south of the city? Not that large, but just as confusing, and impossible to navigate without a pilot to lead you through. A wasteland for sure, with tracks and rolling stock as far as he could see. A place built by pragmatists with no imagination or models in mind.

The Murmansk line itself was a new narrow-gauge railway, a rickety construction. As far as he could see there were signals, and towers and gates and small buildings and people milling about in the snow, the trains all gathered like cattle ready to be shot out of a chute to pasture.

After twelve hours parked on a siding at the northern end of the yard, a delegation of a dozen men in dark suits came and climbed into the car, Jordy letting them in. The delegation entered meekly, and Bapcat wished he could understand Russian the way Jordy did. Had he been able to understand, he would have heard an interesting exchange.

"Zvanka proletariat," a short man with just one hand announced. "We are instructed to assist you to move east, alone and unobstructed. You will, comrade, understand that I can guarantee these conditions only as far as Vologda."

"Instructed by whom?" Dodge challenged.

The man looked nervous. "Let us omit names that need not be said aloud, comrade. My men will help you move your equipment and supplies to your eastbound train."

"How many cars?"

"Engine, coal car, your car, caboose," the man said.

"Crew size?"

"Engineer, stoker, brakeman, signalman, conductor."

"Other passengers?" Dodge pressed.

The Bolo looked at the major and said, "No."

"The conductor stays here," Dodge said. "And the stoker and brakeman. Our crew will now be two men. What engineer cannot read signals?"

"But they are a crew," the man said, objecting.

"And no doubt will be again, but not on this run," Dodge told the man.

The major handed the man his letter and watched him read it. Reading complete, the man sighed and said resignedly, "It shall be as you require, comrade."

"You may show us to our new train, but my men and I will transfer our own gear. Under no circumstances will your men touch anything. I assume you know the way, or do I have to find someone else?"

"We shall do as ordered," the man said. "Shall I wait outside until you are ready to move?"

"Do," Dodge said. "Make your colleagues and bosses aware of our authorization. We will not allow anything to interfere, understood?"

The man bowed and backed out as if leaving a royal presence.

Dodge waited until the man and his delegation were gone.

"Were they expecting us?" Jordy asked.

Dodge said, "Probably not us three, but something heavy. Word travels fast here, and our commandeering the Murmansk train no doubt created a lot of fuss and worry. Two things you do to worry Russians and get them on their back heels: Make a joke; or push them around, and keep pushing, giving them no opportunity to regroup or reassess."

Bapcat watched the men outside disappear between nearby trains, wave a hand at Dodge, and hold up a thumb to indicate they were gone.

"How much time to Vologda?" Jordy asked.

"Two days or less if they make us priority traffic. The letter should move us along, but there's no guarantee. So much traffic these days, with nobody knowing who is in charge, or for how long."

"They think we're real," Jordy said smugly.

Dodge smirked. "The people here are more easily swayed by such fiction than those east of here will be. Further west is a rotten corpse of Bolos, Whites, Old Believers, and only God knows who—or what—else. The Bolos to the east have some pockets of support and are consolidating power every day. In Vologda we will confront our first legitimate officials, and they will be educated men accustomed to dealing with difficult situations, challenges, and problems. They will be especially adept in handling foreigners, and if anyone will see through us, it is likely to be there. They will see and hear with great accuracy and sensitivity."

"Can we go around?" Jordy asked.

"Ah ... Russia," Dodge answered, which was no answer at all. "One line east, and it goes through Vologda; everything and everyone must pass through there, even tsars."

Two hours east of Zvanka they had settled into their new accommodations and were dining on foodstuffs fetched by the locals.

A man interrupted them. He was sharp-bearded, tall, fortyish, vulpine, and crook-backed. Jordy let him in. The man came no more than one step and stood, hat in hand, a supplicant posture.

Bapcat was dying to know what was going on.

The visitor said, "Sorry to intrude, sir, but the engineer wishes to inform your excellencies that Vologda is now under enemy control, and he does not wish to deliver you into their hands."

"Why is he sending *you* to deliver his message?" Dodge challenged.

Bapcat saw the man juggle his hat.

"Comrade Titov believes the engineer's word is God's word."

"You are Comrade Titov?

"*Da.* Yakov Abramovich Titov."

"And the engineer's name?"

"Bezmunyi, sir."

"And what is your job, Titov?"

"I am the stoker, sir."

"Are you a good stoker, Titov?"

"The best," the man said proudly.

"Can you do the engineer's job, Titov?" Dodge asked.

"Yes, comrade, I can."

"You would not exaggerate or lie to us, would you?"

"Never. Titov believes in truth."

"The engineer sent you because he thinks he is better than his passengers?"

Titov took a deep breath. "*Da*, comrade."

"Is he?" Dodge asked.

"No, comrade, but he is certain in his own mind."

"Do you respect his abilities, Titov?'

"No comrade. He is fraud and sycophant."

"Thank you for your courage and candor, comrade. Please inform the engineer that we wish to have his company. You can run the engine while he is with us, yes?"

"*Da*," Titov said.

"And if the engineer is relieved of duty, could you take over and perform in his place?"

Bapcat had no idea what they were talking about, but the Russian was sweating profusely, and it was cold in the car, very cold.

The man was suddenly glassy-eyed, and said nervously, "I shall do my best, comrade."

"You look shaky. Your best is shit to me, Titov. You can and will do the job, or not; which is it to be?"

"I shall do the job, comrade."

"Go now and send the engineer back. Tell me his name again."

"Bezmunyi, sir. Stepan Iosovich Bezmunyi."

Dodge laughed heartily. "You're joking, Stoker Titov."

Bapcat didn't get it.

"No, sir, stokers never lie."

"Is Comrade Bezmunyi loyal to the Party, Titov?"

"Who knows the truth in a man's heart?" the stoker replied.

"Very well. Send the engineer to us at once, and go take over his job for now."

The man rushed away.

After Titov had gone, Jordy laughed and looked at Bapcat.

"*Bezmunyi* is Russian for insane. Our engineer is named 'Insane.'"

Dodge was smirking. "You follow all that?" Dodge asked his sergeant.

Jordy said, "Enemy ahead, the stoker will take over from the engineer, whose name means 'Insane.'"

"Good; perfect. Comrade Titov seems to be ready to do Bezmunyi's job, the enemy really does control Vologda, or there is some other game underway."

"Which enemy?" Jordy asked.

"Exactly. We shall find out. Muskul, be ready, but if we need to apply force to the engineer, fists only, no knife—yet. I want him to continue doing his job if he tells the truth."

Bapcat nodded once, and felt his heart skip as Bezmunyi entered the car. The engineer had the complexion of an aged-out beet.

Dodge greeted him. "Comrade Bezmunyi, it was good of you to warn us that the enemy is ahead, but we are soldiers, and meeting the enemy is our sole purpose in life. Which enemy?"

Bapcat saw Bezmunyi flash a look of momentary confusion, which quickly turned to something else.

"What did that toadying bastard tell you?" Bezmunyi asked, in the high-pitched voice of an adolescent choirboy.

"What he said *you* told him to tell us."

"I said nothing about an enemy. Who *is* the enemy? This is his nonsense, and why he will never make engineer."

"Is he competent to run the train?"

"As long as everything is routine. When things turn sour, he freezes."

"You didn't tell him to tell us about the enemy?"

"I did not. As I said, *what* enemy? I simply told him to tell you he is at your service."

"Why would he make a point of telling us there is an enemy ahead, and why would he tell us that you sent him to relay such a message? This would seemingly be important enough for you to present to us in person, to answer any questions."

"*Da*," Bezmunyi said, nodding.

"Why would he do this?" Dodge asked. "Are you two at odds?"

"Titov is at odds with anyone he thinks he is better than, which is most of Russia. Engineers, comrade, are trained to go from destination A to destination B, to run their planned route, not to bother passengers with practical aspects of the journey."

"Are you committed to a cause, Bezmunyi?"

"Yes; my cause is my family—my wife and my two sons. No more, no less."

"And God?"

"When required."

"Or the Tsar?"

"There is no Tsar."

"In Titov's shoes, who would your enemy be?"

"White Army," Bezmunyi answered.

"If Vologda is under White control, what do you propose we do?"

"I will do what you order me to do, comrade. My name may mean 'insane,' but I am anything but. Bloody Nicholas was a disaster for Russia, he and his German wife. You want genuine *bezmunyi*, look to her and the crazy priest, Rasputin."

"Why would Titov not specify which enemy?"

"Man to man?"

"Of course." Dodge opened his hands to invite candor.

"He wants my job."

"Is he qualified?"

"As I said, for routine operations, but nothing more, and even that level of routine would put him at the edge of his mental capability. He goes to pieces quickly, and over nothing; even as a stoker he is stretched as thin as delicate glass."

"Titov seems to be running things all right at the moment?"

"The road is straight and easy for this part."

"Why did you send Titov to us?"

"I did not. He volunteered."

"He said you sent him. You take issue with that?"

"Of course I take issue with that. The conductor was briefly an engineer, but demoted for incompetence, and the signalman wants to move to my position. Titov is a sniveling liar. I don't know who you are, comrade, and I don't care, but you know less than shit about railroad operations and railroad politics and personnel."

"You are a blunt man, Bezmunyi."

"*I* am the engineer."

"We do not need to go through Vologda if there is no need, or if it will be too difficult. We are trying to verify the whereabouts of the Romanovs."

"They are not in Vologda," the engineer said.

"What's the railroad grapevine saying?"

The man smiled. "I heard from several people that the Imperial train was in Tyumen, and that passengers off the Imperial train got on a ship bound for Tobolsk."

"Credible voices?"

"My wife Olga," Bezmunyi said.

"What is your Olga's source?"

"She is secretary to the director of the Zvanka Yards."

"Where?"

"She is in Petrograd. I am assigned to Zvanka. We live in between. I take a train in one direction and she, in the opposite."

"How long has she been in this position?" Dodge asked.

"Four years as secretary, and chief secretary to the director since April sixth, last year."

Just after the abdication. "What happened to the former assistant?"

"Arrested and executed. The body was later delivered to his family, dumped in the street."

"A message?"

"The former assistant was a Royalist."

"But not Olga?"

"No, my wife and I are pragmatists and familyists."

"You concur with the man's execution?"

"No, it is the sort of thing the Cheka does, and in the Tsar's name. May I ask, sir, what are your orders?"

Bapcat understood the word Cheka from his years with Zakov. This was the Tsar's hated and brutal secret police force.

"If one wanted to go all the way to Tyumen by rail, could that be arranged by you?"

"One could, and I could arrange it, but rail regulations will require you to change trains in Vologda."

"This train can't go through?"

"This is not allowed. It is forbidden."

Dodge showed the man his letter of authorization. "If I order it done, will this make a difference?"

"Why should I agree?"

"Because I am in command."

"Not of me, comrade. I don't know you, and the letter could be—and is quite possibly—a forgery. I believe and trust no one and nothing in these terrible days."

"Pride is a sin, Engineer Bezmunyi."

"An engineer must be proud, confident, and in charge."

"I have the power to order you to do this," Dodge said.

"I am a Bolo engineer, and the Whites may want to arrest me and execute me as a traitor."

"I will not allow that to happen."

"You have no power over the Whites. You expect me to bet my life on your promise?"

"Or we can throw you off the train and let Titov take over."

Bezmunyi grinned sardonically. "Better you throw yourselves off the train before he puts it on its back, and if he does not, he will report you at the first opportunity to anyone he thinks can get you out of his hair."

"You're a Bolshevik?"

"I am a railroad man, and I object less to them than the Whites and Royalists who are reduced now to no more than the Tsar's dog-pack of blind followers."

"And Titov?"

"He changes sides by the moment. He is an opportunist."

"Do you need a stoker to run this thing?"

"Not once we are moving. There are stokers in Vologda, better men than Titov, and I can recruit one of them in short order."

"Even with the Whites in control?"

"It doesn't matter who is in control. All sides need rail stock."

"Please return to your cab and ask Titov to dismount."

"We are moving."

"Do you wish to stop and start again?"

"No. And if Titov won't go?"

"Throw him off the train."

Bezmunyi pulled back. "I can't do that, sir. I am a professional engineer, and a nonviolent man."

Dodge looked at Bapcat and pointed at the engineer. "Go, comrade. My man will take care of this." Dodge pulled Bapcat close and whispered, "Throw the stoker off the train."

Bapcat gave the major a questioning look, but followed the engineer forward.

Lute Bapcat saw Titov turn white when they climbed into the cab. Bapcat jerked the man to an open space on the deck, faced him forward, and gave him a hard shove. Pushed backward, the man would have faced certain death. This way he had a small chance, which was better than the alternative.

Bapcat didn't like the kinds of orders he was getting from Dodge. The mute part of this role was easy compared to what Dodge was ordering him to do.

Winter, 1918. Vologda

"A handshake is a deal, and a deal is a deal."

It is almost counterintuitive unless you are inside the process. While a game warden obviously needs to understand the ways of game and fish, even more importantly, he also needs to know the ways and means and motives of men who seek other creatures for their pleasure, comfort, and profit. Of all species, mankind is the most difficult to understand, much less predict. Early in life Bapcat had learned that he had the ability to size people up immediately. He seldom found that further contact altered his first conclusions in any way.

His supervisor Horri Harju called his ability one that all game wardens needed, but few possessed, which put them in danger more often than was reasonable. Zakov was equally adept at gauging people, though he came to his judgments more slowly and deliberately. Rarely did the partners' conclusions disagree. No doubt the Russian had good reasons for requesting Jordy and Bapcat's presence, but until he heard it from Zakov's lips, Bapcat couldn't even begin to imagine how he could help in a place where he lacked familiarity with everything, especially the language. It was a very strange request, and maybe one that hadn't even been made.

Although Bapcat couldn't understand a lick of the Russian's conversation with Dodge, he knew Jordy and Dodge would fill him in. He also knew how to watch eyes and facial expressions and a hundred other physical clues that might reveal a man's inner climate and emotional state.

Bezmunyi, the Russian train engineer, struck him as forthright and honest in how he carried himself. The man didn't strike him as hot-tempered, but something made him think he was the sort of man, once committed to a course of action, who would not easily be swayed from his goal.

Bapcat knew he could take Jordy aside and easily get him talking about the details of what had gone on, but this would be unfair. The military helped young men to grow up fast and part of that was following orders. Bapcat was supposed to be mute, and Jordy was to speak only Russian. Living with ambiguity and incomplete information was a big part of life, evidenced by this whole strange operation.

Exactly what was happening remained a mystery, and no doubt would until they found Zakov. He expected Dodge to occasionally pull him aside and bring him up to speed on various goings-on, but this hadn't happened in a while. Jordy, who was ordered to speak Russian only, but sometimes disobeyed Dodge and whispered to his father in English, would explain the best he could what was going on.

Tonight they had stopped in the middle of nowhere, *nowhere* seemingly *everywhere* in Russia. After they stopped, Dodge and Jordy and the engineer went off the railroad bed to a small fire where there were a dozen or more men gathered. Bapcat couldn't get a count because the only light was a lantern held by one of the men and the flickering, nervous light of the small fire at their feet. He thought he saw one man at the head of the group, short and burly in a greatcoat, with the massive head of a bear, hat off, hair thrusting in all directions.

Something poked Bapcat's ribs and startled him, enough to make him take a half step back from the touch.

"*Allo,*" a voice growled in Russian. "*So grazh dane!*"

Bapcat saw that it was their signalman, now also serving as stoker, and backup engineer. The American pointed at his mouth, made a talking motion with his lips, and shook his head.

The man slapped the American's arm and laughed. "*Ty byt nemoi, da?*" The signalman pointed at his own mouth, shook his head, and said, "*Nemoi?*" and again patted Bapcat's arm.

Nemoi. Did that mean "mute"? Had to be. Lute the mute, he thought, and stifled a sigh. This act was ludicrous, and difficult, but the Russian's voice and gesture seemed genuine. Bapcat smiled to thank the man as they watched what was going on near the fire.

If Jaquelle could see this charade she would spot its humorous aspects, of which there were plenty, but overall, this was anything but funny. It was deadly serious. They were in a foreign land and he had injured citizens here, and they were pretending to be something they weren't, which had to be illegal.

Meanwhile, Jordy and Dodge were engaged with the Russians, leaving Bapcat and the signalman in the dark. Mute and blind, Bapcat thought. This just keeps getting better. How in the world did Dodge obtain his so-called authorization letter? And who exactly did these other Russians think they were? This was frustrating, and growing more so as time passed.

The signalman disappeared as Bapcat watched Dodge listening carefully to the Russians. Eventually the pack melted into the black night and the two Americans and the Russian engineer trekked back to the engine and clambered aboard. Dodge immediately lit a Russian cigarette and offered one to Bezmunyi, who refused.

The chain-smoking habits of Russians of all ages amused Bapcat, and the thought of following their lead appalled him even more, but in such circumstances, when in Rome . . . do as Romans do made sense. One of his comrades in Cuba once gave him a cigarette during a break in the action and he'd asked the man why.

"Gives us something to do until we die."

Soldier humor, always dark. It felt like that here.

Jordy pulled Bapcat aside and leaned in close. "The major wants me to interpret as they talk."

Finally, Bapcat thought. Is Dodge less concerned about avoiding English now? No matter. Let Dodge worry about it. It's his call.

Jordy converted the overheard words in a whisper and without hesitation.

Dodge was speaking. "Your comrades seem to favor the Provisionals."

Bezmunyi didn't answer right away. Bapcat thought: Here is a calculating, precise man, careful, an engineer.

The Russian engineer said. "Sanity savors stability."

"Even at the price of Bolshevik power?"

Bezmunyi smiled wryly. "There is no stability in that gang. They are a bag of snakes, criminals, lifelong ne'er-do-wells and scoundrels, who have found purchase with the Reds, or opportunity, perhaps, to reverse the direction of their miserable lives and vault over legitimate and law-abiding citizens. Bolos are a mass of degenerates and deplorables grabbing at power, a dangerous thing," Bezmunyi concluded.

Quite a speech, Bapcat thought. What's the engineer's angle?

Dodge took a puff on his cigarette and exhaled. "It's easy enough to get out of Russia to another place. The borders here are long, gaps wide, and border guards, few."

"I am fully aware of our geography," the engineer said, "but I am Russian-born. Are you not?"

Interesting question. Does the engineer suspect the truth with them?

Dodge ignored the man, and asked instead, "Do you have a family?"

The man looked irritated. "We discussed this earlier. A wife, and my two sons."

Bapcat was focused now. A wife and *my* sons, not my wife and *our* sons. Is this what's really being said, and is Dodge paying attention? If he already knew this, why did he ask the man again? For my benefit? Interesting. Or did he forget? That would be troubling. God, I hope Jordy is interpreting this stuff right. He's so young, and Russian isn't his first language.

"Four can move as easily as one," Dodge pointed out.

"You are not Russian," Bezmunyi declared in English, which startled Bapcat. "You cannot be Russian. You have no grasp of the true Russian heart."

"The Bolos are in the process of cutting out that heart."

Bezmunyi grimaced. "Your point is sound, but even that is just one more air castle, and we are wasting time. You need to get through Vologda. If you are an agent of the Bolsheviks, I will not ask why and how you carry a Red *pass-billet*. You talk of leaving Russia, yet here you remain."

"I have things to do before I can think of leaving."

"Alone or with your men?"

"Some alone, but we are all in this together—the Three Musketeers; you know them?"

"Mais oui; Dumas, n'est-ce pas?"

Bapcat blinked. *The engineer speaks English and French, and Russian—and what else?*

"And you are in this now, as well, Comrade Bezmunyi, *deeply* in this."

"May I speak candidly, comrade?" the engineer asked in English.

"I prefer it."

Bapcat's thought: *Dodge isn't exactly embracing the engineer.*

"Tvoi nemoi," Bezmunyi said gruffly in Russian.

"Your mute," Jordy whispered.

"What about him?" Dodge replied.

"He makes me uneasy. You say he can hear and understand all, but he shows no sign of understanding anything. He is devoid of emotion, and he is calculating. He pushed the stoker off the train."

"As I ordered," Dodge said.

"But he allowed the man to go feet first, which made his survival more likely. *You* lack Bolo fire in your eyes, but your mute has it. His eyes burn holes in others. So why such leniency with the stoker? Who's leading who here?"

"Our mute is a soldier," Dodge said decisively, "a very hard soldier who follows orders. Can *you* follow orders, my friend?"

Bapcat was anxious for the man's answer. *The engineer thinks my eyes burn holes in others? Jaquelle didn't think so.*

Bezmunyi said, "I can deliver you to Vologda. I may have many professional tricks, but I am not a magician, and I don't believe in magic or miracles."

"We want to get into the city and have a few days to do some things, after which we want you to get us out and on to Tyumen in your train, with you as engineer. Will you continue east with us?"

The engineer tugged on the ends of his mustache. "I have a job, my wife has a job; why should I do this?"

Dodge switched directions, an old trick Bapcat had learned from interviewing people.

"Can you take the train through Vologda, yes or no?"

Bezmunyi scratched at his chin. "I cannot. You know this. All trains must stop here. All passengers must transfer to different equipment."

"Never an exception?"

"Never," the engineer said. "Track gauges are different."

The major laughed. "Of *course* there are exceptions. You already told us that the royal train went through, and I doubt if general staff or other governmental authorities are required to act like simple citizens. So you see, while authority to go through is possible, it is perhaps not routine, and possible only in an occasional way, yes?"

"Privilege can move through with the right authorization, but these tend to come from the west on the same-gauge tracks."

"Our authorization will get us through," Dodge said confidently "Besides, in your train, we are on the correct gauge. As I just told you, I can get us some days here before we push east."

"You talk nonsense," the Russian said. "You babble about theory, but our lives are lived practically. The royal administration controls all authorizations for travel. But our dear Tsar has abdicated and turned tail, and until a new Tsar is crowned, there *is* no royal administration."

"But *you* are still working, so someone must be making the practical decisions," Dodge countered.

"The Bolsheviks have established a hold here and there, and they issue orders and exceptions, at least for now. Tomorrow? Who knows." Bezmunyi shrugged.

Dodge showed him the letter of authorization again. "You think this isn't enough?"

"This is not a question I can answer, but it seems to me that your paper is good solely where the Bolsheviks have control."

"Vologda; Tobolsk?"

"There is no rail connection to Tobolsk at present. One must take a riverboat from Tyumen."

"But there is rail service east, from here to Tyumen?"

Bezmunyi nodded thoughtfully. "*Da.*"

"You could take us from here to Tyumen."

"Theoretically."

"What stops theory from becoming reality?"

"I am not currently appointed to operate east."

"*Were* you appointed at one time?"

"Yes, I have worked everywhere in my time. I was an engineer on the Transib. This was before I was married, of course."

"Tyumen would not stretch your abilities?"

"Not in the least."

"Good, it's settled then. You shall carry us to Tyumen."

Bezmunyi stiffened and made a loud sighing sound. "Excuse me, my new comrade, but are you a fool, sir? You didn't strike me as one until you began this unrealistic talk."

"Would a fool possess a letter such as this?" Dodge asked, brandishing the document.

The engineer waved a finger at Dodge. "You would see me stood against a wall and shot, comrade."

"You would not lack company."

Bezmunyi twisted his chin to the right. "You stole this authorization document or counterfeited it?"

"Do I look stupid?" Dodge countered, avoiding a direct answer.

"Stupid is rarely in appearances, but in actions taken."

"You do not trust me, Comrade Engineer?"

"As much as you trust me."

"I shall demonstrate my trust, my engineer friend."

This was twisting in ways Bapcat couldn't figure out as he listened to Jordy translate. Hearing this, he now thought he might be better off as mute and unhearing.

"You are gambling?" Bezmunyi wanted to know.

"Life is a gamble. We are Americans," the major said, and Bapcat felt his knees go weak. What in the hell was Dodge *thinking*?

The engineer did not waver, did not take a reflexive step back. If anything, he leaned subtly in. "American Bolsheviks?"

Dodge said in English, "Not Bolos; American military. You know that American, British, French, and Japanese troops are landing in Russia as we speak?"

"To what end—to restore Nicholas the Bloody?"

"On the contrary. And let us leave it at that. I assure you, we are not here to restore the Romanovs."

Jesus, Mary, and Joseph, Bapcat thought.

"There is no mention of foreign troops in the newspapers," Bezmunyi said.

"Russia is no longer in the war against the Germans. The Bolos are pulling troops out and have pulled back from the fight. With the Tsar gone, there is a vacuum, and no more eastern front to pull the Germans in two directions. The Bolos have signed a peace pact with the Germans."

Bezmunyi stiffened and turned red. "Never. Impossible. The Bolsheviks are not authorized. They do not run our government. Peace with the Kaiser? Never!"

"Nevertheless," Dodge said, "what I am telling you is true. We digress, Bezmunyi. Will you or will you not take this train, and us, to Tyumen?"

"The question is, why should I risk my hide and that of my family, which is what I will be doing?"

"You assess it correctly," Dodge confirmed. "Life is a gamble, and a better life is a gamble with even longer odds."

"A better life in Russia?"

"Not in Russia; not in our lifetime. If the Bolos come first in this contest, you can find the life you want in America. It is what we are about."

Bezmunyi laughed nervously. "You lie. You are testing me, and if I agree, your henchmen will rush in and haul me away to be shot."

"These *are* my henchmen, and *you* are my henchman. Yes, I lie, when circumstances dictate. But this is not such a time."

"Go to America?" the astonished Russian asked.

Dodge said, "*Da*, America; why not?"

"It is filled with Jews and cowboys who hang and burn Africans," the engineer said.

"Yes, it is filled with every kind of the worst—and the best—of human creatures," Dodge said. "There is nowhere in the world like it."

"I could do this . . . *with* my sons?"

Bapcat was listening closely. Again, *his* sons. What about his wife—*our* sons?

"And will, of course, if you choose. It's up to you."

"And, if I choose not to?"

"I will have to think about it. Our lives are for the moment more in your hands than they were just an hour ago."

"Does that give you pause, comrade?"

"It does," Dodge said.

"When would we do this thing?" Bezmunyi asked.

"America? As soon as my men and I are done with our business in Russia."

"And, if your business concludes unsatisfactorily?"

"As long as we are alive, we will keep our promise. We have a saying in America: 'A handshake is a deal, and a deal is a deal.'" Dodge extended his hand.

Bezmunyi took it in his paw and said, "God protect me."

Jordy spoke, "God protect us all."

Lute Bapcat thought, We're in a lunatic asylum.

12

Winter, 1918. Vologda

"It means Corpse Street."

A nervous rail official met them at the railyard and told them they were summoned to meet leaders of the *Komitet Sovetskii*, the local town council, which had sent a guide to show them the way. The escort wore a mixture of uniforms and had Asian features, with deep smallpox scars that left his eyes puffed and pinched to the size of pinheads. His sun-browned flesh looked like it had been unwashed since the Great Flood, and he wore a chest-length mustache whose tails hung down like Siamese snakes.

Dodge declined the escort, who did not argue, but paralleled them as a distant flanker, rifle in hand. The three Americans made their way into the city while Bezmunyi took care of water, fuel, and finding other supplies.

Bapcat was wary as they moved into the city, which reeked of horse shit, fires, death, panic, and defeat. The people were draped in black and shuffling, their boots shushing like small plows. Bodies were strewn in the streets or piled at intersections, and in the center aisle of a wide bouvelard, a massive row of dead had been stacked like firewood. They were being removed by sluggardly people with black cloth masks over their faces.

The bodies were beside a large hand-painted street sign that said *Merivets Ulitsa*, which meant nothing to Bapcat. Jordy whispered, "It means Corpse Street." The Cyrillic lettering of the makeshift sign was bright red, hastily painted and already turning brown, given no chance to

85

dry. Drips migrated down the board to pool on the snowy cobbled street below. It was too cold for flies.

Dodge told the railroad greeter they would be fine in the city, whose streets were as familiar as his hand. How? Bapcat wondered.

"What do they want?" Jordy asked their major in English before catching himself. Bapcat noted that their discipline was already beginning to fray, specifically their peculiar major's insistence that he and Jordy always speak Russian among themselves.

"They will try to intimidate us," Dodge answered in Russian. "Steady as she goes, Sergeant."

Bapcat had no idea what the words were, but the tone was one of "keep cool."

"You know this place?" Jordy asked, slipping into English again.

Dodge closed his eyes and groaned, and answered in English.

"Not well. Most Western embassies moved their operations here from Petrograd. The German salient was not far south of the capital, and this caused widespread fear that the Germans could strike quickly and easily take the city. The Russians also moved their government inland—to Moscow. But the Brits, Swedes, and English are here, or were."

"What about our embassy?" This from Jordy.

"Probably in Archangelsk. Last I heard, the American ambassador was thinking it would be safest to be closer to American troops—in case. Vologda is a city without soul or identity. It is controlled by politicians who are no better than professional thieves, *voryi nyi*. Everything here is about gold, if it can be had, or money, or trade if there's no gold available. Nothing moves here without money to power and push it along."

Bapcat wondered how Dodge knew all of this.

Jordy asked, "And us?"

Dodge said, "Our currency is better than gold, and can be used to ace all the gold and platinum we might need."

Bapcat would only realize the significance of this comment later in the mission.

"There was a sign by the dead," Jordy told Bapcat. "*Gripp mertvyi*—it means 'influenza dead.' The flu is here."

Dodge said over his shoulder, "Dead is dead, and I doubt burial crews make any distinction between causes, which to the dead are quite irrelevant."

They saw sickly-looking men and women trying to haul the dead onto a sledge. There were body parts strewn about in the street, a veritable trail of fleshy crumbs through the urban forest. The people handling the bodies looked little better than those they collected, but Bapcat saw how they kept at the grisly business. This was disease, not war, but it looked, smelled, and felt similar.

Dodge steered them around a pyramid of stiff bodies into a tall white building with the word *Gosbank* chiseled in Cyrillic letters into the marble facade. The interior boasted a massive open lobby filled with soldiers and cookfires and stacks of weapons, swarms of people yelling and moving around frantically. Two goats were hanging nearby, skinned and dripping blood.

A man in a coarse dull gray suit met them and pointed at a wide bank of marble stairs. They ascended to a wraparound balcony and went through a set of doors that led into a large room filled with desks. Sounds assaulted them: the clickety-clacketing of typewriters; telephones ringing; and ponderous teletype machines, buzzing and thudding mushily. The sight and sounds of so much equipment made Bapcat uneasy. The side with the best communications in a war usually prevailed. This had been true in Cuba, where the other side held all the premium high ground, but could not marshal and move their forces quickly enough. The Americans had smashed into them and broken their lines with what amounted to lightning speed.

But this place, no matter which side might turn out to be in charge, looked far better prepared.

The three Americans were shown into a large conference room with an exotic polished-wood table and chairs. A huge silver samovar sat on one end of the table, small russet-colored clay cups arranged in lines like tiny soldiers.

Eventually seven men and a woman filed into the room from another entrance, all of them sporting bright red cockades on their suit lapels. They were all dark-skinned and stoop-shouldered, and they avoided eye contact. The sole woman had long hair the color of ripe corn, skin as pale as the room's walls, and eyes the hue of sun-bleached slate. As striking as her appearance was, her eyes had no visible life or light in them. The Russians clustered en masse at the other end of the table, nobody speaking or moving.

Bapcat was edgy and on full alert, his nerves sparking.

The woman separated from the others and floated gracefully the length of the table to Jordy Klubishar. Her hair was so yellow it seemed to bounce light off of Jordy's dark tunic. But if light flew off her hair, nothing showed in her eyes, and Bapcat braced himself.

"*Ya starosta,*" the woman said quietly as she examined Jordy's face. "*Ya marushka.*"

Bapcat knew one of the words, as Zakov often threw it around. *Starosta*—leader. Was Marushka a name? The woman's? Her presence and apparent role as leader, if real, were a surprise. His sense was that this place was no less welcoming of women in positions of authority than the United States, which had little interest in such things. This made Jaquelle Frei unique, a virtual freak in the almost exclusively male commercial world.

The blonde snarled.

That was clear enough. What was her interest in Jordy, and what was she up to?

"*Pritti so menya,*" she said softly, her meaning clear enough. She wanted Jordy to come with her.

No chance.

Bapcat pushed between the woman and his son and pressed his knife-point against her stringy white throat. She smiled and folded her upper lip back, showing broken green teeth and gaps.

Bapcat immediately felt something pointy pushing against his heavy parka. Unlike the woman, he was dressed in heavy winter gear, and she, only in a thin robe. She would feel his blade long before she could get her knife through his clothing layers. No contest. He pushed the point hard enough to draw a drop of blood and raised an eyebrow for emphasis. He felt her point pull away from him.

The woman looked over at Jordy and said "*Potem pozhalui?*" but Jordy stood fast. She withdrew to her group, went to the door through which they had entered, paused, looked back, and leered. She blew a kiss at Bapcat, who by now was keyed up beyond reason, his mind yelling *This isn't over yet!* Green rotten teeth in that beautiful package of woman? God.

Bapcat kept his eyes on the group and the door and stepped back beside Dodge.

One of the other men advanced halfway and began to talk in a tone barely above a whisper, and Bapcat, understanding nothing, focused on the men behind the spokesman. The language thing—the whole situation—were wearing on him, but he had no trouble staying focused.

When various conversations with Russians were explained after the fact to Bapcat, they made little sense to him, the Russians tending to ramble on at length. It would be annoying to have to deal with them full-time over a long period, and now, with his brief experience in the country, he could see that his friend Zakov was unique for his tribe: a man who could get directly to the point or fall back on endless platitudes and meaningless words, as needed. He missed Zakov, and now, having had some glimpse of where Pinkhus Sergeyevich had been born, he had a better sense of how Russian Zakov was, and wasn't. His Russian friend had adapted well to American ways. Was he equally comfortable and adept now that he was back here?

One thing about Zakov had always irritated him, and this was that his friend gave him almost nothing about his family or childhood, and only scant facts, as it suited him, about his military career and experience. He was neither yappy nor tight-mouthed, his friend.

Bapcat caught something moving just to the side of the group of men, and his eyes quickly locked on the very large bore of a black revolver in the hands of the green-toothed woman. She was gliding toward him, her weapon raised, her corn-colored hair flopping behind the revolver. She was chanting, "*Pomeshannyi chadovische, pomeshannyi chadovische.*"

Bapcat calmly raised his rifle, placed the sight on an area between her eyes, and squeezed off two rapid shots, leaving everyone's ears pounding with the reports and resounding echoes. The woman lurched to one side and crumpled, and the revolver clattered across the floor and went off accidentally, clipping the upper leg of the exotic wood table and shattering it into numerous splinters, some of which stuck in Bapcat's hand and face. He did not react. Instead, he swung the weapon over to the spokesman, who had dropped to the floor, as had all the other men. They were all prone, looking panicked and, with the woman down, anxiously staring at each other to see who might lead them.

Who the hell were these people? Not leaders. Sheep at best. And who the hell was she, and why this unprovoked attack?

A reluctant spokesman struggled to his feet and surged to Bapcat and threw his arms around him, clinging to him like a bear as the other men charged forward and joined them. Bapcat found himself dancing around and someone shouting, *Blagoslovit nash spasitel, blagoslovit nash spastitel!*"

The game warden tried to peel the men off him and saw Jordy grinning as seven grunting, chirping creatures squeezed him. Finally he raised his rifle straight up, broke the hold, and shoved them away. They kept smiling and nodding. God. This whole country was nothing but lunatics!

Dodge stared at the dead woman, who only had half a head now. Large, loose clumps of hair were spattered on the white plaster wall. Bapcat saw that the Russian men didn't look down at her. They acted as if her death were a gift.

Several soldiers came flying up the marble staircase and into the room, but the three Americans had their weapons at the ready. The spokesman yelled at the soldiers to calm down and, having stopped the soldier threat, led his group away. The soldiers came in and looked at the body, and the first three or four grinned and spat on the remains.

Bapcat was amazed. Not a popular leader, then.

Jordy looked poleaxed, and though he had his weapon up and ready, Lute sensed that the boy's mind was elsewhere. His own mind was trying to take off and hide. He'd just shot a woman in the head. This was crazy; not war, but something else.

Dodge stared at the body.

"*Bog,*" he muttered as he leaned over, picked up the revolver and gold dagger, and handed them to Bapcat. "*Vash,* comrade."

"*Vnimanie, puskat!*" Dodge growled at the soldiers, waving them back to where they had come from. "*Vnimanie, puskat!*" The soldiers bowed their way out and Dodge pushed his comrades and nodded that they should get out of the building, fast.

They left and made their way directly back to the railyard, speaking to no one.

When they reached their train, Dodge waved Bezmunyi to their car as they mounted the metal ladder steps. They went inside and began to throw off their outer clothing.

The engineer arrived quickly, looking calm.

"Chaos in the city," Dodge said in English. "A woman was in charge. No idea who she was or what."

Bezmunyi answered tentatively in English. "Was?"

"We had to kill her." He pointed at Bapcat, who was glad for the language change.

Bezmunyi looked out a window.

"There's no mob coming," Dodge said. "They hated her, and I think we did them a favor. She wanted a fight, but the rest of them had no stomach for it."

The engineer said in English, "They will find the stomach soon enough, and then they won't be able to stop themselves. Power is as catching and deadly as influenza."

Bezmunyi looked at Dodge. "Did the woman have straw-colored hair, beautiful, until she opened her mouth?"

Dodge said, "You know her."

"*Da—of* her," the engineer said. "She goes by *Zelenyi klyky*. She's Rasputin's cousin, crazy like him. The Tsar's people had a hard time killing that holy bastard."

Jordy leaned close to Bapcat, whispered, "*Zelenyi klyky* means 'green fangs'—like a viper's."

"It took only two bullets for this one," Dodge said. "The second round was redundant."

"Are you sure? They had to kill the monk several times to make it permanent."

"*Da*, dead certain. She now has two heads, neither in operating order."

"The Bolsheviki are not in control here?" Bezmunyi asked. "I understood her to be loosely a Royalist."

Dodge said, "No one seems to be in charge. It's up for grabs. Are we coaled, watered, and supplied?"

"The coal and water, yes; food, what I could find in this short time. Ready for orders."

"Fire us up."

"Destination?"

Dodge told the engineer, "Take us outside this madhouse for now—and eventually, to Tyumen."

Thirty minutes later the train lurched and sighed with strain as it began to gather momentum forward. As they moved through the sprawling railyards, Bapcat began to let himself relax.

Who the hell was this Rasputin character they were referring to?

13

Winter, 1918. On the Road to Tyumen

"I am called *Volshebnik*—the Magician."

Bapcat felt the brakes begin to slow the train. The car was as dark inside as out, and peering outside, he could see expanses of old gray snow, nothing fresh.

"Why are we stopping?" Dodge muttered sleepily. "Goddammit, what's going on? I issued no orders to stop. Sergeant, get up to the engineer and tell him I want to see him *now*," adding, "and when you get up there, stay and help the stoker. You awake, Sergeant?"

"Awake, yessir, on my way, Major."

Bapcat heard Jordy leave the car and closed his eyes, not yet wanting to wake up. Not because he'd been having a good dream. He supposed he dreamed, and Jaquelle insisted all people did, but if so, he rarely remembered any of his. Too tired, he guessed. Sometimes he wondered what not remembering meant, if anything.

He hoped Jordy was all right. The catwalk to the engine and coal car was narrow, and there were no safety straps or even grab-bars along the way. If you slipped, you were on your own, and if you fell . . . He didn't want to think about that.

"Captain?" Dodge asked.

"Awake," Bapcat said, grudgingly sitting up and setting down his feet. "Why are we braking?"

"I mean to find out," Dodge said. "This was not in my instructions."

Bapcat had no idea what the major had told the engineer, because he had done this away from Jordy and him. Instructions implied a plan, and this ought to be encouraging, but so far the plan felt pretty much like it was being made up minute by minute as they went along. This didn't necessarily make it good or bad, workable or unworkable, but it felt uncomfortable.

Something else bothered him more. We're not at war with the Russians, yet we've killed Russians who are not legally our enemies. What does that mean? Are we still looking for Zakov, or the Romanovs, and in what order of priority? So many questions, no damn answers.

Fifteen minutes later, Bezmunyi slid open the carriage door and stepped inside. He was wearing black oilskin and looked like a drowned rat, snow cascading off him like dandruff.

"Why is there no light?" Bezmunyi asked.

Bapcat was shocked to see Jordy right behind the engineer, given Dodge's order.

"Is there a problem I should be aware of, Comrade Engineer?" Dodge said, in English, ignoring the engineer's question.

"We are being signaled to stop."

"A trap? Ambush?" Dodge asked.

Bapcat had wondered the same thing, and tried to see outside through the filthy window.

"A personal signal," the engineer said. "Years ago we railmen realized that the State lied regularly to us about anything and everything—lied about things we needed to know or neglected to tell us things of interest. It occurred to us that trainmen knew more about what was going on in the country at any given time than most regular citizens, so we devised a signal code to help us spread factual, accurate information."

"Like semaphore?" Dodge asked.

The major was dressing as he talked, and Bapcat began to do the same. He was grateful that Jordy had come closer, in order to translate.

The engineer said, "Different, yet similar, reduced to a few signals conveying real safety information that should not be passed by mouth if one doesn't want to get sideways with the official government position, *da*?"

Dodge seemed irritated, his mind occupied. "Fine, of course; message, not paper, no record, matter of security. What the hell are you doing here, Sergeant?"

Jordy didn't cower. "The engineer said there was no need for me forward. The stoker can handle it alone."

"I ordered you to stay forward," Dodge said, sharply rebuking the boy, who immediately moved to leave the car once again.

But the engineer said with a growl, "Stay here, Sergeant. *I* decide who is in my cab." Then, turning to Dodge, he glared. "There is no need for that boy up there. He can be of more help here."

"As to your inquiry about our location," the engineer said, "we are about eighteen hours west of Tyumen, approaching the Bad River, *Giblyi Rechta.*"

"A location of consequence?" the major asked.

"There is a severe valley, a land formation important to various military tacticians and strategists. It is the sole aspect of note for the *Giblyi.*"

Dodge said, "Are you going to stand here all night, or are you going to find out why we are being signaled to stop?"

"The snow is already turning to rain," the engineer said, "and it will be heavy. It is of course far too early for us to move from winter to *rasputitsa,* the mud season, which history teaches was the beginning of the end for Napoleon."

"*Rasputitsa,*" Dodge said. "The season of bad roads, then no roads, and little movement; when the world stalls, all at the same time. But we are on tracks, not dirt roads, and Bonaparte's dragon tail was far too long to maintain, unlike ours, which is contained here, with us. Napoleon could hardly maneuver, while we have few limitations—is this not so, Chief Engineer?"

Bezmunyi shrugged and departed while Dodge was still talking. Bapcat was pretty sure the major hadn't even noticed.

Jordy had left with the engineer, leaving Bapcat alone with the major.

When the game warden started to light a lantern, Dodge said, "Keep it dark for now."

Bapcat hoped Jordy was all right. Who had signaled them to stop?

Another half-hour, and Bapcat heard noise. The slider opened again and Bezmunyi came in, as drenched as he'd been before.

"Where is the light?" Bezmunyi asked, in English.

"Never mind that. What is happening?" Dodge demanded.

"My colleagues inform me that there is a Bolshevik force five *versts* ahead."

"How large a force?" Dodge wanted to know, staying in English, and making Bapcat feel more relaxed. Where was Jordy?

"A thousand men, perhaps, heavily armed."

"Why are they there?"

"They are attempting to cross a bridge held by a large force of Whites on the opposite span. The Bolsheviks want to move eastward to meet the Royalists, who are advancing from the west. There is, it seems, a stalemate at this bridge."

Dodge said to Bapcat, "Hear that, Captain? We are approaching a fight over a bridge. Reds on one side, Whites on the other."

Then, turning to Bezmunyi, Dodge said, "Our letter should get us past both sides, should it not, Chief Engineer?"

"Alas," Bezmunyi said, "it is your letter, not mine. I should think it will get us through the Red line, but it will have no value on the other side."

Dodge grumbled to himself. "I suppose we shall have to take a side in this thing, at least temporarily. Can your colleague get word to the Bolo commander ahead and ask for a parley when we arrive?"

"The system does not work that way, sir. It has served its purpose in alerting us to the problem ahead, and now it is up to us to solve it. This is the Russian way."

Dodge seemed to swallow his irritation. "Get as much information from your man as you can regarding the Bolo force, thank him for warning us, and let us steam forward to find these red *warriors*." The last word dripped sarcasm.

Soon after the train began to move again, Jordy returned.

"Bolos and Whites are in a scrap ahead," he said excitedly. "We going to pick a side?"

Dodge said confidently, "We shall play Red *and* White, cover all possibilities, as in roulette. Whatever happens, we *will* keep moving eastward."

They were in a sea of Bolshevik fighters who looked like cartoon Indians to Bapcat: furs, feathers, bells and beads, red ribbons, bandoliers, swords, knives, and a mix of modern and ancient firearms. No two soldiers were armed or dressed the same, but all of them were smiling and seemingly happy for the train's arrival.

When Dodge went outside to meet the Bolo leader, the revolutionaries immediately put up a dilapidated tent and began pouring vodka and offering tin plates of *zakusky*, various cold meats and fishes, all of which Dodge officiously turned down, while a burly man in a dark bear fur kept trying to hug and kiss the major's whiskered cheeks.

"*Zakusit, zakusit*, have food, a snack," the Russian in the bearskin urged.

Dodge finally pushed the much shorter man backward and looked down at him. "Can you read?"

The man laughed. "I have no need personally, but when we as a group need this thing, I have Comrade Niedbalski, *nash krasnyi evrei*, to manage that for us."

Jordy leaned close to Bapcat. "He's calling the man their 'Red Jew.'"

"How do your men read their orders?" Dodge wanted to know.

"Like birds, we sing it to each other," the bear man said, and all the men around him began tweeting and whistling until he raised a hand and cut off the din. "Read, who needs to read? We hear and then we do. Or we choose not to do. This is our way. We are a brotherhood, and I am the military leader, *polkovo dets*."

"Do you have a name, Military Leader—a rank?"

"I am called *Volshebnik*—the Magician—and I need no rank. Here the Magician commands, just as on the taiga, the bear rules."

Dodge grabbed the authorization letter and held it out. "Where is your Red Jew?"

The Magician sniffed at document, looked it up and down, and handed it to a wolfish man with a long white beard and thick spectacles, a black patch over one lens.

Niedbalski took the paper in a steady hand and read quickly, moving his lips. When finished, he held it out to his leader and told him, "It's a kind of wolf ticket."

The Magician grinned. "A wolf ticket, eh?"

The bearded man grinned insipidly and began nodding wildly. Bapcat gripped his rifle tighter. Dodge stood with his usual impassive face and the Magician began talking.

"I like wolf tickets, last chances; that describes us all. It is Boss God who puts us in this position in life, not with the help of the Romanovs and their ass-suckers. Do you know the story of the Spain-man who landed in Mexico and immediately had his men burn all their ships so they would have no choice but to follow him and go forward to seek gold and treasure? Now, *that* is a wolf ticket, comrade."

Dodge said, "Where did you learn this story, Comrade Magician?"

The Bolo leader scowled. "Am I telling it wrong, or was it told to me wrong?"

"Umm," Dodge said, "it is fine as told."

The Magician's face suddenly became bright red. He yanked a Nagant revolver out of a shoulder holster, walked over to a smooth-shaven man with salt-and-pepper hair, and shot him in the head. He then turned to Niedbalski and the other Bolos.

"Erase the story this nonperson told us. He is erased, his story erased; we shall tell this story no more and refer never again to the creature who told it."

All of this was in Russian, and Jordy, leaning close, was keeping up, but Bapcat knew he was tired.

The Magician had just shot another man. Why? Something to do with a story, and if it was the story the Magician had told, Bapcat had heard the same one from Roosevelt long ago, on the ship to Cuba. The story the Magician told was identical to the Colonel's, yet this maniac in the bearskin had shot a man in cold blood over it. This place was far worse than anything he could have imagined. In Cuba, at least, they had fought real soldiers, not babbling lunatics.

The Bolos stoked a huge fire while their leader talked to Dodge. Bapcat saw the major looking over at him several times, making eye contact, but keeping his face impassive.

Bapcat got ready to do something if the major called for it.

"We shall need to cross the bridge," Dodge told the Magician, who clapped his hands together.

"As do we, comrade. This is a meeting of good fortune!" The Magician spread his arms. "We shall deliver you safely across, comrade."

Dodge said, "Your offer is greatly admired and welcomed, but we have no need for assistance, comrade. We do not need you to cross over with us."

"One for all and all for one," the Magician said. "We shall go across together and kill the pretenders. Of course you need us! *God* has sent you to us!"

"Perhaps so," Dodge said. "And who would I be to question the will of God? But as generous and brave as your offer is, we neither need nor want your help."

The Magician continued to grin, though his voice dropped an octave.

"Ah, God sent you to us, because *we* need *your* assistance, and if you will not willingly give us what God has declared ours, we shall prevent you from leaving here. You see?" he concluded brightly. "We have common interests."

Dodge rattled the letter in the Bolo leader's direction and the Russian spit in the fire.

"Paper is for wiping shit." The man brandished his Nagant. "This is steel, and real. Are you a paper man, comrade, or a real man?"

Bapcat sensed the moment was at hand. Dodge touched the side of his head and pointed. The Michigan man struck the Bolo leader in the side of the face with the butt of his rifle and pressed his dagger to the man's throat as he lay on the ground, bleeding profusely and shaking his head as if trying to clear cobwebs.

The Magician looked up at Bapcat and smiled. "Now we understand each other, comrades. We are all men of action here, real men, not paper toys. I would never stand in your way," he said, "but we are Bolsheviki, the majority by name and definition, and so I will do as I must and confer with my men, who shall democratically decide."

The man struggled to his feet and turned to his men. "Shall these new comrades help us attack the White devils or go free on their own?"

A single answer from the ragtag group: "Attack!"

"And if they refuse to help?"

The group, again: "Kill them!"

"You see," the Magician said, "this is how it is, how we are—and who am I to go against those who have elected me to lead them?"

"Yes, of course," Dodge said, his tone softening.

Bapcat had known the major long enough to understand that he was mulling over options as he tried to buy time. Clearly the Russians had an edge in this negotiation. How would Dodge handle this? Attacking the man had not turned the situation in their favor.

The Bolo leader became assertive. "You must choose one side or the other."

Dodge said, "I have a job, and a task; fighting here with or against you is not what I am sent to do, Comrade Magician. But perhaps there is middle ground."

"I think you will fight with us," the Magician said, "or you will no longer be able to fight anyone."

Dodge sucked in a breath and let out a soft sigh that Bapcat was certain the Magician had not picked up on.

"Yes, of course there is a middle ground where we can assist each other," Dodge said. "A deal."

"Make your proposal, comrade."

"You have Lewis guns?" Dodge asked.

"Four," the Bolo leader said.

"We will take two of them and ammunition in return for our services in getting you across the bridge."

"You must stop and fight when we are across. We can do great things together, your great iron beast and my iron men." The Magician turned to his men, who raised swords and axes and rifles in unison and let out a grunt, heavy with violent intent.

"*Skhoditsa*," the Magician said. "We agree!" He turned to his men. "They will fight beside us!"

The soldiers cheered, shot off their rifles, and more vodka flowed, bottles appearing from all sides.

Russia or the old Wild West? Bapcat asked himself. What here was real? Thus far, almost everywhere they had gone they had encountered seemingly loose and out-of-control mental cases.

"Two guns plus ammunition? You ask a high price," the Magician said, taking a long pull on a bottle and passing it to Dodge, who took an equally long pull before handing it back.

"I pick which two," the major added.

"*Nyet, nyet,* I pick. I lead here. These are *my* guns."

"Not your men's guns—collective property?"

The man made a face and pushed his tongue out. "I am no fool. I choose."

Dodge again touched the side of his head, but before Bapcat could attack, the Magician held up his hands. "Of course, you shall select. I should have it no other way. And may I tell you, comrade, that we shall cross at last light, to put the sinking sun in their eyes."

"Why so soon?" Dodge came back. "Full darkness is the aggressor's best friend."

"The devils live in darkness," the Magician declared.

"More superstitions," Jordy whispered behind Bapcat. "They want to attack at last light before the spooks are out and about."

"Very well," Dodge said, "Nay—you pick which two guns, and I say we go across in the dark. Enough talking. Now show me *our* Lewis guns."

Bapcat knew a few things about Lewis guns, which had been designed in the United States and mass-manufactured in England. The guns were barely more than two feet long, and steadied by tripods. The range was said to be a half-mile with a fifty- or hundred-round pan magazine. The gun could be carried and fired by one man. Why Dodge wanted Lewis guns was obvious. It took two men to operate other automatic weapons.

The Magician refused to show them the guns, but acceded to the major's insistence on attacking in the night.

"Tell us about the bridge," Dodge said to the Magician, with Jordy interpreting quietly.

The Magician lifted his chin slightly. "You are trainmen with the big paper; you should know this better than my soldiers and me."

"Humor me," Dodge told the man. "Two sources are better than one, and my only one is quite new to me, so I welcome any help, you see?"

The man in the bearskin said, "Wooden trestle, thirty-five Markovian fathoms deep."

"What is that in meters?"

"Sixty-two?" the man said, looking to the Red Jew for confirmation.

Niedbalski nodded solemnly. "Six-one-point-nine-four, Comrade Magician."

Jordy said, "Two hundred feet is high and deep."

Dodge looked up at the rainy sky and at his watch and told the Russian, "We assemble for the attack in one hour. Have your men bring the Lewis guns with us now so we can prepare for the attack."

The Magician waggled a finger. "In one hour, two hundred men with your guns and your ammo. That is the deal."

"I see," Dodge said. "One hour then, comrade."

Bapcat and Jordy followed their major back toward the train as the Russians resumed drinking, this last fact not lost on Bapcat, and leaving him not a little anxious.

14

Winter, 1918. A Bridge Over Neutrality

"All words are elastic, Sergeant."

Had Virgil dragged Bapcat into the Underworld for a tour of all mankind's sins, he could not have done a more thorough job than Dodge. But Dante's fantasy netherworld had neat levels and gradations, where the Hell that was Russia seemed to have none, and Bapcat, who had never heard of Dante Alighieri, and was unlikely to ever hear of him, knew Hell when he saw it.

Bapcat knew Jordy was mired somewhere between bored, fascinated, and scared, and that their mission seemed to have no focus, which was not how he grew up thinking about soldiering and war.

When the major told Bezmunyi what he wanted done with the caboose, the engineer nodded and raised no concerns. Seemed to Bapcat that the engineer was standing off to the side, wondering how the Americans would pull off this crossing.

"Do you understand, Chief Engineer?" Dodge asked.

"*Da.*"

"Then do it," the major ordered.

When the engineer explained to the stoker what was to happen, the latter scratched his head. "Are we going to die here, Engineer Bezmunyi?"

"We all die in due time, Comrade Elpikovny. We are born dying."

The time came and the Magician arrived leading two hundred fighters, who brought with them two Lewis guns and ten wooden cases of magazines, all of which were hurriedly stashed in the train's spare carriage.

Dodge and the Magician stood behind the train, facing each other.

"Load your men in the caboose, comrade."

"Even the Magician cannot manage that! They will fall off. There is no room."

"There is ample space, and if they are way back here, the enemy will not see them until it is too late. We shall have the element of surprise," Dodge explained. Jordy translated quietly for Bapcat.

The major added, "If we spread the men over the entire train, they may be seen quickly and the Royalists will annihilate us, so this is your choice: Put your men in back for maximum tactical surprise, or spread them out for tactical destruction. It's your decision, Military Leader."

The Magician looked around at his men and after a sigh, conceded. "All of you onto the caboose like monkeys on the rocks in the zoo."

The men grumbled but began climbing aboard, scuffling lightly for what they thought would be a place with a secure hold.

The Bolo leader looked at Dodge and grinned. "I love this plan! But I shall ride in front with you."

Dodge said, "I am surprised that an elected leader would not ride with the men who elected him to lead."

The Magician obviously did not like hearing this, but Dodge's point was clear, and the Russian was nervous.

"I shall lead my men from being with my men not apart from them," the Magician said. "God is whispering to me that this is a fine plan, the best, the greatest ever."

"It is admittedly more comfortable with us," Dodge said, but the Russian barked resolutely, "I have made my decision and God confirms it. Do not argue."

"As you wish, Military Leader Volshebnik."

"In our company, failure is punished by death," the Russian leader said.

"That seems extreme," Dodge told the man. "Even wasteful. Some failures are not one's fault. They are made by fate and nothing more than that."

"This is our way," the Bolo leader said. "Someone must pay. This is God's way, too, but he calls it sin, not failure."

The Americans went forward while the Bolsheviks settled on and in the caboose. Bezmunyi began to move the train forward. It was several *versts* to the bridge, and although the Russian leader wanted last light, Dodge's insistence on darkness for the the attack had won out, and in the Reds' minds, would succeed or fail on the element of surprise.

When the engineer got the machine to full power and began to move forward, Jordy and Bapcat retreated to the car ahead of the caboose and watched. Signalman Elpikovny had installed a chain between the cars, and as the strain of movement increased, the chain snapped, disconnecting the caboose and almost slingshotting the remainder of the train forward, engine, coal car, and two carriages.

Bapcat expected pandemonium from the freed caboose, but there was nothing. He suspected the Magician's tactical instincts had taken over, and that as the train flew forward, the Russian would be moving behind them with his men, hoping for cover. Would he suspect this caboose separation had been planned by the major?

"Do Russians believe in God?" Bapcat asked Dodge.

"Russians, yes; Bolos, no—at least, not officially."

"And the Magician?"

"The Magician recognizes only one God: himself."

As they approached the White-held bank on the other side of the bridge, Dodge, Jordy, and Bapcat dropped off the train, which kept slowly edging forward. Dodge told the leader of the Whites, "To arms, to arms! The Bolsheviks tried to use us to get to you. They are crossing the bridge behind us in the dark as we speak, two hundred men led by one who calls himself the Magician. He has perhaps eight hundred more men on the far bank. This is only his advance guard." Jordy whispered to Bapcat what Dodge had said.

Dodge held out his authorization letter for the White officer to read, but the man was excited, kept looking back past the train, nodding. "You are one of us, *Gospodin?*"

Bapcat could not understand the Russian exchange and cringed. This crossing scheme was a crazy gamble.

"I am done here," Dodge told the man, pointing across the bridge, "and that seems to me the only salient fact of the moment. You are warned and we are moving on, sir. Good luck to you."

The White Russian officer saluted. "Go with God. We are about to give the Magician a large dose of lethal magic."

The Americans climbed back onto the train as the White Russians began to open fire on the bridge.

"The White officer and the Red leader both talked of God," Jordy said.

"God pays no attention to men," Dodge said, smirking. "The Magician is about to be put in a place where magicians seek to place others."

Bapcat was tired of playing the mute. Where the heck was Zakov? He then asked in English, "What *about* Tyumen?"

"Next stop," Dodge grumbled, shedding his tunic. "Let's go back and assemble the Lewis guns while we have time."

The Americans found the gun crates empty, and the magazines in the wooden boxes empty as well.

Dodge looked backward and smiled. "God hates thieves."

"You gave up the Bolsheviks," Bapcat said. "Are we now on the White side? Or neutral?"

"We are not formally at war with Russia, and it does not matter which faction claims to be in charge. That is all I can say on the matter at the moment."

Jordy said, "Not formally at war; that means neutral, by definition."

Dodge said, "All words are elastic, Sergeant."

"Let's stay with English, and exasperated Bapcat added.

15

Winter, 1918. New Day Dawning

"All rivers and railroads run in two directions."

Morning light was flooding in as Signalman Elpikovny scrambled back from the engine to inform the Americans: "There are horsemen approaching from our rear; I see at least five."

How had the men in the engine seen this? Bapcat wondered.

The Americans' car, now relegated to caboose position, afforded the advantage of an elevated platform behind them. They went aft to see their followers.

Bapcat counted only four horsemen in pursuit—a pair on one flank, another rider on the other flank, and a fourth one, barely visible directly behind them, probably between the rails.

"The one behind us will break his animal's legs," Bapcat said, He had seen cowboys in the Dakotas try to race their horses on railroad ties and the end was almost always the same: a dead horse, either during the fall, or later, as a result. Often the rider too.

Bapcat saw the faint outline of a fifth rider approaching on the flank, with only one pursuer. "There's number five; his horse is fresher and stronger than the others."

"Who are they?" Jordy asked in English, then switched to Russian.

Elpikovny said, "This is White territory, and the land of Count Borzich—not a Romanov, but of that ilk."

Dodge explained. "Borzich held office at the Tsar's state level, a minor official with land, no more."

"You know him?" Bapcat asked.

"Of him," Dodge said. "He is of no consequence, a playboy at best, toying with life."

Elpikovny laughed and said in flawless English, "'Minor state official' is ironic. The word you read translated as *state* in English, in Russian means 'lordship' or 'masterdom,' and the English word *power* in Russian comes from root words meaning 'to possess or own.'"

Jordy said, "Your English is incredible."

The little stoker grinned. "Yet imperfect, like your Russian."

Bapcat liked the man, but couldn't say why.

"I was a teacher," Elpikovny explained, "but this was long ago. I was forced out and found refuge with trainmen. On the whole, I am happier here, where I have time to read and study and think, and not bat-thick students in the head to hold their attention. I don't miss any of the politics in education."

"Why are these horsemen following us?" Dodge asked.

The fifth rider had now drawn much closer and continued to close the distance. Bapcat could see the horse's flared nostrils and wild eyes.

"A nobleman's foolish and mindless game to test manliness," Elpikovny said. "They chase everything and wager on results. We've seen it before. It is almost always Count Borzich's men and boys. He is a rich fool." The signalman thought for a moment. "What is new here is that usually we see this game only in summer, not in winter."

"You just let them chase and catch us?" Dodge asked.

"No," the former schoolteacher said.

He went inside the carriage and came back with a fourteen-foot-long wooden pike, small pieces of metal flopping on the end like little wings.

"A bargeman's pole," Elpikovny said.

The men stood in silence, sensing the heavy sound of the hooves of the approaching horses over the many sounds of the train. When the closest man was near, Elpikovny thrust the pole straight back forcefully, causing metal plates to open in a small metal shield. With one solid pop, the Russian was unseated from his horse, which stumbled and veered away from the tracks while the rider bounced several times and came to a stop across the tracks, not moving. The other four riders immediately terminated the chase and veered toward their downed comrade.

"And so the game finishes," Elpikovny said.

"Will the rider be all right?" Jordy asked.

"Perhaps, perhaps not. God will decide—if He cares."

Bapcat was disgusted. God again. There was God and violence side by side everywhere they went in this country. The Russian's English was damn good. Did this mean he could drop the mute game on the train? Bezmunyi already knew the truth, and if Elpikovny was on their side, shouldn't he know, too?

To hell with Dodge. The mute role was finished! Bapcat offered his hand. "I'm Lute."

"Lee-oot?" a wide-eyed Elpikovny answered.

"Close enough."

"Lev Danielovich Elpikovny," the signalman said.

"Elpy," Jordy said.

The Russian laughed. "*Da*, Elpy."

Bapcat caught Dodge giving him an angry look.

"How much longer to Tyumen?" Bapcat asked.

"With luck, late tomorrow in the afternoon, or early night," the signalman said.

"Luck?"

"Luck is part of railroading and all of Russian life," Elpikovny said. He made a *pfft* sound to emphasize his words. "We will soon be approaching Vyatka."

~·~

Bezmunyi stopped the train not long after that and came aft to confer.

"We have red flags ahead," he told Dodge and the others.

"Is this significant?"

"Perhaps," Bezmunyi said. "It seems that Vyatka has gone Red."

"Can we skirt it, go around by another track?"

"Given railroad traffic and reality in Russia, no routes may be altered. These matters are ruled by an iron hand in Moscow. They were in

Petrograd, but they moved. Their control has not changed. All routes are managed from and by the center."

"This track we're on will lead to Tyumen?" Bapcat asked.

Bezmunyi answered, "To Tyumen, eventually, but first, to Vyatka, Perm, and Yekaterinberg, all *before* Tyumen."

"How far to Tyumen?"

"Many days from here, assuming no delays or route changes from the center."

Dodge said, "Let's pause here and let me determine conditions in Vyatka. Perhaps we can move through, perhaps not."

The two Russians went forward, leaving the three Americans alone.

With the Russians gone, Dodge growled at Bapcat and Jordy.

"You two need to keep your damn distance from these Russians, and I have not approved English for you," Dodge said with a snarl, staring at Bapcat.

Bapcat shot back, "These men are risking their lives for us, and to hell with that mute business except when it is absolutely needed."

"Believe me," Dodge said, "Our Russians will preserve maximum options for themselves, and we must do the same. As Russians in their own land, their options are far more numerous than ours."

Bapcat said, "What if the Bolos behind us have had contact with the Bolos ahead of us?"

Dodge exhaled, saying, "All rivers and railroads run two directions, which means in Russia there is always a way"—an open-ended statement that left Bapcat feeling uneasy. River water flowing two directions? With a tide, maybe. This close-in supervision by Dodge was eating at him. In his job for the State of Michigan, he had only nominally reported to his supervisor Horri Harju in Marquette, and in his daily life and routines he had almost total freedom to do as he thought best. Russia was slowly teaching him about his own desperate need to control circumstances. Here and now he had no control, none.

Something about Dodge still felt off. The man was decisive and had shown courage, but there was something missing, and though Bapcat felt this uneasiness, he could not give the anxiety a label. Considering what they already had gone through, the Lewis guns might have proven useful in the future, but the Magician had taken care of that. With a little more firepower they might increase their impact in unavoidable confrontations, though three men, or five, could be easily overwhelmed and overrun by only marginally larger forces. Taking on a train, of course, was not something most soldiers wanted to attempt. They would blow tracks, but to successfully charge what was a fortress with higher ground—quite unlikely. There was some security in sticking close to their fortress as they moved deeper into Russia.

Bapcat knew that even in a hopeless war, there were always men who would take the hard jobs. If and when the time came for a fight over the train, the Russians would find some men willing to take the risk. This was the reality of soldiering in wartime, and having seen and done such things himself, it remained part of something he knew would remain with him for the rest of his life.

Jordy should not be here. No American should. The country was at war with Germany, and now Russia seemed at war with itself.

16

Winter, 1918. Glazov House of Mutter

"The zookeeper knows to keep lions and zebras separate."

The approaches to the city's rail depot prominently displayed dozens of red flags, mostly poorly dyed rags, but the Americans passed through without incident. Bezmunyi wanted to stop for water and coal, to keep resources close to full, but Dodge kept them moving through the huge, expansive, and cluttered yard until they were on the other side of the city, grinding eastbound again.

Bapcat kept after Dodge regarding the Magician having sent messages ahead, but Dodge didn't seem interested. "The Magician's dead," said the major, "killed by the Whites or by his own tribe. His own words, 'There's a price for failure.' Most of these outfits aren't trained army units."

Dodge and the engineer got into a semi-heated argument in Russian, which Bapcat couldn't follow.

Elpikovny leaned toward the American, grinned, and whispered, "This spat comes down to who shall be boss. The Chief Engineer refuses to surrender his authority as long as we are aboard. They are like a married couple."

"We are coming soon to Glazov," the major said in English.

For now, Bapcat's mute role was in abeyance when they were on the train, which was a relief.

"Glazov? I don't remember this name being mentioned before," Bapcat said.

"It wasn't, and now it is," Dodge said. "The Chief Engineer contends it is a former timbering center on the banks of the Chertsa River, a flat plain with rolling hills covered by birch forests. The Chertsa is a tributary, which flows into the Kama and eventually into the Volga, which gives Glazov immense strategic military value. I cannot imagine why I have never heard of it before." Dodge seemed beside himself.

Bapcat had noticed two logging camps since they had left Vyatka, neither looking much different than logging camps back in the Upper Peninsula, and as they neared Glazov he thought the area looked very Upper Peninsula–like, with rocky outcrops, black spruce swamps, huge stands of stunted birch and poplar, here and there, aspen and ash.

"Who is in control here?" Dodge asked the engineer.

"On the train, it is I," Bezmunyi said decisively.

"In Glazov," Dodge said with irritation. "I already know your view-point of command on the train."

"It may not matter who controls Glazov," Bezmunyi said. "The rail-yards are far north of the city center."

"Illogical," Dodge said.

"Not at all," Bezmunyi said confidently. "A city is one thing, militarily and politically, and the railroads are an altogether different thing. These are separate creatures, you see. The zookeeper knows to keep lions and zebras separate."

"I've never heard of Glazov."

"Neither have most Russians, unless they are railroad men. It's a significant area of exchange and rolling stock. The yard director here is Kunikya, who is famous among railmen and as powerful as Lenin with his Bolsheviks."

"Famous and powerful? As Lenin?"

"He is called by many the little emperor of neither-nor and here-nor-there. He runs this operation with an iron hand in an iron glove, employs a pack of mad-dog Cossacks for security, and makes all decisions based on what is best for him, beginning with . . ." The engineer rubbed together the first two fingers of his right hand.

"*Vzyatka*," Dodge said. "Bribe."

"*Da*, Kunikya is a ruble-driven miracle worker. What is impossible in God's name one minute is done the next in Kunikya's name, and on his order. He is a rather loathsome creature, our little emperor."

"You've dealt with him?"

"Sorry memories, all."

"Do we have to stop here?"

"Until the man's palm is slathered with grease, here we shall sit."

"Perhaps others have never tried to reason with him in more-compelling language," Dodge offered.

"His bodyguard is there to assure one language for all transactions—his."

"What about his security?" Dodge asked the engineer, who proceeded to give him a detailed explanation, answering several questions.

Dodge then turned to Bapcat. "We shall no doubt need the skills of Muskul here."

Bapcat felt that he had volunteered as an American soldier with a military mission, not a thug in some vague cause, but he hid his disgust and gave a single nod to let the major know he would do as ordered.

But not forever. There would come a time when there would be a line he would refuse to cross.

—◆—

The Glazov yards were expansive, engines everywhere, miles of tracks, hundreds of empty freight and passenger wagons, some of them looking ancient and rotten. This was a city of trains with people moving through the area like dark ants. Steam and noxious smoke hung over the landscape, making the labyrinth even more confusing and challenging.

"Kunikya's Kremlin," Bezmunyi quipped as they pulled in and were directed to a parking location.

Dodge grumbled. "Let us pay our respects."

"*Ne mozhno*—this is impossible," the engineer said. "All audiences are only at night and by his invitation, no exceptions."

"There are always exceptions to rules, no matter who makes and controls them," Dodge said. "He's in his fortress?"

"Never leaves it."

"Family, wife, concubines?"

Bezmunyi chewed the inside of his cheek. "*Rukavitsa*—you understand?"

Dodge grunted. "Mittens. What the hell are mittens?"

The engineer arched an eyebrow, made a fist, pumped it once, and winked.

"Kunikya keeps a male . . . mistress?"

"His *rukavitsa*, his mittens, but none kept long, and all of them here without their consent, taken by his thugs who search far and wide and are paid well for their young prizes."

"He *buys* boys?"

"From their families."

"This is the twentieth century," Dodge said.

"Elsewhere, perhaps," the engineer allowed.

"Nobody tries to intervene?"

"He holds a royal appointment, bestowed directly by Nicholas."

Bapcat asked, "Is the Tsar . . . of the same . . . persuasion?"

Bezmunyi smirked and guffawed. "No, it would appear he prefers unhinged German females."

Bapcat did not like hearing any of this. He knew, of course, that there were such people in the world, but he had never been forced to confront it. He had known men who kept to men, but not those buying children like slaves or animals. What next in this insane country? Buck up, he told himself. You're here, this is real; deal with it one thing at a time.

Dodge to Bezmunyi, "The *rukavitsa* is in the Kremlin with Kunikya?"

"No, visits only, brought each day by Kunikya's special guards. The pleasure boy goes to Kunikya every day around noon and entertains him until the chief is ready for business in the evening. Usually the mitten is taken back to his quarters at half-five. Rail business commences around six, and stretches until after midnight, or later."

"How large an escort?" Bapcat asked.

"One man, but not a normal man," Bezmunyi said.

"Not normal how?" Dodge asked.

"*Vory v zkone*. Understand?"

Dodge said, "Thieves-in-law," and looked at Bapcat. "The Russian criminal class, the *Vory*. They operate a separate nation-state within the country, with their own laws and rules and ways. They cover their bodies with tattoos which highlight their criminal careers. Even the Tsar's Cheka treads lightly when *vory* are involved." Dodge looked upward. "What is it about criminals who take on their own *noms de guerre*? It happens everywhere, not just here."

"Does this man have a name?" Dodge asked the engineer.

"*Nogot*—the Nail," Bezmunyi said.

"The Nail. Of course, and Kunikya is the hammer."

Bezmunyi nodded.

Dodge said, "I don't understand what it is about this man in Glazov that makes him so powerful."

Bezmunyi said, "Kunikya controls the movement of every train from here across all of Siberia, all the way east to Vladivostok. He wields power over thousands of *versts*, while other yard directors control much smaller areas."

"But what distinguished him, to be appointed here by the Tsar?"

"His prodigious memory for names, faces, facts, dates—anything and everything. It is said he can accurately recite daily yard logs reaching back forty years."

"Appointed by the Tsar's minions?"

"No, by Nicholas himself."

"Why?"

"The Tsar wants the east populated. Peasants are found guilty of minor offenses against the State and exiled east to serve out there for many years. All exiles, in time of war, POWs included, move through here and are under the direct control of Kunikya."

"No other railyard chief has this power?"

"Kunikya controls the transportation of all exiles and POWs in Russia, and all other regional directors follow orders that come from here in Glazov. Because this is the rail hub for the center of the nation, Kunikya can put the touch on POWs and exiles for added income. He has become a very, very wealthy man, richer than most nobles and court hangers-on."

"Everything in Russia is Byzantine," Jordy remarked.

Bapcat asked, "This *vory* who escorts the boy is of the same bent?"

Bezmunyi extended the palms of his large hands and shrugged.

Dodge said, "I want to see the place where these mittens are kept and the path from there to Kunikya's headquarters. When you have done this, you will remain outside and wait until we call you inside. Can you write and prepare the necessary *reis bilet*?"

Bezmunyi answered, "Every engineer with any experience can do this. The *reis bilet* is the central document of our professional existence, our license, professional birth certificate, everything."

"Could you do Kunikya's job here?"

"Why should I *want* to," the engineer came back. "I am already happy in my work."

Dodge asked, "If not you, who?"

Chief Engineer Bezmunyi pondered this and answered, "There is an engineer from Novgorod who has an exceptional mind, and who is, by nature, a leader of men. He is known as *Paporotnik*."

"The Fern?" Dodge came back. "A pathetic and frail name."

Bezmunyi smiled demonically. "Ice, snow, heat, wind, anything, no matter what comes along, the fern survives. It goes dormant when need be and reappears when circumstances are more favorable. Would that more men could learn from such humble beings."

"Does this *Paporotnik* come through here?"

"Yes, he is often on the long eastern runs."

"He could do this job now done by Kunikya?"

"I have no doubt."

"When we get to Kunikya's fortress and go inside, go find Paporotnik and bring him to us—but don't enter until you are called in, understood?"

"As you wish, Major," Bezmunyi said. "But if Comrade Paporotnik is not here?"

"Pick the next best person to do this work."

"I hope Paporotnik is here. There is no better choice."

"Can Elpikovny see to water, fuel, and supplies while we are engaged?"

"Of course."

"Good, tell him to see to the train's needs. And then you can show us this House of Mittens."

Jordy stayed with Elpikovny while Bezmunyi led Bapcat and Dodge to an unusual carriage that sat alone on a hundred-meter segment of track. The railcar was painted green with red trim, and unlike most everything else in Russia, was freshly painted and well maintained. Bapcat and Dodge each carried a revolver and a rifle and wore ammunition bandoliers crossed over their chests, in the Russian manner.

As soon as they saw the special car, Dodge ordered Bezmunyi away and the two Americans continued on. There was a sleepy-eyed tattooed man at one end of the car, and Dodge spoke to him sharply in Russian. A *vory?* The man answered in a voice that sounded like it was scraped over broken ice.

Bapcat would only later learn the content of the exchange, which went like this:

Dodge: "We have come to see *Nogot.*"

Tattoo Man: "Go away. He is busy."

Dodge: "We are here by order of the Tsar."

Tattoo Man, snorting: "There is no Tsar. Be gone or be dead."

Dodge, smiling perniciously: "Can you be certain of that, comrade?"

Bapcat watched the man processing the major's words. After a long delay, the man said, "Wait here," and climbed a ladder to the wagon's platform and knocked.

Dodge moved behind Tattoo Man, Bapcat following right behind him. The major got a knife to the man's throat and roughly pushed him aside. "All yours, Captain."

Bapcat pushed Tattoo Man against the side of the car and put the barrel of his pistol to his forehead. The man grinned toothlessly until Bapcat pulled the hammer back, dissolving the insipid grin.

An undressed man opened the door and thundered, "You know we are not to be disturbed when we are preparing for the procession."

Dodge hammered the side of his revolver into Naked Man's head, dropping him. He stepped inside and growled to Bapcat, "Get in here, and secure the latches."

Bapcat manhandled Tattoo Man through the entry and closed and locked the door. When Tattoo Man tried to pull away, he struck him on the head and dropped him beside the naked one.

A boy of no more than twelve stood in the room before them. He was thin and baby-faced, wearing a red silk robe.

"What's your name, boy?" Dodge asked.

The child said, "Whatever you wish it to be, sir. Have we met?"

Dodge said in what Bapcat thought was a surprisingly sympathetic tone, "This life is ended. What name did your mother give you?"

"I have no mother. She sold me, which is her right."

Only later when Bapcat heard this exchange translated did he react with anger and sadness. Now, as it was unfolding, he was limited to gauging tones and expressions. What he felt as it happened was deep sadness from the boy, and Dodge too, which surprised him.

Dodge said, "Pick the name you want, boy, and be quiet."

"Anton," the boy said immediately. "I have always admired the name of Anton," the boy chirped. "It sounds regal."

Dodge said, "Anton it shall be. Get dressed, Anton."

The boy: "I am dressed, sir. I need only my slippers."

Dodge grabbed Tattoo Man and lifted him. "Where are the boy's clothes?"

"He needs no clothes for what he does."

"Take yours off," Dodge told the man.

"You have no right to my clothes; they are mine, and I need them," the man said with a snarl.

Dodge leaned over, held the *vory's* chin, and stared into his rheumy eyes. "You and your boss stole this boy's youth. You owe him everything, including your lives."

"You would kill me over . . . a piece of spoiled *meat?*"

Dodge said, "I will kill you just for the pleasure of it. Your clothes."

The man grinned. "This boy is nothing. He is to be shed soon and replaced."

Dodge shot Naked Man in the head, turned to Bapcat's charge, and ordered, "Your clothes—now."

Tattoo Man quickly undressed and threw his clothes toward the boy.

Dodge said, "Get dressed, Anton, and be quick about it."

"Am I leaving here, sir? Have you bought me?"

Dodge turned red. "You are done being bought, boy. Get dressed now."

As the boy dressed hurriedly, Bapcat saw fear in his eyes and felt for him. He was glad Dodge had done this dirty work, but the summary execution sickened him. He was a lawman and soldier. What was Dodge?

The boy went with them to the tower, where whatever security there might have been seemed to have disappeared. Bapcat wasn't surprised. They had left the door to the boy's wagon open, and as they departed, Bapcat saw people going inside, looking, and then come running out. They knew something big was afoot, and none of them wanted to be any part of it.

People got out of their way as they walked, and Bapcat couldn't blame their skittishness. Word was traveling fast in this railroad world. Even the emperor's paid guards had fled.

In their shoes, Lute wasn't sure what he would do. Where did duty end? Was duty to the State deeper and more compelling than duty to a mere employer? As always, his head was filled with more questions than answers. What exactly did Dodge intend to do with this boy? You could see he was frail. He couldn't stay with us, could he? Damn Dodge.

The major led them into the tower where a pop-eyed servant pointed at a staircase.

Dodge climbed them quickly, with Bapcat and the boy close behind, Bapcat taking care to watch for threats from behind. When they reached a tall, heavy double door, Dodge shouldered it open and charged inside.

A dapper little man with a pencil mustache tilted his head with curiosity.

"I assume there is a compelling reason for this egregious breach of protocol."

The man stood no more than five-foot-three, with dark hair and a silver mustache. He wore a well-fitted black suit and tie and sat on a large chair resembling someone's notion of a throne.

"Explain your presence," the man said, his voice confident. This had to be Kunikya.

Dodge said, "Come with us, *sobukurvat*."

This word had no meaning for Bapcat at the time it was spoken, but the tone was unmistakable. (He later learned it meant "dog vomit.")

The little man momentarily cringed before recovering control.

"All this is about that ... *creature* you have there," said Kunikya, laughing. "There are thousands more like him. If you wish to have him, take him. I give him to you as a gift." The man shrugged. "I have been contemplating a change."

Dodge pointed his revolver at the man. "Outside, now."

The man did not move. Instead he said calmly, "Security."

"There are no ears to hear your pathetic voice," Dodge said, snatching the man from his throne and throwing him toward the double door.

No one challenged them as they emerged into the graying day. The snow-and-rain mix had turned to snow. A crowd had gathered at a distance to watch, as docile as grazing stock.

Bapcat didn't know exactly what had happened and stayed alert. He had no doubt the body of Naked Man had been discovered by now. Was retaliation coming?

Kunikya stood, grinning confidently, and said quietly to Dodge, "You have a fine sense of showmanship. I could use a man with your skills. What is your name, *Gospodin*?"

Dodge ignored the man and scanned the gathering crowd until he saw Chief Engineer Bezmunyi with a clean-shaven, decrepit man wearing a rabbit-fur *shapka* and horn-rimmed glasses that made him look owlish.

Bezmunyi brought the man to them. "Paporotnik."

The man bowed his head.

"Dodge and Bapcat," the major answered. "You understand that you are about to take over here?"

"I understand this is a possibility."

Dodge took Kunikya by the collar and frog-hopped him forward. He placed his revolver behind the man's head and shouted to the crowd, "This man is a pervert, a stain on humankind, on Russia, on you, on me."

"Exquisite sense of theater," the little man said calmly. "A true thespian. You must work for me. I insist, now; let's be done with this show and get on with real business."

The snow thickened and fell harder. The crowd grew larger and pushed toward them. There was no talking, but a lot of open mouths and astonished looks.

"This bag of dog vomit is no longer in charge," Dodge announced and pulled the trigger, spraying brain, skull, skin, and hair.

The shot caught Bapcat by surprise. He found himself holding his revolver too tight.

Bezmunyi raised Paporotnik's arm. "Here is the new director, appointed not by the Tsar, but by we railroad people. He is one of us, not political, neither royal, White, nor Red, nor *menshivik, the minority or Provisionals*—ours. He is not self-serving; he is a man for all. Now you must vote to make this official. Paporotnik as rail director—yea or nay?"

Rhythmic clapping began, the Russian signal of agreement.

Paporotnik raised a hand and the clapping stopped. "Work will begin inside immediately," he said. "After today we will be available from early morning, and we will refine the schedule further to serve the majority, not the few. Give me some minutes to clear my head and then we shall begin," he concluded, and the clapping resumed.

Dodge nudged Bezmunyi, who nodded to Bapcat. "Bring the boy," Dodge said, leading them through the crowd. Bapcat looked back and saw the crowd beating and clubbing the body of the dead director in the black suit.

What will we do with this boy? What is Dodge thinking? And yet again—why are Jordy and I here?

Lute Bapcat felt a tug on his shirt. It was the boy. Lute shook his head and tapped his throat, then poked the boy's shoulder and the boy said, "Anton."

Bapcat shook his head, pointed at his throat. The mute game again.

The boy looked sad and patted Bapcat's arm.

The boy mumbled something and the boy's sympathy was clear. Consolation from a pathetic young boy? Bapcat wasn't sure how to take this.

17

Breaking Spring, 1918. Hell Everywhere

"All traders and businessmen are mutes, with no mind
for anything except money and profit. They speak with
their fingers for numbers. It's their universal lingo."

Bapcat saw that Jordy Klubishar was angry and frustrated. Dodge had pushed Anton toward Jordy and growled, "Take care of him," and Jordy had been in a pout ever since. Worse, he was following Elpikovny around, and the Russian, having little opportunity to speak English, was talking Jordy's ears off. All the while they were adding a second coal car and water wagon to the train to increase their range and running time.

"I'm a sergeant," Jordy moaned to Bapcat.

"Sometimes rank is irrelevant," Bapcat told him. "We are all privates in this world, Jordy. All that changes are circumstances."

"I don't want to take care of this boy," he said, pointing at Anton, who followed him around like a puppy. "Has he told you what he is?"

"Has he told you?" Bapcat asked.

Jordy groaned. "He called me *beautiful*. He says he is a pleasure boy. What the hell, Lute? What the *hell!*"

Bapcat said quietly, "He is young, still a child, and he was forced to do things over which he had no control."

"He doesn't act like it was forced. He brags about it like he's a big shot."

Bapcat knew Anton was damaged and might never recover, but he deserved a chance.

"He's twelve, and he's scared. He's going on survival instincts alone, and his mind is desperately trying to find some small sense of control."

"Boo-hoo," Jordy said. "That sounds like all of us. I remember when I was twelve."

"*You* are not Anton. You were born with a strength he may not have, but consider this: When Zakov and I found you on your own, you were alive and coping, and this boy is in the same position you were in."

This gave Jordy pause.

Bapcat added, "Here's reality: Life is just one set of circumstances after another, and we have to play the hands we're dealt. There's no magic carpet to elsewhere, and no point in hoping or praying for one. Don't be harsh with Anton. He's just a boy."

"Why is he even with us, and where are we taking him? He belongs with his family."

"Did you belong with your family?"

Jordy Klubishar went silent. His father had been a violent drunk who beat him and did things to his sister. Their mother was dead. From a young age, Jordy had separated from his father as much as he could and lived mostly on his own.

Bapcat said, "Dodge said something about Perm."

"Anton told me he is a Piter boy. What's that mean? Is that what he does? I don't understand."

Dodge came in just in time to hear.

"Piter is what Russians called St. Petersburg before it was renamed Petrograd. Anton said he was born and raised in the city, but getting him back there is out of the question. His mother sold him, which means she doesn't expect him to return, and she doesn't want him back. Later he told me he's from Perm, so he tells you one story, and me another. Your first job, Sergeant, is to get the truth out of him, assuming he can even recognize it now or has ever had any sense of what truth means. You will find out for us, and then we will go from there. In a sense, his fate is in your hands."

"I don't want this," Jordy said.

"It's an order. Own it and deal with it, Sergeant."

"I'm not a goddamn nanny, Major."

"Then think of yourself as a mentor-teacher."

"I ain't neither of them things."

Bapcat smiled. "*Au contraire*, Sergeant. You are, and I won't abide any more whining in the ranks—and that's also an order."

Jordy sighed.

Bapcat asked Dodge, "Why are we still here?"

"Because Signalman Elpikovny decided we should add the second coal and water wagons to extend our range."

"Shouldn't that be Bezmunyi's decision?"

"The engineer concurs. He happily allows his signalman the initiative and delegates authority for him to make decisions."

"Was it your idea originally?" Bapcat asked.

"No, it was strictly the Russians' idea—*they're* the railmen—but I approved as soon as I heard it."

Bapcat watched Jordy, who said nothing. The idea had been his son's, and Elpikovny had jumped on it as soon as he'd heard it. Jordy had spent time with railmen in Houghton and Red Jacket and had listened to them talk about how they organized their cars for various reasons. Railroaders loved to gab about their work.

In fact, Elpikovny had not even waited to confer with the engineer, had on his own started the process to add rolling stock, grinning the whole while. "Better to ask for forgiveness than permission," he told the Americans.

Bapcat interrupted Jordy's reverie. "Put Anton to work; take his mind off himself. Give him a job to do, but make sure it's a real chore, not make-work. And while you're at it, teach him to shoot, if he doesn't already know how."

Jordy Klubishar hesitated and scowled.

Bapcat said, "Get to it, Sergeant. We can't take the boy with us if he can't carry some of our load. From each what he can do, and to each, an equal share."

Klubishar looked at Lute. "That's the kind of crap we hear from Pitelli the Red in Red Jacket. He preaches junk like that all the time."

"You think I'm a Red?" Bapcat asked.

"I'm just telling you about Pitelli. He's a joke, mostly."

Dodge looked over at the captain and sergeant, and Jordy interpreted the look correctly and left the car to the two men, saying, "I'll find Anton."

Bapcat told Dodge, "I signed on as a soldier, not an enforcer."

"There are no Queensbury Rules in this neck of the woods, Captain."

"Tell me exactly what we are doing here," Bapcat insisted.

Dodge had an easy way of deflecting things back to those who challenged him in any way, and to any degree. "We're finding Zakov, your partner and friend."

"I'm a game warden, Major. I get paid to sniff out the full story, not rely on the empty words of others."

"I presume that you are dependent on the process of law."

"Only after my bones and nose confirm a scent."

For once, the major had no rejoinder. Bapcat could tell that Dodge was irritated.

"Paporotnik has sent a message telling us he wants a parley before we push eastward."

"Where *is* the new yard director?" Bapcat asked.

"The more-relevant question is when. He is busy dispatching trains and will not be available until tonight, is all I know. Bezmunyi tells me this delay is fortuitous. Our equipment needs attention. The time helps him and Elpikovny do what must be done."

"And us?"

"The sergeant is taking care of the boy and you are free to relax, even though this is a concept you are clearly not comfortable with."

"You can tell this how?" Bapcat asked.

"I have the same shortcoming," Dodge said.

Interesting admission. "And how do you deal with it?"

"I find something to do," the major said, stretching out on a wooden side bench and draping his arm over his eyes. After a moment he lifted his arm and looked at Bapcat. "There should be a local market. Go amuse yourself. There is some Mexican silver and two gold pieces by my hat. Take them. All prices here are inflated in normal times, and the inflation now is preposterous. We don't need anything, so drive a hard bargain."

"I speak no Russian."

Dodge smirked. "All traders and businessmen are mutes, with no mind for anything except money and profit. They speak with their fingers for numbers. It's their universal lingo."

The arm went back over the major's eyes, and within seconds he was buzzing like an irritated bee.

Bapcat had the same gift for sleep, anytime, anywhere, under any conditions, and he felt for those who lacked such ability. Jaquelle was one of them. She could sleep deeply and quickly only after making love, and since he saw her only once a week or so, she had a lot of sleepless nights—or so she complained every time they got together. Her lack of sleep seemed to cause her to throw herself into the pursuit of profit and money with even more intensity, something she was very good at, and never let him forget.

The local market? Why not? You could learn a lot from what people bought and sold, and especially by how much they were willing to pay. Neither skinflint nor spendthrift, he had learned the value of money the hard way and was by nature a frugal man. He had been astonished to find that Jaquelle, for all her wealth, was at least as frugal as him.

———

Walking alone through the railyards Bapcat felt free for the first time in months. Railmen were scurrying around, shouting at each other, pounding iron-headed mallets on various metal train parts, the din a deep industrial orchestra mixed with angry, busy voices. He passed one man on all fours, like a pig, vomiting in misery, probably from too much vodka the night before. But then it occurred to him—what if this was influenza? This thought made him move faster.

Back in Dakota he'd been friends with a young Kansas City cowboy everyone called Birdfoot, who was partial to a drink called Popskull, the most potent of home-brewed blends. Each bottle had a rattlesnake head in it, and although Birdfoot had assured Lute it was more a matter of thespianic hogwash than reality, the cowboy had died after a particularly lethal batch some of his comrades later thought might have contained actual rattlesnake venom for flavoring.

Did Russians put snake parts in vodka? Were there poisonous snakes here?

These questions reminded him that he knew virtually nothing about this country or the people who lived here, except that right now, they all seemed bent on killing each other.

The market was a huge wide green space trampled down to mud by people and hundreds of hobbled long-haired horses that looked more like fat swaybacked ponies than full-grown animals. Near the hobbled pack animals were huge wooden sledges, the kind loggers used in the Keweenaw. Many of the vendors wore fur capes and had thick cloth or skins wrapping their feet, making them look lumpy and clumsy.

It had been raining when he left the railyard, and this rain now turned to pelting sleet. Where traders had rough-hewn tents, he could hear ice pellets steadily bouncing off canvas, the sound like that of tiny snare drums.

There were no Western goods in the market, but he saw salted fish and meats and every kind of fur imaginable. Many traders wore peculiar skin coats, cobbled together in a rainbow of textures and colors, both natural and dyed. Bapcat wondered if these were unofficial trading uniforms.

Some traders wore wolf and fox skins cured and tanned, with faces and noses in place, which they tipped down over their own faces to make it look like two-legged beasts meeting to trade with each other. The eyeless animal pelts hid the depth of human eyes beneath them. Several traders had sledges with cargoes of knives and axheads displayed, some in iron, some in black obsidian, and the workmanship was exquisite. He was tempted to buy blades for souvenirs, but held back. In England they had heard a Frenchman quip that Germans fought for honor; the French, for survival; the English, from stubbornness; and the Americans, newly arrived, for souvenirs.

Bapcat meandered until he came to a sledge piled with bearskins. He felt them. Brain-cured, soft as the Indians in the Dakotas made, and ranging in color from white and dark blue to cinnamon and obsidian. The furs were bulky, the tanning exquisite, and with more winter yet ahead, he thought long and hard. After a while he picked at the corner of polar bear skin and turned to the trader, opening his hands as a signal for *How much?*

The trader was short and dark, his skin the color of walnut, only a few teeth, the high cheekbones of Asia and flashing black eyes. His thick, unkempt black beard was split in the middle and the two tails draped over each shoulder through military epaulets, held in place in back by gravity and small sparkle-arkles—Jaquelle's word for cheap jewelry.

As he engaged the trader, Bapcat felt eyes on his back, a sixth sense good game wardens developed.

The trader flashed several fingers against the palm of his hand and Bapcat shook his head, making a chopping motion with his right hand. Too much; lower. In his cowboy days he had traded with the Northern Cheyenne, who considered trading a form of low-level warfare and took the outcomes personally.

This man with high cheekbones gave him a look, and Bapcat wondered if Indians had been Russians before they had crossed into North America. Roosevelt had told him a story when they were on one of their first bear hunts—how people first developed from apes somewhere in Africa and then spread all over the planet. People began as apes? He had laughed out loud that night. It seemed to explain a lot, and nothing, but the whole idea of mass migration of humans over the top of the world had fascinated him ever since. Talk about tough, determined people.

The finger flashing of offers and counteroffers went on for a while, and several times Bapcat had shaken his head angrily and started to walk away, only to find the trader pulling his sleeve and restarting the bargaining process. No matter which way Bapcat moved to escape, the surprisingly spry trader managed to block his way or pull him back. Finally, after much emotional and spirited finger flashing, the trader beamed and nodded and put his fist in the palm of his hand, and Bapcat did the same. Deal made.

Bapcat yanked eight polar bear pelts from the pile and put two gold pieces in the trader's hand. The man grinned so wide Bapcat could count his sparse teeth. Clearly the trader felt triumphant. Because the money he'd spent wasn't his own, he felt no sense of loss or gain. The trader pulled on Bapcat's sleeve and handed him a magnificent ninth white pelt and bowed. A bonus?

It was only when he tried to shoulder the weight of nine great white pelts that it dawned on him that he had a problem. Without Russian lingo, he had no way to ask the trader for help, but he looked around and spied Elpikovny at a tent a few paces away. Had Elpy been watching him, shadowing him? On whose orders—Bezmunyi's, or Dodge's?

Having been seen, the signalman rushed to the American's side.

"Dear Captain," Elpikovny greeted him. "You need assistance?"

Bapcat nodded, directing Elpikovny to take some of the furs.

The nine pelts were thick and large, six or seven feet wide by nine or more feet long. If they were still in Russia when next winter arrived, they might come in very handy. Wearing white fur in snowy conditions could render a careful man close to invisible, especially if he were on foot away from the train. Jordy could make first-class bear coats as well as anyone he'd ever met. The boy was a natural with furs, both in trapping them and evaluating them—a skill all its own, and possessed by few of any age.

Bapcat still coveted the obsidian knives, and returned to the bearded trader with filthy hair tied with a rainbow of faded ribbons.

Bapcat picked up a knife and a voice said, "You're slipping, and sloppy. You *finally* saw the signalman following you. Why did it take you so long?"

That voice! He stared at the trader's face. No, not possible. A scar ran the length of the left side of the man's face, not an old scar, but relatively new, from what he could see.

The voice said, "You are in the role of a mute, a suitable role with little need for you to improvise."

"Pinkhus Sergeyevich?"

"It is about time you and Jordy got here," the voice said. "I've been waiting."

"I have a thousand questions."

"Ask one to start."

"What in hell's name are you doing here—are *we* doing here?"

"That's two. You take directions poorly. I have been waiting for you. Where is Jordy?"

Why had Zakov met him here, and not at the train?

"He's with the major."

"Short, dark hair, intense, rarely smiles?"

"That's Dodge. You know him?"

"What's his function?"

"His job was to bring us to you. Beyond that, we have no idea what he's about. He's not one to share."

"Fluent Russian?"

"Yes."

Zakov grinned. "You who cannot speak it, now judge fluency, Comrade Mute?"

Bapcat spluttered. "Is this some kind of damn game to you? We came all this way to Russia to save you, and you make jokes."

"Who said I needed saving?"

"They all thought you were dead."

"Clearly, I am not. All I did was ask the Swedish ambassador to get a note to the Americans that I needed you and Jordy here, and now you're here."

Bapcat was speechless and shook his head disgustedly.

"Life's a game. Where did you land?"

"Somewhere north of Murmansk, place called Pechenga. Dodge is not forthcoming with information, including charts and maps, but he seems to know his way around." Bapcat related what he knew of the major's background.

"Military intelligence attached to the State Department. Men of that ilk can't help themselves. All information is currency and central to security, if managed properly, which is no easy thing. What brought you to Russia? American vessel?"

"English submarine."

"Equipment cached in place when you arrived?"

"Just one, so far."

"Submarine . . . with *your* claustrophobia?" Zakov grinned crookedly.

"I managed."

"You always do."

"Why *are* we here, Pinkhus Sergeyevich?"

"History has taken an ugly, predictable turn, which is to say we are going to do what we can to change said hopeless course or administer justice, whichever is in our power."

His Russian partner had an annoying habit of clouding over all situations.

"Care to be more specific?"

"*Da.* I was sent to determine the fate of the Tsar and his family."

"And?"

"They are all alive so far, together under house arrest in Tobolsk."

"Are we to go there?"

"No, we go to Yekaterinburg."

"Why?"

"Because the lunatic inmates are now managing the asylum. This country is a disaster, getting worse by the day. There is only the illusion of central control, and several groups all claim to be steering the ship. At the local level there is competition for control and endless homicide, paranoia, and sadism. Each local group is dedicated to putting right imagined slights from opponents, from the days when Nicholas ruled. They talk of national goals, but few are thinking or acting in any way but locally and personally."

His friend was seething. Bapcat remained silent.

Zakov said, "The Siberian White Army under Admiral Kolchak will soon capture Tobolsk, and the Bolsheviks will be forced to move their human treasure to Yekaterinburg for safekeeping."

"You know this for certain?"

"I know how those people think and who is doing their thinking for them."

"And Dodge?"

"I know the type, if not the man."

Had Dodge said he knew Zakov? Bapcat couldn't remember.

"What is Dodge's role in the mission?"

"I don't know, and I've not yet decided. Perhaps he can help us, perhaps not. I withhold judgment for now, but don't tell him you've seen me."

"Even Jordy?"

"Don't burden the boy with a secret he'll have to hold in. How is he?"

"Frustrated, disappointed, and angry. I assume you will step forward at some point."

"Where and when I'm ready, and not before."

"How am I to convince Dodge to go to Yekaterinburg? He is aiming for Tobolsk."

"I am working on that. Don't worry yourself, wife."

"*Still* not funny."

"What do mutes know of humor?"

No sense jousting with the man. "Where will you be?"

"Here, there, everywhere."

"Seriously."

"Where I need to be is where I will be."

"You are moving around as a trader?"

"Today, yes, but it is easier to move as a holy man."

"A what?"

"*Starets*—a holy man. My countrymen are superstitious. They fear things they don't understand, and holy men are, in the people's minds, as unknowable and mysterious as the Savior or the Devil. Their ignorance and superstitions are my license to move largely unhindered."

"Russians still believe in God?" Bapcat asked.

"Deeply, even if their God does not reciprocate. When did you land, Lute?"

"Late February, early March. Not quite sure. The submarine really disjointed me. What's the date now?"

"Date? No idea. I believe this is May, or is it April? River ice is breaking, spring is coming. It happens fast here. Do you think those white bearskins will repel mosquitoes?"

"They will repel cold if we're still here come next winter."

Zakov went silent and finally said, "We shall still be here—if we are still alive, which is by no means a certainty."

"How long have *you* been here?"

"A year."

"You've seen the Tsar?"

"Twice."

"Talked to him?"

"Not possible yet."

"You know where he is held in Tobolsk?"

"I know, and his family is with him, along with their servants."

"How many people?"

"Two hundred, including guards on their perimeter, perhaps two dozen more inside and in close."

Bapcat tried to think what to say next, but Zakov spoke first.

"A hint, my friend: Almost all of the Russians you meet are entirely illiterate. They judge your papers by how official they *look*, not what they say. Appearances are everything in interacting with these people. When challenged, the simple ones fold immediately. Those who don't fold immediately will do so soon enough. Even military officers on the Red side grovel and give up, but the political commissars, these people will not relent so easily. Some are both literate and smart, and all are true believers."

Zakov pointed into the distance and Bapcat turned and looked, and when he looked back, Pinkhus Sergeyevich was gone, vanished, as obscure and mysterious as ever. Damn the man.

Jordy would not be happy to learn that he had had contact with Zakov and withheld it from him, and he wouldn't blame his son; he would feel the same in Jordy's place. How will Dodge react if he finds out, and why is Zakov avoiding the major?

Right now playing mute felt like a safe harbor. He'd been to the market, bought pelts, and that's all. Bapcat fought a smile. Zakov was right. Playing the mute was not such a reach for him.

Catching up with Elpikovny, Bapcat said, "We should get some bread for the larder."

The signalman nodded. "*Da*, keep going, and I will find a baker and they will bring bread to us." Elpikovny had found a set of wheels from somewhere in the market, and they loaded all the pelts, securing them with cording.

To hell with Zakov; he would tell Jordy the truth. He owed the boy that.

As they approached the train, Jordy Klubishar and Anton ran to meet them. Anton grabbed the cart handle to help Elpikovny. Jordy fell in beside Bapcat, who leaned close and whispered, "I've seen Zakov."

"I know," Jordy said. "Me, too. He told me not to tell you."

Sonuvabitch.

PART III: BEYOND BEYOND

A lie told often enough becomes truth.

—*Vladimir Ilyich Ulyanov (aka Lenin)*

18

Signs of Spring, 1918. Black Angel

"I should think it comes down to what you
Americans call the chicken-or-egg thing."

The woman was tiny, with tawny skin, hair matted in dry blood, huge glazed-over eyes. Bapcat couldn't begin to read all that was under this surface, and he was not sure he wanted to. His biggest concern was Jordy, who couldn't take his eyes off her, nor she off him.

Her sudden arrival startled both of them, a reminder that they had no real security on the train. The woman's face was covered with blood and looked like a black mask in the poor light of the railcar.

"Hello, there," she said in perfect British English, which to Bapcat's untutored ear sang of privilege and class, and reminded him of the Englishman, Churchill.

"You have a name, Dear Captain?" she asked, switching her eyes from Jordy to Bapcat.

He wore no uniform. She knew he was a captain, but not his name? How could this be?

He pointed at his mouth and shook his head.

The woman broke into a smile, flashing perfect teeth. In Bapcat's experience, only the rich had enough money to keep all their teeth, much less keep them any shade close to white, and this, too, added to his impression of the woman, whose age he couldn't guess.

The woman said, "Ah yes, Dear Captain, I sensed this from the beginning, that you are the famous American, the one they call Muskul.

Muteness is a tragedy, you poor creature. Is it physical or shell shock? So many of our boys have come back from the German war with fewer parts and capabilities than they had before they left."

Famous mute American and his Russian tag. How did she know these things? Who was she? More importantly, why was she here, and what did she want? He needed to stay alert.

Jordy, who had been dog-staring at the woman, appeared to have drifted into some sort of reverie, but now he woke up and pointed a revolver at her. He said something in Russian, and she waved him off dismissively.

"Let us have no dissembling here, Beautiful Boy. I love the great English language, and although it is not my native tongue, it seems so full of . . . possibilities that Russian does not offer; no limits, so few rules—it is a lovely and plastic tongue. But to your point, Beautiful Boy, you wish to ask who I am and what do I want with you and your captain, *da*?"

Jordy nodded, his mouth hanging slightly open.

The woman pursed her lips, drew in a deep breath, and exhaled dramatically.

"Behind my back where lives my shadow I am called *Chernyi Angel*. I serve the dying and the dead, and wherever I go, people are dying. There are people who insist death follows me, and I counter that I only wish to serve." She made a face of consternation. "I should think it comes down to what you Americans call the chicken-or-egg thing. Do they die because I come to them, or do I come because they are dying? It is a conundrum, *da*?"

Finding his voice, Jordy challenged her. "Who here is dying?"

The woman tilted her head. Was she in pain? Bapcat couldn't tell. All he knew was that she felt like big trouble, but a trouble he couldn't yet identify and this bothered him. As soldier and game warden, he had always had the ability to quickly assess trouble.

"Your name is Angel?" Jordy said.

She made a spluttering sound and spit out some of the blood curling around her lips and chin.

"How rude of me. I am Marilka Monikova, graduate of University of Michigan Medical School. Regarding your question concerning death, all of us are obviously dying, in both biological and existential frames of reference, but to be more specific regarding you Americans, I confess I don't yet know the answer, Beautiful Boy. Who or which of you or us is dying first, or soon? Perhaps all of us, perhaps none." She shrugged. "I am a physician, not a philosopher or seer. I can, when lucky, clearly see the fate of one broken body."

"I'm a beautiful boy too," Anton said in English. He had become Jordy's shadow.

Bapcat thought, this boy speaks English?

"Silence, child!" she told the boy.

"Your face," Jordy said to the woman. "Are you hurt?"

She sighed and smiled. "All women are destined to be hurt," she said. "That which you see is the result of a largely inconsequential collision of lead with bone. A bullet, I should specify. Said bullet grazed my forehead ever so slightly and caused me—as such wounds are wont to do—to bleed profusely and prodigiously, albeit superficially. This injury, despite appearances and barring infection, is of little consequence in God's grander scheme. Given current events in Russia, one may be forgiven for suspecting that God intends for us neither grand nor petty schemes, other than chaos, which some mathematicians might loosely term a schema, but for normal people like us, it is anything but. Am I making sense?" she asked.

Jordy said, "Some. We have soap and can heat some water." He lowered his revolver and Lute pointed his at her. Anton chirped, "I will get water," and ran out.

The whole situation was disturbing Bapcat's sense of order and control, the latter, on shaky ground since they had left the British submarine. No outsiders were allowed in this carriage, but this prohibition, he now realized, was more hope than reality. The train had no guards, no security, which made them vulnerable whenever they were stopped.

She told Jordy, "Soap and hot water would be quite useful. Thank you for offering, Beautiful Boy."

"Anton will bring it," Jordy told her.

But she had turned to Bapcat. "I know, of course, that your muteness—your *condition*—is feigned, and I am guessing this is intended to hide your lack of Russian language. Am I correct?"

Bapcat pointed his revolver at the floor and opened his other hand.

"I must say," she said, "you've been quite impressive in your charade up to and including this present moment. It has been most convincing to almost everyone, and your patience in adhering to this role borders on astonishing. Such pretense takes so much energy! But let me assure you, Dear Captain, that you have nothing to fear from me. You may speak, and I shall not, as you Americans put it so aptly, spill forth the beans."

"You've got it wrong, ma'am," Jordy said. "He's mute as a mime. I should know. He's my father."

The woman clapped her tiny doll hands together.

"Yes, Beautiful Boy, this is a charming touch, delivered with perfect timing. It really could not have been better. Ordinarily I go where fate and serendipity carry me—or perhaps they send or summon me—but whatever the reason, I am blown in the wind like a dry paper birch leaf in deep autumn."

Bapcat felt her eyes boring into him.

Jordy raised his pistol again. "We will be happy to help you get your wound cleaned, ma'am, but then you've got to move on. You can't be on this train."

"Yes, of course; let us first attend to this mess. But I must tell you that I've not been blown to you by chance. Rather, I am here at the direction of our dear friend, who wishes to have the company of his wife and son."

Bapcat suppressed a gasp. Good grief! Zakov sent her? Why?

The woman sat down and began clawing at her hair. "Please, young man, now would be the time for that hot water and soap. I am certain your dear captain can keep his pistol aimed at me, if that is the sort of thing Americans equate with security."

Jordy left, looking confused. Anton hadn't returned yet.

"Ah," the woman said, "now we are just two adults in the room. Your sergeant seems a conscientious and dear boy, but quite innocent, I should think. On the other hand, you, Dear Captain, you are far from an innocent. You and I should speak before your major called Dodge comes back from wherever he has gone. You see, I can read the tension here—you and the boy on one side, Dodge on another. I smell a conflict raging. The military and oaths and blood all breed loyalty and blind obedience, which is not synonymous with trust or love. Obedience is superficial and temporary at best."

Her speech complete, the woman began to undress, going about it calmly, in a direct and unashamed manner. When she stood before him in all her glory, she got a funny look on her tiny face. Panic? Bapcat wondered.

With wild and wide eyes she muttered, "Oh my," and fell to the uncarpeted floor with no more sound than the nomadic leaf she had described earlier. Sent by Zakov?

Bapcat looked at her nude body and was reaching for a blanket when Jordy and Anton came back with a basin of water. His adopted son stared for a long time at the woman, grinned, and said in English, "Shall I come back later, Father?"

Anton laughed, and Jordy pushed him back.

Bapcat threw a glove at his son, and Anton laughed. "What happened to her?" Jordy asked.

"I don't know. Fainted, maybe. She was still talking just before she keeled over. Could be she's lost too much blood, or she's hungry, or any of a hundred other reasons."

"You think she's really a doctor from Michigan?" Jordy asked.

"In this place, I'm inclined to believe almost anything, even the most unbelievable. Let's get her onto a cot and covered."

"For such a small person, there's a lot of 'woman' there," Jordy said.

This had not escaped Bapcat's notice either, and he felt guilty. What would Jaquelle say if she knew he was looking at, and not turning away from, an undressed woman?

"Naked and beautiful," his son said. He set down the water basin and he and Anton left the car.

Bapcat draped a blanket over her and the woman opened her eyes.

"You see, I heard you talking. The game is up; I believe that's Dr. Watson's line?"

"Doctor who?" Bapcat asked. "We need to get you cleaned up."

And dressed, he was thinking.

"Yes, of course. Why not?" she said softly. "I was quite fine when I left your Colonel Zakov, but along the way I passed through a village of *izbas*, and there was a sniper, Red, White, or of this earth or not, only God knows, and He obviously doesn't care. I was quite lucky that my sniper took but one errant shot, and when I awoke—I'm not sure how long I was out, it was dark—I focused on getting away from that horrid place, finding you and Jordy. It is a soldier's job to finish her mission, yes?"

"Yes," Bapcat said. *Izbas?* And snipers?

"Where were you when you woke up?" he asked.

"A traditional peasant's log house, what you in Michigan call a log cabin."

"You're sure it was a sniper?"

"*Mein Gott,*" she said in German. "There are snipers *everywhere* these days. They kill randomly, like God or boys. Surely you remember Shakespeare's marvelous line? 'As flies to wanton boys are we to the gods. They kill us for their sport.' This is Russia now."

"I don't read much," Bapcat admitted.

"Yes," she said, "Zakov was quite clear on that point. He says you don't read books, but you read people with a scholar's eye."

Damn Zakov.

Bapcat moved the basin close to the cot and began to clean her face and neck and hands. She soon fell asleep and did not stir. The skull wound was superficial, but she had bled a lot, and her hair was so badly matted there was no way to clean it without a lot more water and a brush with stiff bristles.

Jordy came back alone. "What do we tell Dodge?" he asked.

Bapcat had no answer. Zakov had individually made contact with both him and Jordy, and now he had sent this woman. Why?

"Where is Dodge?"

"Gone when I woke up this morning," Jordy said. "Elpy said he's seen him only once since we stopped last night. Elpy thinks the major and our engineer went ashore at first light this morning. He doesn't know where, or why."

How and when they'd begun referring to anything off the train as "ashore" was lost to Bapcat. It had started a few days before and had persisted, and why not? This train journey slicing into the heart of Russia was like an island-hopping sea voyage, each city where they stopped turning out to be not just a separate city or island, but almost an entirely separate country, with its own rules and form of governance.

"Did Elpikovny say why we are stopped?" Bapcat asked. The night before, Dodge had hardly seemed to notice.

"Some sort of traffic from the opposite direction. We've taken a siding to let it all pass and then clear our way forward."

"First time that's happened since we got on the train."

"Elpy says there are fewer tracks and fewer choices the farther east we get, and that this is normal out this far. How're we going to hide the lady doctor?"

Clearly his son and the Russian signalman were bonding. Bapcat was sick of the cloak-and-dagger crap, pretending to be something and someone he wasn't.

"We're not hiding her."

"Odysseus," Jordy said.

"What?"

Jordy explained, "Who, not what. It's our mission name, and it also relates to us. The original Odysseus wandered from island to island, trying to make his way home after the Trojan War. That's us, trying to get our mission done and then get home. That's the goal for all military missions, to get everyone back safely, right? Fight the enemy and come home."

The boy was in many ways wise beyond his years.

"Goals and reality often aren't the same thing," said Bapcat. "The reality is that often, not everyone makes it back."

"Odysseus lost every last one of his men, and it took him twenty years to get home."

"But he got there, right?"

"He made it, and he found his wife had a hundred suitors hanging around, trying to make time with her."

"How did he handle that?"

"He killed them."

"All of them?"

"Yep. I don't think Widow Frei would tolerate a hundred men. She hardly puts up with you and me."

Bapcat smiled. It was like the young to feel immortal. This is why they made such good soldiers. They always assumed the best for themselves, imagined disasters as the province of others.

"Did Odysseus ever have to hide a woman on his trip home?"

"I don't remember, but naked women on his voyage were a dime a dozen. Cannibals and monsters, too."

Cannibals and monsters and naked women?

"I suppose we'd better hide our doctor until she can tell us what Zakov wants and why he sent her to us."

"Dodge is in command," Jordy Klubishar said.

Was he? Bapcat clearly remembered talk that indicated when Zakov was found, leadership would pass into Bapcat's and Zakov's hands. Was that time now? What would Dodge's role be after that? This had not been made clear.

Jordy said, "Elpy has a small space in the second water car. He goes there to be alone, to think, to read, to dream."

"Our signalman has dreams?"

"Doesn't everyone?" the boy said. "He dreams of America—what his future life will be like and where he will be."

"Dodge said Bezmunyi and his family are going back with us, not the signalman."

"That doesn't seem fair. Elpy's risking his life for us, and there's just him, no family. Elpy's more like you and me than Bezmunyi is."

Bapcat felt weary and anxious. The signalman was coming home with them too. How much more was going on that he didn't know about?

"Think he'll give up his secret space for our secret passenger? Do we need a key?"

"Yes, and I know the way."

"Let's get her moved. I'll clean her up more when we get her secure. You wait for Dodge to get back and keep him occupied."

"Me?"

"Good sergeants always have ways of keeping officers occupied when they don't want them to know what's really going on. It's almost an art."

"I ain't no artist."

"I beg to differ."

At this moment Anton came hopping back into the car and saw the woman still there, under the blanket. Jordy growled at the boy in Russian, and he fled.

Bapcat said, "What did you say to him?"

"I told him if he ever expects to see America, he'd better not say anything to anyone."

"See America? *Anton?*"

"We can't very well leave him here with all these Russian assholes, can we? Look what they've done to him already."

This was getting out of hand. He, Jordy, Zakov, Dodge, Bezmunyi and his family, Elpikovny, *and* Anton? How many more merry travelers would they accumulate on the way back to the States? How many *could* they accommodate? How would they feed and protect them?

No, this was not a good thing in the making. Not good at all.

Jordy followed Bapcat, who had carried the Black Angel to the tank car space. Jordy carried the cot, which he put down, and Bapcat laid the woman down and covered her. She was filthy, desperately needing a bath. Only then did it dawn on him that he no doubt needed one even more. How long had it been? He could no longer remember his last bath. England? Good grief. After feeling disgust, he laughed. Smelling like this would no doubt gag maggots and wolves—a good defense, perhaps.

Bapcat told his son to go back and wait for Dodge.

It was getting dark, and when he looked at the woman, her eyes were open. She lifted the blanket, inviting him to join her.

"We can talk much easier," she said.

"I stink," he said.

"I know, Dear Captain, and so do I," she said, and closed her eyes.

Where the hell is Zakov, and why did he send this strange woman? How had she even gotten on board? Does Zakov even *know* her? If not, who is she, and what is she up to? Who really sent her, and what was her game?

He crawled in with her and felt her arms slide around his waist.

As it turned out, Dodge and Bezmunyi didn't come back until much later. The woman on the cot had slept. There had been no talk or anything else. Her body was hot as a furnace, and lying next to her had made him sweat. Bapcat eventually returned to their carriage and asked Jordy and Anton to watch the woman, so she could get some real sleep.

Bapcat was sitting when Dodge came in. "Our business done here?" he asked the major.

The marine rubbed his forehead and tousled his hair. He looked tired, which was a first. Until now, Dodge had acted like his energy reserves were endless.

"The engineer and I met with some of his people today. There is a rumor that the Tsar and his family are alive and in Tobolsk, captives of the Bolsheviks."

"Are we going there?"

"I don't know. There is speculation that the Reds will move them to Yekaterinburg. This rumor says that the Tsar's former military escort will be replaced by Latvian Rifles. These so-called Letts are used by top Bolos for what they call 'wet business,' *mokryi delo*."

A flood of information from the major, and most of it said in a disinterested monotone.

"Wet business?"

"Russians prefer euphemistic misdirection in all things political. They mean *ubistvo i kazn*—political murders and executions. What a country is Tsarist Russia. It's like falling down Alice's rabbit hole, only this is real, not some egghead don's satirical fantasy of modern politics and mathematical theories."

Rabbit hole?

"Alice?"

"*Alice's Adventures in Wonderland*," Dodge said. "Do you not read *anything*?"

"Must be new," Bapcat said, not wanting to seem ignorant.

"Came out during the last year of the War Between the States, 1865," Dodge said in a raspy voice. "It's been around for a very long time, but the point is that innocent little Alice drops into total chaos, which looks organized and reasonable next to this Russian version we're facing. Latvian

Rifles, Captain; this is not a harbinger of good news. These Letts are brutal bastards and were among the first to jump on the Bolshevik bandwagon. If this rumor is true, we should fear for the Tsar."

"What about his family?"

Dodge was slow to answer. "I certainly hope not. They are innocent, especially the children."

Bapcat asked, "With this new information, shouldn't we go to Yekaterinburg rather than Tobolsk?"

The major's voice and tone shifted. "Our mission brief seems clear to me, Lute."

Using his given name? Odd, and maybe a first. "The mission is to find Zakov, who is to find the Tsar, right?"

The major seemed to be losing interest in his captain's questions.

"Implicit in our orders is a charge to retrace and document every step of the Tsar's journey in exile and imprisonment. This means eyes-on, hands-on verification and documentation of every location and stop along the way."

This was utter nonsense. If he knew where a suspect was, he went directly there. He did not follow some long, winding trail that might lead eventually to the same place.

"Seems to me our priority is to get to the place where we are most likely to find them."

Dodge raised his hands and fell back on his cot, hooking an arm across his face.

"My hands are tied. I'm done talking, Captain."

Back to Captain, from Lute. What was Dodge's angle?

"Where are our written orders?" Bapcat asked.

"Nothing is ever put in writing for missions like this, Captain. Everything is verbal, for the security of the mission and all those involved."

Bapcat recognized butt-covering when he heard it. Neither Roosevelt nor the strange Englishman Churchill had said anything about documentation.

"Zakov sent a message through the Swedes, asking for us. That's the *only* reason we're here, you *or* us."

Dodge said, "You don't have the experience in such matters that I have, Captain."

Bapcat was outwardly impassive and inwardly shaking his head. A game warden was well advised to keep his face from betraying his feelings. This practiced game warden's mask tended to unsettle people enough to make them try to fill the silence it created, and usually what they blurted out to fill the void tended to be self-incriminating, a term he had learned from *Tiffany's Criminal Law*, the game warden's legal bible.

"Too damn vague," Bapcat said.

"Which part?" the major asked in a waning voice.

"All of it—everything."

"I can certainly understand your feelings, but our orders are quite specific, and though this is not specifically specified in the specifications, I can say with great confidence that we are almost certainly not in this venture alone. Theoretically there are always assets, friends, allies, sympathizers—more than one can know."

More of Dodge's blather, more puzzles and smoke. Bapcat was fed up.

"With all due respect, sir, I can't help but think you're holding something back."

"Your feelings are your feelings, Captain. You alone own them."

"Puzzles have parts," Bapcat said.

"Some have more parts than you can imagine," Dodge replied.

"Soldiering is not like that," the game warden told the marine.

"Soldiering in Russia *is* like that," the major said, and stopped talking.

Who were these allies and other people Dodge was talking about? Bapcat knew better than to ask. Through trial and error, first as a soldier, then as a trapper, and since then, as a game warden, he had learned that cases often turned on hard, physical evidence, not one's gut instincts, yarn spinning, or wishful thinking. To make a case, you had to stay focused and patient, bide your time, and gather irrefutable evidence. You had to learn to see both what was there and what was missing that should be there.

Dodge lifted his arm. "I suspect you have innumerable questions."

"Only one, sir. Yekaterinburg or Tobolsk? And if the latter, how? There is no train service there, according to Elpikovny."

"We shall emulate the birds," the major said, raising his elbows and flapping them.

Dealing with Dodge was almost as challenging as dealing with the Northern Cheyenne.

One thing he could decide for himself: If Dodge was going to fly to Tobolsk, he could bloody well fly alone. He and Jordy would wait for further contact with Zakov and try to figure out exactly what message the woman doctor was trying to convey by being here.

19

Spring, 1918. Last Stop to Nowhere

She opened an eye and whispered, "The last stop to nowhere."

Bapcat gave the woman water and watched her drink, her eyes riveted on him the whole time.

"You are a patient man," the woman said. "Patience is the gift of saints, healers, and spies. It limits mistakes."

He was not as patient as she assumed.

"Zakov," he said, trying to keep her focused.

"Yes, dear Zakov. You see, he did not send me directly. Bishop Boris dispatched me at Pinkhus Sergeyevich's instruction."

"I never heard of a Bishop Boris," Bapcat told her. Your Russia seems to have a very long cast of characters, wandering on and off the stage.

"No doubt you will never know him. He is a very cautious man, our little bishop."

"Zakov," he repeated. Could no one in this country keep their focus?

"My instruction from the colonel came through Little Boris, the Bishop. You are to come with me. I will guide you to your husband." She was grinning mischievously.

"You're a real jokester for someone just shot in the head," he told her.

She waved a hand dismissively. "Alive, dead, what is the difference? We have no evidence of life beyond. We have only this life at our feet, so let us live it as best we can, for as long as we can."

"Who is Little Boris?"

"The Bishop."

"Bishop of what church?"

"That's a difficult question, Dear Captain. Boris is neither Roman nor Russian Orthodox, neither Baptist nor Adventist, but he leads a congregation which believes in God and Russia, although it seems increasingly evident that God perhaps does not have much interest in Russia's fate." She lifted her blanket. "You look so weary, Dear Captain. Even God rested on the seventh day. You should rest and refresh yourself. A weary soldier cannot be an effective soldier."

He knew that soldiering was entirely about operating on little food or rest, in terrible weather, over impossible terrain. Who *was* this woman?

"You talk much, but say little. I do not like games. Who are you, really?"

"You do not believe I am a doctor from Michigan?"

He showed her his game warden mask.

She sighed. "Very well, Dear Captain. I am actually Baroness Sophie-Marie Lizbeta Moroz."

"So you're not a doctor, then?"

"Oh, I'm a doctor as well. I went to medical school in Michigan, as I said."

"As a member of the royal family?"

None of the titles here, in England, or elsewhere meant much to him. President, senator, congressman, judge, sheriff—these titles he mostly understood, if not precisely how those with the higher titles came to get them. He knew Colonel Roosevelt, of course, had known him before he became president; it had been clear even then that the man was going to some high place he himself would never approach.

"Not the Romanovs, Dear Captain." She smiled. "But yes, I am of the privileged aristocratic class. My late husband owned unconscionably massive tracts of land, and what good did *that* do him? The Germans killed him. I blame Dear Nicky, who *insisted* Mikhail Isodorovich join the military. He was of course appointed general, my late husband, and I have no doubt he was as incompetent a general as he was a landowner and husband. He was a marvelous, charming, enchanting, and astonishingly incompetent human being, but my Darling Michael a soldier? *Preposterous!* Michael could not kill a spider, could not stand to even countenance such creatures. He was afraid of loud noises, forceful people, horses, making decisions, his own shadow. In truth he was the model anti-soldier, truly pathetic, though rather fetching in his general's uniform."

Not exactly her husband's biggest supporter. Very unlike Jaquelle, who promoted him shamelessly to anyone who would listen or could, in her estimation, be of assistance in the future. It was often embarrassing, and early in their relationship he had complained. She had laughed at him and assured him that she knew about planning and setting tables for the future, whatever that meant.

"A marriage of convenience," the baroness said. "He was rich, and I looked quite gorgeous beside him, an arm ornament befitting a baron. He was a nice man, my Darling Michael, born terribly wrong, the weak eldest son of a strong man, which was never good for either of them, do you not agree, Dear Captain?"

"Got no idea what you're talking about, so I can't agree or disagree."

She cocked her head again. "You are a sensitive and thoughtful man, Dear Captain. I believe you find it painful to offend or injure feelings."

"I tend to offend a lot of people in my job," he told her. "Some would tell you that's my *whole* job, and truth is, I don't much think about the feelings of the people I deal with. I deal with what people have done, not so much the reasons why."

She waved a long finger at him. "Then you know yourself, Dear Captain. All knowledge and wisdom begin with self-knowledge."

"You know that, do you?" he asked her.

The baroness winked at him. "Oh yes, Dear Captain, oh yes. Intimately."

A very strange woman, but oddly, he found himself increasingly comfortable with her. Nothing in Russia was ever what it first appeared to be.

"Where is Zakov?"

She said, "I cannot cite a location with specificity. As you surely know, our Pinkhus Sergeyevich is somewhat unpredictable and always mysterious. He prefers to operate in a miasma of ambiguity, which I see as a kind of impure sea, with him either swimming in it robustly or quietly treading water as circumstances dictate. He is quite adept at bold and subtle thinking and action."

What the hell was her game?

"Maybe you ought to be on your way," he suggested.

She smiled. "But I am, as you state it, on my way. I am here at your side, Dear Captain, yours and Dear Jordy's. I am exactly where—and with whom—I am supposed to be. Surely you understand this."

"Surely I don't," he answered.

She let go a long sigh, sat up, swung her shapely legs over the edge of the cot, placed her bare feet on the deck, and hitched the blanket over her shoulders, not bothering to cover her breasts.

"Listen to me, Dear Captain. Your Colonel Zakov—your friend, colleague, partner, *husband*—travels under the protection of the church, which serves as his eyes, his protector, and sometimes, his guide."

"You said Bishop Boris is not of a particular church."

"Of course not, but like the Metropolitan of the Russian Orthodox Church, he has his own impressive resources, none of them attached to the State by an umbilical cord."

More Russia confusion, which was how he was beginning to think of this place.

"You said Boris is not of the Orthodox faith."

"I suspect he is of said *faith*, but not of said *church*. Do you understand such a distinction? We can love our country but not its government. Boris travels in celestial ether the way Zakov does, in shadows, out of sight, unseen, unheard, the bat and cruising owl at night, an old man sitting in a corner by daylight, tucked in an obscure shadow in plain sight."

Was she telling the truth about Boris, and did it even matter?

"My only interest is Zakov," he reminded her.

"Silly man. Zakov is always with, or close to, the Bishop."

"Boris sent you, which means you are also with Boris and Zakov?"

"One may be dispatched without being *with* someone."

Bapcat rubbed his eyes. He needed tea, or sleep, or even better, some black coffee to melt the cobwebs in his brain.

"You are going to lead us to Zakov." Statement, not question.

"I shall lead you and Jordy, Dear Captain, and you shall follow, and in the process of our journey the colonel will intercept us. You see how ingenious this plan is?"

He saw the simplicity, the holes and possible pitfalls. It sounded just like his beloved friend to complicate the ordinary.

"What about Major Dodge?"

"The major is quite capable of carrying on alone," she said dismissively.

"His orders were to assist us in finding Zakov, and after that, for all of us to work together."

Baroness Moroz made a clucking sound.

"He has helped you to find Colonel Zakov. I am here, am I not? The major's job, *c'est fini, n'est-ce pas?*"

"I doubt Zakov will see it that way."

"It matters not how he sees it. My sole interests are you and Jordy. We need to leave this train at the first opportunity."

"On foot?"

"Yes. Are you both mute *and* crippled?"

He shook his head.

"The train will move to another siding tonight, and Major Dodge will be going somewhere to further coordinate future rail movements. Chief Engineer Bezmunyi will be with him."

"How can you know this?"

She smiled. "You think it coincidence that I know the engineer's name or your signalman, your dear Elpy?"

He was never a believer in coincidence at work in the Upper Peninsula, but this was Russia.

"Is it?"

Her eyebrows danced. "All things are possible in Russia in these anxious times."

"*All* things includes both good and bad?" he said.

"In Russia, of course."

"When do we leave?" he asked.

"When Dodge leaves you to sleep, I will come for you. Sleep while you can, because you will need great energy for what looms before us."

"And you?" he asked the baroness.

She lay back on the cot. "I shall sleep the sleep of innocent babes in Paradise. You may go now, *mon capitaine.*"

He paused and looked outside the tank car. "What lies ahead?" he asked her.

She opened an eye and whispered, "The last stop to nowhere."

—◦—

"She okay?" Jordy greeted him back in their carriage.

Bapcat nodded. "Where's Dodge?"

"Gone with Bezmunyi, something about obtaining permission to pass through. The major is not happy. He hates red tape."

The train had slowed a couple of times but had not stopped. When and how had Dodge gotten off? No point asking. Some things happened for which there was no explanation.

"We're leaving."

"When?" his son asked.

"Tonight. The baroness will fetch us. We're to sleep until then."

"No argument from me," Jordy said, slumping to his cot. "Baroness? I thought she was a doctor. Is she someone important?"

"She is to us. She's taking us to Zakov."

"That wasn't my question."

"But that's my answer."

20

Early Spring, 1918. Perm

"In a land of wolves there are no sheep."

Four days, or was it five since they had left the train? Time and life had become so jumbled over recent months, Bapcat wasn't sure whether they were still in Russia. *Somewhere* was not a precise enough answer for him, but it seemed the best he could do as they trundled along behind their erstwhile pathfinder, waiting for Zakov to find them. They took care to avoid villages and other pockets of humankind, but everywhere they went, most days, they heard the reports of rifles—sometimes single shots, sometimes frantic fusillades—and the sounds made Bapcat think of deer season near Red Jacket.

From a distance they could see fires in the streets of villages, and occasionally they came across bodies, some shot and some with no marks and no way to determine cause of death. More than once they got close enough to burning structures to hear the death moans and howls of domestic animals, and Bapcat found the whole thing disconcerting. It was clear the baroness was picking her way along carefully, perhaps to spare them from seeing the worst of what was happening, but as he thought about this, he decided that imagined horrors were often worse than reality. What they were seeing and hearing was pretty bad in its own right, and the thought that their guide kept steering them away from more extreme things made him shudder. He worried about what Jordy was thinking.

Carefully stepping over and around the wounded and dead bodies of your own men and the enemy all tangled in the death vise was bad. This he had seen and done in Cuba. But there it had been clear who was friend or foe; here, it was not. Save for small pieces of red ribbon on some of the corpses, presumably Bolo troops or their sympathizers, most of the bodies had no means of identification—no standard uniforms, weapons—nothing. It had taken five years after Cuba to stop seeing the dead, and in his first year as a game warden, his brain sometimes turned dead animals into dead human beings, especially skinned and caped animals.

This Russian mess might be like hunting season, but prey and predators alike were armed and killing as thoughtlessly as breathing. There seemed no limits here on carnage: men, women, children, infants, the elderly, all civilians and onetime neighbors, even swarthy priests in gaudy gilt gowns and long, thick beards were crucified on trees here and there, and not a church anywhere in sight. Some bodies had been disfigured by their killers, some by death itself. The whole thing felt like a huge message, but to whom, and what exactly was being said? Everyone seemed to be intent on killing others. It made no damn sense, but it was real; his eyes and nose affirmed this everywhere they went.

The whole thing reminded him of the stories his friend All Things had told of US Army raids on Indian villages when warriors were away, with only innocents slaughtered, the old, the young, and all women, even the sick. Bapcat had been confused by the raid stories. The army raids were not simply white men trying to eliminate red men, because the military also employed hundreds of red men—not just to help them locate certain tribes, but to help with the killing, which meant the thing was more nuanced than red against white. All Things told him that Indian scouts working for the army killed with great enthusiasm. As they hiked behind Baroness Moroz, Bapcat began to think of the carnage in Russia as something like the army raids in the West: one side intent on wiping out the other.

Once in a while in Red Jacket, someone would jabber about races as if they were different sides in a game, but if this were true, how to account for people of your own color killing you? The Civil War was said to have been about slavery, but near as he could tell, it had been whites slaughtering whites.

They had stopped for fifteen minutes. The baroness rolled a cigarette and held it out to him.

"The worst of all this," she said, "is the filth and corruption which will follow. It hangs in the air like poison fog, and we walk through it all day long. How wonderful it would be to sit in the hot mineral waters of Vyatka, forty-five degrees centigrade, day in, day out. So hot it would burn the filth out of our flesh. I wonder if I shall ever feel truly clean again."

He sensed she was not talking about simple dirt and the need for soap.

"You've killed no one," he told her.

She exhaled a smoke snake and grimaced.

"There are sides here, Dear Captain, at least two, and both sides share collective guilt. I cannot imagine what will emerge when all this is finished. Thank God I won't have to see it."

What did she mean by that?

She seemed to read his mind.

"I will be in America," she told him. "Russia will have to figure it out without me."

"But you're Russian," he reminded her.

She flashed a thin, pained smile.

"No longer. I am now, like you and Jordy, and the major, and Zakov, as American as apple pie. Do you like apple pie, Dear Captain? Do all Americans eat this sugary delicacy every day? If they eat it every day, does this not disqualify it as a delicacy and turn it into regular daily fare?"

"No clue," he said. "I never think much about apple pie. You went to school in America," he reminded her.

"Medical students have no time for simple delicacies of life such as apple pie," she lamented, and added, "Or for making love. Is that not also an American delicacy?" she asked, looking directly into his eyes.

This woman!

"I don't know where apple pie comes from, if it's an original American thing or if it came over from Europe or somewhere. Almost everything in America comes from elsewhere—except Indians. They're our only originals, but they don't get treated that way. Here you are all Russian."

"You are blind, Dear Captain. Russia, like America, is a polyglot, a cauldron of stew with many, many ingredients. Have you not looked at the faces of the dead? Asiatic, European, Pomors, Tatars, Cossacks, many, many races and colors. We are alike, Russians and Americans—mongrels."

"If we're alike, why not stay here? This is your home."

She sighed. "Home is not a fact of one's birth, it is the place one must choose. We are born with relatives and ancestors, over this we have no choice. But friends, we choose. For me, home is friends, and apple pie," she added.

"You may not like it. The United States is always changing."

"I shall adjust. At least you Americans are not running around trying to exterminate all who disagree with you."

"We have done that in the past," he told her.

"Your Civil War is long done, and ours has just commenced, under-way, and I have no idea for how long, or even what is being decided by all of this nonsense. I despised the royal and class system, even though it surely benefited me." She jutted out her jaw. "I shall learn to love America, Dear Captain." Much about this woman reminded him of Jaquelle, but Jaquelle was honest to the core, and this woman? He doubted it.

"There is something we must discuss," she said, fumbling with her tobacco pouch and rolling a cigarette, which she passed to him before rolling another for herself. "I hope American tobacco is better than this Russian . . . *pomet*. That means dung."

"You didn't smoke American tobacco while you were in medical school?"

"No time for apple pie, or making love, or smoking tobacco." She was smiling.

"*Pomet*," he said. "Your dung, the dung of animals and people. We call it shit."

"*Da*, shit. I like this word, but doctors are more circumspect and call it feces. I like shit better than both of the other words, yours and ours."

They both laughed quietly.

"I think, Dear Captain, that our living in this disgraceful abattoir has given us equally filthy and disgusting minds."

"No apple pie?" he joked.

"Nor making love," she added.

He changed the subject, guessing there was more on her mind.

"You want to talk of more than apple pie and *pomet*."

"Yes, Dear Captain. To this point I have tried earnestly to navigate the path of least resistance, but I seem to have failed. The next two or three *versts* offer our little company no safe harbor and no friendly faces. I fear we shall have to fight in order to advance."

Bapcat rubbed his eyes.

"America is neutral. We are not at war with Russia or the Russian people."

She pursed her lips.

"There is no Russia now, Dear Captain. The Tsar is yesterday, and there is a contest to determine who will control and define this country tomorrow. Until this contest is settled, Russia does not formally or legally exist. There are, at minimum, Red and White armies, and who can even tell them apart? You have seen the bodies, the lack of uniformity in anything except violent death. Even the combatants can't tell each other apart at more than fifty meters. Each side behaves the same: It kills anything in its path."

"And it's happening everywhere, in villages and in cities," Bapcat said.

"These are local fights, the settling of long-standing grudges—getting even, I think you say in English. Some are White sympathizers and some prefer Red, but the armies have not yet reached them, so they kill each other for personal reasons, long forgotten by most people around them. This may be said to be political in nature, but it is not, and most of what you are seeing is not ordered from 'on high.' If we must fight today out here, we do not kill Russians; we only remove brigands, opportunists, and obstacles to our progress."

He accepted yet another cigarette, puffed and thought. The Russian stuff tasted worse than Indian tobacco. He did not consider himself a thinker in the way Zakov was a thinker, or his friend Judge O'Brien, or Jaquelle, but he had always had a knack for solving real-life problems. The United States was not at war with Russia. Official Russia did not exist, the baroness insisted. Was either fact relevant? Would this logic for fighting be upheld in a court-martial? Of course, if they got killed fighting, there would be no court-martial. It would be what Colonel Roosevelt called "moot," as when they passed a sniper he had shot and Roosevelt would grin and proclaim "Another moot, Corporal Bapcat." There was no way to predict the reactions of the brass if they got through this. To get court-martialed, first they had to stay alive, and if that meant killing, then so be it.

He was not happy with such logic, but there was no choice. They seemed to be caught in what cowboys back in the Dakotas called a dang box canyon.

"How will we know who to kill and who not to kill?" he asked the woman.

She exhaled dramatically and smiled. "There will be no not-kills where we go. If it attacks, blocks, or challenges us, we must quickly kill it."

He tried to keep calm, but couldn't and frowned. "This is shit," he said disgustedly.

"The tobacco?" she asked.

"That, too; everything here, all this."

"You include me?" she asked with a concerned look.

"No." He hoped.

<hr />

It seemed apparent that they were in the outer part of a town, whose name he did not know. He could see fallow fields and expanses of larch, and suspected that if they could get into the forest he would breathe easier.

For more than three hours, they had moved cautiously through a series of ruined buildings, and been confronted by no one. There were bodies, of course, and the lingering stench of dead and burned flesh, both human and livestock, and there had been shooting all around them as they advanced behind the baroness. Occasionally they heard angry voices or screams, and at one point the woman stopped and put her mouth near his ear and told him something that unnerved him.

"We are being watched, but we are being left alone. They don't know who we are or what to make of us. This will not last," she added quietly.

He suspected she was right and wished she wasn't, but this was always the way in war. Expect the worst at all times.

"How far to open country?" he asked, then corrected himself. "To the forest?" He glanced at Jordy, saying, "Stay alert."

"One *verst*," she said, "perhaps a little more."

"How far, in English, Jordy?" he said quickly.

"About two-thirds of a mile . . . call it twelve hundred yards."

"Russians don't think in distances," the baroness said. "They think in terms of time, how long it takes to reach a destination. I fear we have come as far as we can without conflict. The area just ahead is impossible. It was recently in a frenzy of bloodlust."

Bapcat heard flurries of shots and tried to read the tactical realities, but what he heard didn't sound like signs of trained, disciplined soldiery. These were erratic, wild, without plan, patience, or discipline, marks of rank amateurs, most likely civilians.

Throughout his life, all his jobs had taught him patience and the importance of standing back and gathering information to help understand what he was dealing with. If there were to be a fight, there would be unwritten rules in play, rules learned the hard way, the first and foremost being to kill your opponent quickly, without hesitation, and move on. But no one ever knew how they would behave until they faced a situation. Was Jordy up to this? Probably. If something happened to the boy, Jaquelle would kill him. And Baroness Moroz? Could *she* handle it?

Lead, he told himself. Jordy and the woman will have to fend for themselves. This is the first rule of war: Take care of yourself first.

Baroness Moroz tugged softly on his sleeve, showed four fingers, and motioned slightly right with her hand.

"Moving toward us?" he mouthed silently.

She shook her head, whispered, "I'm not sure if they have seen us and are trying to clear the path for a surprise or if they are not aware we are here."

"What kinds of communications do these irregulars have?" he asked.

"Runners," she said. "Only messengers."

Good. Runners in an open fight were weak links in coordinating an attack.

"Do you have a route in mind?" he asked her.

"*Da*," she said, pointing to a gaudily painted green log building with salmon-red window frames. "Behind the building, then at angles to the green space. You can make out the treetops. Not large, but dense." She pointed.

He saw it. "From there?"

She shrugged. "Let us get there first and take another look."

"All right," Bapcat said, "You out front, then Jordy. I'll secure everything behind us, keep ten or twelve paces between us, no more than that. If we run into a block or threat, fire, no hesitation, and move forward."

"Red, White?" Jordy asked.

"In a land of wolves there are no sheep," the baroness said. "This is Danteland, understand?"

"Hell," Jordy said.

The woman smiled, seemingly touched by the look on Jordy's face.

"Shouldn't I go first?" the boy asked.

Bapcat said, "The baroness is leading this detail. We're in support. She knows the way. We don't."

"I can take the last position," Jordy tried.

"This is not as easy as it looks. With you between us there is strong support for either of us, both of us, all of us."

Bapcat saw the woman grinning.

"What?" he asked her.

"You have a poet's heart, Dear Captain. 'Either of us, both of us, all of us'—you sound almost like Comrade Lenin, who prefers to fight with words and let others do the dirty work and take the risks."

"Lenin?"

"Leader of the Bolsheviki," she said. "A monster with a snake's cold blood, a rich man's son who wants to destroy the world and remake it in his image. He will make himself the new tsar and change only the title. He will be the same absolute power, on a par with God Almighty."

The name and description meant nothing to him. Bapcat had never before heard the name, and he was no poet, whatever the baroness meant by that. He had little patience for tricky words that didn't get to the point.

Jaquelle would read things to him and then explain what they meant, how A was really B, which was really something else. He'd object: Why doesn't he just say B is B and say what he has to say? That's not art, she'd counter, and he'd laugh. And then she would tell him A is a more beautiful way of stating B, and his retort was always, 'Not to B it ain't,' and they would both laugh. He liked direct, not indirect, and was never comfortable with double-talk, be it from a violator trying to lie his way out of something or some fancy lawyer playing the same game before a judge.

The truth was that as a game warden, he was a sailor on the sea of ambiguity; not knowing everything or, sometimes, even enough was a perpetual condition of the work. He didn't like it, but it was the unreality of the job's reality. Which made reading poetry in his private life not something he cared for. Too damn unclear, what most poets meant, and sometimes he wondered if even they knew.

As he was thinking Bapcat felt intense heat just below his right cheekbone, then a loud report. Only then did he react and flinch. He felt his face, saw blood on his fingers. No real pain. A bullet had grazed him, and he felt the baroness's hand land softly on his.

"There is some blood," she said, "not much. It has broken the skin, but not deeply. I can sew it together quickly, but for now we need a bandage to keep out as much dirt as we can. The thought of all this disgusting air and dead and poisonous cells floating about gives me pause, but let us do what we can. The most insignificant wound here can kill, so we must treat each as if it is major. I will wash it with carbolic lotion for now and wrap some gauze over it. The gauze will be soaked in the same solution. When I can find it, I use bismuth iodoform paraffin paste to clean a wound, but I have only carbo at the moment. Let me do what I can for now, and later I will stitch it."

"A great plan," he said with a snarl. "After we get out of the line of fire." He looked for Jordy, saw where he was slightly to his right, and seemed fine.

The three of them slithered quickly to a chunk of cement nearer their destination and pulled up there. Bapcat was sure more rounds would come in, but none did. He did not relax while she blotted at the wound.

He did not like sitting. Done was done, and close was close. To stay alive in a fight, you had to keep moving, and they were anything but in motion.

"All right," the baroness said. "That will hold for now. Shall we make our way to the building with the red windows?"

Bapcat nodded, and she took off with Jordy behind her, and he followed Jordy, who seemed a natural at soldiering, maintaining perfect interval spacing behind their guide. Had the boy been born with this, or had he and Zakov given it to him? Jordy had come into their lives when he was only twelve, and they had treated him as a comrade and an adult almost from the start.

As they hopped through broken buildings and brick piles and debris, Bapcat caught movement out of the corner of his eye and froze. The motion soon came into focus as a picture, a wolf dragging a small human body. He felt no sympathy for the human or revulsion toward the wolf.

Wolves, reviled by all mankind for all time and despite massive efforts to eradicate them, were still around, the ultimate survivors. He admired their ways—not the foolish myths about them, but the realities of wolf life: strength, discipline, endurance, patience, loyalty to their pack, ferocity when needed, stealth when ferocity was not propelled by hunger. This wolf was hungry, and why not human meat? Meat was meat: venison, moose, beaver, bear, all edible, all meat. Eating was nature's way, even for humans.

His friend Judge O'Brien in Laurium liked to say, "We're all talking monkeys, only we know that we're just animals, and we can recognize our own ridiculousness." His learned friend read even more than Jaquelle and told him such stuff had been written by some German. Although Bapcat no longer remembered the man's name, he remembered what the judge said, and in his mind, part of that ridiculousness was in how humans thought of and treated wolves.

In the midst of thinking about wolves and men, he had an idea. Ludicrous? Maybe. But what was there to lose? He'd just been grazed by a bullet that he was pretty sure had been random, and that he was not the target, but simply an obstacle on the way to the bullet's final resting place. What would be their chances, the three of them, if and when they became the intended targets? Not good, but maybe there was a way.

He used his fingers to make a shrill whistle, which froze Jordy and the baroness in their tracks. They both looked back. Bapcat pointed at the wolf, making slow progress with its treasure. He signaled with his hands for them to lay flat, and when he saw that they were down, he lay down in place, and saw that the wolf was watching him. His idea: lay back and wait for darkness. This would not eliminate being killed randomly, but it would decrease a hostile's ability to see an easy target and, thus, increase their survivability.

He knew for certain that only the wolf would find a safe way out of all this, so he waved Jordy and the baroness back to him. When they were close, he began following the wolf as best he could into the gloaming, the woman behind him and Jordy dragging the rear.

It took five exhausting hours to cover just twelve hundred yards. A snail would have thoroughly licked them in a race, but finally there came a moment when they were together and away from the buildings, across the open space, and deep into dense larch, black spruce, and birch stands.

When they had entered a small clearing, the baroness said, "Here we make tea, and I'll see to your wound, Dear Captain."

Jordy used his knife to dig a small hole and build a tiny twig fire while the baroness washed Bapcat's face with carbolic lotion. Then, satisfied that the wound was as clean as she could make it for the moment, she opened a small leather pouch, took out a needle, sterilized it over the fire, threaded it, and with a sure hand, put his face back together.

"Will it leave a scar?" he whispered.

"Does it really matter, Dear Captain?" Then she said, "There, done." She cupped his face gently with her small hand and kissed him, grazing her lips over his. He was so taken by surprise that he did not react.

Jordy made tea and broke out chocolate for all of them. Before leaving England, Dodge had procured reserve rations for them, most of which were on the train, but some of which they had in their packs. The rations included bacon, one-pound cans of corned beef, hard chocolate, tins of hard bread and hardtack biscuits, packs of sugar and salt, and separate cigarette rations, which initially had to be hand-rolled but were now made by machines. Bapcat had forgotten about the ration cigs until Jordy dug some out and passed them to the baroness, who sighed audibly as she lit up.

"In the sweet name of Jesus," she whispered, inhaling deeply. After a pause, she said, "North of here it grows less dark this time of year; by June and July, there are no more than three hours of partial darkness per night, certainly no more than four. Here we have only marginally more."

It seemed not unlike the Keweenaw to Bapcat. Summer dark coming around eleven p.m., and sunrise around four in the morning. And the terrain was very similar.

The baroness lit another machine-rolled cigarette and sat back against a tree.

"When light comes, I fear we shall find more of the same as yesterday. It is the same everywhere."

"Mass murder," Bapcat said. "I see no patriotism in this country."

The woman shrugged. "War is brutal; civil war, more so. What began as a revolution to oust the Tsar and stop all our men dying in the fight against the Germans has now become a civil war in earnest."

"A war of survival," Bapcat observed. "You saw the wolf yesterday? It makes no distinctions when it comes to meat. Its only prohibition is to not eat its own kind."

"I wish we could say the same for men," the baroness said. "I have heard many reports of starvation and cannibalism in our cities and towns."

Jordy said, "That's disgusting."

"Not at all," said Bapcat and the baroness in unison.

Bapcat asked, "Have Russians not tried to eradicate wolves?"

"Of course," she said. "An endless struggle of epic proportions. Did we really follow the wolf to safety?"

Bapcat was pleased. "The wolf wanted to get that meat to a cache, or to his pack, or to a safe place where it could eat in peace. I thought, if anything can safely make its way through the maze, it would be the wolf."

"This would never occur to me," the woman said, "and I must boast that my imagination is large and sometimes surprising, even to me. Still, to think to follow a beast out of the city, this is brilliant, even though it carried human flesh."

"Meat," Bapcat said. "And even though I saw the wolf initially and could follow it, I saw it no more than four times after that. It is a creature that can easily become invisible."

"And yet, you were able to follow it," the baroness said.

"It's what Lute does," Jordy said proudly. "Follow animals and people. Zakov says Lute can smell the shadows of butterflies and follow them. He's the best."

Bapcat sipped his tea, made a face. "*Pomet.*"

They all laughed. "We're clear of the city," Bapcat said. "Where to now?"

"Toward Yekaterinburg," the baroness said.

"How long?" Bapcat asked.

"Difficult to say, Dear Captain. In your American miles, say, one hundred and eighty *kutcha letnyi.*"

Jordy said, "What is *kutcha*? I don't know the word."

"I should have used the word *voron*," the baroness said. "*Kutcha* is a word of the old people, the Old Russians."

"*Voron letnyi,*" Jordy said. "Raven flying; this means direct," he said, looking at Lute. "Same as how the crow flies."

"One hundred and eighty miles direct—if we go in a straight line, which, of course, we won't," Bapcat said.

Baroness Moroz smiled.

"There are no straight routes or lines anywhere in Russia, Dear Captain. The old Russians believe *kutcha* was their ancestor, and a very naughty boy, a trick-maker."

"Like a magician?" Bapcat asked.

"*Da*, why not?" she said. "His pleasure sometimes makes life difficult for his human kin."

Bapcat sniffed the air. The breeze had shifted, and even deep in the forest, as they were, he could still smell smoke and death.

"Seems like *kutcha* is hard at work in these parts," he said. "What is this place we've gone around?"

"Perm," Jordy said.

The woman had slid over and was leaning against Bapcat, resting her hand on his leg as she fell asleep.

Jordy lit a cigarette and looked at his father. "I think she likes you."

"She likes who is most convenient."

Jordy grinned.

21

Late Spring, 1918. Kungur

"What, pray tell, is *your* plan, Dear Captain—to keep pushing on?"

It was a five-day slog to the town where Baroness Moroz said there was a world-famous cave, and violent hard rain the whole way, which cleared away the snow and stirred up a gooey thick muck that lay like liquid cake dough on everything, turning the ground slick as ice.

"World-famous cave?" Bapcat asked Jordy.

"Never heard of it," Jordy said. "Not famous in the Upper Peninsula, I guess."

No surprise, Bapcat thought. The Russians, it seemed, were like many Americans, assuming narrow local interests stretched across the world.

The baroness was as hardy as the Americans and not only kept their pace as they pushed her, but upped the tempo at times. Once she landed on the subject of caves and caverns, the woman talked incessantly of stalactites and stalagmites and other sundry bits, all of which Bapcat tried to tune out. He hated caves, mines, unlit basements, privies, submarines, and attics, anything confined and dark that might trigger his fear of being closed in and trapped.

"Where is this cave?" Jordy asked her one night.

"Near Kungur," their guide reported, adding, "And before you ask how far to Yekaterinburg, I don't know. It is neither close, nor far."

The undulating terrain approaching Kungur was a series of gentle rolling hills and flat, densely wooded sections, and although they were soaked from rain, they managed to find and carry enough small dry kindling to make fires. It was easy enough to skirt villages and avoid people, but they were hearing distant gunshots all day, every day, and still finding bodies here and there. Despite the cleansing hand of the heavy spring rains, the stench of death lay everywhere.

Elsewhere, in consistently flat country, Bapcat felt like they could easily make twelve miles a day, and though this rolling, wooded country was less than flat, he felt they were pushing close to that rate. He guessed they had made sixty miles since leaving Perm.

Over their fifth-night fire the baroness allowed that the remaining distance to Yekaterinburg was "in the neighborhood" of four hundred kilometers. Bapcat cursed. Why could not the entire world work on the same system of weights and measures, and what did "in the neighborhood" mean? Pretty big neighborhood, he told her, as she again settled down to sleep beside him under a lean-to of logs and spruce branches he and Jordy had thrown together.

"Is four hundred in the same neighborhood as three-fifty?"

"You're such an angry man, Dear Captain," she whispered. "You should vent your passions in more positive ways." Her hand was on his leg again, and he pushed it away. She rolled her eyes and swatted at him in a dismissive gesture that needed no language to understand.

Meanwhile, Jordy converted the distance from four hundred kilometers to two hundred and fifty miles, which set Bapcat to calculating again, and this frustrated him even more. No way to know what kind of ground lay ahead. If the terrain got steeper, more uneven and difficult, their day-miles could range between five and ten, which meant it would take them between twenty-five and fifty days to complete the trip. This took no account of weather. In steep country, the heavy rain of the last five days could make travel almost impossible. Having lived so long in the Upper Peninsula, Bapcat knew that weather was always a major factor in travel and even large trains had trouble bucking snow.

If they could increase their pace to fifteen miles, they could shave the trip to two weeks, assuming favorable weather, and that their health, legs, and luck held. Bapcat was not worried about food. They had been able to forage en route, with plentiful snowshoe hares, partridges, and sundry game birds. Baroness Moroz was certain game was plentiful in the area of

Yekaterinburg and that there were plenty of fish in the rivers and streams all through the area. Bapcat wanted to stay clear of fish until hares and birds became scarce. Fishing slowed them down. Game they could shoot on the move and carry as they went.

After mulling distances and travel factors, almost all unknown, Bapcat told his companions, "All this walking is no good."

Jordy said nothing. The baroness sighed and said, "We shall take respite in Kungur with *Babochka*."

"Means 'butterfly,'" Jordy told his adopted father.

Baroness Moroz's head was against Bapcat's shoulder as she whispered, "Babochka is neither Red nor White, Christian or otherwise. She has tried many religions and found them all silly and barbaric notions at best. She feels the same about all forms of government and awaits the day when the country is run by real people, not greedy, power-crazed politicians."

"Your friend dreams," Bapcat said.

"Not merely my friend; she's my sister-in-law. She also happens to be Zakov's sister, and her name is Anya."

Zakov has . . . a sister? This was news.

"She carries a pistol at all times, even when unclothed," the baroness added. "She has used it many times."

"On who?" Bapcat asked.

"An unanswerable question. Zakov characterizes her thusly—as pathologically, emotionally, and mentally unstable."

"And we expect *help* from her?" Bapcat said. "Zakov's sister . . . your sister-in-law?"

"Anya was briefly married to my brother. We were linked, her, Colonel Zakov, and me."

Were, past tense? "Briefly married to your brother?"

"Yes, until she was forced to kill him."

"*Forced* to kill your brother, her husband?" Was she serious?

"Of course. She caught him cheating, *in flagrante delicto*."

"This is a capital offense here?"

"She found him with . . . sheep."

"Wool—mutton, that kind of sheep?"

"Yes, sheep, four legs, baa baa baa. And now you will no doubt wonder whether sister shares brother's proclivities, and sister shall share only that she finds some dogs quite handsome and fine company, but she draws lines, this sister does, clear lines, you understand?"

"No sheep, no dogs," Bapcat said. Good grief.

"No Cossacks either," the baroness added. "They treat their horses better than their women. No Cossacks. I'm quite certain, Dear Captain, that you understand, then, the extreme angst life creates for a woman in possession of, as the Germans put it, *unergründliche* libido."

He reminded her that he had no German, and she whispered, "Unsatisfiable libido," and squeezed his leg.

Once again he changed the subject. "What exactly are you expecting Babochka to do for us?"

"Shelter us, provision us, succor our needs, large and small. She is famously *très généreuse*," Baroness Moroz added.

"Generous—and impulsive," he pointed out, thinking of the husband she shot.

"Quite so," the baroness said.

Bapcat did not like the plan. Succor our needs? What did that even *mean*? He didn't like it.

"We should keep pushing on to Yekaterinburg."

The baroness spluttered, "What, pray tell, is *your* plan, Dear Captain—to keep pushing on? This has neither precision, nor substance."

"I'd wish we had a train," Bapcat said.

"Ah," Baroness Moroz came back with a dramatic, hand-dancing flair. "Your plan is a *wish*? *This* is how American soldier captains think and plan, they . . . wish?"

"Hardly ever," he said sheepishly. Why was she in his face?

She said haughtily, "I propose we migrate directly to Babochka's manse and rest there. We can create a plan while we rest. She has contacts everywhere. Perhaps you will agree to this plan for the moment?"

"I guess," Bapcat allowed, thinking that maybe their leaving Dodge had not been such a capital idea, *capital* being Jaquelle's word for big-good-satisfying events, even small, sweet personal moments.

The baroness reminded him in some ways of his wife.

Wife? What had he done? He was still not mentally adjusted to the sudden change in his legal status, other than that he'd sworn to stick it out till death do us part, and this bloody *stupid* mission, this fool's errand, might do that very thing. This could make their marriage one of the shortest ever, in fact, a mere eight hours, which is all they had enjoyed together before he and Jordy had gotten on the train to head east. Eight hours seemed no more than an eye blink. How long ago was that? He no longer remembered. How long had they been in Russia? Months, was the best he could estimate, but not the specific number.

Hours later, Jordy snoring, the baroness poked at Bapcat's chest.

"Is your wife beautiful? Jordy says she is a 'looker,' but I do not know this word. Is she indeed a 'looker'?"

"A real looker," he whispered. "Everybody says so."

"And you think this as well?"

"Of course," he allowed. Why was she pushing this? "I'm married," he added, not sure why he'd felt the need to tell her. He was sorry as soon as the words were out.

"Pish," she said almost inaudibly. "I, too, am married," she announced.

"You said your husband died."

"I speak of my second husband," she said.

"You *are* married or *were* married?"

"I am married until I see him again, and then I shall shoot him dead."

"Another sheep problem?"

She sighed. "He's gone over to the Reds. This baron and general of the Tsar's Royal Army has gone over to the Reds; is that not ludicrous? At least my first husband was decent enough to die bravely in service to the Tsar."

"You spend a lot of words," Bapcat said. A second husband, a Red, a baron, and a general? Good grief.

"And you, Dear Captain, hide inside your head and say little. You are a direct man, a disciple of the religion of black and white, either and or, yes or no. You are wholly divorced from the entire philosophy and reality of life called gray. Am *I* a 'looker,' Dear Captain?"

"Yes, ma'am," he said.

"Most lookers know they're lookers," Jordy said.

"You're *supposed* to be sleeping," Bapcat told the boy.

"It's more interesting to listen to the baroness's sales pitch."

"Do you hear the corporal's words, Dear Captain, that 'lookers' *know* they are 'lookers,' and I that I am engaged in a sales pitch?"

"Do you think you are beautiful?" Jordy asked her.

"This is, of course, a fact known to all who can see," she said. "What is it that you think I am trying to sell?"

"I ain't talking about money or nothing like that," Jordy said. "It's none of my business what you two got between you."

Bapcat had heard enough.

"There isn't anything *between* us," Bapcat said. "And there's not going to be."

The baroness settled against his chest and whispered so Jordy couldn't hear, "The greatest military campaigns are always slowest to develop."

"Are we moving out?" Jordy asked. "We're burning daylight."

"It's not daylight yet," Bapcat said, but he could see hints of morning twilight in the east.

"I'll make tea," Jordy said.

Bapcat left the baroness and helped his son build the little fire.

"'Looker'? That's your *mother* you're talking about."

"She was a looker before she was my mother, and she's still a looker, *Dad.*"

Bapcat playfully swatted his adopted son.

The baroness stood up and slid on her pack.

"We have tea," Jordy told her.

The baroness lit a cigarette. "I am ready."

Bapcat could see dim eastern sky light now.

"We're ready, too, soon as we finish our tea. Explain this to me: Zakov's sister Anya is a mental case and shot your own brother, and you don't care, and now you're going to shoot your own husband, if and when you see him again. You and Babochka must drive him crazy."

"Second husband," the baroness corrected him. "This is not the same as a first husband, who is generally meant for practice purposes. It is my view that Zakov is not fully mentally balanced, and that he is a true genius—that is, by the currently developing psychiatric definition of such

174

things. This means he lives by different rules than most of us. You know what happened when he was against the Japanese?"

Bapcat said, "The outlines."

"Dear Zakov took his commanding general into the heat of battle on the front lines, marched him directly into enemy gunfire to make sure the man did not survive. His commanding officer was a coward who hid behind his men and ordered them forward to die stupidly. Zakov would not allow this to happen again and removed the problem, but in the process he was seriously wounded and almost died. This surely is not the mark of a mentally and emotionally stable person.

"Here is the irony: Zakov's men loved him, and still do. He was the only aristocrat they had ever met who treated them as equals and humans. Many of these same soldiers have now declared Red, but continue to carry affection and loyalty for their brave colonel. Legend, of course, says Zakov died that day, and most of his men believe that, but still hope it's not true. When he encounters these men, they immediately fall to their knees and swear allegiance to him. It is quite a remarkable phenomenon. It shows the power of myth, the story of an aristocratic soldier who treats his men well, a royal White, if you will, and yet they will turn from Red to Zakov in a blink. This is the power of leadership, and, I suppose, a mentally unstable man."

Baroness Moroz sighed. "This is Russia's third national upheaval. First came Genghis Khan and his barbaric hordes of city-eaters. Then Napoleon came, and now, after three centuries of Romanov rule, we have Lenin and his loutish lot. If God on high cared a wit about this country and the Russian people, we would not be in the midst of such a disaster, but obviously God does not care that the Romanovs ruled for three hundred awful years, topped off by Bloody Nicholas, and I ask, what will the Russian people have next?"

She talked as much as Jaquelle did and with equal passion.

"I'm sure I don't know," he said. The truth.

Their destination was a large house that Bapcat would call a mansion. There were several striped onion-domed turrets and many pointed gables, the whole thing constructed of giant logs, a massive cabin, in effect, gables painted bright green, and here and there, dabs of recent paint. The house was every bit as large as the mansions of the mining barons in Copper Country. Where they stood, there was a horse skull outside the entrance. It was planted snout down in the ground, like a flower pot, and filled with cigarette and cigar stubs.

The baroness barged into the place without hesitation, set her rifle against a wall, and hurriedly began shedding her outer clothes. Bapcat and Jordy Klubishar held on to their rifles but dropped their packs by the entrance. It was odd that there was no sound in the house. A shiny pink, hairless cat appeared and stared at them before ghosting away. Jordy gave his father a what-the-hell look.

"I am famished for civilized food," the baroness announced, adding, "which is not to demean partridge breasts and delectable wild hare meat. Such fare has its place and purpose, and would be near perfect if there were also a bottle of vintage French or Georgian red. Alas," she concluded.

She led them through a series of hallways and rooms, all paneled richly in shiny brown woods, and at some point Bapcat heard a voice. Moaning? Pain?

Baroness Moroz threw open a massive double door and the source of moaning lay before them, a scantily clad male holding a tourniquet to his left thigh. The baroness talked to the man in fast Russian, and Jordy whispered, "She asks if he had an accident, and he informs her it was more a shortcoming in personal judgment, saying, 'And I should know better than to come to this *pryut*,' which means asylum."

"Explain what has happened here," the baroness demanded.

The injured man pointed at another door and muttered, "Ask *pistold Koroleva*."

"Pistol queen," Jordy translated.

Jordy asked the baroness, "Should we help this fellow?"

She said, "He came here of his own volition, and he can show himself out."

"But he could bleed to death," Jordy pointed out.

Baroness Moroz was dismissive. "They each and all know the reality of this place, and yet they come."

"Each?" Bapcat asked his son. "What the hell is going on?"

"You're asking me? *You're* the captain," Jordy said.

The baroness looked at the bleeding man and shook her finger. "Get out and don't come back. This is always the fate of those who come here."

The man began crawling toward a door, trying to keep the tourniquet tight.

Bapcat said, "Be sure to loosen that thing every twenty to thirty minutes, unless you want to lose the leg."

Jordy translated.

They passed into a new room with dusty plush carpets everywhere, and dusty wall hangings of bloody scenes of wolves killing moose. Bapcat looked around the room and at first did not see the woman, who was seated on a throne-like chair, an ornately carved thing with gold leaf and the carved heads of small monsters. She held a long-barreled Colt pistol in her left hand. Her hair was auburn, her eyes, ghostly blue-green, and she had the heel of her right hand pressed to her forehead as if she were plugging a leak. She wore a black toga-like garment, thick as brocade, and with all the style of a curtain. The room was lit by dozens of candles, some of them three or four feet tall and thick as grand piano legs.

"Anya, *darling*," the baroness greeted the woman, in Russian.

"Sister-in-law," the woman replied without emotion. "Is that fool out there bleeding in my home?"

"He is leaving as we speak. He stanched it with a belt."

"Why do I shoot him in the leg?" the woman called Anya asked rhetorically. "I should be shooting his little middle leg that he felt compelled to wave at me like a magic wand."

"Your aim is off?" Baroness Moroz asked, with a smile in her voice.

The woman raised the pistol and shot out the wick of a candle.

"Jesus!" Jordy yelped, and Bapcat felt himself flinch.

"My aim remains sure," Anya said. "My problem is the softness of my heart. I have no wish to destroy what is such an important part of a balanced life for men, their *muzhchina zmeya* is their identity. It represents their sole purpose in life, to procreate."

Jordy sniggered as he translated.

"What the dickens?" Bapcat asked.

"She is talking about a man's . . . snake . . . you know."

Bapcat understood and felt uncomfortable. "I know what she meant."

Now what? This was to be their place of *succor*?

Anya waggled the pistol at Jordy. "Are you laughing at me, boy?"

The baroness said, "Here stands the godson of Pinkhus Sergeyevich."

The woman popped to her feet. "You are the one called Jordy, *da*?"

"*Da*," Jordy said.

"My brother failed to inform me that you were so tall—or so handsome."

"*Anya*," the baroness said with a hiss of disapproval.

Anya threw her head back and laughed. "I have no designs on him. *Yet*. Besides, he is like kin."

"You've seen your brother?" the baroness asked.

"Months ago, not since. He is not one to share his plans. He's not here, if that's your purpose."

Baroness Moroz said, "We did not think he would be. We seek refuge."

Anya smiled, nodded once, and held open a hand, "*O kurs*, you are always welcome, *zolovka*. So you want to find my brother."

"We do," the baroness said.

Anya threw her hands up and cackled with delight. "You might as well seek audience with a cloud or a ghost. He is without substance and invisible as air."

The baroness said, " He is around, and he will appear when he is ready, not before."

"Yes, always the master manipulator of dramatic effect," Zakov's sister said dismissively. She wheeled toward Bapcat and shook her finger, and said in English. "Pinkhus Sergeyevich thinks you are a fool not to marry your woman. A widow, *da*?"

How did she know these things?

"I took care of that. We're married now. Since just before Jordy and I left America."

"My brother, of course, will take credit for said union. It's his way."

"Let him," Bapcat said. "Credit doesn't matter."

Anya said, "We agree, and I think I shall like you, comrade."

The baroness continued in English, "Comrade? You've gone Red, Anya?"

"Not exactly, but I have the most magnificent man—Red Army, a giant in all ways. He is called Milochovsky. Trotsky has summoned him to join the Sixth Red Army near Kotlas."

Dodge had led them to believe that the Reds had only a small following, and here the woman was talking about the Sixth Red *Army*? This sounded neither small, nor unpopular. Knowing that Dodge had not told them the truth irritated him.

"Trotsky?" Bapcat asked. This was a new name, easier to remember than most Russian names they had encountered.

"The so-called Bolshevik minister of war," the baroness explained. "Lenin is the Red brain; Trotsky, the Red mouthpiece and its muscle. The third man is Stalin, a Georgian viper. Trotsky can move crowds with speeches or order his men to destroy them with guns."

"Trotsky is in the field, personally leading his Sixth Red Army?"

Anya said airily, "Details are so boring, ambiguous, and inconclusive. I love only the excitement this brings, the sweet sense of how temporary we all are—the need to act, to not put anything off, because there may never come another chance."

"Kotlas?" Bapcat asked.

"It is en route to Archangelsk," the baroness said. "Why do you ask? Our interests are elsewhere."

"It's upriver from Archangelsk," Jordy added, his study of maps during their submarine voyage still fresh.

"What *are* your interests?" Zakov's sister asked.

The baroness said curtly, "The same as Pinkhus Sergeyevich's."

Anya clapped her hand over her mouth and guffawed. "You seek the Romanovs! Surely by now they are headless, mere worm food in the black soil of the Motherland."

"We seek your brother," Bapcat corrected the woman. Whatever her source, she was wrong. Zakov was sure the royal family was still alive, though being held captive.

Anya said, "He will most certainly be around Yekaterinburg."

"Yekaterinburg, of course!" the baroness exclaimed.

Bapcat was puzzled. She already knows this. Why was she making this show? How did Zakov's sister know what was going on? Her Bolo boyfriend? Do Trotsky and the top Reds know this, too, or is this only a local thing? Impossible to say. Zakov would know.

The baroness looked at Anya. "How do you know where the royals are?"

"Milochovsky told me."

"And he knows this, how?" Baroness Moroz asked.

"He says that the army's fighting leaders are waiting to hear that the Tsar and the Romanovs are dead. This they expect any day now."

"They are to be executed, then?" the baroness asked matter-of-factly.

"They wouldn't *dare*," Anya said. "Murder the Romanovs? I should think they would be shot while attempting to escape. There are rumors upon rumors of rescue schemes for the royal family. Milochovsky says this cannot and will not be allowed to happen. The Whites are disorganized, and nothing must be done to help rally them or bring together disparate sympathies and factions."

Anya looked directly at Bapcat. "It is even said that the Americans are mounting a rescue. Would you know anything about that?"

"No, ma'am," Bapcat said. "The upper ranks do not share their thoughts or plans with the likes of me."

"Pity," said Anya. "There would be more adventure and romance in rescuing the Romanovs and the Tsar than trudging to the front with Milochovsky." She sighed. "Yes, a pity indeed. In any event, any such attempt shall certainly fail."

"*Shall* fail?" Baroness Moroz asked. "You are Cassandra now?"

"Not at all, dear sister-in-law. It is quite elementary. The Allies would use the Tsar as a rallying point, to keep Russia in the war against the Kaiser, a war the people never wanted to fight in the first place."

"The people are in revolt against the Tsar. Why would they rally back to him?"

Anya sighed. "We revolted against Kerensky, the government creature who succeeded the Tsar, but there are many people who still share sympathies for the Romanov line, and they would support a returning tsar, even one who is a puppet of the West—even a weak and incompetent fool like our dear Nicky."

Anya paused.

"No, this must not happen. Nicholas the Bloody must die. This is a political certainty, and it would be no less than a small miracle if he and his awful family were still breathing."

The baroness glared at Anya, then said without a trace of an edge in her voice, "You said earlier that surely they are feeding worms and rotting in the black earth of the Motherland. And now you say they are alive and awaiting execution."

"These are Comrade Milochovky's thoughts."

"You would condone such murder, even of children?"

Anya closed her eyes and held her pistol out to the side. "With this I can right most wrongs done to me, but it holds only six bullets and my reach is limited. The Romanovs will die, one way or another, and there is nothing anyone can do to stop it."

Zakov's sister was now talking as if it were certain the Romanovs were still alive. Zakov had told Jordy the same thing. Was her brother as much a source as the Red she called Milochovsky?

Again the baroness led the questions.

"To be clear: Your man Milochovsky told you that the Romanovs and the Tsar are alive?"

"Only last week," Anya said.

"When did you last see Pinkhus Sergeyevich?" the baroness asked Zakov's sister.

"I no longer dwell or think in past terms," Anya said. "Better to keep all eyes forward to the future, to the new Russia. We are all going to be reborn under the Bolsheviks."

"Reborn?" the baroness countered. "The Reds are in the field killing everything in their path. How is this a rebirth?"

Anya said calmly, "The shooting shall end. Think of this as an earthly preview of death and St. Peter."

Bapcat watched something flash though Baroness Moroz's eyes, and her voice turned calm and appeasing.

"Lenin and Trotsky as two-headed *Sankt Peter*, deciding who lives or dies or goes to Hell or to Heaven? You may be right, Anya."

"Well," Zakov's sister said, "let us get you settled in and fed. I don't know how long I shall be able to remain with you. My magnificent Milochovsky will be coming to fetch me away at any moment."

Then, looking directly at the baroness, she said, "The Bolsheviks will disappear soon. They are renaming themselves 'Communists.' Is that not romantic?"

"Why?" Baroness Moroz asked.

Anya shrugged. "Great Invisible Leader Lenin believes this new name better encapsulates the qualities they seek to be known by—all together, communally, no classes—you see?"

"You believe such tripe?" the baroness asked. "That such is even possible?"

Zakov's sister smiled thinly. "Of course not, but who am I, with only six bullets in my gun?"

"And yet, you will give yourself over to this Milochovsky character?" she added.

"Happily, as often and anywhere he wishes," Anya said, clapping her hands together.

Bapcat and Jordy were offered separate rooms, but chose to stay together in one. The baroness went off with Zakov's sister, leaving the Americans alone.

"Feel good to speak English so openly?" Jordy asked his father. "You've been quite talkative for a mute."

"What have you heard from all this talk?" Bapcat asked the boy.

"We're safe here, I think, at least for now. And this sure beats walking."

"No, what did you hear that is *most important*? The tsar is *alive*."

"But Zakov already told us that."

"But his sister claims her Russian boyfriend is the source, not her brother, and that the information from that source is as recent as last week. What does this suggest for our mission?"

Jordy shook his head and exhaled.

Bapcat said, "Her boyfriend has been called to serve in a numbered army, which tells me the Reds are better organized than we've seen so far. We also heard that the Red Army, if Anya's soldier is right, knows where the Tsar and his family are and that they will die soon because the Reds can't risk them being rescued."

"She also talked of an American rescue. Do you suppose that's us?"

He didn't know. Their mission was to locate Zakov and follow his direction regarding the Tsar. If there were to be a rescue, wouldn't it best be coordinated with White Russians?

"Our orders, as I understand them, are to help Zakov find out if the Tsar is alive, and if so, where he and his family are located. Beyond that I know nothing for certain."

"Is war always like this—the left hand not knowing what the right hand is doing?"

"No. Sometimes the left hand doesn't even care if there is a right hand."

"We need Zakov to find us, and the sooner the better."

Zakov had said that he had seen the Tsar, but hadn't actually talked to him. Was this still the case, or had he since found a way to make contact? If he had talked to the Tsar, then they were probably about to make for home, unless the Tsar had asked for help. Did Zakov have authorization to rescue the Tsar? Was Zakov crazy enough to think he could rescue the Romanovs from the middle of desolate Russia?

Good grief.

"What?" Jordy asked his father.

"I like working in the dark, not being kept in it."

"Do you and Zakov talk the way you and I talk, asking each other what was hard, and that kind of thing?"

"All the time. Two brains and four eyes beat one brain and two eyes, and the way to make both brains stronger is to make sure they both always know the same things."

Jordy looked at his father. "Are we going to die here?"

"Not willingly," Lute Bapcat said. Not if he was to have a say in it.

"Where do we go from here?" Jordy asked. "Back to boot leather?"

"At ease," Bapcat said. "We just got here. We'll eat and sleep, then see what's next."

"But the Tsar and his family could die," the boy said.

"Everyone dies, Jordy."

22

Late Spring, 1918. Marooned

"*Mon capitaine,* dearest Lute—mere *breathing*
can get one killed in this country."

The next morning Bapcat felt vibrations, something quiet and nearly inaudible, yet distinct, something not there the night before. Was Jordy hearing it? Better to act alone than to try to wake the boy, who sometimes slept like a corpse.

He eased back the hammer of his pistol and raised the weapon. There was a hint of light in the darkly furnished room. Near dawn, he guessed, early, sleep heavy in his eyes, his first night in a real bed in how long?

From the far reaches of the room, a faint, but distinct, sound.

"I know you're in here," he said. "Step out where I can see you."

Bapcat heard the hammer click on Jordy's revolver. The boy was awake too.

"Show yourself—hands in the air," Bapcat said.

Jordy grunted something in Russian.

There was no reaction from what he thought was a crude human shape, a barely visible silhouette. "Step left to the window light."

The figure stepped left and Jordy yipped, "Elpy?"

"And Anton," a small voice squealed happily from the dark as a second figure joined the first. "It is I, Anton, senior signalman's junior assistant."

"Elpy, you've been promoted?"

The Russian chuckled. "One cannot have an assistant if one is not a senior something."

Jordy said to the boy, "So you have a new job now?"

"I know how to do many things," Anton boasted.

Elpy and Anton? Strange, but this was Russia, where all that would be considered strange elsewhere could be quite common here.

"Of course you know how to do many things," Bapcat told the boy. "What is going on, Lev Danielovich; why are you two here? How did you find us?"

"Chief Engineer Bezmunyi sent us. He says you must come quickly."

"Why?"

"Engineers do not explain."

Bapcat told Jordy, "Find the baroness and tell her to saddle up."

Jordy left immediately, buckling his gunbelt as he went.

"Bezmunyi is on the train?" Bapcat asked Elpy.

"We have a new train, a fortress," Anton said proudly. "It has armor, like a brave knight."

Armor on a train? "A new train. Is this Dodge's doing?" Bapcat asked.

"*Nyet*, Dodge is gone," Elpy said. "Soon after you disappeared. Chief Engineer Bezmunyi believes we will be more secure with this new equipment. It was Trotsky's train."

Trotsky's? "Was?"

"The Great Fighter and Orator has left it, so clearly he no longer has need of it. Does the man himself not preach 'from each according to his ability, to each according to his needs?' The Chief Engineer believes our need to be greater than Trotsky's at the moment, and now the train is ours."

So many questions . . . such as where the heck was Dodge?

"How did you find us, Elpy?"

"The baroness told Bezmunyi where you were heading before you departed. We've been near here, waiting for you, and today the Chief Engineer woke us and said, "Fetch the Americans; it is time for them to return."

"We can take this train to Yekaterinburg?"

"Bezmunyi will explain all. I am only the messenger."

"And I am *assistant* messenger," Anton added.

Jordy came back moments later.

"Baroness Moroz says, 'Be so kind as to inform the Dear Captain that a lady, having lived rough for so long, now requires her beauty sleep, and she intends to have it.'"

Good grief.

To Elpy, "Who let you in here?"

The signalman pointed at the boy. "He is the assistant in all things, including housebreaking, our Anton."

"The mistress of the house doesn't know you are here?"

Elpy said, "Does this mistress of the house have red hair?"

"She does," Bapcat said.

"She left with a giant hairy beast of a man who looks like a bear, or a giant bear that walks like a man—it was difficult to tell."

"You saw her with this man?"

"He was not alone. There were at least a hundred other men on horseback, Bolsheviks, red ribbons on their horses' harnesses."

These were no doubt the vibrations that had awakened him.

Bapcat asked Elpikovny, "How far is the train?"

"One hour's walk, more or less. It is early—few citizens are out."

"Get our things together," Bapcat said.

He went to find the baroness, who was sprawled in a bedroom with a bare floor and no furnishings except a large bed, dwarfed by the space. She was sprawled naked on the bed, snoring quietly.

"I know you're awake," he told her, standing by the bed.

"You cannot possibly *know* this," she whispered. "You are guessing."

"I can tell a fake snore. I am a soldier. I have lived among legions of snorers."

"I've been told that my snores are as convincing as my kisses."

"Not this time."

"*Ach!*" she said. 'You've not even tried to kiss me, so you cannot possibly know." Baroness Moroz added, "There are two kinds of intrusions into a lady's boudoir, her *spalnya*. If you intend to remove your clothes and slide under the coverlet with me, this will be not only welcomed, but also deliciously rewarded. If this is the other kind of intrusion, where you plan to roust me from my beauty sleep, it is entirely unwelcome, and I will curse you all my living days—or at least all the rest of this day, assuming we are still alive when it concludes."

"Getting light fast," he said. The room was in morning twilight, her perfect figure a ghostly white. "We are moving out. Bezmunyi is nearby with an armored train that belonged to Trotsky at some point. Anya and her giant Milochovsky are gone, on horseback, with a hundred others."

"And here I thought the horses I heard were a dream."

She could not possibly have heard them from this room.

"There were a hundred of them."

The woman stretched slowly. "This is *not* the morning I hoped it would be. Must you always be soldiering?"

"I have no other reason to be here," he told her.

She threw a small pillow at him and defiantly pulled up her covers. "I am not leaving," she said, her voice muffled under the coverlet. "*Ever!*"

He ripped the covers away again, and she closed her eyes and said with a hiss, "*Bastard!* Now I'm chilled! It is a gentleman's duty to warm a cold lady."

"I'm no gentleman."

And I'm married.

"But you are a captain. All officers are gentlemen."

"We do things differently in the States. Get dressed," he told her. "We'll find food on our way out."

"I require something *before* food," she said.

"Whatever it is, you'd better find it now, because we are going to eat as we move."

The baroness was yawning as she stumbled downstairs. Bapcat watched her eyes sweeping everywhere. She might be trying to look sleepy, but he saw that she was wide awake and on alert.

Elpy and Anton came into the hall and dropped two large bags beside three other similar ones. The signalman froze when he looked up and saw the woman.

She smiled.

"You two know each other?" Bapcat asked.

The baroness said, "Lev Danielovich, what, pray tell, is the story behind that dreadful . . . growth," she said, touching the flesh above her upper lip. "*Ty, usatyi?*"

"I have been promoted," Elpikovny said, as if that explained everything.

Jordy joined them, wearing a bright red leather uniform with a pointy red leather hat that looked like an inverted funnel on his head.

"What in the world?" Bapcat said.

"Promoted to engineer," Jordy said to the signalman, ignoring his father.

"*Ne belo kurii,*" the baroness said forcefully.

"No, I'm not blond anymore, Baroness. I am promoted to chief actor," Elpy said.

"What in blazes is that silly red getup?" Bapcat asked his son.

"Elpy says we all have to wear these to the train."

Bapcat frowned at his son and the Russian. Elpy's hair and mustache had been blond when last he'd seen him. Now both were dark, almost black.

Bapcat instinctively touched his own upper lip. How long since he'd even *thought* about shaving? Months?

Elpikovny smiled. "The Chief Engineer says I must resemble Comrade Trotsky, at least from a distance. I have a pointy chin and bulging eyes; we might be identical twins."

Baroness Moroz said, "Yes, I can see that now. Surely I do not have to wear one of those ridiculous red leather costumes."

Elpy pushed a canvas bag between the baroness and Bapcat.

"There is red leather for each of you."

"What nonsense is this?" the baroness asked.

"This is deadly serious, Baroness Moroz, and we must hurry. Put on your costume, please. There are boots, too. I hope they fit. Put the clothes you're wearing now into the bag and carry it with you."

When the baroness did not move, Elpikovny barked, "*Now!*"

"This is no promotion you throw around," the woman said, snarling. "It is a demotion to something less than the pathetic creatures who collect dog shit from city streets." Then, "You expect me to undress and re-dress in front of you men?"

"We are all soldiers here," Elpikovny said.

"Shameful," she said, smiled, and began to take off her clothes.

Bapcat saw Anton watching the woman, and when Elpy noticed, he cuffed the boy on the head. "Outside!"

"Am I not a soldier in red?" the boy objected.

"You may be wearing red, but you are not a soldier. Do not confuse the two." Elpy lightly cuffed the boy again and laughed, and even the boy smiled as he left the room.

"We are all promoted to actors in our red costumes," Elpy said, opening his bag and pulling out black leather, with the same red hat with a large red star.

"You even sound a little like Trotsky," the baroness said as she wriggled into her leather.

Jordy asked, "What of our rifles and gear, our packs?"

"Bring them along with the clothing duffels, and let us move. The Chief Engineer will be getting nervous, and that will only agitate him. He expects things to be done on time and on schedule."

The baroness said, "What schedule? All I've heard is 'hurry, hurry.'"

Elpikovny said sheepishly, "Bezmunyi is Chief Engineer. He does not offer explanations or reasons. *Nas idti!*" the signalman said in a new, deeper, more confident, and clearly commanding voice. "Our fate awaits us."

"Is that a line from something?" Jordy asked.

"It is original," Elpy said.

Jordy said, "Excellent. You may have a career as a *pero*, like Shakespeare."

"I prefer Gogol."

"Have you *read* Shakespeare?" Jordy asked.

"Why should I when I have Gogol?" Elpy came back, and waved his arms. "*Move!*"

Jordy looked at his father and rolled his eyes. "Gogol?"

Bapcat said nothing. He had neither read Shakespeare nor heard of a Gogol. He was more interested in the red leather outfits, especially the ornate metal badges on their left sleeves, below the shoulder.

"What do these insignia mean?" he asked Elpy.

"*Krasnyi Stoyna*—Red One Hundred. Trotsky's chosen one hundred, his elite guard."

The baroness saw Bapcat looking at her red costume and said haughtily, "I think it rather becomes me."

Bapcat said, "I have the feeling that wearing these fancy red outfits could get all of us killed."

The baroness laughed out loud and touched his arm. "*Mon capitaine,* dearest Lute—mere *breathing* can get one killed in this country."

23

Late Spring, 1918. The Red One Hundred

"Do you think this is a tragedy or a comedy?"

Bapcat was surprised how effectively their gaudy red outfits seemed to push people away, but by the time they reached the train, he was fed up with yet another pretense. Where *was* Zakov?

"Chief Engineer Bezmunyi, explain the logic behind these silly costumes," he demanded when the Russian climbed down from the engine to greet them.

"Costumes? This is no village theater troupe; these are Trotsky's own Red One Hundred."

Bapcat said, "You know very well that if Trotsky has his own Red One Hundred, we are *not* them."

Bezmunyi grinned.

"We know this, and perhaps Trotsky will one day know, but he is not here, and those we encounter cannot possibly know, which means that for all practical purposes, we *are* the authentic Red One Hundred wherever we go. Our Elpikovny is as close to a perfect doppelgänger as we could hope to find. Who dares to step forward and say that *our* Trotsky is not *the* Trotsky? Thus, red leather and Elpikovny afford us great advantage."

Bapcat was tired, and even more tired of this charade.

"This is the kind of secret that can easily be found out," he said. "Playacting is not reality. Do you think this is a tragedy or a comedy?"

The engineer said, "Plays *are* real in the minds of an audience. Shakespeare wrote long ago, 'Think when we talk of horses, that you see them

Printing their proud hoofs i' the receiving earth; For 'tis your thoughts that now must deck our kings, Carry them here and there; jumping o'er times.' What one sees, revolves around what one *wants* to see. With our red leathers and Elpikovny, we help them see Trotsky. Tragedy, comedy? The end of our play will determine this, Captain. If we all die, it will be tragic for us. If we succeed, it will be a fine comedy. So you see, Captain, how well we act will determine what kind of play we are presenting."

Shakespeare, plays, actors' lines?

"I need a real explanation," Bapcat said disgustedly.

"Trotsky has two armored trains, and each train has two engines. Trotsky uses these great devices for visiting and directing military units. Sometimes he personally delivers messages and orders or even assumes direct command locally; other times, he remains with the train. He is known to be highly secretive, restless, impatient, volatile, and continuously on the move from front to front, so who is to say that we are not him on the move? Between Major Dodge's letter, our red leathers, this fine equipment, and Lev Danielovich's uncanny resemblance to the Bolshevik warlord, we are very well covered."

"But Elpy is *not* Trotsky," Bapcat said.

"Do you *know* Trotsky?" Bezmunyi challenged him.

"You know damn well I don't."

"Which is my point. Almost no one has met Trotsky. Few know what he sounds like, though many may have seen pictures. Almost every Bolshevik strongman we meet will be illiterate and nervous in the face of having to make what might be a deadly political miscalculation."

"Someone has only to telegraph the real Trotsky," Bapcat argued.

Bezmunyi crossed his arms. "And where exactly would he receive that wire? Trotsky has no fixed land base. He keeps moving. Even Lenin doesn't know where the man is until he deigns to report to Moscow."

"The security people are illiterates?"

"Most so-called officers, too; illiterates, elected by mass deplorables."

Could this really work? The engineer seemed confident, and so far he had been right about virtually everything.

Bapcat sighed with resignation. "We Red One Hundred are going where?"

"Yekaterinburg, where we tell officials we need to see the Tsar because White forces are closing in and the Tsar must not fall into Royalist hands."

"You think they will tell us where he is?"

"It is possible they will even hand him over to us. Nobody wants to risk capture by the Whites and be accused of being the Romanov family's captors."

"Where's Dodge?"

"Tobolsk, I presume."

"Why?"

Bezmunyi shrugged. "He believes this is what was ordered. Have you seen his orders?"

"Nothing written." At least, none he'd seen.

"A different drummer drives that man," the engineer remarked. "We must ask: Is our major performing solo with his own music or within the context of an orchestra's score?"

"Is it good or bad music?" Bapcat quipped.

"Irrelevant," the Chief Engineer said. "It all depends on audience and outcome."

"Yekaterinburg first, then where?"

"Fate, Captain, fate. We shall see what God has in store for us."

"All right, Yekaterinburg it shall be. Tell me, how in the world did you come up with the idea of borrowing Trotsky's train?"

Bezmunyi cocked his head. "My wife."

"Your wife what?"

"She made this possible, gave this to us—the train, the leather uniforms, ammunition for the guns, all of it."

"Why?" Bapcat asked.

"Because she wants her sons to be safely in America, not here."

"But she is going with us."

"Impossible. If she tries to join us, the Bolsheviks would turn the world inside out to find and make an example of her."

"Why?"

"She is the chief scheduler and manager of railroads for the Bolsheviks."

"She's a Red? You never told us."

"I have only recently learned. Her five predecessors were shot for incompetence or political unreliability."

"She just handed this train over to you?"

"She is trapped in the maelstrom. The truth is, she is unsuited for motherhood. She knows this, has always known it. She loves our boys in her own way, but has no time or patience for them. I told her I wanted to take her and our sons to America and she said she would help us, but that she must remain here, where the Motherland needs her."

"She's been Red all along?"

"I had suspicions, but she never said specifically until I told her the plan for America. I argued that her sons need their mother, but she scoffed at this, said, 'They need only Stepan Iosovich Bezmunyi; he is all they have ever needed.'"

"Did she ask how you plan to get the boys to America?"

"No. She knows that if I told her and she had this knowledge, and her comrades found out about it, they would rip it out of her, along with her heart and guts. Better ignorance than knowledge in some things."

"And with that she handed over Trotsky's train and red leathers?"

"She told me where to find them, and we went and took them."

"And your boys?"

"Now on board with us, to share our fate, whatever it may be."

"Have the train and uniforms been reported missing?"

"Not yet, and when they are, my wife will smother the information for as long as possible."

"Eventually the Reds will start asking questions, investigating."

"But not quickly," Bezmunyi said. "This is the new Russia, and in the Red Army it is treason and a capital offense to lose military assets, so nothing will be reported stolen because that would then necessitate that someone be judged as culpable. And then the Reds would shoot someone, guilty or not."

"But they wouldn't shoot your wife?"

"They would shoot her, too, but unlike the less powerful, she is able to keep it under wraps for a time."

"A lot rides on the theft not being reported."

"What theft? We are Trotsky and his One Hundred."

"This is absurd." The only word Bapcat could think of.

Would Roosevelt approve such a wacky plan? Probably. It was not much worse than charging uphill into enemy guns.

"Yes, of course, absurdity is deeply Russian from all angles. Have faith, Captain, and remember your Shakespeare: '*Think* when we talk of horses, that *you see them*.' Shall we proceed to Yekaterinburg?"

"May we assume your wife has cleared the track ahead of us?"

"We may, Captain."

"How many people on this train?" Bapcat asked.

"Men, women, children—I would say, almost ninety."

"How many of them think they are ultimately bound for America?"

"All of them, Captain."

Bapcat was astonished by the number, and asked, "Just who is the magician who thinks he can pull such a large rabbit from the hat?"

Baroness Moroz came in and said, "Abracadabra, *mon captaine*."

"None of us are legitimate. These damn costumes are stolen. Our Trotsky is a look-alike, a, what, a . . . doppel—? All to go along with this charade. How will Zakov see this business?"

"I am certain he will be much in favor," Baroness Moroz said.

Had she seen him? When and where? He and Jordy had been with her almost every minute for—hell, he couldn't remember how long it had been. "You know this how?"

The woman waved her hand dismissively.

24

Early Summer, 1918. Unscheduled Meeting

"Are all American men as bloody literal as you, *mon capitaine?*"

They were no more than two hours out of Kungur when Baroness Moroz walked into Bapcat's car still wearing her red leather and looking as fresh as a spring morning.

"You are entitled to know that the engineer is being forced to stop the train so we can vote," she announced.

Her calm unnerved him. "Vote on what? Who is stopping us, and who is to vote?"

"The Red One Hundred—although our actual count is under ninety. I cannot say why that is, and, of course, when I asked, I was rebuked. If it is learned that we are less than one hundred, we shall be found out."

"Vote about what?" Bapcat asked again.

"You," she said, "this mission, the reward, all of it."

He fought the temptation to chase her away.

"Are you saying this is our own people stopping us."

"Yes, of course, Dear Captain."

"This, then, is mutiny."

"Yes, I suppose that is true, technically."

"And when is this to take place, technically?"

"As soon as I deliver you to the Chief Engineer."

"This is his brainchild?"

"Of course not."

"Am I under arrest?"

"Are all Americans so foolish?"

"In these same circumstances, probably."

"America is a democracy. Do you not vote to solve problems collectively?" she asked peevishly.

"Not exactly. We vote for a person who along with others works to solve problems for the people."

Had she learned nothing in her time in Ann Arbor? Or was this one of her games?

"This seems to me to be rather a lot to impose on one soul. Does this elected one have the power of the Tsar?" she asked.

"We elect one person to lead many others we have elected, to solve problems together."

"Do you shoot or exile them if they fail?"

"No, we vote them out of office."

"This seems quite inefficient."

"It is that."

"I see," she said, with a tone that suggested otherwise.

What in the world was this all about? Bapcat pointed at the door, but the Baroness did not move.

"You must wear your red uniform," she said.

"It makes me look like a clown."

"Not to our people, it doesn't. The red and your badge tell them you have authority."

"But I don't."

She shrugged. "All that matters most of the time is appearance, not substance. If you wear the red, they accept you. If not, they will not."

"None of us are legitimate. These costumes are stolen. Our Trotsky is a dopp . . . dopp—"

"*Doppelgänger*," she inserted.

"Right. We can be shot for all of this. In fact, we probably will be shot, the lot of us."

"No doubt," the baroness said. "Please dress in your uniform."

"Turn around."

"So you can bash the back of my head and flee, *mon capitaine*? Do you think me a simpleton? Get dressed, and stop playing the spoiled child."

"You know this is all insane," he said. "The uniforms, the stolen train, Elpy as Trotsky."

"Yes, yes," she said, waving her hand. "Dress, dress."

He stopped talking, not caring if she watched or not. He began removing his clothes, and when he was finished, she said, "I shall enjoy even more watching you undress when the right moment arrives."

"There won't be such a moment," he said. "I'm married."

"So too am I, but it will surely happen. You must trust me in such matters."

"You're going to *kill* your husband."

"Which is entirely his fault, not mine. A lady must defend her good name, *n'est-ce pas*? How do the British put it when they wish to change the subject—'Let us find another topic to talk about, tra la?'"

She was a strange and oddly compelling woman.

They walked to a train car called Long Gun, which had no gun, long or short. Gathered there were about eighty people, men and women mostly, with a few children.

"This isn't everyone," Bapcat said to the baroness.

"The others are on guard, Dear Captain."

On their way to the meeting Bapcat had studied the armored train. He and Jordy had taken a quick inspection walk earlier, but this time he tried to put everything into perspective, militarily.

One car held ten-inch guns on rotating platforms at each end. How would that work? Didn't the operation of such guns require specialists? Were such soldiers aboard? One carriage had a twelve-inch naval gun with shells twelve inches in diameter and two feet long, which could hit targets ten miles away. Who would operate these weapons? Two cars held ammo for small arms, the many mounted machine guns on the train, and for the artillery. How much, and for how long could they fight? And at what firing rates? Had anyone thought about such details? The ammo carriages were roofed with slanting plates of British and Swedish steel, and he noticed some bends and odd angles, and wondered where incoming would be deflected.

The Long Gun meeting place had no arms in sight. Bapcat saw people standing patiently, the way he had seen Russians queue in other places, somber and silent.

"This is everyone?" he asked Elpy, who was waiting with Chief Engineer Bezmunyi.

"These and the guards," the signalman said. "And us."

Bapcat looked through the fighting slits in the steel plates and saw civilians gathered about a hundred yards from the siding where the train was parked. There were yellow and white birch immediately behind the gathering place, easy escape to cover if it became necessary. So different than back home. Here people had to be on guard for their lives all the time. Had it always been like this under the Romanovs?

The baroness brushed his leg with her hand to catch his attention, pushed hair off her face, and said, "They think Trotsky is aboard. They dare not approach any closer. If a great man wishes the company of common man, he will have them summoned. This is behavior all Russians know. It was the same under the Tsar."

Her voice had a bitter element.

So what is all the fighting accomplishing, he wondered. So many dying, and for what—the status quo?

Elpy bade him step onto a piece of wood set on top of some large boxes, announcing to the crowd, "Our American captain."

There was no reaction, all faces blank as dead dogs. Why was Elpy doing this? Wasn't Chief Engineer Bezmunyi in charge here?

The baroness clambered up onto the platform and pressed close to him.

"Say what you have to say in English and I will translate to Russian."

"I'm a mute."

"That charade is last week's fish."

"What the hell am I supposed to tell them?"

"The truth," she said.

"Will they know it if they hear it?"

"We shall see. Stop stalling, and tell them how you will take them to America."

Damn. He took a deep breath and looked at the masks in the crowd.

"Stay alive," he said. "That's the first rule. We can't get to America if we are dead."

No response as the baroness said his words in Russian, although he noticed a few people whispering to others.

"Do they understand what I am saying?" Bapcat asked.

Elpy inserted himself. "A few of them speak some English, but they understand the baroness quite clearly."

"They don't look like they're even hearing," Bapcat told the signalman.

"You haven't said much yet," the Russian trainman said.

"This is your idea for me to speak, not mine." He looked at the baroness. "Her idea?" Then at Elpy. "Yours?" And at Bezmunyi. "Yours?"

"All of us," Elpy said. "Each of us," he added, with one of his insipid grins. "We *are* the real Red One Hundred, *your* Red One Hundred, and we wish to hear your plan for getting us safely to America. What do we have to do, here and now, to get there, and when?" The grin stayed pasted to the little signalman's face.

"This whole idea of the train was sprung on me," Bapcat said. "I have no idea how Zakov will react to it."

Baroness Moroz said, "He will be much in favor."

"You've seen him? He told you this?"

The baroness made a sniffling sound and wriggled her nose. "It is all in the air," she said.

"What is?" Bapcat asked.

"Don't be silly," she said. "It is quite unbecoming for a leader. They want to know if we will find the Tsar and his family and put them on the train with us, and if they will join us on our trip to America. I humbly suggest you tell them that this is the plan."

"*But there is no plan.*"

"There is always a plan in God's mind."

"God is not here," Bapcat said. "I think."

"But you don't *know*," the baroness pointed out. "Better to play it safe and assume he *is* here and involved."

Bapcat shook his head. Good grief. Would this never end?

"Baroness, how about you tell them what *you* think it is important for them to hear?" he said.

"But these would not be your words."

"I'm delegating. You may speak for me, and your words will be my thoughts."

"Shall I tell them how we make love, how often and how intensely, how we can't keep our hands off each other?"

This jolted him. What? *"We never did that."*

"Are you certain?"

"Yes."

She smiled. "We shall agree to disagree. My memories are quite different."

Good grief, he thought. We're all going to be killed in the middle of nowhere.

Jordy and Anton came and stood beside him.

The baroness said, "All here support rescuing the Tsar and his family and bringing them with us to America."

"What if the Tsar and his family want to stay here?" Bapcat asked.

Baroness Moroz laughed. "The Romanovs are not stupid, *mon capitaine*. The handwriting is not just on the wall here; the walls have all been torn down, and there is no formal record of anything. They *will* leave, I assure you. The people also wish to know if we will fight the Red Army, and when, or where? The answer I recommend is that this is solely in God's hands. Russians understand and accept this ambiguous concept.

"They also wish to know if you will lead us east to join the Czech Legion, and then move to Vladivostok in order to go to America. Or will you choose to lead us north through both the Red and White Armies, and exit north via a waiting ship or submarine. Some of the people are interested in traveling under the ocean's ceiling, and others will refuse. This is a contentious issue, the where, how, and when of transportation."

"Tell them whatever you want," Bapcat said. "It will be as solid as any story I could come up with. Nothing you say is of any consequence until we can find Zakov."

Surely he knows this armored train gambit is afoot. Why is he not showing himself? Damn him.

The baroness brushed her hair out of her face again and began rapidly talking in Russian. Bapcat watched her audience and saw no change in expressions, no indication that they were taking on anything she was saying, even though she seemed to be speaking passionately, almost angrily, banging her fist again the palm of her other hand. When her long harangue was done, the crowd applauded in weird, cadenced clapping, and he noticed some smiles.

"What was all that about?" Bapcat asked.

"I told them our American captain has no time or inclination to feed swill to the herd, that all their questions will be answered in time, by God. Meanwhile, they should return to their duties and stations and stop annoying the American captain with their whining. Our captain has too many critical duties facing him to be drowning in the cries of a whining crew."

"You gave them the kiss-off."

"Yes, a royal kiss-off, I should think."

"And they applauded?"

"*Mais oui, mon capitaine.* You have the attitude of a strongman, and all Russians want a strongman as their leader, especially in the perilous times we live in. They have seen you now, heard your voice; you are no longer an issue. They will do as you ask or die trying."

"A well-played part," Elpy said, and left with Bezmunyi as the crowd broke up.

"Is this no more than a stupid play?" Bapcat asked the baroness. "And if so, who is directing?" Not him. Of that he was certain.

"You pose the correct question for the moment. Let us withdraw to private quarters and discuss this, as coleaders should."

"Coleaders. You and me? What about Bezmunyi?"

"The Chief Engineer and signalman have their roles. It remains my job to stay with you until Zakov finds us."

"Or Trotsky finds us first," he corrected her.

The baroness smiled. "Only after I quietly whispered to our esteemed engineer to ask after such assets. He knew nothing of these things. You see?"

He didn't see anything at all. He was not blind, but little that had happened made sense, starting from the meeting with Roosevelt in Marquette. Who the hell was this woman, and why was she even here?

Baroness Moroz squeezed his arm as they walked, and when they reached the car, he saw that all of Jordy's things had been cleared out and hers moved in. He paused at the door and she said, "Coleaders should cohabitate. Is it not a simple matter of egalitarianism? We are equals, Dear Captain. Shall we retire?"

Bapcat planted his feet and shook his head, and she said scoldingly, in a soft, sweet voice, "*Liberté, égalité, fraternité*—this is the philosophy of the French: 'Liberty, equality, fraternity.' You and I must practice this philosophy as an example to our ship's company."

"We aren't on a ship!" he said harshly.

"Are all American men as bloody literal as you, *mon capitaine*?"

"I'm not all American men," he pointed out.

She smiled. "I rest my case. Which side of our bed do you prefer?" she asked.

"*We* don't have a bed." This woman is not right in the head.

"*Au contraire, mon capitaine*, we soon shall. It is being delivered."

"I prefer my own cot."

"It is to be removed."

"The floor will be fine," he said.

"You are a stubborn man, Dear Captain."

"This is not the first time I've heard that."

Looking around he saw that indeed, his cot was gone. She handed him a cigarette, and he accepted and lit up to think. She smoked her cigarette in a long ivory holder. This time the tobacco made him cough.

"Turkish," she said. "Stronger than Russian, which is redolent of potato fields. Shall I pour us a brandy to facilitate conversation and discussion?"

She was a natural talker and schemer. Same as Jaquelle.

He nodded, and she poured two glasses from a bottle which had not been in the car when he left.

"Where do we stash the train in Yekaterinburg?" he asked her.

"Chief Engineer Bezmunyi shall see to that. I have instructed him to put us in a location which will allow us to come and go easily, on our own terms, not those of the Reds now in control of Yekaterinburg. We shall possibly need our second engine to serve as a shuttle for various purposes."

"Did you work all this out with your previous coleader?" he asked.

"*Mon dieu*," she said. "*Est-ce que mon capitaine et mon co-leader déçu ou faché avec moi d'avoir pris des initiatives?*"

"You know I'm not handy with foreign tongues."

She smiled. "Foreign tongues—yes, of course, I see. Let me rephrase in English: Is my captain and coleader disappointed or angry with me for taking initiatives?"

"What initiatives?"

"Suggesting that Bezmunyi see to the train location and security."

"You think he wouldn't have done that on his own?"

"That is irrelevant. He and I agreed this would be the proper step."

"Did you allow him to suggest alternate ways?"

"But why?" she said snippily. "This is decided and off the table. We can move on to more important things, you and I."

"Such as?"

She poured a full tumbler of brandy and pushed it toward him. "Let us begin anew, *mon capitaine*. Is this not the finest brandy you have ever tasted?"

He left it sit.

"I've not tasted it. I don't usually drink when I'm supposed to be working. In fact, I doubt if I've ever tasted brandy." He lifted it to his lips, sipped, and slightly raised an eyebrow. "Got a little heat on the trip south."

"*C'est bien?*" the baroness asked.

What was her game, with him, with Jordy—and Zakov? Nothing so far was clear or felt right. She was all over the place. Why? You can't know everything, he cautioned himself. Accept this reality and keep going.

Back with the enlisted Rough Riders, their rule was to go along to get along. He held out his glass and so did she.

"*Za zda-ró-vye.* To your health."

"Down the hatch," he said, and drained the glass.

"Oh my," the baroness said, and did the same.

Five brandies later, his coleader was passed out on the floor, her mouth wide open, and he was dizzy and needed sleep before he passed out. He was just about to find a place on the floor when Jordy walked in and looked at the woman.

"What happened to her clothes?"

Bapcat tried to focus. She was undressed? When did *that* happen?

"We've got trouble," his son said, still staring at the woman.

"Tell whoever is asking for the great leader that he is unavailable, and that the problem should be handled by the person wanting help from on high. I ain't no babysitter or priest."

Jordy grinned and looked again at the woman, then at his father.

"No, sir, you sure ain't no priest."

"Get the hell out!" Bapcat yelped, "and next time, knock before you come in."

"We're not roommates anymore?" the boy asked.

"Tell somebody to bring back my dang cot."

"Were me, I'd think that cuddling with the beautiful lady would be better than your dang cot."

"You ain't me," Bapcat said, and threw a mukluk at him, which missed.

Only then did he notice that the brandy bottle was empty, and that he, like his lady friend, was as naked as God made them. This was an unsettling discovery on too many levels to think about without sleep.

25

Summer, 1918. Yekaterinburg

"Are you suggesting Dodge is a treasure hunter?"

The air had been getting increasingly uncomfortable for three weeks and was now at near-unbearable levels, the kind of damp heat that sucked all oxygen out of the railcars, almost as bad as Cuba—perhaps worse, Bapcat thought. He, Jordy, and the baroness tried to sleep outside on the railcar platform, but Russian mosquitoes were the size of hummingbirds and as carnivorous as the ones back home in the Keweenaw.

Jordy showed the baroness how to rub black mud on her skin to create a barrier against insects, but she dismissed the suggestion. "We Russians have no need for magic potions. Mud? This is disgusting, boy."

"Doctors have no remedies for such pests?" Bapcat asked.

"Yes, we stay in our surgeries; otherwise, we learn to endure the curse. *This* is the Russian way."

Bapcat thought her ungrateful, moody, and flighty.

They were now on a siding outside Yekaterinburg, and Bezmunyi had launched inquiries. An answer came back quickly, which was as Bezmunyi foretold. In Bapcat's mind the Tsar's location should have been a closely guarded state secret, but they had learned the information in a matter of mere hours.

Russia, Bapcat thought.

"It works," Jordy said, rubbing more mud on his hands, face, and neck.

Baroness Moroz said, "Foo, Beautiful Boy, leave me be."

The Tsar and his family were being held in a house commandeered by the Reds from an engineer named Ipatiev. Bezmunyi's source reported that a double log palisade had been erected around the white stone building.

With directions from Bezmunyi, Bapcat and Jordy went to see for themselves. Bapcat thought the makeshift log walls made it look like newspaper drawings of old cavalry forts out west during the Indian Wars.

Having seen Ipatiev's house, and no sign of the Tsar, Bapcat said nothing to the others about where they had been or what they had seen. They would wait for Zakov. One critical note was the five-man patrol making a circuit on the outermost wall fifteen minutes before and fifteen minutes after the hour. Poor security was always predictable. Were there other holes and weaknesses in the security setup?

"We ought to go get the Tsar," Jordy suggested.

"We wait for Zakov. He knows the man."

"What if he never shows up?"

Which was possible. "We still wait," Bapcat repeated.

"We do that a lot," the boy complained.

"The army way is hurry, hurry, then wait."

"They don't tell you about this part before you join up. You and Zakov never said a word about this stuff," the boy grumbled.

"Stop whining. Zakov will come when he's ready."

"You seem sure. Seems to me he's cutting it pretty damn close."

"I am sure," Lute Bapcat said.

He was also nervous. Pinkhus Sergeyevich could be counted on to do as he promised. This was unquestioned. Never mind that his partner had abandoned him a year ago without a word. Roosevelt, no longer in government, may have been behind it, and somehow Roosevelt was in cahoots with the Englishman, Churchill. How one could maintain power over the government without being *in* government made him wonder if the country was somehow run by a small crowd of the rich and power-ful, elections and voting just so much window dressing. If so, no wonder there were so many wacky anarchists and Communists among the miner immigrants in Copper Country.

Zakov appeared the next night, in the small hours of summer darkness. He told Jordy and Bapcat to dress in their normal clothes, not the foolish red leathers. He looked at the baroness sleeping on the ground and whispered, "What is *that* doing here?"

Bapcat whispered, "Baroness Moroz? *You* sent her."

Zakov shook his head. "Never."

"But you know her, yes?" a confused Bapcat asked.

"Let us move quickly and quietly. Leave her."

"You know her?" Bapcat asked again.

"Yes. Be quiet and move."

Outside, Bapcat tried to engage his old friend.

"She told us her first husband was killed in the war."

Zakov said, "I suppose he was, figuratively."

"She called him a coward and a brute."

"She embellishes. She is a maestro of distortion and disinformation."

Bapcat said, "She claims her second husband is a Tsarist general who has gone over to the Reds. She insists she will shoot him the next time she sees him."

"I doubt that," Zakov said. "How did she find you?"

"The Bishop—Little Boris."

Zakov grunted.

"She says you instructed the Bishop to send her to lead us until you intercepted us."

"Did I?" Bapcat's partner came back.

"She told us that you asked the Bishop to send her and that somewhere along the way you would find us."

"*Bishop*? Who *is* this Bishop?" Zakov asked.

"We assumed you knew him." Why else would he have sent her to guide them? "She told us he has a following, but no church. She calls him a Russian nationalist."

"Did you sleep with her?" Zakov asked pointedly.

"I'm a married man."

"That has never before stood in her way," Zakov said and stopped. His eyes widened. "Married to whom, and since when?"

"Jaquelle."

A huge smile crossed the Russian's face. "It's about time. Congratulations. Still, I must know: Have you slept with the baroness?"

"Define *sleep*."

"When did you become a lawyer? You know very well what 'sleeping with her' means."

"No, I did *not* sleep with that woman in that way. Which is not to say that she didn't try to entice me."

"Ah, that's the woman I know. Please tell me, my friend—how many ways *are* there to sleep with a woman?" Zakov asked.

Before Bapcat could answer, Zakov said, "An old game, the honey trap; this is how it works. You sleep with her, and she slowly drains information from you, until the Cheka has a case built. She is one of their trained vampires. The Bishop is her boss."

"Cheka?"

"The Tsar's security apparatus, his secret police."

"I know who and what they are. That should put them, and her, on *our* side, right?"

"*If* they're not sympathetic to, and controlled by, the Reds. There is some considerable evidence and much rumor that the Chekists have almost entirely gone over to the Reds. Did you meet my sister Anya?"

"Yes, she's taken off with a Red named Milochovsky."

Zakov snarled, "Of course it would be Milochovsky."

"You know him?"

"My sister has been running away with Milochovsky since she was a child. Bad chemistry, those two. He has been a soldier, a cop, a professional thief, and now he is a Bolo warlord, one of their more ruthless fighters. Most Bolshevik volunteers are less than worthless. She will tire of him after a short while and abandon him, or he will tire of her. It has always been thus. My wealthy sister has done well for herself, and she is entirely insane—like the country itself, driven by impulse, anger, and lust, but never by logic or any interest but her own."

Bapcat said, "Baroness Moroz told me she is Anya's sister-in-law and that Anya killed her brother."

"Something to do with sheep," Zakov said, smiling. "The upper class in Russia tends toward one of two strains: devout followers of church and

Tsar or those who drown themselves in licentiousness. My family is of the second strain."

"But not you," Bapcat pointed out.

Zakov drew in a deep breath. "Even I have not entirely escaped it, but I chose to serve as a soldier, for whom people's moral expectations are somewhat lower. Baroness Moroz is my wife, Lute."

Lute Bapcat was speechless, until he finally managed, "Is . . . your . . . *wife?*"

"Was. She is not as young as she appears—nature has been especially kind to her. She is very intelligent, is Marilka Monikova, and a master schemer. I was declared dead during the Manchurian War, my estate divided between my widow and sister. Both are opportunists, which, in this country, is the only sensible way forward for most women. Otherwise, a woman is born chattel and remains so."

"Like sheep," Bapcat said.

"The woman has a nature so malign and evil that she never sates her greed for anything, and each time after she gets that which she seeks, she grows hungrier than before. It never ends."

Jordy spoke. "That's sort of a thought from Milton! You know, that thing about eating and still being hungry?"

Zakov slapped the boy on the back. "Good, you are still reading!"

Jordy nodded. "Until I got here."

"You will learn more from this experience than any book can teach," Zakov said. The Russian smirked and turned back to Bapcat.

"My sister is politically whatever works best for her at any given moment. Tomorrow is a place too far for her thoughts to reach. Today, this moment, this second, is past, present, and future. She does what she wants, when she wants."

Bapcat said, "She told us Milochovsky was on his way to join Trotsky and the Sixth Red Army in Kotlas."

Zakov grunted. "Bloody hell! This means Trotsky is north and cannot get here soon enough."

"Why should we want Trotsky here?" Bapcat asked.

"The Tsar is here, and there is considerable consternation among local Bolos about what to do with him and his family and their entourage.

Admiral Kolchak's Czech Legion is steadily hammering its way west and will soon capture Yekaterinburg. Trotsky might very well stop Kolchak here, but the local military and militia? Impossible. They do not have what it takes to hold, and the Tsar will suffer for this."

"Surely the Yekaterinburg Bolos are talking to Trotsky?"

"Yekaterinburg talks solely to Moscow, where Lenin cowers like a cat in the rain."

"You're sure of this?"

"Russians love to talk. Add vodka, and my countrymen will talk about anything and everything."

Bapcat asked. "Who is this Kolchak? I've heard that name before."

"Kolchak and the Czechs were recruited to help us break the alliance between the Austro-Hungarians, Turks, and Germans. In return for this, the Tsar agreed that after the Germans and Austro-Hungarians were pushed out of Czech territory, Kolchak would be given the Tsar's blessing to work with his countrymen to create their own independent country. When the Provisionals and Bolos pulled Russia out of the German war, Kolchak objected and wanted to keep fighting."

Zakov continued, "He has fifty or sixty thousand highly motivated, trained, experienced officers and soldiers under him. The new regime reluctantly agreed to let Kolchak withdraw east to Vladivostok, where the British would transport his forces to France to fight, but along the way some soviets, the local government units, took exception with Moscow's decisions and began to resist the Czechs, who then wheeled back to the west and decided to forego France and take Russia from the east in order to assure their national future. Kolchak and his men are formidable foes. The Czech Legion is still moving steadily west, and the local volunteer Reds have so far been helpless—and hapless—against them."

Zakov took a tired breath. "Red theorists, amateurs to the man, think a professional army is bourgeois, a remnant of the Imperialists, and therefore they want an entirely volunteer force with *elected* officers. But this . . . pathetic air castle of an army . . . this is a formula for failure against professional soldiers with a working chain of command. Trotsky is now leading the Red armies. He is not such a grand military strategist or tactician, but the man understands how to motivate troops, how to build an army, how to keep it supplied, and, most importantly, how to discipline it."

Bapcat's partner glared, and continued. "Kolchak has troops in various places all the way to the ocean in far eastern Siberia. He is a tough and brutal bastard, but a fine fighter and leader. His men are loyal to him alone. A force this size can play a critical role against the largely poorly led, trained, and equipped Red Army. Kolchak has sided with the Whites against the Reds and is punishing the Bolsheviks in every fight. He is now said to be surging toward Yekaterinburg and could arrive any day now. If Trotsky were here, he might hold up Kolchak and see the Tsar to safety. But Trotsky is not here, and cannot get here in time. As a result, Lenin will order the locals to kill the family and cover it up. We must find the Tsar, and quickly." And, after a pause, "We may already be too late."

Bapcat said, "They are in Ipatiev House. We've been there, and seen it. We have come a long way because of you, Pinkhus Sergeyevich."

"Yes, and you traveled in high style. I rather like your armored beast on wheels. It may prove of great value when we withdraw."

"When will that be?"

"After we complete our mission. We must get to the Tsar and assess the situation."

"If we are too late?"

"Let us pray we are not," Zakov said. "Do you know why I was sent here?"

Bapcat said, "Only what Dodge told us. I am still having difficulty deciding exactly what his role is in this whole thing."

"I am equally puzzled," Zakov said. "It is possible that his remit is similar to mine—to find the Tsar, liberate him, and help put him back in power in order to keep Russia in the war, which will keep the eastern second front alive. I harbor doubts about the marine major's dedication, judgment, and his interests. He knows the Tsar is here in Yekaterinburg, yes?"

"He knew the royal family was to be brought here from Tobolsk, but he chose to go on to Tobolsk alone."

"You objected?" Zakov asked.

"He was supposed to help us find you. It seems that he has been evading that duty, and I don't understand why."

Zakov, who sported pointy whiskers in his graying beard, pulled on them.

"Makes no sense, unless . . ."

"Unless what?" Bapcat pressed.

"There is a great deal of speculation about how much treasure the abdicated Tsar and family carried along in their westward flight. Rumors suggest it could be considerable."

Bapcat processed this information for a moment, and when the light of understanding began to come on, he did not like what it brought to mind.

"Are you suggesting Dodge is a treasure hunter?"

"I'm not suggesting anything. Neither am I ruling anything out, but Dodge is Dodge, and with his own agenda, it seems. We, however, are together now and shall remain so."

"You think we can actually liberate the Tsar and his family?" Jordy asked.

Zakov sighed. "In Tobolsk, it might have been possible, but here, so late in the game, with Kolchak closing in and the Reds on the verge of panic, the chances are slight. I learned only days ago that the Tsar's personal guard has been replaced by Latvian Rifles."

Bapcat said, "I think Dodge said something about this a while back."

"We have Latvians in Red Jacket and Houghton," Jordy said. "Some of them are mouthy, quite a few militant Communists and anarchists."

Zakov smiled. " A misnomer: Few Latvian Rifles are *actual* Latvians. Many are Germans, or Lithuanians, Poles, Finns, or Estonians. The thing they have in common is that they were early supporters of the Red movement and are fanatics who will do anything, following all orders they're given without question."

"You know a lot," Bapcat told his friend.

"There was a poorly hatched plan to spirit the royal family from Tobolsk to Moscow for safekeeping. Although the Yekaterinburg soviet is notoriously erratic, they somehow managed to intercept the escape train and move it here, assuming control of the Romanovs. The local soviet is violent and unstable, and they are being made more so, knowing Kolchak is breathing down on them from the southeast."

Following his partner's line of thought, Bapcat said, "They're afraid the White Army will free the Romanovs and put them back in power."

"Exactly. When Kolchak and his White allies strike in force, I suspect the Reds will melt away and disappear."

"If they do something to the family, there will be evidence," Bapcat said. "There is always evidence."

"In America, I would agree," Zakov said. "Not here."

Jordy said, "We have to *do* something."

Zakov said quietly, "We lack the wherewithal."

"We have an armored train and firepower."

"We must forget this train for now. I fear that its appearance could be leveraged by the local soviet to exterminate the Tsar and deny Moscow the advantage of holding the royal family for its own purposes."

Mind spinning, Bapcat asked, "Are you thinking the Yekaterinburg Reds believe the train is here to free the Tsar?"

His stomach was beginning to curdle as he worked out the implications. *They* could be the cause of the Tsar's death? It was a chilling thought.

"Were the train not here, the situation might not be so explosive?"

Zakov said, "Irrelevant. What is, is."

"Isn't there something we can do?" Jordy asked.

"We will watch and hope for an opportunity," Zakov said.

"This is not even a *weak* plan," Bapcat told his companions.

It jarred him that his agreeing to the relative safety and comfort of the armored train might speed up what was about to happen to the royal family—the exact opposite of what their mission was supposed to accomplish. He blamed himself. It was his fault for not thinking ahead. Damn it—Dodge might have been right about not hurrying to Yekaterinburg, albeit for different reasons than he'd originally entertained.

Zakov said, "It's not a plan. It's a hope, and not a strong one, but that's our reality. Soldiers are trained to face reality as it unfolds."

The Russian looked over at Jordy, who was smoking a cigarette.

"All grown up now, vices and all?"

"Smoking ain't much of a vice," the boy said sharply. "Where are we going, and when do I get to learn more about everything you two are talking about? I *am* part of this . . . whatever it is, right?"

"You are," Zakov said. "We are going to *helan*; you know this word yet?"

"It sounds like hell," Bapcat said.

"*Helan* is an old English verb," Zakov explained. "It means to hide or conceal. The English took the word from the Germans. It is a verb, but the root of the word *hell*, the hiding place of the dead."

"It doesn't have to be an actual place," Jordy said.

"No?" Zakov said. "You're a theologian now?"

"I'm just thinking that the mind is its own place, and in itself can make a heaven of a hell, or a hell of a heaven."

"John Milton," Zakov said, smiling. "Well done. The Widow Frei has done well by you."

"I started reading when I was living with you two," Jordy said, "but you were mostly too busy chasing fools to pay attention, and since Lute doesn't read much at all, it wouldn't mean much to him."

"We need to hurry," Zakov said, squeezing his partner's shoulder. "You know the way to Ipatiev House?"

"I do."

"Let's move. Lives hang in the balance."

His friend's words sickened him.

The armored train, Trotsky to the rescue; this was *his* fault.

26

Summer, 1918. The Engineer's House, Yekaterinburg

"Yekaterinburgers are calling it the House of Special Purposes."

The Romanovs were held in an ornately decorated white stone building. Bapcat and the others could see only the top floor of the house over the two new log palisades ringing the structure, the log walls so new that sawdust and bark piles cluttered the ground around them. The palisade tops had been sharpened like spear tips to make it difficult for intruders to climb over. It seemed to Bapcat that the log walls had been stripped of bark and painted black.

They were four hundred yards away in a thick aspen copse, about the only trees in the area still standing. All else for hundreds of yards had been stripped and logged to provide a wide field of fire from the house.

"Why did they paint the logs?" Jordy asked.

Zakov said, "They didn't. If you strip certain kinds of pine logs, they darken on their own within twenty-four hours. No one knows why. Peasants are convinced it is a harbinger of evil, a bad omen, and in this case, the people may be right. Yekaterinburgers are calling it the House of Special Purposes."

"*Plukhoi predznamenovanie*," Jordy said. "Bad omen."

"More *likhoi* than *plukhoi*," Zakov muttered. "More evil than mere bad. *Gvarddeets.*"

Bapcat asked, "How many guards?"

"Difficult to know from this distance," Zakov said with a glance at Bapcat. "You were here before. How many did you count?"

"Not nearly enough. Most of them must be inside the walls. There is one outside patrol twice an hour, at fifteen before and fifteen after, no variations that I could see. Some guard personnel appear to be boarded in a building across the avenue." He pointed at an ugly gray boxy wood building across the cleared area.

Zakov said, "The Tobolsk building was different, much larger, more expansive. The family had their own house guards from Tsarskoye Selo. Their own people watched over them, but with light reins. The family had almost normal freedom. It was not as much of a prison as this place appears to be."

"How long were you in Tobolsk?" Bapcat asked his partner.

"Long enough. Most of what I know, I got from villagers and neighbors, who watch such things and gossip. Here there is no liberty, only prison walls. It is rather easy to find information about the Tsar and his family. They are too big a secret to be contained. Some watch, many speculate, and none *do* anything."

"But you talked to the Tsar?"

"Once, briefly, in Tsarskoye Selo, before the family was sent east, and again when I caught up to them, in Tobolsk."

"You actually talked to the Tsar himself?"

"Briefly, both times."

"What shape was he in?"

Zakov shrugged. "He seemed fine physically, but mentally, he is—and always has been—rudderless. He finds it difficult to come to decisions, and invariably second-guesses himself. In this regard he is the same as always: poor Nicky. He is a disaster, with neither the head for leadership nor the stomach for it. He makes the worst choices for his advisors. He is largely a good and loving father; in fact, his crazy German wife and children have always come before the country's interests."

"What did you talk about?" Bapcat asked.

"I told him he needed to get away, and all he would say is, 'All is in God's hands.'"

"It's normal to care for wife and kids first," Jordy said. "Isn't it?"

Zakov answered, "Tsars, kings, presidents—people in high positions—they are not allowed such normalcy. When a leader begins to focus almost exclusively on his personal interests over the national interest, his more important responsibilities fray, and eventually this tears apart the fabric of the country or kingdom. History reveals this pattern over and over."

"Why is the family even with him?" Bapcat asked. When US law enforcement personnel locked up a criminal, it was just the accused, not his family, unless they were criminals too.

Zakov chewed on this for a moment. "Simple: blood succession. In terms of power, the Tsar and his family are a single unit. It has taken me a while to piece it together. The local soviets, all of them, are cauldrons of anger, anxiety, and abject fear. Each local leader operates alone, based almost solely on how he thinks those above him *want* him to act. Everything is reduced to guesswork. There is no effective central control from Lenin; none. Trotsky is closest to an effective national leader, but he is engaged in organizing and rallying the Red Army and has no time for the rest of it."

Zakov continued, "On top of this, there is a blanket of mass paranoia which began when Kerensky's Provisionals and Lenin's Reds both feared Petrograd might fall to a German assault, or even one from the Finns. To avoid either disaster, the government fled east and south, toward the Russian center. The price of such panic has been disjointed actions by the local soviets, who, having no clear, direct, or regular contact with the master comrades in Moscow, do what they please, and what pleases first and foremost has nothing to do with the country. What they do is wreak havoc on all opposition, real and imagined, current and historical."

Zakov paused for a breath.

"It is no different in cities controlled by the White Army. Retribution is the disorder of the day, as *de rigueur* as it is in the Red-held towns and cities. Bodies are piling up everywhere. The reason's the same, with no logic to any of it. Meanwhile, those citizens who manage to avoid capture and torture, or being hung or shot, are starving and stealing and killing to stay alive, and if they are captured, they are hung or shot as criminals, and sometimes, as political saboteurs. They are executed locally, without tribunals of any kind. Russia is, for the moment, no longer a country. It is at best a loose confederation of city-states, like old Italy, Germany, and Greece—all of Europe, for that matter, before cities surrendered to national direction and control."

Zakov squinted. "The most radical and uncontrollable of local soviets is in Yekaterinburg, which it appears will soon fall to the Whites, and retributions will begin anew. The Romanovs are, of course, a grand bargaining chip. As long as they live, the Reds can, if they so choose, use them to negotiate. The question is, will they?"

Bapcat asked, "But if the Whites free them?"

Zakov answered, "They will certainly try."

Jordy asked, "And if the Whites succeed, then what?"

"The Whites will push to rally all sympathies to their side, but I'm quite certain the Tsar and his family are doomed to die."

"Not if we can free them," Jordy argued.

Bapcat knew Jordy was listening intently, and when Zakov stopped talking, the boy said, "When Cortez landed in Mexico, he ordered his ships burned and sunk. His men then had no choice but to follow their commander, inland and overland, wherever he chose to lead them."

Bapcat reminded his son, "You said this same thing in Murmansk."

"I'm saying it again," Jordy replied. "The Tsar and his family are the Reds' ships."

Bapcat didn't know what to say. His son thought on an entirely different plane than him.

Zakov said, "Therein lies the problem. For the greater good of the national Red cause, the Romanovs belong safely in custody, in Moscow. But they will never get there."

Bapcat asked, "The one called Lenin is in Moscow. Can't he order them brought there?"

"Burn the ships," Jordy said.

Zakov looked at Jordy. "Yes, but not as Cortez did, to propel the fight forward. That was tactical. This decision is strategic. Better to kill the Tsar and his family quietly and invisibly, and then, even if the Whites carry on the fight, there will be no added motivation for them to crush the Reds in Yekaterinburg, which will become just one more city to deal with."

Bapcat asked, "Do the Whites know the Tsar is here?"

"Undoubtedly, but *which* Whites?" Zakov countered. "Like the Reds, the Whites are not a single entity with consolidated leadership. The White Army is made up of many fighting groups, mostly operating independent of each other. It seems that the civil war has now expanded to fourteen or fifteen different fronts, with different foes lined up against each other and almost no coordination. Tsar or no Tsar, chaos always reigns for the common people of Russia. The Yekaterinburg soviet will soon kill Nicholas and his heirs."

"When?" Jordy asked.

Zakov sighed and rubbed his face. "I should think they won't wait to see the legs of the Czech Legion's soldiers through the smoke. I think the end of the Romanovs is imminent."

Jordy said, "We have to get the Tsar and his family out of there."

"To where—and then what?" his father asked.

"We have a wheeled fortress."

Zakov said quietly, "No train is invincible. But if we could reach the Crimea, escape might be possible. *If . . .*"

Jordy said, "Or north to Archangelsk or Murmansk, where we have American troops to help us."

"North may be too physically demanding," Zakov said. "Winter will be arriving soon to the north. Too many unknowns in that direction. There is Vladivostok and the Far East, where there are also American troops, but there are many thousands of miles between here and there, and still there is the bite of winter to face. Crimea would be our best choice. There is in Crimea a large pro-Tsar Cossack contingent to connect to."

Bapcat said, "You talk about what our best bet would be, not what it is."

"Indeed," Zakov said. "We lack the force to overwhelm the Ipatiev fortress. The Letts are fanatics and will not cave easily."

"Non-Russian Europeans, right?" Bapcat asked.

"Yes, Letts, Latvians—they are the same."

Jordy added, "Who are not all Latvians."

"Exactly," Zakov said.

"Are we just going to sit here and wait for the royal family to be murdered?" Jordy asked, his eyes bulging with disbelief and passion.

Zakov said, "Think of a mine disaster. The first step afterward is to rescue survivors, and the next logical phase, recover victims."

"We're going to *let* them die!" Jordy complained.

"We shall do what we can with the smallest loss and greatest gain," Zakov calmly told the boy. "This is always the soldier's choice and priority: Never spend your men's lives ignorantly."

"But we're not *at* war," Bapcat reminded his compatriots.

"No?" Zakov came back in a flat, cold voice.

After a while, Bapcat asked, "House of Special Purposes, as in murder?"

Zakov raised his hands in recognition of their helplessness in the face of what seemed inevitable.

Bapat felt both sick and sad. To come all this way, for what? Most lawmen got called in after criminal events happened, but game wardens were paid to know where violators would act and to be there to stop them before they broke the law or while the crime was in progress. Game wardens were the opposite of reactive.

He tried to rationalize their circumstances here. They weren't empowered to intervene. This was Russian business, a problem for Russians, not Americans.

His stomach refused to settle.

27

Summer, 1918. Crazy Ivan

"In Russia, we trust nobody."

Zakov reacted immediately to a summons from Chief Engineer Bezmunyi to "Come quickly," the message delivered by Elpikovny. Zakov asked Bapcat to come with him, and left Jordy to keep an eye on the House of Special Purposes.

Bapcat thought he detected relief in Bezmunyi when they arrived. The man was sitting among four severe-faced soldiers in different dark, uncoordinated uniforms.

"Black shades of white," Zakov whispered as they climbed the ladder to the main engine.

Bezmunyi greeted them in English. "These gentlemen are emissaries from their commander."

"From Admiral Kolchak?" Zakov asked with the hint of a smirk.

The conversation then switched to frantic Russian, and Bapcat would not understand any of it until Zakov explained later. What he saw and knew was that his partner was directing everything he said, no matter who he was speaking with, to only one of the four men, an unimpressive, somewhat pudgy little fellow with bulging eyes, with bags and deep creases below them. The man had thin hair and a wispy mustache; compared to the other soldiers, with their bushy clumps of whiskers, the man looked almost youthful.

Later, when Bapcat heard his friend's playback of the meeting, he understood.

"Why have we been summoned?" Zakov asked Bezmunyi.

"These gentlemen wish to inform us that by the Tsar's direct order, this train is to be appropriated for use by the White Army."

"Do they wish me to understand that this is a *direct* order of the Tsar?" Zakov asked. "And if so, how is it that our esteemed visitors have had contact with a Tsar no one has seen since the spring of 1917? Some believe he is dead, which makes it truly impressive that these gentlemen assert they have spoken with him. They can talk to the dead? This is surely a miraculous skill, and could provide a significant military advantage. I would suggest that they talk to the generals who turned back Napoleon. I should like to talk to them even more than the missing Tsar. Can the esteemed gentlemen arrange this?"

Bapcat could see that the three kept glancing toward the pudgy younger officer with the passive face. Zakov talked only to the engineer for a while.

"How do the gentlemen plan to appropriate the train now in our possession?"

Bezmunyi said, "By superior force, of which they wish us to be informed."

"Informed, or threatened?" Zakov challenged. "Never mind, Chief Engineer. Please inform these intrepid fellows that it would be wise for them to look around carefully. This armored beast is the high ground from which we can reach out and bite hard, close, and far. To assault this monster is to be as a fish beating against the bottom of a boat—a lot of noise with no effect. But if these gentlemen wish to be on-the-knives with us, let it be so."

Zakov explained later that "on-the-knives" means to point swords at each other with open hostility and intent—a state of war.

Bezmunyi said, "They wish to complete this transaction without bloodshed."

"If they are ordering us to give up our train, would it not be proper procedure to negotiate terms?"

A thick-bodied man in a green uniform and a beard glistening like wet coal said, "Our commander will, of course, offer fair compensation to avoid bloodletting."

Zakov continued to direct his words to the Chief Engineer.

"What is fair compensation?"

"A billion," the black-bearded soldier said.

"One can't wipe one's arse with a billion in Red scrip."

"Gold," Blackbeard hastily amended.

Zakov laughed. "Very well, the price is five billion, gold."

Bezmunyi's eyes bugged out.

"This can be done," Blackbeard said calmly.

"Negotiations are at an end," Zakov said, looking at the youngest soldier. "Tell your commander to face me, commander to commander. I do not deal with or through lick-spittle surrogates and proxies."

Blackbeard pointed to the north. "Please look," the man said.

Bezmunyi leaned over to a window and looked out.

Blackbeard blew a shrill whistle.

Bezmunyi reported, "Armed men coming from the north."

Zakov continued to look at the younger officer. "How many, Chief Engineer?"

Bezmunyi squinted. "Two hundred, five hundred—they keep coming out of the forest."

"Our men are ready?" Zakov asked.

"They are, sir," Bezmunyi reported.

"Give the order," Zakov said.

Blackbeard said quickly, "We came under a flag of truce. By the rules of civilized war, you must guarantee us safe passage."

Zakov laughed. "There are no such rules in Russia."

"*Ten* billion, gold," Blackbeard came back, upping the offer.

"Gold coin?"

"Bullion."

"Guaranteed by whom?"

"Tsar Nicholas."

"Authorized by him when?"

"Within the week."

"Where?" Zakov pressed.

"Tobolsk."

Zakov ignored the man and said instead to Bapcat and the Chief Engineer, "We have nothing more to discuss with these imposters." He added. "Give them safe passage, three minutes before we commence fire."

Three of the men began to move, but the younger, frumpier one sat where he was, scowling and grimacing.

Zakov asked, "Who is this commander of yours?"

"General Paloonik," Blackbeard answered.

"General Pilgrim," Zakov said. "A nom de guerre. Listen to me well: The Tsar and his family are captives of the Red soviet here in Yekaterinburg. They have not been in Tobolsk for many weeks, and the Tsar has had all authority and rank stripped from him for more than a year."

Neither Blackbeard nor the frumpy one said anything.

Zakov said, "I knew a captain in the war with the *Yaponets*, a brilliant young officer destined for future command at the highest levels, but he made the fatal mistake of criticizing senior officers as being too predictable, without imagination, and without balls. *Byt' n'e ko d'voru*—unfit for the courtyard. He did not fit in, this young and brilliant officer. The reality was that most of the captain's decisions succeeded beyond expectations, but as all officers do, he sometimes failed miserably and spectacularly. I lost track of him after a time, but continued to hear reports of the latest antics of one Crazy Ivan, who had done this and done that. There was, of course, no official discussion of Crazy Ivan, who had become a legend, but was considered an exiled ghost."

The thick-chested young officer smiled.

"I recognized the colonel right away," the man said. "Colonel Zakov, sir. Had I known this was your train, we would have never approached."

"Crazy Ivan Kazmirofvich Sornyak," Zakov said. "You lead this rabble?"

"*Da*, they fight better than they parade."

"As it should be," Zakov said.

"They are not rabble," the man said proudly.

"With you in here and them out there, they are no better than a mob. You've taken a gamble to commandeer this train. You cannot overwhelm it with arms. You are writing in the water with a hayfork, my dear Ivan."

The man smiled grimly. "I am talking to a dead man."

Zakov replied, "Every man is ultimately a dead man."

Sornyak nodded. "But you died in Manchuria, sir. Have you risen like our sweet Jesus?"

"Never mind Manchuria. You are hanging hair here. Where's the dog buried, Ivan Kazmirofvich?"

"There is no one White Army, no single White Guard, no consolidated leadership. Everything is fragmented, disorganized, not even a vestige of White government. We are reduced to children of anarchy." The man continued: "You are in possession of one of Trotsky's two armored trains. Your men wear the red leathers of Trotsky's Red One Hundred, but you and your men are neither Red nor White. I need this train to carry the fight to Trotsky."

Zakov raised an eyebrow at this point and said, "The unexpected gambit has always been your specialty, Sornyak."

Crazy Ivan lowered his voice to a conspiratorial tone. "Here is reality from our snooper agents. The local Reds and soviets are untrained, have tunnel vision, harbor local grudges and priorities, but Trotsky is beginning to bring together disparate elements and shape them into a fighting force. The time to fight him is now, before he pulls it all together. If I can confront him now, I can sever the head of the dragon."

"There's still Lenin," Zakov said.

"And that bastard Georgian Stalin, but it is Trotsky who builds and leads the army, not Lenin or Stalin or any of their stooges cowering in Moscow."

Zakov said, "I am inclined to concur, Sornyak. You may not have this train . . . yet."

Sornyak said, "Yet?"

"Hear me out: You and your men join us, and when we have completed our mission, you shall have the train."

"We have no gold to pay you," Sornyak admitted.

"Imagine my disappointment. Your word is gold enough for me, Sornyak."

"What, sir, is your mission, and when shall it conclude?"

"We are here to affirm that Nicholas and his family are alive, to examine how we might free them in order to help restore him to the throne."

Sornyak said solemnly, "If you think this will keep Russia in the war against Germany, you are mistaken, Colonel. That ship has struck its sails and dropped anchor. The people loathe the Romanovs, and none of us,

Red or White, will renew the fight with the Krauts for the royal family. You may very well restore the man to his throne, but Russia is done fighting the fucking Germans. And, it is general now, not captain, Colonel Zakov."

"Who is this Sornyak?" Lute later asked his friend.

"A doomed man, almost a Romanov by birth and a personal friend of the Tsar when he was growing up. Unlike Nicky, Sornyak possesses courage and a brilliant military mind, but he has always been too much the risk-taker for the old lions."

"Including you?"

"I tried several times to have him transferred to my command, but I had my own problems and disconnects with the general staff."

"You trust the man?"

Zakov rolled his eyes. "In Russia, we trust nobody."

"He's one of the Tsar's generals?"

Zakov sighed. "I am guessing he is self-declared—like most of them now—but unlike others, he is willingly followed. Ivan was born to lead men in battle, but there is no Tsar to dispense promotions and advancements."

"Which means you are no longer Colonel Zakov?"

The Russian smiled at his partner. "I have been a long time without rank, Lute. For the moment I think of myself as a kind of first violin in a primitive band, and when we return to Bumbletown, I shall happily and willingly revert to second fiddle to my partner's first."

"We are equal partners, you and I, Pinkhus Sergeyevich."

"Only on paper. On the Keweenaw ground, you are first fiddle."

Bapcat changed the subject. "We know Nicholas is alive. How do we free him and his family?"

Zakov squinted at the White Russians trickling back into the birches, and sighed. "When the crayfish whistles."

"Does that mean never?" Lute asked.

"It sounds less depressing as an idiom," Zakov said solemnly.

28

Summer, 1918. Ipatiev House

"The swan flies, the crawfish scuttles backward,
and the pike heads for water."

A breathless, hard-eyed Anton came, barking shrilly, "Sergeant Jordy says you must come now—bad things are happening!"

"What things?" Zakov asked their wisp of a messenger.

"I am but a humble servant, sir," Anton said. "The sergeant humbly begs you to hurry, please."

They found a somber Jordy slumped against a larch tree, a rolled cigarette hanging from his lower lip. Bapcat was still not accustomed to seeing his son smoking, much less the foul-smelling Russian tobacco.

Zakov spoke first.

"Your smoke is redolent of shit," Zakov said. "Explain why are we summoned with the frantic 'come now, come now' by this rude boy."

Jordy shrugged. "If you mean this tobacco stinks like shit, it tastes like it too."

Bapcat saw that his son was disturbed, his eyes distant and glazed. Did Zakov not see this too? He glanced at his partner and spotted the same concern.

"Things are happening here?" Bapcat asked.

"Happening, happened, underway, in progress, over—pick your own verb."

Zakov knelt. "Talk to us, Jordy."

The young sergeant stared straight ahead at the engineer's house, and spoke without emotion. "A Bolo officer escorted three stumbling, very drunk guards over to the Popov House," Jordy said, pointing, "which is directly across from Ipatiev, and where they billet some of the guard detail."

"How do you know this?" Zakov challenged.

"They came out of the compound and I followed them. I wasn't ten feet behind them when the officer dropped them off and ordered them to stay away. I listened to them talk; they were difficult to understand, but I think I caught the gist of it."

"What did you hear?" Zakov asked.

"They talked about the Letts and the slaughter and expressed their disgust with that, but then they began talking about the 'Seventh Lett,' and it seemed that whoever—or whatever—this was, it was too disgusting for them to even speak of, even in a drunken stupor. They went to sleep after that, and I went back outside and saw the gate to the engineer's house standing open. I went inside to see what was happening."

"These guards you heard were Letts?" Zakov asked.

"No, Russians—locals. The Letts were inside."

"Where is your red leather?" Bapcat asked, and felt stupid as soon as he'd said it.

"I left it behind and dressed for the woods, and after I found the drunks, I took some of their clothes to help me blend in. I figured it might give them pause if we met, and give me a small edge over their reaction time."

Zakov said, "Did it work?"

"By the time I'd crossed the open area, the main gate was closed and locked, but there was nobody in the main sentry port, so I walked into the compound and through an empty guard post in the inner palisade. That gate was also closed and locked. Strange. It was like a plague had swept through and erased everyone in the citadel. I saw no one, but I kept to the shadows and found a sentry post at the house with the guard curled up like a napping cat, drunk, snoring, and covered with vomit. Two empty bottles on the floor, vodka. The post looked directly down into a small room, like a half-cellar, not twenty feet long, narrow, no furniture, no people—nothing but white paint."

Bapcat glanced at his partner, who was showing little emotion, and at Anton, who stood to the side like a small dog with its tongue hanging out, awaiting its next command.

Jordy took a long time before he spoke again.

"Not long after I got into the sentry post and found the passed-out guard, a man in a black leather coat entered the room below me and looked up at me."

"Did he challenge you?" Zakov asked.

"No, based on what was to happen next, I think. Black Coat was nervous, excited, and overwhelmed, and he halfheartedly waved for me to stay at the post. I decided to play along, but I had my pistol in hand, just in case. It felt like time was frozen. Have you ever had that feeling?" Jordy asked Zakov.

"It's normal during a fight, before, or right after it is over," the Russian said.

Bapcat could only nod. He had been in such circumstances and had felt the same unreal freezing of time.

Jordy said, "I watched the room fill with slow-moving men and women, and a sick or very weak boy, carried by one of the men. All of them looked dressed for a trip. They milled around, and Black Coat talked to them quietly. Then he said something to a guard who came into the room. The guard left and came back with a chair, and after several trips, more chairs, and Black Coat got some of the travelers seated, like they were to have a group photograph before a trip, with one row standing and one sitting. Black Coat stood in front of them like the conductor of a band. I knew something was about to happen, but not what."

He paused for a moment. "Did I say there were girls, sort of young, bundled up for the trip, young like me, maybe a little younger? All the girls carried little pillows, like hand-warmers; I thought this strange, it being high summer. Why do they need hand-warmers? Mosquitoes? I didn't know. The boy was thin and listless, white as flour. He looked sickly."

Jordy paused and swallowed loudly before continuing.

"All of this is like a series of small pictures in my mind, disjointed, all part of one thing and yet separate. After Black Coat got the people in chairs, he talked for a while to the man holding the boy. The man had a pale blond beard and clueless eyes. Very strange, I was thinking, and Black Coat took a paper from his coat pocket and read, like he wanted to get it over with quickly. I couldn't make out a word, but he was barely finished when a small mob of men brandishing pistols pushed into the room behind him and began shooting at the travelers. It was chaos! Gray smoke, girls screaming, men yelling and shooting, bedlam. Seemed like it went on for an hour, but it couldn't have been more than a minute. When the shooting stopped, some of the travelers were moaning or screaming and crying. Some were writhing and flopping in pain on the floor, and one girl was trying to drag herself toward a door, but one of the men went around with a bayonet, stabbing anyone who moved, and Black Coat followed, putting one round into each head."

Jordy caught a sob, exhaled loudly, breathed in.

"All through the shooting bullets were ricocheting off the walls and several came through my opening and hit the drunk sentry's body, one right in his head, which made a small hole but did not go through. He never felt anything, but his body lurched with each hit, absorbing the lead with the sound of a fist against a flour bag. *Whack-whump.*

"I kept my head down until the salvo stopped. When I could look again, the knife man and Black Coat were ghosts floating around, finishing off the travelers, one at a time, and the other men began pulling up the women's clothing and groping their bodies. Disgusting. There was still some whimpering and crying going on as the ghosts went about their business, and from time to time there were muted curses. The one with the bayonet kept stabbing as he moved around."

Jordy stopped talking and stared off into the distance.

"Finish it," Zakov said quietly.

"There was a wooden wall behind them—did I tell you that? It was painted white, not a proper plaster wall, but wood which splintered under ricochets and sent slivers flying like deadly little darts. Did I say that some bullets hit the drunk guard next to me? Maybe slivers, too. He was dead."

Then, "They're all gone now, you know. Not here anymore. The girls were lined up just like sheep and didn't say a word. Just before the shooting began, a very noisy truck started up outside, and someone kept revving the engine, maybe to keep the noise high? Do you think they were trying to muffle the sound of the shooting?" he asked his father, and then turned to Zakov and said, "Twenty seconds, fourteen minutes, two hours, not long at all, yet a very, very long time. Is that even possible?"

Zakov nodded and patted Jordy's arm. He said to Bapcat, "A brutal and bloody end to three hundred years of Romanov rule."

"The barrage didn't kill them all outright," Jordy said. "Some tried to get away. The moaning and crying and shooting went on until I heard hammers clicking dry over and over, the men still trying to shoot empty and too excited to realize it, like stones striking stones?" the sergeant said.

"I decided it was time for me to get out of there. Before I went, I watched the shooters roll up the man with the pale beard in a sheet, and start getting other sheets spread out for the other bodies. The outside sentry posts were still empty, and both palisade gates were open and three trucks were parked close to the cellar, their motors still running. I kept to the shadows and took a roundabout way back to the woods. Anton was out here the whole while."

Zakov looked at the boy. "Did you hear shooting?"

"No, sir, but I heard trucks," the boy said. "Does Sergeant Jordy mean they killed people?"

"Yes." Zakov patted the boy's head. "You did well to hold your position while the sergeant was inside and in fetching us. Thank you for being such a good soldier."

He turned to Jordy. "Where're the trucks now?"

"I don't know; still inside, maybe? This didn't happen but more than an hour ago. As the smoke cleared I saw blood everywhere in the room, spattered on walls, floors, on the shooters . . ."

"What happened to the drunk guards at the Popov House?" Zakov asked.

"I couldn't really see, but I think one of the men stumbled into the woods. He could hardly stand, and I think he was probably looking for a place to sleep it off, so he wouldn't be found by his officers." Jordy nodded toward some birch trees.

The gate opened shortly after three a.m., and a loud green truck and two black ones raced noisily onto Ascension Avenue.

"Follow those trucks," Zakov ordered Jordy Klubishar.

Bapcat knew his son could run all day, if needed, and at a punishing pace. With his ability to track and read sign, he was not likely to lose sight of the trucks.

Anton volunteered to go with him. "The sergeant and me, sir—we're good runners and observers. Sergeant Jordy may want to send back a message. I can do this, sir. Please?"

"I'd rather be anyplace but here," Jordy said quietly. "Anywhere."

Bapcat took his son by the shoulder. "Follow the trucks only, and *don't* interfere. When you find them, send Anton back to us, and hold your position."

Bapcat turned to Anton. "No risks, your *only* job is to come back here to tell us where Sergeant Jordy is, understand?"

"*Da*," Anton said, nodding solemnly.

Jordy seemed to stay in his trance as Bapcat and Zakov led them to the cobbled avenue where they had last seen the trucks, then raised his nose into the breeze and sniffed like a hunting wolf. "Blood and petrol, blood and petrol. Got it."

With the boys gone, Zakov said, "Let us find that sleeping guard."

———

The gaunt man looked malnourished. He had a rodent's face, smallpox scars, slow-blinking eyes the color of snail slime. Zakov rubbed wet grass on the man's face, making him splutter.

"Wake up, little dead man," Zakov said with a snarl.

"Am I dead?" the man came back. "Is this . . . *Paradise?*"

Zakov said, "Not quite, comrade, but I am at this moment your God, and I'm about to determine your fate and future relationship to eternity. Who are you, and why are you drunk so early on this fine summer day?"

The man put a hand over his eyes. "Summer? Is it?" The man put his left fist against his left ear.

Zakov said sternly, "A drunk sentry is no sentry at all. In the army we shoot men for sleeping while on duty."

The man frowned, tried to lift his hand again, but seemed to have no energy.

Zakov leaned down. "When the ax swings, chips must fly, comrade."

"*Da,*" the man said forlornly. "It had to come."

"It?" Zakov asked.

"Nicholas the Bloody and his spawn."

Zakov pressed in a firm but gentle voice, "Nicholas is no longer Tsar. He abdicated a year ago. Why do you talk of him?"

"His death, theirs—it's the people's will, comrade. We could all feel it coming. Few of us were talking, except the Seventh Lett, who wouldn't *stop* talking. That bastard says to us, 'Tonight's the night, boys. Tonight it shall be done. We await the order from Moscow. The decision has already been taken here. Tonight's the night, and then, alas, no more *shushy,* no more *tselina* for Oyars.'

"Only the Seventh Lett talked, but we all knew what he was about, and some of us wanted nothing to do with it or him. Those four girls . . . sweet sisters," the man mumbled, choking up.

Zakov turned to Bapcat, and said in English. "I sense regrets in this sad excuse for a soldier."

"What is *shushy*?" Zakov asked the prone guard.

The man moaned. "I will not talk about this. This was the Seventh Lett's business, and only his."

"You wanted the Romanovs dead?" Zakov asked the sentry.

"The Tsar and Rasputin's whore, yes, of course; the heir too, I suppose. Not those sweet girls. Some of us told them to leave the girls be. They're just girls, with no power. Kill their mother, father, and heir, but put the girls into exile, let them fend for themselves, find husbands. They are handsome girls, all of them."

"How was this suggestion received?"

"We were thanked, given vodka, and shown to the other house where we are barracked. How did I get *here*?" the man asked, looking around.

"You left the Popov House after it was done."

"I did? Finished? All of them?"

"*Da*," Zakov said.

"*Chetveren'ki*—all four?"

"*Da*," Zakov said, "the family, and others."

The man closed his eyes, rolled on his side, and gagged. When he recovered, he wiped his mouth with his sleeve, mumbled, "Servants and friends, all evidence."

The man started to doze again, but Zakov shook him vigorously with his boot, and the man came awake.

"*What?*" he cried with a startled yelp.

"We are not done talking, comrade."

"I know nothing. I am a mere sentry in the House of Special Purposes."

"It would seem there is no longer a special purpose."

"No, but there will be evidence."

"What about evidence?" Zakov asked.

"Is this how Paradise works—we sit around, answering questions? Bah. Give me hell, then."

"What about evidence? You have said this twice now."

"I have? Evidence—what evidence?"

"From the liquidations."

"There have been liquidations?"

"*Da.*"

"I missed them?"

"Yes."

"Good. I couldn't bear to see that."

"*Evidence*," Zakov repeated sternly.

"What evidence?" the man replied.

"Of the shootings."

"What shootings? I saw no shootings, I heard no shootings. To this I can swear in court, before God. I know nothing, can testify to nothing, or against anyone."

Zakov said with steely authority, "Your testimony is now, comrade. *I* am your God, not the Cheka. I am far above that, and this is not court. You are dead. I am now weighing the cleansing of your soul for eternity, or the leaving of it in the thick muck of sin and filth. You swear you did not participate in the killings?"

"What killings?" the man said again. "I swear."

"We know you were not there, comrade. Tell us why."

"I already told you. I won't shoot girls. They said I lacked patriotic fervor. Is that like fever?"

"They brought you over to the Popov House and what did they tell you?"

"I think the officer said to us, 'You neutered scum know where the dog is buried. Were I you, I would run now, and keep running. The Whites will hunt you like the dogs you are.'"

"But you drank instead of running," Zakov said. "What will you do now?"

The man puffed his cheeks and blew out air. "Must I run even in Paradise? Am I not dead and free of all that mess?"

"The Whites will come for you," Zakov said.

"God would let this happen?"

Zakov shrugged. "Not God, me. If I let you go, you must run if you are to save yourself."

The man nodded slowly. "*Da*, they will kill me if I stay, but they can't kill what they can't find."

Zakov added, "We found you easily enough. If they were going to kill you, wouldn't they have done that when you refused their order?"

The man's doughy face was red, pained, breaths coming in deep wheezes, his eyes bulging. "It was *not* an order. It was a request for volunteers. Some of us did not wish to volunteer."

"And they took you to Popov House when you refused."

"Commander Nepotkin said, 'You who cannot do what must be done, must leave.' But first he made us drink vodka, a lot of vodka, *excellent* vodka."

"Just you?"

"No, everyone had vodka. It was a celebration of the thing to come."

"How do you know they wanted you to shoot the royal family?"

"They tried to give us revolvers. Only officers carry revolvers. The intended use was clear."

"You could go back and tell them you are now sober and wish to report for duty."

"There is no place for me here. I am not going back."

"What is your name, comrade?"

"Luk," the man whispered.

"A nom de guerre," Zakov said.

Bapcat saw that whatever Zakov had said, the man had not understood.

Zakov added, "It's your Party name, not your given name."

"*Da*," the man said. "Luk."

"It means onion," Zakov told Bapcat.

"Comrade Luk, I admire this name. An onion has layers, as do you, as does the Party, as all lives have layers. The execution and liquidation of the Romanovs is only one layer, comrade. If they needed you to do what they planned to do, they would not have let you go to Popov House. They asked for volunteers and did not order you to do something against your conscience. You should return to your unit."

The man had wary, feral eyes.

"I lacked courage," the man confessed. "They will neither forgive nor forget."

"You will demonstrate courage if you return to help them with what must be done next."

"I don't want to go back," the man said in a clipped voice.

"Which is why it takes courage—or I could shoot you now and save them the effort and the bullet."

"But you are God, and I am dead. Why would you shoot me if I am already dead? I don't like this. I am tired of this. You are not the God I believe in."

"You are certainly dead if you stay here, and then run. You will be considered a traitor. They will think you are deserting the cause."

"But if you send me back to that life, I will no longer be dead, in Paradise?"

"Or in Hell," Zakov said.

The man grimaced, "The swan flies, the crawfish scuttles backward, and the pike heads for water."

Zakov said quietly, "And the cart those creatures were pulling remains where it was. You should return to your cart, comrade."

"If I don't?"

"You know the answer."

The man suddenly stood on unsteady legs and drew in a deep breath. "What is it you want, comrade. Who are *you* in life?"

Zakov said to Bapcat, "He asks who we are in life? This is a common Russian threat, which implies we are nobodies and therefore can be ignored."

Zakov told the man, "Your choice is to live or remain dead."

The man tried to steady himself on his feet. Bapcat couldn't believe he was even upright considering how he smelled and how much he must have imbibed.

"What is it you want of me, Comrade *Bog*?" the man asked with resignation, using the Russian word for God.

"Names: every prisoner, every guard, every Party official involved in this, every soul, dead and alive."

"In return for my life?"

"We shall see."

"*Bog* is as slippery as the comrades."

"The Seventh Lett."

"I don't know his full name. He once called himself Oyars. He left before us."

"Perhaps he had no stomach for shooting girls either."

Luk closed his puffy eyes. "His stomach was for violating them."

"Do your best. If you can't learn his real name, try to find out where he has gone."

The sentry stared at Zakov. "The Lett fucked them; he didn't murder them. Why do you care?"

"*Bog* cares," Zakov said. "What was the relationship of this Seventh Lett to the other six?"

"I don't know. They came in a few weeks ago. Everyone said they were a special killing squad, but even the six-man squad was deathly afraid of number seven." The man suddenly sat down.

"The Lett commander?"

"Not a commander. A minder of sorts? I don't know. They don't talk much except to their own Lett kind."

The word *Lett* was squishy. Technically it meant Latvian, but it also meant Austro-Hungarian prisoners who had come over to Russia as fellow revolutionaries, generally spoke their own languages, kept their own counsel, had their own special uniforms, and followed Red Russian orders precisely and completely. No one in his right mind got in the way of uniformed Letts.

"But the Seventh Lett did not take part in the killings. He left before they happened."

"*Da*, before we were even led away by the political officer."

Zakov looked at Bapcat, and explained in English, "Our man here refused to shoot the four sisters and was brought over here by his officer, called a coward, and told to run because the Whites will hunt him. There is an old Russian saying—to find oneself between two fires. One fire is the Whites hunting him, the second fire is the liquidators, rejecting him as wanting in patriotism."

"What other evidence?" Zakov asked the man.

"Evidence?" the man said. "What are you talking about? And now, I fill my mouth with water."

Zakov broke a smile. "He fills his mouth with water."

Bapcat asked what this meant, if anything.

His Russian friend said, "One cannot talk when one's mouth is full of water. He is done talking."

Zakov leaned closer to the man. "Do you mean there is no evidence, comrade?"

The man crossed his arms and stared at the darkness. Mosquitoes swarmed his face and he frowned, but did not try to slap them away or resist them. It was much the same back home in Michigan, Bapcat thought. You tolerated pests, did not battle them. There was no point. There were too many. Learning to endure made you stronger, harder.

Zakov said to the man, "They will bury the remains and there will always be evidence, comrade. You are mistaken in your assumption."

The man glared at Zakov with a crooked sneer. "Lime, acid, and the ax."

Zakov looked at his game warden partner.

"They will dismember the bodies and use lime and acid to destroy the remains in an attempt to make the evidence disappear."

"I thought he was done talking?"

"He wants to prove to God that he is not stupid, so he gives us more information. He is still drunk."

Zakov asked, "This Seventh Lett, this Oyars—was he supposed to be a shooter?"

The man kept his arms crossed.

"So you don't know. Why were you so concerned about the royal sisters?" Zakov continued, "Have you considered, comrade, that the White Army will not want you dead as much as the Seventh Lett—Oyars—will want you dead. As long as you live, you are a threat to him."

The man rolled on his side and sighed. "Are you going to bring me back to life?"

"I am considering it," Zakov said solemnly.

Bapcat could not believe the stench rolling off the man. The alcohol fumes coming from him were enough to make others too close to him get drunk on the fumes alone. He had seen and smelled drunks of this magnitude before, but always they were truly dead by then. He didn't understand how it worked, but too much alcohol could kill. Why was this creature not dead?

"He will not hunt us," the sentry said. "The Seventh Lett will run to Boat Mountain and his own kind."

"His own kind—meaning other Letts?" Zakov pressed, but the man had gone to sleep and was snoring loudly.

The man awoke with a start and mumbled, "They said they would march them down the twenty-three steps to the basement, and kill them all."

The game wardens pulled the drunk to his feet, steadied him between them, and escorted him to the tree line, where they pointed him at the palisaded white building.

"*Bog* grants you life, Luk. You know your job. I will come to see you so you can tell me what you have learned."

"You won't know where to find me," the man tried.

"*Bog* knows your whereabouts at all times. Did I not find you in the forest?"

The man slumped his shoulders and began shuffling across the cobblestoned space toward Ipatiev's house, but he'd gone less than halfway when he suddenly wheeled and ran clumsily off into the forest again.

Zakov looked one last time at the drunk and nodded for Bapcat to follow.

"He's running."

"We could easily bring him to heel again."

This time when they caught him and knocked him to the ground, Zakov took out his pistol and pressed the barrel against the man's forehead, between his eyes.

"We are done playing, comrade. The Seventh Lett. Oyars what? Truly a Latvian, or just a Lett?"

The man shrugged. "Foreigners are foreigners. They all look and sound alike."

"Tell us the Seventh Lett's full name, comrade."

The man closed his eyes and said, "Oyars Kaspars Arajs."

Zakov said, "A Lett who is actually Latvian?"

"But not human," the man said. "I spit on him!" He staggered into the forest.

"Shall I bring him back?" Bapcat asked his Russian partner.

"No, we have what we need."

"Who were the killers?"

"Hush," Zakov said. "It doesn't matter."

—◆—

They had a name, and all they needed now was word from Jordy and Anton.

Bapcat closed his eyes and imagined Jordy and Anton out there on their own. Would it have been better to let him go to France to serve with other soldiers? This question would not let go. Had he been selfish? What if he died here? Jaquelle would kill him. No, if *he* lost him, he would kill *himself*. He wouldn't deserve to live.

Zakov grabbed his partner's arm.

"Don't worry; Jordy will be fine. He is young, and already better at what he is doing than we were at his age."

29

Summer, 1918. Koptyaki Forest

"Here is here and there is there, and this there-there has
different rules than the here-here back there."

Jordy was gone three hours before Bapcat and Zakov were ready to follow,
both of them dressed as raggedy Russian peasants. They made their way
into the abandoned Ipatiev compound and took a close look at the half-
basement. They found six old women trying to clean the room, scrubbing
to erase all evidence of what had happened. Buckets of fresh white paint
were standing open, to be slopped on the walls.

The game wardens decided not to wait for a message from Jordy. Bapcat insisted he could follow the boy, who would, by training, leave subtle
signs along the way in the old Indian tradition. Unlike his son, Bapcat
could not smell the mix of blood and fuel spewed by the trucks, but he
could read his son's sign like the local newspapers.

Bapcat estimated their steady pace at three to four miles per hour, and
when his Russian-made watch showed they had been advancing for three
hours, he estimated they had made eleven miles from Ipatiev House. They
kept moving along a faint dusty trail that paralleled the railroad tracks
and eventually led to a dark hut, one of hundreds situated along Russian
rail routes to provide water and fuel.

Nobody seemed to be stirring in the shack. No one came out to greet
or challenge them, which Bapcat found strange, as for months, he had
seen many similar huts and they had always been occupied.

Zakov said, "Landmark for us, crossing station number 185."

A short distance further on, the dirt road curved into a marshy area, and they saw a black Fiat truck like the one from the House of Special Purposes. It was sunk to its axles. Lots of footprints and cart tracks led from the vehicle to the forest ahead. Was this truck one from Ipatiev's?

Bapcat looked at the dark muck and said quietly, "Blood in the truck bed and in the muck."

Zakov leaned into the truck, swept his hand around, held up something the size of a pea.

"Diamond," he announced. His hand swept around several more times, and he said over his shoulder, "Five total."

"Meaning?" Bapcat asked.

Zakov shrugged. "We shall see."

Not a minute later, Anton came loping out of the forest, waved to them, looked solemn, and beckoned for them to follow him.

Bapcat saw that the boy moved swiftly and effortlessly, with a predator's gait. After a few minutes they saw Jordy, standing in a raggedy black spruce stand. Bapcat's son had situated himself just inside a tree line that looked out on a grassy knoll. Bapcat sensed a lethargy in Jordy. Not good. Dark eyes, fear—revulsion?

Jordy pointed.

"They got the truck stuck back there and had a helluva time. Wagons were summoned from a village up the trail from here, and the bodies were moved ahead on farm carts. It was a quagmire."

Bapcat said. "We saw."

"What village lies ahead?" Zakov asked.

"Koptyaki," Jordy said. They were talking in normal voices, not whispering.

"Where are the men from Ipatiev's?"

"Most are gone. They left three men to secure this place. The villagers brought carts, but the Bolos took them and sent the villagers away, told them they'd be shot if they talked or tried to see what was going on."

"That would never stop Russian villagers," Zakov said.

"It didn't," Jordy said. "I saw several of them creeping around, even when the killers were still here."

Zakov asked, "Did they dig graves?"

"I'm not sure. If they did, the bodies aren't in them. I saw bodies and parts bobbing in a water-filled hole."

"I don't' understand," Bapcat said.

"Remember the old Indian copper mines up our way?" Jordy asked his father.

"A shallow mine?"

"Probably."

"Why would they put bodies in water and not sink them?" Bapcat asked.

Jordy shrugged, said, "I found what looks like two old mine entrances, and maybe there're more. This place is called Four Brothers, but I see only two old black stumps."

"How do you know what it's called?" Zakov asked.

"I heard the men talking when they were working on the bodies."

"*Working* on them?" Bapcat asked.

"They began with axes," the boy said, looking away. "Both mines are flooded, and if the other place is a mine, it's also flooded."

"How deep?"

"No way to measure," Jordy retorted. "It's murky, muddy-black water. Who knows how deep? Who knows, and what does it matter?"

"Where are the victims now?" Bapcat asked.

"First the Bolos chopped them up—with axes, did I tell you that? I watched them."

"How large a force?" Zakov asked.

"Force?" Jordy answered, staring at the Russian. "Maybe thirty? I didn't count, but they were all around here for a while, all yelling at each other and passing around bottles. The main group took off and left six or eight men behind, but that's shrunk to just three. Force of three. Can three even *be* a force?"

"The execution squad?" Zakov asked.

"They were all here, I think. I didn't really study faces or anything like that, you know? They were all chopping up bodies."

"Did Anton see this?" Bapcat asked his son.

Jordy said nothing, shook his head once.

Bapcat asked Anton, "What did you see?"

"Men running around. Sergeant Jordy would not let me see what was happening. He made me stay back, but I heard what you said about chopping. I heard axes."

Bapcat wished his son had seen none of this.

Zakov took Anton's arm. "You remember the rail crossing near where you found us?"

"Where the lorry is sunk in mud is crossing station number 185. Anton remembers everything."

"Exactly, number 185. We want you to hurry back to Bezmunyi and tell him to send Second Brain to number 185, and be quick about it." Trotsky's special trains each had double engines. Bezmunyi referred to their main unit as First Brain and the second one as Second Brain. "We may need support. Tell him Second Brain should include one gun carriage."

"Who shall bring it—Elpy or the Chief Engineer?" Anton asked.

Zakov said, "Bezmunyi decides, but we need one gun carriage for a show of force."

"Is Anton to return with Second Brain?" the boy asked.

Zakov said, "*Da.*"

Bapcat said, "*Nyet.*"

The partners locked eyes and Bapcat said, "He is too damn young."

Zakov countered, "This is Russia, and age is irrelevant. Being young is not allowed here at present. The boy is strong and resilient. He has already shown this."

For now, Bapcat thought. How long could that last? War eventually wore down all but the crazies and committed professionals. He could see it in Jordy, who over the months here had wasted to a skeleton, ready to disintegrate into a pile of loose flesh.

Zakov gave the boy a gentle push. "On your way, now. Go quickly, and keep in mind, this is not a race. Do not take foolish chances. Your job is to get back to our people as quickly as you can, but safely. This is your job. Now go, and bring Second Brain."

The boy said, "Yes, comrade," grinned, and took off to the south.

Bapcat watched him run, lithe as a deer, lacking only a white flag marking his path through black spruce and dark forest. Sick, how some

Russians had used the child. Was he doing any better? Cuba had been one thing, but the situation in this country was entirely different, something unimaginable. Why had he let Colonel Roosevelt talk him into this? Why had he brought Jordy? Would the boy have been better off on the front lines in France?

Stop second-guessing, he told himself. Deal with what is. You think and worry too damn much.

Zakov said to Jordy, "We need to determine precisely how many guards are here. When did the main crew leave?"

"Right after first light, for the big group, an hour or so later for the others. But people seemed to come and go all night; it was nearly impossible to track, let alone keep count."

"No matter," Zakov said, looking at Bapcat and signaling with his eyes. The two men had been partners so long that they rarely needed words to know what the other was thinking or needing.

"Stay here and watch our backs," Bapcat told his son.

The two men moved off alone. Even with the sun about to rise, the forest was dark and thick, with few trails. The place called Four Brothers was a grassy opening in the trees, sunlight not quite on it yet.

Bapcat saw one bearded guard sitting on the grass, his blouse loose, bandolier out of reach behind him, his back against a birch tree, rifle across his lap. The man was smoking and looked half-asleep. Too much work and emotion last night? This whole thing seemed poorly planned, as if it had been cobbled together at the last moment.

What happened next would later be explained to Bapcat in English by his partner.

Zakov stepped forward, pushed his rifle barrel against the guard's head.

"Freeze, comrade. Do not even breathe. Spit out your cigarette."

The guard complained, "But I just lit it."

Zakov swatted the side of the guard's head with the forestock of his rifle. "Quiet unless instructed to talk."

Bapcat picked up the man's rifle and ammo belt and tossed them out of the man's reach. There was some blood showing on the guard's head from Zakov's blow.

"Tell us about the Seventh Lett," Zaklov said with a snarly voice.

The guard shrugged. "He's gone."

"What was his job at Ipatiev House?"

"They never told us," the guard said.

"But you saw him at his work."

The guard nodded. "With the girls."

Zakov asked, "How long have you been guarding the former Tsar?"

"Weeks. They asked for volunteers at the brickyard."

"Who asked?"

"Yekaterinburg soviet leadership. They wanted men they could trust."

"You are one of them?"

"There is not much choice when they point at you and say, 'Come with us.'"

"You were *inside* Ipatiev House the whole time?"

"Five months. It was boring. The girls were sweet, but spoiled. I spoil my wife too. Women should be spoiled, especially when they are young."

Zakov: "The Seventh Lett was also a volunteer from the factory?"

Guard: "*Nyet*, he is Lett, a foreigner from elsewhere, but would not say where."

"This Lett's name?" Zakov asked.

"OK," the guard said.

"What is it?" Zakov asked again, irritation in his voice.

"OK," the man repeated, then amended it to "Oyars Kaspars something—O. K."

"The last name?"

"I don't remember," the man said.

Zakov took two rolled cigarettes out of a tin, gave one to the man, and lit it.

"Will you blindfold me before you shoot me?" the man asked calmly.

"I do not plan to shoot you if you are honest. When did this Lett visit the Romanov sisters?"

"Only at night."

"Did he visit the Tsarina as well?"

"Don't know. She was held in a different part of the house, had her own guards."

"The Seventh Lett visited just at night?"

"*Da*, only at night, always late," the guard said.

"Where is this man now?"

The guard shrugged: "Asleep? Who knows? The man bends the stick, understand?"

Zakov would later explain the meaning of this to his partner.

Zakov answered the guard: "He is the goat in the kitchen garden."

"*Da*," the guard said, "truly a goat."

"The Seventh Lett was not part of the execution?" Zakov asked.

"He finished with the girls before midnight, and we've not seen him since."

"Was anything different that last night?"

"Only that he quit early. As I said, he was usually at them all night long." The man's chin dropped, "They are spoiled but nice girls, sweet. Sorry—were."

"Did your comrades share your feelings for the girls."

"Some did. Most wanted what O. K. was getting, but only he was granted that."

"Why and who gave him orders to do these things to the girls?"

"We don't know. Not our commander; he was very nervous around the man."

"Oyars Kaspars, that's all you know for the name?"

The man looked at the rifle barrel in his face and whispered, "Arajs. He told us this word means 'ploughman' in his language, which he called Livonian."

"The Seventh Lett is Oyars Kaspars Arajs, and the last time you saw him last night was when?"

"Between eleven and half-eleven; I'm not certain of the exact time."

"What happened after Arajs left?"

"Commander Yurovsky came and told the family to dress for a journey. He said we were all about to come under attack, and he would not sacrifice their safety in the chaos of battle. They were to be moved to a safe place."

"You heard this?"

"We all heard it."

"Were they given a destination?"

"No," the guard said, "and we were not allowed to ask questions. We dealt only with what was immediate and in front of us, not what might be."

"Who was in the shooting party?"

"Finally? I'm not sure, because I was not down there."

"Who do you *think* was in the party?" Zakov asked, continuing to press for information.

"I heard it was Yurovsky, Nikulin, Kudrin, Ermakov, Vaganov, and Kabakov."

The man hesitated here.

"Kabakov was from the Tsar's Life Guards, a monster, that one. I heard the two Medvedevs also were shooters."

"Two Medvedevs? Related to each other?"

"No. Mikhail, who also used the name Kudrin, and Pavel, was head of the Ipatiev House Guard in name only. Also it seems likely that Goloshokin, Voykov, Beloborodov, and Didkovsky were in the room. I didn't hear if they were shooters."

"There were twelve men in the liquidation detail?"

"How could I count? I wasn't there. What does it matter now?"

"You swear you were not a shooter."

"I don't murder girls," the man said. "Romanov or otherwise. Nor does the white crow, Arajs the ploughman."

"Because?"

"He took off—was not there. A weather-maker, that one." Meaning someone with influence. A white crow was an outsider.

Zakov looked at Bapcat and caught him up on the high and low points in English.

Zakov took out his pistol and pressed it to the prisoner's forehead.

"Where did the white crow go?"

"Where all men go when they are between two fires and doomed in all directions."

"Does such a place have a name?"

"Boat Mountain on the other side of the Grove of Special Fruit."

"The Seventh Lett told you this?"

"No, but this is the place that has always welcomed the lost, the dregs."

"Where is this grove that leads to this mountain?"

"Up the River Iset, beyond Aramil, toward Dolmatovo."

"Aramil?"

"Twenty kilometers south of Yekaterinburg, on the River Iset."

"Aramil is a village?"

"No, a holy man's grave and pilgrimage place, with a small chapel."

"How far from grove to mountain?"

The man shrugged.

"There's a road?" Zakov asked.

"One gets there only by rail or river. The rail runs beside the Iset. And there is a trail just inland of the rails, but this is the Urals, where nothing is easy or hospitable."

"You've been to this place?"

The man laughed. "Those who go there rarely come back."

"Get up," Zakov said, "and go back to your company. Did you help prepare the bodies?"

"I am a soldier, not an axman," the guard said. "And I'm not going back to my company. I have failed as a guard. Yurovsky would have me shot."

"What will you do?"

"Follow the wind," the man said.

"There is no wind," Zakov said.

"There is a cyclone inside my chest," the guard said.

"How many are in your security detail?" Zakov asked the obviously nervous man.

"Three, including me."

"But there were more before, yes?"

"We had sixteen inside under Avdeev, but Sacha was soft on the family and removed by Commander Yurovsky, who replaced the inside guards—all but me."

"Why were you the exception?"

"I follow orders."

"You would have shot the girls."

"No, I already told you—and I was not alone. Andras Verhas, an Austro-Hungarian soldier who came over to us, and two other men also refused to take part."

"You said all but you were replaced in the guard."

"Yes, July 4; I remember the date."

"How large was the total security detail?"

"Sixteen inside, more than fifty outside the palisades, and many more with other tasks and duties, more than five hundred in all."

"All gone now?"

"Most were ordered away before the shootings. Fewer witnesses, a matter of security after the fact, *da*?"

"You're certain Arajs left before the executions—that he was not one of the shooters."

"He was gone before midnight."

"To Boat Mountain on the other side of the Grove of Special Fruit?"

"I should think."

"Go, comrade, and do not stop until you are far away."

The guard didn't need a second invitation. He took off through the forest, leaving his rifle and ammunition behind.

Bapcat stood beside his partner. Neither spoke, until Zakov said, "Oyars Kaspars Arajs. He has fled to Boat Mountain."

"Which is?"

"A refuge for scoundrels."

The mine water was a virulent greenish-brown, streaked with gray contrails and pink lily pads floating on the top film. The lily pads turned out to be patches of swollen human flesh, pink as boiled shrimp. Severed limbs floated like small boats scattered from their moorings by an angry wind.

Zakov sighed, whispered, "Nothing more to be done here."

"We're going to leave them, like *this*?" Bapcat said.

"They are beyond our help, Lute, and beyond pain now . . . at least, any pain *we* might know."

"Our mission is done?"

"Not quite," Zakov said.

"Now what?" Bapcat asked out loud, knowing full well he would get no answer from his partner.

Jordy intercepted them as they left the watery grave.

"Visitor," Jordy whispered, and gestured toward the grassy area of Four Brothers.

They followed him, and after five minutes saw a gray figure hunched down in the grass, a bear, perhaps, looking for wild berries? The figure clawed like a bear in the Keweenaw, feeding on lowbush blueberries.

When its head popped up, Bapcat gasped. "Dodge!" Then, aloud, "No berries here, Major."

Major Dodge looked up from his hands and knees as his left hand grabbed for his revolver.

Jordy growled, "I hope you're planning on cleaning that weapon, Major. Otherwise you're going to die right there on your knees." The sergeant racked a round into the chamber of his rifle.

"No call for such animosity, Sergeant. You startled me." The marine refastened his holster strap.

"You've been gone a long time," Bapcat told Dodge, who got to his feet and brushed off his trousers with his left hand, his right hand balled into a fist by his belly.

Bapcat said, "Sergeant, let's see what the major has in his right hand."

Jordy reached, but Dodge kept his fist closed.

"You forget who commands here!" Dodge snapped.

Zakov pointed his rifle at the marine. "Open your hand, Major."

"Zakov," Dodge said. "I should have known."

"How did you find this place?" Zakov asked.

"Nothing in this country is wholly or permanently a secret."

"Open your hand," Zakov said. "Now."

Jordy took the major's hand and held it open. There were three small opaque stones in his palm.

Dodge said, "Diamonds and topaz."

The sergeant searched the man's pockets, found a small leather pouch with a dozen more stones, all uncut diamonds, some pea-sized, a couple as large as acorns.

Bapcat asked, "*These* are in your mission brief, Major?"

"War souvenirs?" Jordy quipped.

"War reparations," Dodge came back.

"For whom?" Zakov challenged. "The United States and Russia are not at war."

"American supplies and weapons are here. These need to be paid for. The Russians owe us. In addition, the Russians pulling out of the war against the Germans caused the president to speed up the deployment of US troops to France."

Zakov said derisively, "You think raking taiga grass with your hands will recover the country's expenses? You are a blind optimist, Major. Or a damn fool. We shall call you Quixote. How did you get here?"

"I walked."

"And miraculously came exactly to this very secret place. I don't believe in coincidence, or lucky guesses."

Dodge told them, "The Bolos are on their way back and will be here any moment. We can't be here when they return."

"Who is *they*?"

"Yurovsky."

"Why would this Yurovsky come back here?"

"Evidence remains," Dodge said. "There is dissatisfaction with the disposal operation. The remains are to be moved."

"Remains? You've seen them?" Bapcat asked. "They are hardly remains—only body parts."

Zakov asked, "How many are with Yurovsky?"

Dodge shrugged. "He won't be alone."

"There was a five-hundred-man security force at Ipatiev House. Where are they now?"

"Who knows? Most likely they were scattered to fighting units to confront the Czech Legion," Dodge said, adding, "There is only one guard here."

"There were three," Bapcat said.

"Now there's just one," Dodge said. "I took care of two."

"You have astonishingly detailed information, Major."

"I know how to blend. A professional chameleon, you know?"

"Especially if you are one of them," Bapcat said.

"Mind your mouth, Captain. Here is here and there is there, and this there-there has different rules than the here-here back there."

There-there and here-here? Dodgian drivel.

Bapcat said, "Did you find other reparations in Tobolsk?"

Dodge nodded. "Some. Nicholas and his family left Tsarskoye Selo with considerable 'assets.'"

"And now you are cleaning up behind the royal family," Zakov said.

"As best I can," Dodge said. "The Reds are doing the same."

"You have so many interesting details in hand," Bapcat pointed out, his voice thick with skepticism.

"I am a professional in the game," Dodge said.

Zakov jumped in, "So claim *kriminal'nyi, Blatnoi mir Russkii*—the Thieves Society."

"I am a soldier, not a criminal," Dodge said firmly.

Zakov said, "I smell *zapolo*." He translated the word for Lute: shady business.

"Our mission is complete," Bapcat told the major.

"Only I will decide that," Dodge said.

"You are both wrong," Zakov said, ending the discussion.

Minutes later Anton and Crazy Ivan came running and the soldier told Zakov, "There are lorries headed this way."

Lorries, Bapcat thought. Why not just say trucks?

Zakov didn't react. "Is Second Brain at crossing station number 185?"

"Above it a *verst* or two," Ivan said, and pointed. "Our direct path to it is that way," he added, pointing west, "or do we stay and fight?"

Zakov smiled at his old friend.

"Fish seek a deep place, men a better place. Let us go to Second Brain now. We are done here."

"I'm not," Dodge said. "I'm staying. Seconds count."

"As you wish," Zakov told the American marine.

"What the hell is Second Brain?" Dodge asked.

Anton grinned, said, "Choo-choo," and made a dirty hand gesture as he scampered away with the other three.

Bapcat saw relief finally sweep over Jordy's face.

30

Summer, 1918. Near Rail Crossing Station No. 185

"You are Trotsky, Signalman Elpikovny."

Ivan and Anton led them across the tracks and around a sharp curve, beyond where Second Brain awaited them, and into the forest, which gave them cover on their way back to the train. When they saw the engine, Ivan left the others inside the tree line and waved his rifle at the train. Someone in the engine waved a small green rag—their signal to approach.

The five of them ran, and as they got closer Bapcat looked under the carriages and saw that a group of men had gathered on the other side. Bapcat tapped Zakov, who grunted "I see them" as they ran on, hurriedly climbing aboard past two of Ivan's guards.

"Trouble on the other side?" Ivan asked his men as he leapt up.

"They demand to talk to Trotsky."

Bapcat couldn't understand the exact nature of this exchange, but the name *Trotsky* was clear enough.

The five of them were aboard and making their way back to the caboose, where some of Ivan's men were gathered, watching and listening.

Elpikovny was clad in his black leathers and standing on the caboose platform, talking and gesturing to a crowd of haphazardly armed men. Elpy had on his pointed red leather hat, his arms stretched out like God on high.

Zakov told Bapcat to stand back, and he stepped out behind the signalman, who did not turn around to acknowledge him.

Bapcat could see the men at the back of the mob, and it looked like they were listening intently.

Zakov intermittently stepped inside to report.

Said Zakov, "They are rapt, and Elpikovny has them in the palm of his hand, hanging on his every word. As Trotsky, our signalman tells them, 'Disband and hide. Comrades, my brothers in arms. Kolchak is fast approaching and will capture Yekaterinburg. It could even be tonight! We lack the strength to resist Kolchak and his barbarians. They are many more than us, perhaps sixty thousand, all trained, all veterans.'"

Elpy's little speech brought protests and questions from the assemblage, which Zakov relayed: "'How will we stop them?' one man calls out, and Elpy answers, 'You won't and can't stop them. Those who do not go to ground immediately must hurry north and west to join the main arm of our army, which is rallying this way.'" Zakov grinned and continued. "Another man asks, 'Shouldn't we just wait here for them?' And our Elpikovny answers scornfully: 'They will find you and kill you here. You must go north to the gathering force. The Whites will hunt you down here. Do not linger with your decisions, comrades. The Motherland is under attack from without, and only we together can push these monsters back.'"

Zakov shook his head.

"Another man shouts, 'Our commanders ordered us to hold and fight.' Our Trotsky laughs derisively at the man. 'And where are these illustrious commanders who give such orders. Are they here among you?'"

Bapcat heard not a sound from the gathering, and Zakov reported in a whisper, "Our little Trotsky answers his own question, 'Of course they are not here. They are in their safe HQs, packing and getting ready to run while you die at the hands of the invaders, which will buy time for your leaders to escape with their families and treasure. This is a new day, comrades. We Communists are all equal. We do not recognize arbitrary rank. We elect our commanders from our own ranks, and we all run the same risks and share the glory and potential rewards.' A superb speech and conclusion," Zakov told them.

Then another man yelled out and Zakov reported, "A Yekaterinburger points out, 'But Trotsky is commander, and *he* is not elected.' Elpy laughs and roars, 'Trotsky is appointed and elected by Comrade Lenin, and yes, I am the commander of the armies, but I do not hide in safety. I am like a turtle. My headquarters is wherever I am, this train, my boots, they are the traveling fortress. Where I am, decisions are made by me, and I am telling you again, comrades, go north and west and join us for the fight to come. Your leaders here are worthless. Go now and tell anyone you meet that you have seen Trotsky, and he has ordered all soldiers north. Take everyone you can find with you. If they don't have weapons now, they will be given them when you reach our army.'"

Elpy's speech done, Bapcat watched the crowd nod with grim, determined faces.

Elpy repeated, "Go now, comrades. Seek the army. You will be welcomed."

A new voice called out, and Zakov translated. "'But where will you go, Comrade Commander?'" And then Zakov whispered Elpikovny's reply: "'I go southeast to rally and warn others. All of you must keep moving. You will soon see me again, and make no mistake, comrades. With your great courage and skill, we shall prevail!'"

The irregulars cheered lustily, and Elpy yelled a command, translated by Zakov: "North, comrades, go north—go north *now*!"

"We want to kill the enemy now," a voice shouted.

"And you shall, comrade, you shall help them die in their misanthropic, antisocial cause. Go north, comrades, go now!"

The crowd of fifty or so lingered for a while before they moved off, paralleling the tracks.

Only when the group had disappeared into the distance did Elpy step inside the caboose and throw aside his leather hat. His head was drenched in perspiration.

Zakov greeted the man with a hug.

"You are Trotsky, Signalman Elpikovny. You should be an actor."

"We are all actors," Elpikovny said with a slight smile. "Sometimes we are given large roles, and often they are small, but all roles matter in this theater of life."

Zakov grinned from ear to ear.

"And a philosopher too! You are a man of many hidden talents."

"In Russia all men are onstage all the time, a stage that moves and sways and changes under our boots—and in any event, I would rather be a chief engineer than the great Fyodor."

A smiling Zakov looked at Bapcat, Anton, and Jordy, and told them that Fyodor Volkov was the great tragedian, founder of Russia's first public theater—in many minds, the father of all Russian actors and drama.

"The theater in Yaroslavl was named for him seven or eight years ago."

Bapcat blinked. Had Elpy, in fact, been an actor before becoming a railroad man? The Russian onion again: Peel a layer, find what lies underneath.

"Are we returning to First Brain?" Elpy asked Zakov.

"Eventually. Right now I'm more interested in conditions between here and Dolmatovo."

Bapcat saw Elpy's face freeze. This had obviously caught him off guard.

"Are you joking?" the signalman asked.

"I'm quite serious," Zakov answered in English.

"Nobody goes willingly to Dolmatovo. It is a mining district, mountainous, outrageous, unpredictable weather, a place full of antisocial creatures, violent outlaws, grass bandits."

"Good," Zakov said. "You know the place. How might we get there from here? I understand there is a railway along a river."

Elpy answered, "We follow this line to Aramil, south of Yekaterinburg, and then we take the Sverdlovskaya Line eastward—if the tracks are in repair. The bandits are famous for derailing their victims."

"How far?" Zakov asked.

"One hundred and sixty *versts*, I should think."

"You've made this run?"

"On occasion," Elpy said.

Bapcat wondered about his answer, which seemed tentative.

"How far from Aramil to the Grove of Special Fruit and Boat Mountain?"

Elpikovny sneered. "Not as far as Dolmatovo, and an even worse place once you are there."

"I've not heard a distance," Zakov came back.

"Not quite halfway between Aramil and Dolmatovo."

"You say you have traveled this route?"

"I have traveled it," the signalman said.

"Not happily, from your tone and sour face," Zakov said.

The signalman frowned. "It is a place of *straniki*. It is *antisanitarnyi, nemadeshnyi, polumerdvyi, khsoticheskii, likhoi mrachnyii*."

Zakov replied matter-of-factly and calmly. "I hear what you say: There are wanderers, it is unsanitary, insecure, dark, half-dead, chaotic, and evil. Please explain to me how any of that is even remotely different from here and now, or from anyplace else in our country these days?"

Elpikovny made a fist and shook it. "This is not a place one goes to if one wishes to remain alive."

"Can you take us or not?"

Elpy closed his eyes. "If you order it."

Zakov said, "So ordered. Good. Now let us get underway."

"The Chief Engineer needs to know where we're going," Elpivovny said, peeling off his leather garb.

"He will, eventually—if we don't all die," Zakov told the signalman.

"This is not a place to joke about," Elpy said unhappily.

"Ah, I am disappointed," Zakov said. "I have heard Trotsky is famous for his bonhomie, his legerdemain, his sense of humor."

"No doubt," the signalman said, "but I am *not* Trotsky," and headed for the engine cab.

31

Deep Summer, 1918. Beyond the Grove of Special Fruit

"Now we are in the real unreal Siberia."

The rail siding struck Bapcat as odd, the tracks at a 30-degree angle off the main line and pointed at tall rock walls stretching beyond into a leaden sky. Only a narrow black cleft broke the clean line of the massif, a notched opening that looked like someone had made an attempt to run rails into the mountains and given up.

Elpy had been unusually pensive and reserved since his Trotsky performance, and edgy, which was even more unusual. Bapcat was curious, but decided to let him be.

With the train stopped and on the siding, Zakov assembled his company in the caboose before they dismounted and walked to the cleft between the gray cliffs.

Elpikovny remained behind, standing with his arms crossed and speaking only in clipped English. He told them, "Look around and down, at what you are walking on."

The path to the opening was pale white, chalky.

"Through there," Elpy said, "is *Shlyupka Gora*, Boat Mountain. It is at the end of the white way, which you must stay on. If you get even slightly off the path, you will violate the Holy Grove's taboos. Nothing can help you then. This place is not Russia, not even Earth, not human—not in the least. It has been here for centuries, a kingdom within a kingdom, run by women and served by men. In charge here is a creature called *Provodnik blik.*"

Jordy stood beside his father, said, "Light conductor, or conductor of light—something like that."

Elpy said, "You must address it as *Provodnik*, no exceptions. It will call itself Mother."

Zakov said in English, "Mother? Your unease is clear and palpable, Signalman Elpikovny, and so too is our duty. We believe a man we seek is here, and we cannot complete our mission until we have found him."

Elpy said almost in a whisper, "Provodnik is mother, and now we are in the real unreal Siberia."

Bapcat did not interrupt his partner. What this jaunt had to do with their mission eluded him. The Seventh Lett was no doubt their quarry, but why? Zakov had not shared his thinking.

The group consisted of Zakov, Bapcat, Crazy Ivan, and Jordy. Zakov had asked Elpikovny to accompany them as well, but his only response had been, "Never."

"We stay on the path all the way?" Zakov asked the signalman.

"*Da*," Elpy said.

"How far to Boat Mountain?"

"I don't remember," Elpikovny said miserably.

"You've been and don't remember, or you've never been before, or you've heard from another traveler and don't remember?"

"Nobody told me anything," Elpy said. "Few who enter here ever come back."

"And how do you know this preposterous fact?" Zakov asked.

Elpy bowed his head. "I don't remember."

Zakov glanced at Bapcat and caught his eye and said nothing, but Bapcat got the message. There was something seriously peculiar here. He had never seen Elpy like this. The man was deeply spooked.

"Any final guidance, Signalman?" Zakov asked.

Elpy shook his head and whispered, "I would wish you all to go with God, but God has abandoned this accursed place."

Like Russia itself, Bapcat thought.

Not knowing why, he looked down at the path and let his mind fill with what he was seeing, and said out loud, "Bones."

Zakov and the others turned to him, and he pointed down and said, "This path is made of bones."

Elpikovny said, "See that yours are not added to them," turned, and swung back up onto the caboose's steps.

"What the heck is Elpy's problem?" Jordy asked—what Bapcat suspected they were all thinking.

"Never mind that," Zakov said. "We have work to do."

The path led them two hundred yards through dark wall shadows before it opened into a boulder-strewn valley, perhaps a quarter-mile across. The path ascended gradually through a forest of gray, leafless trees. Late summer and no leaves? Trees should be full by now, perhaps one or two early-bird leaves hinting of fall, but this valley should at least be a deep green, not the color of soot. Disease? Something else? How was this even possible?

Reading his mind, Jordy nudged his father. "What's with these trees?"

Bapcat had no answer, decided the trees were some kind of deciduous species, but what? Their bark was smooth as skin, and it looked like muscles rippling close to the surface. Seeing this, it dawned on him: hornbeam—also known as blue beech, muscle-wood—hard as stone and just as durable. What was it doing here? Usually these grew near water, on floodplains. Another Russian peculiarity.

Zakov walked slowly and deliberately up the gradually rising path, Crazy Ivan close behind him, his soldier's eyes all over the place. Jordy was in front of his father, who found himself at the rear of the small formation, where he automatically assumed responsibility for security against surprises from behind.

The path continued to be of compressed dry bones. As they hiked, Bapcat soon saw piles of bones underneath the trees, including what looked like human skulls. What in the world? An ancient burial ground? Some tribes in the Dakotas placed their dead on platforms so that wild things could feed on them.

Further on he saw human remains hanging from tree branches, the flesh of the desiccated remains wrinkled yellow-brown by time, and as he scanned, he saw shredded ropes, dozens, perhaps hundreds of them, hanging from branches in the heavy air. Some of the remains showed an odd purplish color to the dried flesh, some not yet wrinkled and smooth as a baby's skin.

He and Colonel Roosevelt had once come across a prospector who'd hung himself in the Flair Hills, not far from the outer reaches of the Colonel's ranch. The body had been hanging six months and looked a lot like what he was seeing now.

The higher they climbed, the more bodies they found, none looking recent or fresh. The path continued on a straight line, but after thirty minutes of walking they hit a small plateau, and the path began to bend slightly.

Suddenly Anton was at his side, grabbing at his hand and trying to pull him.

"Come," the boy insisted, "Come. I show you."

Bapcat stopped. "You're supposed to be in the train with Elpy."

Anton tugged on his hand. "Come, come—I know this place."

"You know *this* place?"

"Mother sold me to Kunikya."

"Slow down. This is the mother who sold you? This is where that happened?"

"Yes, Mother here, not birth mother who is dead. Nobody must stay on this path. Too dangerous."

Bapcat shook his head and said, "Elpy told us to not leave the path."

But he couldn't let go of of what Anton had just said:

Mother, not your birth mother, who is dead

"Elpikovny doesn't know what Anton knows. *Lovushkas krytyt, zasada, pohyat?*" The boy called in an anguished squeak, and Jordy came back to his father.

"Go back, Anton. This place isn't for you," said Jordy.

The boy's voice turned deep. "*Lovushka krytyt, zasada, pohyat,* understand?"

Jordy stared at the boy, "*Where?*"

"*Da, zasada.*"

Jordy translated for the boy. "He says there are hidden traps ahead and an ambush."

"How can he know that?"

Anton spoke for himself. "Because I was here. I know this place. Not safe on this road. Must get underground."

"What underground?" Jordy asked.

"Caves, rooms, roads, rivers."

"Under here?"

The boy nodded, "Everywhere, starting soon. We must get off this road *now!*"

Zakov joined them.

"What's holding us up?" When he saw Anton, he said, "You! What are *you* doing here, boy?"

The boy and Zakov went at each other in frantic Russian, and when they were finished, Zakov said, "The boy will lead. Jordy and Ivan, stay close. Lute, drag point."

Bapcat would continue to secure the rear, but put some space between the others and him so that he could guard his rear and any attack against the six o'clock position of the others.

Anton led them to an opening beyond a tree full of human remains.

"If there are bones, there is an opening close by," the boy explained.

The tree of bodies was redolent of rancid hay. The opening was a narrow squeeze ten or twelve feet along smooth canary yellow sandstone, into a large room. There was another path just like the one outside, paved with chalky bones.

Zakov whispered to the boy, who said, "Women make all decisions here. Some men are welcome, but must pay their way in."

"*Pay* to get in?" Crazy Ivan said.

"They must pay a quarter," Anton piped up.

"A quarter of what," the Russian soldier asked.

"A hand or foot; each can choose."

Ivan laughed nervously. "What the hell for?"

"Protection," Anton said. "To become part of Mother's family."

Who exactly was this Mother? Bapcat wondered.

Zakov said, "Protection in the collective womb."

Bapcat wanted to get on with whatever Zakov had in mind. He did not like the closed-in feeling pressing on him. "Arajs, the Seventh Lett— he's here?"

"We shall see," Zakov said.

"Let's get on with it," Bapcat grumbled. "I don't like this."

Zakov asked, "You all right back there?"

Zakov knew his friend's discomfort in closed spaces.

Bapcat said, "We'll find out."

"You want Jordy to drop back?" his partner asked.

"No." Rear security required serious experience. He would push away the claustrophobia and keep his wits to do the job. "How far?"

"The boy says we are close. He says we should see for ourselves. There is a vista."

"Of what, more trees?" Bapcat said.

"Boat Mountain," Zakov told them, "the place ruled by *Provodnik blik*, a kingdom of women."

Bapcat asked his friend, "Why would Arajs come *here*?"

"Lifelong anonymity?"

"A high price," Bapcat said.

"Perhaps," Zakov said, and to the boy, "Show us."

The boy led them along a twisting path which suddenly turned straight.

Bapcat heard scurrying and movement around him and said in a loud whisper, "We've got company back here." He tried to see what it was, but whatever it had been was gone or had hunkered down.

"Steady," Zakov called back.

Minutes later they came to an opening above a flat, chest-high boulder. They looked out over the giant stone at a tight canyon filled with boats of all descriptions and sizes, in every imaginable condition. It looked like a pile of discards dropped from the sky by God. *Russia!*

"Bizarre," Bapcat whispered. "A place of dead boats."

"It is a city," Anton said.

It didn't feel like that to Bapcat, or like anything he had ever imagined.

32

Deep Summer, 1918. Shlyupka Gora *(Boat Mountain)*

"Ah, my favorite imp!"

"There must be hundreds of derelicts," Jordy observed. "How did they *get* here?"

Bapcat wondered the same thing.

Anton spoke up. "They steal them and bring them here," the boy said.

The others looked down at their guide.

"*Who* steals them?" Zakov asked.

"Men with the trains come, and it pays them."

An irritated Zakov came back with "Trainmen steal boats for this *Provodnik?*"

"She pays them in gold."

"Interesting," Zakov said, changing his tone.

Bapcat wondered if Elpy had been one of the trainmen selling boats to this eerie place. Or had Bezmunyi?

"What are we looking for?" Crazy Ivan asked.

"Who, not what," Zakov said. "Oyars Kaspars Arajs, the Seventh Lett."

"What's he done?" Ivan asked.

"The unspeakable," Zakov came back.

"This puts him in rather large company these days," Ivan said. "Is this Lett dangerous?"

Zakov bit his lip. "Let us assume so."

"Why do you seek this Lett?" Ivan asked his old comrade.

"To reward him."

"For what?"

"The Latvian will know."

Bapcat wondered why Zakov was singling out this one man. Arajs had not even been one of the royal family's liquidators. Zakov was sometimes difficult to understand. He had been away for a year, and by the looks of it, largely on his own. Both of them had been trappers leading solitary lives, and Bapcat knew such circumstances could take a high toll, even on a loner such as himself. New wife Jaquelle had helped him realize this.

Anton climbed the flat boulder to take a look.

"Where does the leader live?" Zakov asked the boy, who pointed at the hull of a ship

"It's the color of Noah's Ark," the boy added.

Jordy corrected him. "Nobody knows what Noah's Ark looked like, or even if it was real."

"Mother knows," Anton said officiously.

"Natural planking," Jordy said. "And caulked with pitch."

Anton grinned and pointed. "Over *there*, that one."

Bapcat tried to follow the boy's arm. "The one with three masts?"

"Yes. It calls it *tsarstvo ob tselovstyi.*"

Jordy said, "Kingdom of Kisses? Why?"

"Mother does not explain. It is *Provodnik blik*," the boy announced.

Bapcat frowned. Why was this person, apparently a woman, referred to as It, not her? Elpy had said this too.

"How long were you here?" Zakov asked the boy.

"Three years. It seemed longer."

"How do we reach the kingdom boat?"

"There are many ways, but I know all the best ones which will bring us right to the place. It won't see us until we step out."

Bapcat found the continuing reference to "It" unnerving.

"We?" Zakov asked.

"Yes. It always liked me, and seeing me will allow a short time when It will not shout orders."

"How long to reach Its place?" Zakov wanted to know. "Maybe routes have changed. It's been a long time since you were last here."

"Nothing changes down here," Anton said. "It will not allow it."

"Lead on," Zakov said.

— ∾

Was this a woman he was looking at? Bapcat had no idea.

It was a lithe, bald figure, knotted with stringy flat muscles and pale, almost chalk white skin. Sizewise, It was no larger than a child—but with unusually large hands. Strange to behold, but hardly imposing. How could such a small and insignificant creature hold such power? And over whom? He'd heard sounds and assumed people were watching them, but he'd not seen anyone since they had entered the canyon, except for the hanging dead.

It sat in a large chair with an ornately carved fan-back, a virtual throne. Its eyes moved slowly as It examined them, sniffing rapidly like a dog.

Anton whispered, "Only Colonel Zakov and I talk. The rest of you must not talk unless It talks to you through me. It never talks directly to anyone except those It allows this gift."

Anton stepped toward the throne and gestured for the others to spread out.

Bapcat's mind was racing. Where was Its security, guards, anything? This felt like a dream.

Finally It spoke, "Ah, my favorite imp!" No emotion in the voice, totally neutral, aloof emotionally.

Anton said, "You sold me, Mother."

Bapcat wondered again why It was called Mother.

"Did we get a good price," It asked.

"The goods are not told such things," Anton said.

"Probably better that way," It said.

Bapcat was puzzled. It seemed entirely focused on Anton. Had It not seen the rest of them?

"Why are you back, imp?"

"Our colonel wishes to address Mother Light, in English?"

Mother Light?

"Is this colonel-thing English?" Mother asked.

"He is Russian," Anton said.

Bapcat knew Zakov was studying the creature, who began to address him.

"You, I assume, are this colonel-thing the imp refers to. Tell me in English why the imp is not too young to be soldiering with your men?"

"Some are older than their years," Zakov said.

Anton added, "Speak to me and I will tell Mother. This must be the way."

Zakov looked at Anton, and said, "Some mature quickly and not by choice. They have it imposed upon them: grow and cope, or die."

Anton repeated Zakov's words and It said, "Yes, I do understand. What is this the colonel-thing seeks?"

"A man," Zakov told Anton, who passed it on. "We seek a man."

Bapcat was nervous, but Pinkhus Sergeyevich seemed his usual calm self.

"Why do you seek a man?" It asked.

"Justice," Zakov said to Anton.

"Mother understands justice. Who is this man you seek?"

Zakov said, "A Latvian, Oyars Kaspars Arajs."

It stared at Zakov. "What does your Latvian look like?"

"I don't know," Zakov said. "We've never seen him."

It laughed at Anton when he parroted Zakov. "You come for a man you have never seen?"

Anton looked at Zakov, who told him, "Justice is blind."

It tilted Its head to the left. "Does the colonel-thing expect Mother to parade all of her things through here?"

Zakov said, "How many things might that be?"

Anton repeated his words.

It shrugged. "I keep no count."

It waved her hand and gestured for Anton to come closer. "Who *are* these things you travel with, Imp?"

"Soldiers; my comrades. They rescued me."

"Reds or Whites?" It wanted to know.

"American," Zakov said, and Its jaw dropped.

"*Amerikanets*," she said, using the Russian word. "Should I be honored or threatened?"

Zakov said, "Tell It that our feelings are Its feelings."

It waved Anton off. "Are the *Amerikanet* things friends of the Tsar?"

"The Tsar is dead," Zakov told It. "Intimates and royal servants too."

It went silent, then asked, "When?"

"Days ago."

It closed Its baggy eyes.

It didn't know, Bapcat was sure of it.

Mother said, "And the war against the Germans?"

Zakov said, through Anton, "Russia has withdrawn and made peace with the Germans, but the war goes on."

It whispered, "Men-things start wars. Men-things fight wars and women die. Men-things are the problem, but Mother thinks the Tsarina and her big-pricked monk led the Motherland into this. It is good she is dead. She was a German-thing, not of our blood."

Bapcat sensed It was not well connected to goings-on outside this place. He eased closer to Zakov and whispered, "Ask It how often new people arrive. Arajs can't have been here that long if he's here."

Zakov looked at Mother on Its throne. "How often do you receive visitors?"

"Never," It said emphatically. "People come here to stay. We are sanctuary. There are no visitors."

Zakov said, "*We* are exceptions. We have no intention of remaining."

Bapcat's uneasiness remained high, his nerves sparking. This place felt evil.

"Your status remains to be determined," It told Zakov.

Zakov took a new tack. "Who came here just before us?"

It shrugged. "I don't keep track."

"But you used to," Anton chirped, butting in. "The Book of Mother Light—you have all new ones write their names in it."

"Clever Imp," It said. "Your memory is unimpaired, unlike your grasp of reality."

"The book is under Mother's throne," Anton said, pointing.

"You were too young to understand things you saw then, Imp. People come here to stop being who they were before they came. They sign false names."

Zakov interceded. "Arajs would have been here within the past few days."

Mother looked at Anton. "You remember where new things are kept?"

Anton nodded.

Irritated, It said, "Tell Nashivka to fetch the new ones—all of them."

Anton scampered away and came back with a surly-looking group, a dozen in all, one woman and eleven men. Nashivka was a soap-white woman of indeterminate age, a wiry, sinewy walking skeleton with black eyes that blinked furiously in the low light of Its throne room. The woman had a pinkish-orange scar that stretched all the way across her forehead. Like It, she was bald; it was clear she'd been recently shorn.

Jordy whispered to his father, "*Nashivka* means 'stripe.'"

Zakov studied the new arrivals, including the lone woman.

"The woman can step away," Zakov said.

Mother retorted, "It decides who steps aside."

Nashivka stayed put.

Bapcat stared and saw the hint of a smile on the woman's face, and then it hit him.

It was Anya! Zakov doesn't recognize his own sister?

It said in Russian, "All Latvians will step forward one pace."

All eleven men took a step forward.

Jordy said, "It asked Latvians to step forward. Can it be they are all Latvians?"

"Probably not," Bapcat said.

It was smiling benevolently.

"We seek truth here. Prove yourself to us by using your native language. If you try to fool us, you will be taken to the trees immediately."

Mother pointed to the nearest man. "You first."

The man shook his head, said, "*Nyet*," and stepped back.

Bapcat was taken off guard. All had declared they were Latvian by stepping forward. Now this one was taking it back. Was the step-out some kind of prisoner's gamble?

The second man stepped back, but the third one remained steadfast.

Bapcat wondered how Mother would determine if the man's Latvian was legit? He knew some Latvians in the Keweenaw, from the mines and the farms, and knew a few words of the language, but there was no way he could tell if someone truly spoke the tongue.

Jordy raised an arm and looked at Anton. "May I speak, Mother?"

Anton passed on the request.

"Why should you?" It asked back.

"I speak Latvian."

"How well? This is a foul thing to Mother's ear."

"Well enough to know if it is real," Jordy said.

It waved its hand. "They're yours, boy-thing. Fail, and we shall have you treed."

Bapcat lurched at these words. Who the hell was this demented creature?

Jordy looked at the third man and said, "*Tu runa latviski?*"

The man paused, said, "*Es esmu pilsitga dzimus, i Riga.*"

Jordy said, "He claims he's a city boy, born in Riga."

To the man he said, "*Sarkana vai bolta?*"

The man came back, "*Esmu patriots.*"

"He says he is a patriot," Jordy told the others.

"Ask him who his president is," Zakov directed.

"*Kas ir jusu prezkleuts?*"

The man answered haughtily, "*Oku pejayi kruviga. Mums nav prizidenta. Krievi mus aiznem.*"

Jordy interpreted. "He says he has no president as long as Russians occupy his country."

Jordy looked down the line at the eight remaining men, asked in Russian who wanted to try next. No takers. They all took a step back.

Jordy looked to Zakov for direction.

"Ask him who is responsible for his country's occupation," Zakov said.

Jordy looked at the man. "*Kas ir at bildigs par jusu valsts nodarbos anos?*"

The man answered, "*Jas anas Romanovs.*"

Jordy said, "He says it was the fucking Romanovs."

Stepping closer, Jordy said, "*Vai esat at bildigs par niko lassu un vina gimeni?*"

"*Vairs nav,*" the man answered, smirking.

Jordy told Zakov, "I asked him, Even Nicholas and his family? And his answer was, 'No longer.'"

Jordy turned back to the Lett, asked, "*Ka tu vairs?*" Then, translated, "What do you mean by no longer?"

"*Nikolajs un vina prostitute atteicas.*"

"The man tells me, 'Nicholas and his whores abdicated,'" said Jordy.

Zakov said, "Keep pressing him. Why are they whores?"

Jordy said, "You have loose language. How can you know they are whores?"

This brought another smirk. "*Mans gailis nekad nav.*"

Jordy said disgustedly, "He says his cock never lies."

"What is the meaning of all this?" Mother demanded with a growl.

"Tell It what you saw in the House of Special Purposes," Zakov instructed.

Jordy did not even attempt to talk through Anton, and instead, spoke directly to It. He described the murders in the basement room.

It listened impassively.

Zakov took over. "The Lett we seek did not take part in the murders, but every night for months he came to the rooms of the daughters and had his way with them."

It pushed out a cheek with her tongue. "Had his way with them? On orders from whom?"

"We don't know," Zakov answered.

"Did they submit willingly, welcome his attention?"

"No."

"Are you certain this is the thing you seek?" It asked, then added, "This thing understands English. I watched its eyes."

Bapcat was startled. Mother said *its* eyes, not *his* eyes? Who was this man, the Seventh Lett? What was all this about?

Zakov turned to the man. "You speak English?"

The man blinked, rolled his eyes toward Jordy, said in English, "Better than this bumpkin who slaughters my language."

The woman who was Anya suddenly jumped on the back of Arajs, grabbed his hair, pulled back his head and slashed his throat with a long-bladed knife. Cut made, she held the head back to further open the gash and speed up the bleeding. When he had bled for a while, she let go of him, leaped to the throne, and did the same to Mother, who died without making a sound. Anya had moved like a feral cat on crippled mice.

No one spoke until a startled Jordy said, "What the *hell* is going on here?"

Zakov let loose a growl, grabbed his wild sister, knocked the knife aside, and shoved her toward Jordy. "Crazy before, crazier now!"

"She's insane," he he said to Jordy, who stumbled as he stepped back from her.

"I am not touching a crazy person. What if she has another knife?"

Bapcat grabbed Anya from Jordy, and she smiled at him, as Jordy took Anton's shoulder and pushed him forward. Until then the boy had just stood there with his mouth agape. His eyes locked on the prone figure of Mother, Its hand pressed on Its lethal wound. It gurgled hoarsely, "Take . . . them . . . to . . . trees."

"We are leaving, and we're bringing her with us. Anton, you take the lead. Get us out of here the fastest way possible, no stops. Go, go!"

Anton pulled loose from Jordy, yelped, "Follow me," and scampered into the subterranean tunnel with the others in close pursuit, the only sounds their breathing and the staccato hammering of their boot soles on the hard white path.

Bapcat was both livid and unnerved and hoped they would make it back to the train without further trouble. But when they burst up into the light in the grove, he saw dozens, perhaps hundreds, of people dodging through the trees, all holding weapons: axes, spears, knives, clubs, or rocks. They were coming through the dead woods in total silence. Their hair was long and wild and they wore no clothes.

As he ran Bapcat saw the trail start to enter the cleft between the two cliffs, and he heard a mass snarl from the armed crowd as some began moving to cut them off at the exit point. Running behind the others, he saw that five pursuers were past, moving along the path. He used the barrel and stock of his rifle to hammer three other challengers who tried to block and grab him. Second Brain should have been but a short sprint from here. They should have been able to make it with time and space to spare.

But as Bapcat cleared the path and looked ahead, he saw no train. *What the hell?*

He immediately looked west and saw the black nose of a locomotive on the main track, not Second Brain, but another train, and from it, sinewy streams of men in green uniforms all brandishing rifles. As Bapcat watched, the green soldiers began to open fire and he ducked instinctively, only then realizing the uniformed men were firing at their pursuers.

He looked left and saw Second Brain, at least two hundred yards east of where they had dismounted earlier.

What was Elpy doing? Why the hell had he moved the train? *Damn Russians!*

The six sprinted to the train and clambered aboard. Bapcat arrived last, and as soon as he was on the caboose platform, he heard Zakov yell at Elpikovny, "To First Brain, as fast as we can get there."

Elpy gawked at Anya. "Is this lady with us now? What happened to her hair?"

"Move the bloody train!" Bapcat shouted.

Jordy said, "I'll help," and the two of them headed forward.

Zakov and Bapcat watched the soldiers slaughtering the pursuers from the grove.

"Who are they?" Bapcat asked Elpy.

"Czechs. The Legion is here. I thought they were more to the south and east of us. I think they will reach Yekaterinburg sooner than we anticipated."

Five *versts* to the west they stopped the train. Crazy Ivan and his men laid demolition charges under the tracks where a bridge crossed a stream that ran north to south at the bottom of a deep chasm. When the charges went off, most of the timber bridge fell in a heap as they continued west to rendezvous with the Chief Engineer and the rest of their crew, on First Brain.

Bapcat looked at Zakov. "The train was not where we left it."

"I saw," Zakov said, and left it at that.

Anya stood nearby, caressing her bald head. She looked at Bapcat. "They shaved it," she said, almost like she had just noticed.

"Better your hair than your throat," he told her.

She dismissed him with a loud puffing sound.

Part IV: Back to Beyond

The only thing that makes battle psychologically tolerable is the brotherhood among soldiers. You need each other to get by.

—*Sebastian Junger*

33

Late Summer, 1918. Yekaterinburg

Bezmunyi said, "I have been thinking our most promising escape route is north."

Bapcat saw something in Bezmunyi's face and demeanor he'd never seen before: a hint of panic, raw fear. Why? Zakov seemed to sense it, too, as the three of them gathered in the cab of First Brain while Ivan and Jordy were seeing to securing Zakov's sister. Elpikovny was out completing tasks to ready them to move.

The Chief Engineer said, "Trotsky has moved south to give some backbone to the fight against the Cossacks."

"Source?" Zakov asked. "Is his army with him?"

"My wife, and no. She says he is moving between armies, trying to organize and inspire them, and changing generals as needed. His northern army is driving east toward Yekaterinburg, but he is not there to lead it. The army's drive toward here is designed to block and turn back Kolchak and his legion."

Zakov said, "Some of Kolchak's forces are driving due west. We saw them. Tell him, Lute."

Bapcat explained to the engineer what had happened after they learned the Romanovs were dead. He did not mention Zakov's sister killing the Seventh Lett Arajs and the creature called Mother, but he did relate how the green-uniformed Czechs had gone after their pursuers, something that lingered in his mind and still made no sense.

How could the Czechs not have seen the emblem on Second Brain? Trotsky's shield was showy and gaudy, something people immediately noticed and remarked on. Why had the Czechs not attacked Second Brain? There had to be a reason, and his not knowing ate at him, but he had not yet discussed his concern with Zakov.

"The Czechs probably saved us," Bapcat concluded.

Zakov looked at the engineer. "Your wife is in regular contact with Trotsky?"

"There is no schedule, nothing regular. Trotsky talks when he chooses, to whom he chooses. He prefers face-to-face over wires, or wireless, which he keeps brief, and to the point."

"Tell us again why Trotsky has gone south," Zakov said.

"Yesterday," Bezmunyi said.

"Not when," Zakov said, "Why?"

It seemed unlike the engineer to be confused, Bapcat thought. What's on his mind?

"*Da*," the Chief Engineer said. "Trotsky is dissatisfied with the lack of leadership in the south and wants to instill some backbone by leading them for a while."

"Your wife had a wire to this effect yesterday?" Zakov asked.

"The wire said only that he was south. She inferred the rest from the wire and previous conversations."

Guessing at motives and actions? Bapcat wondered. This was disturbing. As a game warden he had acted similarly, but the stakes of failure were far less than they were here.

Zakov continued his questioning. "Other than yesterday, when did your wife have her last wire from Trotsky?"

Bezmunyi was looking less wild-eyed. Was this all that had been on his mind? Bapcat focused on the engineer's eyes and hands. Anxious people often showed nervousness in their hands. His were still.

"More than a week ago," the engineer said. "He was still north then, near Kotlas."

Bapcat cut in. "Yesterday your wife wired you in the early afternoon. Did Trotsky wire her too?"

"They exchanged wires. She wired me afterward."

Bapcat's heart was racing, but he told himself to remain calm.

He thought back to two days ago, when Elpikovny-as-Trotsky told a crowd of Bolo irregulars near the Four Brothers site that Trotsky had gone south. How the hell had he *known* this? And yesterday the signal-man had moved the train after dropping them. Why? For that matter, why had he parked the train so far north of crossing station number 185?

Bapcat continued in a soft voice. "Chief Engineer, what communications capability does Second Brain have?"

Bezmunyi said, "First Brain has a printing press. Trotsky prints his own news as he travels. They have the same telegraphy equipment, except that First Brain can be hooked to a wire from more than a hundred meters, but Second Brain has to be operated close to the pole. Someone has to climb the pole and do the key work there. First Brain has an on-board connection in the communications carriage."

Bapcat closed and rubbed his eyes. "Where is the wire and wireless equipment on Second Brain?"

"Through a metal box mounted above the engine catwalk, just forward of the cab," Bezmunyi said. "First Brain has a metal bridge that can be stretched to a pole for the technical hookup. Second Brain has to send someone to the ground, then up the pole."

There was no pole where the signalman dropped them yesterday, but there was a pole almost next to the engine when they came running back. Had Elpikovny moved the train to be closer to the pole, and if so, why? At Four Brothers, the train had not been parked at the crossing shack, but north of there, around a bend, and he seemed to recall that there had also been a pole close by that location, as well.

Damn. Was Elpy talking to someone? Who, why, and what about?

Careful now. "How long have you known Elpikovny?" Bapcat asked the engineer.

"Years—a long time."

"Did you work together east of Yekaterinburg in those years?"

"No, we were on separate lines in those days. I was on the Trans-Siberian run, and he, on shorter lines."

"Have you ever heard of Boat Mountain?"

Bezmunyi got a crease above his eyebrows. "What about it?"

"Could you find it, if we asked?"

"Possibly. I would have to study the maps and talk to some people. I don't know it offhand."

Bapcat told the engineer what had happened there, and how Elpy had taken them to the location and repeatedly warned them away from it.

Bezmunyi looked at Zakov. "This is true?"

"My partner always tries to speak the truth."

"You're certain the train was moved?" the engineer asked.

Both men nodded.

"Why is all of this important?" Bezmunyi asked.

Bapcat inhaled. "Elpikovny knew Trotsky was moving south. He told the Bolos at Four Brothers twenty-four hours before Trotsky informed your wife."

A shadow crossed the engineer's face. "Let us talk to Elpikovny and clarify this."

"No," Zakov said, much to Bapcat's relief.

Bezmunyi gulped air. "What exactly are you proposing?"

"Our mission is complete. It's time for us to leave."

"Where is Major Dodge?" the engineer asked.

"Scavenging," Bapcat said.

Bezmunyi didn't understand, and Zakov said *v musore*, but the engineer still seemed confused.

"He is searching for treasure," Bapcat tried.

"What treasure?" the engineer wanted to know.

Zakov shrugged. "Who can say what's in a human heart?"

"Is he joining us or not?"

"Maybe he will, maybe he won't."

"Bad luck for him if he misses us," the engineer said.

"Bad luck and good luck push the same sleds," Bapcat said.

Bezmunyi grinned. "You know Russian proverbs?"

"I've heard some of them from Zakov."

"Forget Dodge for now," Bezmunyi said. "I have been thinking our most promising escape route is north. Trotsky's army is battling in the south, and he is no longer on the Sixth Red Army front between Kotlas and Archangelsk. My wife will clear routes for us. Once we're through Kotlas, we should be able to connect to American soldiers."

Zakov was rubbing his chin and pointy beard. "It is August, and Kotlas is what, almost seven hundred *versts* distant?" To Bapcat he said, "About four hundred and fifty miles, crow-fly. It will be much longer by rail."

"Can we go more directly on foot?" Bapcat asked.

Zakov answered, "Easier in winter than in summer, when it is all one massive, endless bog. And on skiis and snowshoes, only at certain times in winter."

The Chief Engineer continued, "Even God cannot defeat a Russian winter."

Zakov said, "We shall not fight winter, Chief Engineer; we will flow with it."

"You have not seen Russian winter."

Zakov smirked. "I grew up in Russia. *You* have not seen winter in the Upper Peninsula of Michigan, where snowfall is beyond your imagination. Let us spend some time with a map and then talk by wire with your wife. Is the line secure with her?"

"Yes," Bezmunyi said. "What about Elpikovny? Are you saying he's an enemy? How could that be? I have known him for years. I trust him completely. He has earned it."

Zakov looked at his partner. "How can he be a Red if he sent the Czechs after our pursuers? Why would the Czechs listen to him?"

"I don't know," Bapcat had to admit. "I know it makes no sense."

"What are your instincts telling you?" Zakov asked his friend.

Bapcat's intuition about unspoken things was often correct, later proven when all facts were brought to light. He said to the Chief Engineer, "We shall keep watch on our signalman. I know he is your friend and colleague, but there is no time here for emotion. Many lives ride on this."

"But Elpikovny wants to go to America."

"He claims he does," Bapcat corrected.

Zakov changed directions again. "Tell us again why your wife thinks north is the way out."

Bezmunyi said, "The Americans and British are trying to link with the Czechs to break Trotsky's defense, but fighting north of Kotlas is almost impossible this time of year. Too hard to move. Trotsky has left only a token force up there and sent the main of his Sixth Red Army east, toward here."

Zakov thought for a moment. "Where exactly are Trotsky's forces now, relative to here?"

"I don't know," Bezmunyi said, "but my wife will help."

"Have the United States and England declared war on Russia?" Bapcat asked.

"My wife will know," the engineer said.

"We need to know now," Bapcat said.

Could Americans and Brits be fighting the Bolos without war being formally declared? What risks were they going to run if they killed Russians in open fighting and were captured?

Turning to another thought, he said, "You promised First Brain to Crazy Ivan after he helped us."

Zakov said, "And he shall have it as soon as we are done with it."

"His fight is here, not in Kotlas," Bapcat said, knowing only that Kotlas was somewhere far north of them.

"He will have his train when it is time," Bezmunyi echoed.

Zakov said to the engineer. "Ask your wife where Sixth Red Army elements are deployed now. Where are they headed, where are their forces deployed in and around Kotlas, and how far have American and British forces advanced south? We shall ask her for answers after we three study the maps and get some sense of what we are dealing with in terms of raw geography."

Bapcat wondered how many people they were going to attempt to move to the United States, and how many would survive, realistically. Before this moment, such a thing had been just words in the air; now it was about to become reality, and he did not like how it set heavily on his head and belly.

34

Late Summer, 1918. Yekaterinburg

"How exactly do you plan to connect with our invisible man?"

They had been poring over terrain charts and railway maps for the better part of three days. As Bapcat sat with his partner and the Chief Engineer, his mind was troubled. Something was weighing on him.

Finally he called Zakov and Jordy outside. They stood on the platform between the caboose and Second Brain, smoking. They could see Crazy Ivan's men on both sides of the train, providing security.

"You look perplexed," Zakov told his partner.

Bapcat got to the point. "We can't leave without Major Dodge."

Zakov said, "We don't know his agenda, his mission, or even his loyalty, assuming any of those apply. Do you doubt that the man would leave you and Jordy?"

He couldn't answer the question. Bapcat looked at his partner and his son.

"What I know is that we arrived here as a unit and he got us to you. We can't ignore that and just up and leave without checking on him. Is he hurt? Does he need our help? He deserves to know that we are ready to go north and home."

"How exactly do you plan to connect with our invisible man?" Zakov asked.

"I'll start at Four Brothers and see if I can pick up his trail from there."

"It's been days," Zakov reminded him. "Finding him is a long shot at best."

"Better a long shot than no shot," Bapcat replied.

"They may be the same thing in this instance," Zakov said. "We can't sit here waiting for him indefinitely. When Bezmunyi's wife tells us we have to move, we'll have to move."

"I want time to look for him," Bapcat insisted.

"How long?" Zakov asked.

"At least forty-eight hours," Bapcat said.

"Starting when?"

"Today—now," Bapcat answered. "I'll take Jordy, Ivan, and a couple of his men."

Jordy asked, "What about Anton?"

"He's a kid," Bapcat said.

"Not in Russia; not in these times," Jordy said.

Zakov said, "Children are largely invisible and can often go places some adults don't dare."

Decisions. Was it right to continually put this boy at risk? No easy answer. There was no normal life left in Russia, just time eerily passing.

"Where are the Czech forces now?" he asked Zakov.

"Estimated seven to ten days southeast of us, but this is no better than a guess repeated by the Chief Engineer's wife. It's unlikely she has access to actual current Bolo military intelligence, assuming they even have such capability, of which I have so far seen little evidence."

"They're stumbling in the dark?" Jordy asked.

Zakov smiled. "Trotsky is using a strategy of continuous maneuver to retard White Army advances, an interesting gambit when one is largely outnumbered. Hit hard at A, then move quickly and hit hard at B, so that the enemy can't get a good read on how strong you are or where or how you are deployed."

"You make it sound like a one-man war," Jordy said.

"It sometimes comes down to that. One man can get into an enemy's head in ways an entire enemy army cannot. Bezmunyi's wife reports the main Czech thrust coming north from Chelabayinsk, two hundred miles south of us."

Bapcat said, "We saw a Czech force less than fifty miles from Yekaterinburg."

"Four days ago?" Zakov said.

"Exactly," Bapcat said. "They could be in Aramil by now; we saw nothing to block them."

"Even if they are close, and no doubt they are," Zakov said, "they won't surge north into the main city until they consolidate the western probe we saw, with the main column, moving north. The Czechs are organized on the Imperial Austro-Hungarian model, meaning all decisions are taken from above and pushed downward. No local decision-making is encouraged or allowed. The local commander or soldier has little authority to make such decisions without orders from above.

"Americans are far superior in this regard, leaving most tactical decisions to the lowest operating level. This gives them flexibilities the Reds, Whites, and Czechs don't have. This means there's no way for them to exploit sudden openings and opportunities.

"Will you take Second Brain and Elpy? It will give you greater range."

Bapcat hesitated, and Zakov said, "There is an armor-plated Packard on Second Brain. Also some motorcycles, and our own petrol supplies."

"We won't need Elpikovny," Bapcat said.

"Take him. The man can fix anything, and we may need our own Trotsky to force something to a head."

Was he wrong about Elpy? Safer to be wary, but having him along would provide more opportunity to observe him.

"All right, Elpy goes. Jordy, let him know, and I'll tell Ivan."

"Anton?"

"He goes, too, but you're in charge of him."

"I'll let Bezmunyi and his wife know the plan."

Bapcat grasped his friend's upper arm. "No. Keep this information here. She doesn't need to know."

"Are you suggesting something?"

"No. I don't know. I'm just following the notion that the fewer people who know something, the better chance it will remain secret."

"Agreed. Bezmunyi wants to move us further north to provide us with more distance between First Brain and Yekaterinburg," Zakov said.

"How far?"

"Kungur—a hundred miles, one twenty, in that range."

"Roads and rail from here to there?"

"Charts show roads, but not their conditions. I'll confirm what I can about conditions with the Chief Engineer."

Bapcat looked at his son, said, "Let's get this rolling," although his mind was still on Dodge.

Where was he, and what was he up to?

35

Late Summer, 1918. Koptyaki Forest

"Which is where, this there?"

Forty-three hours after reaching the forest, the searchers were not in the best of moods. They had gone through the original burial site and talked to peasants who told them the remains had been moved elsewhere, but while they found the new place, and a half-dozen gems as well, they found no human remains. At the new site they had chased off six drunk peasants on horses and talked to at least fifty others who were in the woods or in their hovels around the forest. Only one remembered anyone who might resemble Dodge. It seemed he had been on a motorcycle, the day after they had encountered him at the original mine graves.

Elpy drove the Packard, Bapcat beside him, with Jordy and Anton in back. Crazy Ivan and two of his men drove loud German motorcycles, which roared like gray wolf pups at feeding time.

They were getting close to the time when they would have to pull the plug and head for Kungar to meet First Brain, Zakov, and Bezmunyi, but Bapcat refused to give up until they used the full forty-eight hours.

"Where can the bloody marine be?" Bapcat said, thinking out loud.

Jordy laughed. "*Chert znaet chto takol*—only the devil knows."

Anton said, "I saw *galka* soaring."

Jordy translated. "*Galka* are jackdaws, a form of Russian crow."

"Sir," Anton insisted, "*galka* like shiny things and dead things."

"Where were these birds?"

"In the forest, across the tracks from where Elpy parked the backup rail unit when it was here."

"You saw these birds today?"

"Yes, and yesterday, when we were at the old graves."

Bapcat turned to Elpy, who had been relatively quiet. "How far?" he asked their driver.

"From here? Two *versts*. Not far."

They reached the area and saw no jackdaws or any other birds. Bapcat looked back at Anton. "Both days?"

The boy nodded.

"Think you can find where they were?"

Bapcat told Elpy and Jordy to wait and took just Anton. He told the others, "We'll make it fast. When we get back, we'll make our way toward Kungur."

———

They were in a sizable natural clearing with no jackdaws, but Bapcat's nose picked up on something a hundred yards before they reached the opening.

Bapcat had Anton stand in the corner of the opening while he circled just inside the tree line. He came across a dead body in the early stages of putrefaction. It had been stripped of clothes and had a bullet hole in the back of the head.

Just another unexplained, random execution? Had this been the birds' interest? Maybe.

He examined the site. There were blood spatters on a black spruce, and he guessed the murder had happened here, not elsewhere, the body left at the site. No sign of a struggle, but he could, after carefully brushing away pine duff, make out faint impressions of footwear. Not a clear pattern, more on the vague side, which could be made by wrapping your boots in rags and such. But why?

More searching showed that some small popples had been cut and the branches cleared. There was blood here and there around the cuttings.

One of the branches seemed large enough to serve as a walking stick or a cudgel, but the others were too small.

What in the world was this about?

Bapcat began to follow the trail, which kept inside the tree line. He called to Anton, "We have tracks and a body."

The boy approached, looking down. "I don't see it."

"You don't need to. Concentrate on the tracks. They're very faint."

"Like a ghost?"

"Ghosts don't leave prints."

Bapcat positioned Anton on the outer edge of the clearing until the trail began to move deeper into the forest, and then brought the boy closer and placed him five feet right of the prints while he walked left of them, stopping several times to look and try to form a mental picture of what had gone on here.

The right print did not look normal; maybe it was even being dragged. Why? The small cuttings: A splint? Possible. Wrapping feet in rags to hide boot size and outline was an old woodsman's—and soldier's—trick.

"Do you still see them?" Anton asked.

"Faintly, but they keep going, and so shall we. We'll probably find a drunk ahead," Bapcat joked.

"Or *durki*," the boy said, "Fools."

"Drunks and fools are one and the same," Bapcat said, and the boy giggled.

What they found was a very grim Dodge.

Bapcat spied the outline of a man leaning against a windblown tree that was unique and familiar, a shape of immense size and angles that looked off-kilter, even in the best of times. The major was wearing an ill-fitting green military uniform, and a large canvas pack was on the ground, near his left leg. There was a crude splint on his leg, bound in place with cloth strips and some sort of vines with leaves still attached. The familiar pack was wrapped in braided red cord.

Bapcat got close enough to be sure it was Dodge, and when he announced himself, he saw the man flinch.

"Major?"

The marine looked up at him. "I'm busy."

The man was in his own world.

"You're obviously hurt."

"I am *not* hurt."

"Then you're doing a great impression of it. And you are in a foreign uniform."

"You're suddenly an expert on military regalia?"

"Czech, by the look of it," Bapcat added. He saw Dodge try to hide a grimace as he attempted to shift his weight.

"We ran into Czech troops east of Yekaterinburg a few days ago," Bapcat said. "Same uniforms."

"*East* of Yekaterinburg?" Dodge asked. "Moving west? How long ago, did you say?"

"Five days, to be exact, and I'm not sure they were moving west. They came from the east, that's all I can say. We didn't exactly hold a parley."

"Were they after you?"

"They had something else in mind," Bapcat said, leaving it at that. "Did you kill the man back in the clearing?"

"I found him dead and took his uniform," Dodge said.

Why a Czech uniform? This made no sense. It would make him stand out, a prime target for the Reds, and perhaps even some Whites. Unless . . . unless he *wanted* to be taken for a Czech.

Was the major's action an indication that the Czechs had taken Yekaterinburg? Was he withdrawing and trying to blend in? Why would a lone Czech be this far north at this point? Scouting, or were Czechs looking for the Romanovs' burial site?

"What happened to *your* clothes?" Bapcat asked.

"Stowed."

"Our mission here is done. We're heading to Kungur to meet our train."

"You're going north?"

"Yes."

"Assisted, perhaps, by Bezmunyi's elusive Red wife?"

Bapcat nodded. "First Brain waits in Kungur for us and for her clearance to move further north. We're on our way home."

"It would be much easier to go south," the major said. "Through Crimea."

"How did you get hurt?" Bapcat asked, ignoring Dodge's comment.

"I'm fine."

"You may be fine, but you are still hurt. You need to grab your pack and we'll be on our way. We're wasting time."

Dodge didn't move.

Anton grabbed the man's pack and tried to lift it, but got it only an inch or two off the ground before letting go. "Too heavy!" the boy yipped.

"What's in that thing?" Bapcat asked, stepping over to the pack. When he bent down to try to unbuckle the straps, he found the barrel of a pistol in his face.

"Mine," Dodge said.

"Then pick it up and let's go," Bapcat said.

"I'm not going. Just go away and leave me be. I'm fine right here on my own."

"You're staying in Russia?"

"That's none of your business."

"It *is* my business. I'm leading this mission now, and I am required to report on your location and actions."

"You do not outrank me," Dodge said.

"Nor do I want to, but you are coming with us, Major, unless you can give me a damn good reason to leave you here. Point that damn pistol elsewhere. My son Jordy has a pistol not three feet from your head."

Bapcat had watched Jordy make his way stealthily until he was almost on top of them.

"I'm not falling for that crap," Dodge said with a skeptical grin.

Jordy pulled the hammer back on his pistol and Dodge turned, looked back, and froze.

Bapcat took the marine's pistol, popped the clip, and handed it to Anton, who set it on Dodge's pack.

"I'll want that back," the major said through clenched teeth.

Bapcat shook his head and thought, we'll see about that. "What's wrong with your leg?"

"Broken," Dodge said. "Swollen—I don't dare take off the boot."

Bapcat knelt and looked. "Broken for sure. Compound?"

"Don't think so," the major said.

"There's no blood; that's good. How did it happen?"

"I had a disagreement."

"You killed the soldier we found."

Dodge shrugged. "We don't *know* he was a soldier. I know only he was wearing a Czech uniform. Could be he was a Czech or a Bolo looking to blend in when the Czechs flood into this area."

"You shot him once in the head. That sounds like an execution, not a disagreement."

"I did no such thing."

"Shall we count the rounds in your clip?"

"Wouldn't prove a thing."

"Would in my book," the game warden said.

"All right, the man was already dying when I found him."

"You put him out of his misery?"

"That's a reasonable way to look at it," Dodge said.

"Talk sense, Major," Bapcat said. "If you stay here, you'll die."

"I cannot leave," Dodge said. He looked at Jordy. "You move like a snake."

"That doesn't make me a snake," Jordy said.

"When did you break the ankle?" Bapcat asked.

"Not too long after I saw you at the mines. The Bolos came back early the next morning and moved the bodies, including more work to render them unidentifiable before reburying them. It was a fuck-up from start to finish. The second burial site is a few *versts* south of here. I found more loose jewels there, and some here when I had time to make a more careful search. I broke the ankle right after I stashed my pack. Stepped back on some uneven ground, the ankle turned, and I heard a snap, like a stick breaking, damn it all."

Bapcat looked at the major. "Can you walk?"

"Not fast, and not very damn far."

"Jordy, go cut some poles for a travois. Simple X-design, three cross braces. Lace it with vines. We'll load him in the back of the Packard. You can jump on the back of a motorcycle and Anton can ride in front with me."

"I can also ride on the back of a motorcycle," the boy volunteered.

Bapcat ignored him and sent him running to tell Elpy to bring the Packard closer to the woods.

Bapcat unbuckled the pack, flipped the top flap down, and looked inside. Pulling out a soft leather sack, he guessed it weighed ten pounds at least. It was one of three such bags. Running his hand under the sacks, he felt something heavy and smooth, got hold of it, and clumsily lifted it out into the light.

"What do we have here?"

The light in the forest was poor, but enough so that the object's dull shine gleamed.

Bapcat said, "Gold!" He dropped a gold ingot on the ground and felt around the bottom of the pack.

Dodge said, "There are ten of them, nine-point-six pounds each."

Ten gold bars? What the hell was Dodge up to?

"You've been busy. Where did you find all this?"

"The bags also contain gems from here and there, the gold from there."

"Which is where, this there?"

"Chelabayinsk."

"South of Yekaterinburg?" Bapcat said.

"Your geographic knowledge is improving," Dodge quipped. "Be careful—Russia will capture your soul, tear it out, and eat it."

"Russia captures my turds and nothing more," Bapcat said. "When were you in Chelabayinsk?"

"Some days before I saw you at the mines."

"I saw no pack then."

"It was here and not meant to be seen."

Bapcat studied the pack, saw all manner of needles embedded in the hard fabric. Black spruce, bog spruce, same as back home.

"You buried the pack in a bog," the game warden told the marine.

"Believe what you wish," Dodge said.

"I'll take your pack. Jordy will soon move you onto the travois. Grab your stick. We have a Packard waiting for us."

"How did you come by that?"

"No Fords were available." Bapcat said, glaring at Dodge. "What the hell is going on here, Major?"

Dodge sighed and exhaled. "The gold is from the Russian treasury. When Nicholas abdicated, the new Provisional government feared the Germans would take Petrograd and shipped the national gold reserves to Samara by train, and from there, by boat, to Kazan. The Czechs coming north liberated it."

"You were in this Kazan place?" This was a new name.

"No, I heard this from the Czech troops massing to join the column north to Yekaterinburg. Word of the treasure was on every tongue, and the men were not the least bit surprised that their commander Kolchak turned it all over to the local White government."

"How did you get your hands on part of it?"

"My mission was to find the gold reserve after I helped you with your mission of finding the Tsar."

"You were looking for him, too."

"Only for potential leads to the national gold."

"Did the Czechs or local Whites give you that gold as a gift?"

"They won't miss ten bars. There are at least twenty-eight railcars filled with wooden crates containing gold ingots, not to mention boxes of gems, the royal collection of crowns, currencies from more than a dozen countries, millions of Romanov family gold rubles, Romanov paper rubles, and a massive collection of rare and ancient porcelain."

Twenty-eight railroad cars?

"What's all that worth?" Bapcat asked.

Dodge looked exhausted. "Guessing three hundred to four hundred million in dollars, maybe even north of that figure."

Good grief.

"Where's this treasure now?"

"Sitting quite vulnerably in the Chelabayinsk railyard, with minimum security. I managed to liberate samples to confirm I had located it. The ingots have mint marks, which can be traced."

"*Gold* was your mission all along?"

"Aye-aye," Dodge said. "The United States has dumped millions into Russia to keep them in the war against Germany."

"Are we in this war, strictly and officially speaking?" Bapcat said.

"We've been manufacturing weapons and war materiel, shipping it mainly on British ships to Murmansk, from where it makes its way south to the war front. Or did. Now the plan is to have troops in Archangelsk. The Bolos there have been stealing from stockpiles. President Wilson secretly agreed to support the Tsar and his troops with a promise that we would be paid back. That seems to be out the window now, with Lenin's Bolsheviks running the show. Now that we know where the gold is, and that it's still intact, we can negotiate, even with the Bolos, and if they don't want to cooperate, we can force the issue and come get it."

Bapcat doubted his logic, but said nothing.

Jordy came back with the makeshift travois and together they lay the major on it. Jordy picked up the crossed poles and started forward, dragging his load.

"Hang on tight, Major," the sergeant told the man. "I'll try not to rock your boat too much."

Bapcat hoisted the treasure pack and it nearly buckled his knees. He guessed it was 140 to 150 pounds of dead weight, a tough chore for anyone. He hiked slowly behind the travois.

When they reached Kungur and the safety of First Brain, Zakov came to the Packard and looked at Dodge in back.

"You found him."

Bapcat took the pack from the trunk of the vehicle.

His partner asked, "What's that?"

"As you guessed: treasure. The major is coming home with us."

"That's mine," Dodge said, pointing at the pack.

Zakov replied, "*Mine* is a word that can include more than one's self."

36

Fall, 1918. Kungur

"Let Bezmunyi's wife's competence trump
God's blessings for what lies ahead."

"I don't like this," Bapcat told his partner.

Zakov had buried himself in old maps and charts, holding flash meet-
ings with Bezmunyi and Elpy, during which the three of them went at
each other in hushed, harsh Russian. Best as Bapcat could understand, it
revolved around what seemed to be a never-ending string of expansive yet
seemingly ambiguous telegrams and messages from the Chief Engineer's
wife. Giving up her kids and husband? Was she crazy? What was her game?

"*This*," Zakov snapped back in English, "is too wide a field of play. We
need more specificity."

"Eight days—is that specific enough? I keep remembering what
Firkles used to tell us."

"Jumping Jim? He's hardly a strategist."

Firkles was a well-known railroad man back home.

"Jim says, 'Even when you're on the right track, you'll get killed if
you're sitting still or going too slowly.'"

Zakov smiled. "Like all oracles, our friend dwells in the wide, general,
and ambiguous."

"But he has a point. We're sitting here. We need to be getting out of
this . . . country."

Bapcat wondered whether given its state, Russia could even be called
such anymore?

"What is your concern, Lute?"

"Nothing. Everything. We're sitting still, doing nothing. Do you even know how many people we have with us? Are all of them expecting us to take them back to the States, and if so, how exactly do we do that?"

Zakov looked at his friend. "Do *you* know how many people we have?"

"No."

"Perhaps you should make a count and give some specificity to your concerns."

Was his friend dismissing him with make-work?

"We have been sitting on this siding for eight days. Where are the Reds, the Whites, the Anybodies?"

"Bezmunyi's wife is keeping us informed."

"You trust her?" Bapcat asked.

"You have reason *not* to?" Zakov retorted.

"Our law enforcement experience."

"Understood, but this is more of an intelligence matter, and it takes perhaps a soldier's perspective to evaluate it properly."

"A colonel's eye, rather than a corporal's?" Bapcat said.

Zakov rattled a map. "You are a captain now, not a corporal, but all right, your point is well taken. You do understand, yes?"

He didn't, and he wanted them to get moving. He couldn't put words to what was inside him, but he had felt it many times before—in the war in Cuba, and later, as a game warden. It was an anxiety he had learned not to ignore.

Zakov looked at him. "Eight days. Are you sure it's been *that* long?"

Before Bapcat could answer, his partner said, "Not important, these eight days. It takes time and thought to solve complex problems."

Maybe so, but he'd never seen his partner stew so long over any problem back in the States.

Zakov added, "The reality is that we don't know how much time we have, much less what portion of the unknown time is more valuable than another."

Nonsense.

"I don't like feeling that I'm not involved or helping."

"You aren't helping at this juncture because you can't. We're looking at three choices, trying to narrow them, but good information is almost impossible to get. The country is in such flux that normally intelligent, rational people are acting anything but normal. Chaos turns the simplest things into complex gambles."

"I ask again: Can we really trust Bezmunyi's wife? Is her information solid?"

Zakov smiled. "You be the judge. She's told us we could sit right here for all this time because she can see rail traffic all over the country. She is tied into Red military communications and informs us that for now, this is the most advantageous place we can be."

"She told you that?"

"Not in those specific words, but her meaning seemed clear. She has to be careful what she puts on the wires, to whom, how often, and so forth. The Reds have their own snoops. The woman has limits, and she is running great risks. I truly believe she wants her children clear of this nightmare."

"Yet she will stay?"

"Captains go down with their ships. You think this is because they want that end or see no opportunities to get off alive? No; it's because it's their job to see that the crew and passengers are safely off. The Chief Engineer's wife is in a similar position, only her crew is her husband and sons."

And us. Bapcat shook his head. "It still doesn't feel quite right to me."

"You have no feel for the Russian mind. Bezmunyi's wife has her limits. We all do."

The role and motivations of the Chief Engineer's wife had been bothering him for quite a while.

"How does she keep secret her communications to us?" The technical workings of the telegraph had long eluded his understanding and interest. The technical side of most things rarely caught his attention.

"It's only one wire, yes?"

"Codes," Zakov said dismissively. "One key shared by only two people, the Chief Engineer and his wife, written down nowhere."

"Elpy doesn't know this code? How could that be? He sends and receives all the telegrams and messages."

"Sending and receiving are not the same as encoding and decoding. He sends and receives signals but has no idea what they mean. Bezmunyi decodes and reports content."

"You've watched Elpy transmit?" Bapcat asked.

"I've watched every step on our end. Both men are smooth and very fast. The limits on the process are on message length and speed, and over these things we have little or no say."

Bapcat thought about this. "Short messages are better than long?"

Zakov nodded. "Are you about done with this insipid line of questioning, or must I endure more of your emotional insecurities?"

"You know I don't do well sitting around, and I'm just trying to understand."

"Ask Elpikovny. He knows more than the rest of us about telegraphy. I hope to have our choices reduced to two by tomorrow," Zakov said and turned back to his maps.

⁓

Bapcat and Crazy Ivan shared a British cigarette, a Bronte, from a shit-brown package.

"Are we close to a decision?" the longtime Russian soldier asked.

"Are your men bored?" Bapcat asked him.

The Russian shrugged. "They are soldiers. Hurry up. Wait. Eat. Shit. No talking in ranks, smoke on command only. They act when ordered. Other times, who knows a soldier's mind?"

Bapcat was developing a fondness for Crazy Ivan, the crazy part so far not having shown itself. The man never complained and sometimes took his time answering questions, which was not what Bapcat expected from the soldier Zakov had once described as "wildly impetuous."

Ivan asked, "If we're on a train, why do we sit? I think this is mostly what is on the men's minds."

And no doubt Ivan's mind, as well, and his.

He'd been thinking about Jaquelle a lot these past days, and home. Home? He'd never thought of the Upper Peninsula as home before. Until now, it had been just another place where he'd lived and happened to be. Now it was home? How had that happened, and what did it mean? Did it matter? If they made it, it would be great to get back there. He guessed the first thing Jaquelle would do would be hand him his Krag-Jørgensen .30-40.

"You're no longer naked," she'd quip, knowing how much the carbine from the Cuban War meant to him, and how much he had relied on it. The rifle had been invaluable in Cuba, though shooting a different round than the Norwegian original. It was accurate and packed a wallop. It would be nice to get back, *if* they could get back.

No, don't think that way. *When* we get back, not *if.* Whenever that might be, as we sit here on this siding like turtles sunning on logs.

—— ——

Jordy was with Anton and the Chief Engineer's two sons, morose, stern-looking children with permanent scowls etched into their young faces. Fear or anger, Bapcat wondered, realizing that with children, these were difficult things to know. He'd had his share of both as a boy.

"The boys want to know about America," Jordy said. "Is the *chorney khleb* as good as Russia's black bread?"

"What did you tell them?"

"I didn't. I just smiled. Our Russian friends are unnerved by questions answered with smiles, or worse, answered with outright laughs."

It seemed to Bapcat that he and Jordy had begun to act more like brothers than father and son, or what he imagined brotherly behavior to be. Having grown up in an orphanage, he had never known real brothers. Later he got to know two Northern Cheyenne brothers in the Dakotas, but Indians were not the same as white men in some of their thinking. Indians had their own ways and didn't willingly share them with just anybody who came along.

"We moving out soon?" his son asked.

Ignoring his question, Bapcat asked, "How many people on the train?" Then added, "Sergeant."

Jordy Klubishar rolled his eyes. "I'll get right on that, sir."

"I can help," Anton volunteered.

"Can you count numbers higher than your fingers and toes?" Jordy threw out.

The boy was undaunted. "I can do algebra. You? Can you square seventy-nine in your head?"

"Not in my head," Jordy said.

Anton said. "I can. Anton loves numbers, and numbers love Anton. A strange old professor taught me algebra, and more."

———

Elpikovny rattled on about all manner of things telegraphic, and Bapcat could only stare at the man said to be Trotsky's twin. At times, strangers certainly seemed to take him for someone else. Did the little man have an agenda the others didn't share? Time to put some light and heat on the subject.

"You warned us about Boat Mountain and the grove."

A statement, not a question, a technique he'd learned as a game warden interviewing potential or alleged lawbreakers or people with something to hide for whatever reason.

The little signalman did not react. Not sure how to read that. Boost the pressure.

"Perhaps not your first time in that place?"

Elpikovny remained unresponsive.

"Mother told us all about how It bought boats from railroaders," Bapcat said.

The signalman finally looked up.

"It knew nothing, had no dealing with outsiders. Others did all of this on Its behalf."

Obviously there was firsthand knowledge in this declaration.

"You dealt with such middlemen?"

"As part of a train crew. The engineers back then ran several side businesses and shared only with some of their underlings and mates."

"Was the Chief Engineer such a sharer?"

"Never. This was before he and I met. Why are we talking about this? Are we going back to that accursed place? 'The dead past should bury its dead and be done with it.' That's from an American poet, I think."

Bapcat said pointedly. "You knew the Czechs were coming." From a hunch, not an established fact.

"I knew only that there was a possibility."

"But you put the train near a telegraph line."

"Habit—training."

Could it be so simple?

"How did you know it was a possibility?"

"The brotherhood, as with Bezmunyi's signals."

"Those I understood to be visual, not telegraphic."

"The telegraph is part of it sometimes. As are the codes."

"Code keys you carry in your head?"

Elpy touched his temple. "Certain ones, yes, in here."

"But you didn't warn us about the Czechs."

"The Czechs were the least of our problems in that place. I warned you about the evil in there, and I didn't know about the possibility of the Czechs until you had gone into the accursed mountain."

Sensible, believable answers. Push more, or accept? Change the subject.

"When you talked to the men at the burial site, you told them Trotsky was moving south. How could you possibly have known that? Nobody knew it then. Trotsky doesn't announce his intentions or destinations."

"Bezmunyi knew," the signalman said.

Was this believable? Undecided. Wanted to believe him.

Jordy came in. "The Chief Engineer wants us all forward."

Elpikovny, Bapcat, Jordy, Zakov, and Crazy Ivan squeezed into the engineer's cab.

Bezmunyi got to the point. "Trotsky is racing north fast. Our ally is slowing him as much as she dares, but we have to go now or risk a fight with Trotsky."

"My men will fight," Ivan declared.

"Irrelevant," Zakov said. "Trotsky will stand off many miles and rain steel on us. We can't fight artillery with small arms and warrior hearts." He continued, "Bezmunyi's wife will clear tracks ahead of us as best she can. We have looked at our options: One is to run to Zvanka and go north to Murmansk from there, but this is the longest route, and the Chief Engineer says we are the wrong gauge to operate on that line, so that option is out."

None of the men said a word. All were tense and listening after eight long days of waiting.

"A second choice is to take the railway north from Vologda to Arch-angelsk, but Bezmunyi's wife says Trotsky left his heaviest troop concentrations in that area, and he is resupplying his field operations from there."

"And?" Bapcat prompted.

Zakov loudly drew in a breath and said, "We will run the line from Vyatka north to Kotlas, abandon the train there, and make our way up the Dvina River to Archangelsk. This seems our only realistic option with Trotsky at our heels."

Bapcat looked at Ivan, but said to Zakov, "When does Ivan assume command of the train?"

"Kotlas, under this option, if he wants such a command."

Bapcat looked at Ivan and raised his eyebrows as a prompt.

Ivan said quietly, "Let us assume for discussion that we all abandon the train in Kotlas. Then what?"

"We take what equipment we can use and destroy the rest, along with as much of the train as we can, and then push north to the river to find boats to carry us."

"A risky plan," Crazy Ivan said. "You think we can find boats?"

Zakov nodded.

"Ivan is for this third option."

"You're not taking over Second Brain?" Bapcat asked.

"My men and I have decided to go to America or France—we shall see which."

"All of you?" Jordy said.

"Why not?" Ivan came back.

Lots of reasons Bapcat could think of. "How many are you?"

"My boys, your people, the others, just over one hundred."

Bapcat had doubts. Destroy the train and steal boats for more than a hundred souls and head north?

"Where are the Red troops ahead of us?"

"North of Kotlas," Zakov said. "And we shall find out where our forces are."

This sounded to Bapcat uncharacteristically nonchalant on Zakov's part, especially when it came to military matters.

"How far behind us is Trotsky?"

"Twenty-four to thirty-six hours, depending on exigencies, natural and otherwise," Zakov said.

"And for us, from here to Kotlas?" Bapcat asked, trying to get a better fix on the timing of what felt like impending danger.

Bezmunyi said, "With clear tracks, no breakdowns or problems, twenty to twenty-four hours. We are wasting time talking," the Chief Engineer added.

"Do we vote on this?" Bapcat asked.

Zakov grinned and said sarcastically, "It is the new, momentary, and massively misleading democratic Russian way."

"Bolshevik, not Russian," Crazy Ivan corrected Zakov. "I say we go to Kotlas and fight our way to freedom."

"And Second Brain?"

"I myself shall plant the explosives. It shall never be used against anyone in the future."

"We are a tiny group, not a fire-breathing army," Bapcat reminded his comrades.

Zakov raised an eyebrow. Bapcat had no idea why. Did his partner have something up his sleeve?

Jordy spoke up, "I'm in."

Bapcat nodded.

Zakov said quietly, "Chief Engineer, let us proceed: Perm, Glazov, Vyatka, Kotlas."

"With God's will and blessings," Bezmunyi said.

Elpy began readying the engine to move. He looked over his shoulder as he hefted a shovel full of coal, "Let Bezmunyi's wife's competence trump God's blessings for what lies ahead."

Zakov, Bapcat, Ivan, and Jordy carefully made their way aft to their car. Along the way, Bapcat said to his partner, "A river is seldom ice-free, especially a river we don't know, and which is beginning to kiss winter."

Zakov said, " Simple breathing is not risk-free."

Zakov stopped on the catwalk and faced his partner. "You know about godfathers?"

"Not that I recall." So many names, so many stories; he'd had to stop listening long ago.

"Russia is different, especially among aristocrats and royals, for whom the primary godfather of a child must come from the bloodline. But royals also use what they call a second godfather, who can be from the aristocracy and not necessarily of royal blood. In some rare cases, royals may sometimes serve as primary godfathers to nonroyals. In my case, Tsar Alexander III was my godfather."

"Alexander?" Who was this?

"The father of Nicholas. Alexander loved to hunt the forests, mountains, and swamps, and maintained secret, highly secure camps all over Russia. His favorite was a place he called Cave of Bears, just off the Dvina. The camp is in a deep swamp, the eastern side of it the only higher ground for many *versts*, an area infested by bears. By royal standards this lodge is small, intended to house only a few hundred people."

"This is your plan—to go to this lodge?" A few hundred was *small*?

"I was there many times with Alexander and got close to the cadre of guardians who oversee the place. The guardians have little contact with the outside, except in rare instances when they choose to initiate it. They make it a point to pay attention to everything going on around them. These guardsmen were hand-selected by Alexander, and each pledged to live their lives with their families and offspring in service to the Tsar."

"Maybe the Bolos have gotten to them," Bapcat said.

"Then they will be dead Bolos. These are Alexander's people, and they have a lifestyle far beyond that of regular people. The guardians were created with only one aim in mind: to protect the Tsar and this place."

"But their Tsar is no longer among the living?"

"Alexander's kidneys gave out, and he was only forty-nine. His pipsqueak son took the crown in his place. Imagine the runt son, at five-foot-seven, his papa at six-three, and granddaddy Nicholas I, at six-nine. Small man's syndrome in the late Bloody Nicholas and his wife's closest religious, philosophical, and political advisor, the six-four monk Rasputin towered over the Tsar too."

His friend loved to talk. "These guardians?"

Zakov tilted his head. "*Chernyye volki*—Black Wolves."

"This is bear country, but the Tsar's protectors are wolves?"

"Bears are loners, and wolves live in packs. Both are kings of the taiga, but they share it and are not enemies. They live in peace with each other."

Bapcat shook his head, and Zakov said, "You will see, if we live long enough."

"It's your plan to drop in on the dead Tsar's hunting lodge with a hundred mouths to feed?"

"The place was built in part to hide and shelter the Tsar and his family in the event of a national calamity. Those who guard it are loyal to the Romanovs, and they will welcome us for as long as we need to be there."

"Black Wolves," Bapcat said. "What if they are long gone, the lodge torn down, burned, looted, whatever?"

"I've already made arrangements," Zakov told his friend.

"You what? How? When?"

"I guessed that at some point I, or we, would need protection, so as soon as I came into the country, I went to see the elder of the Wolves, who was a boy when I first came to the lodge with Alexander. Of course, I didn't expect to be bringing a hundred mouths to feed, but this is a minor detail. You shall see."

"Are you saying these Wolves are *waiting* for you?"

"Us, dear wife, us. Friends of my friends and all that, you know."

"That is a saying, and worth what we pay for it, which is nothing. How do we reach this place?"

"Boats, which are already waiting. I shall guide us."

"How far?"

"Ninety to ninety-five miles north into the narrows, just upriver from where the Kodima River joins the Dvina."

"Boats in winter?" Bapcat asked.

The coming of winter had been eating around the fringes of his mind for the past eight days.

"We should be just ahead of it," Zakov said. "The camp usually gets its snows in October, but winter hits first to the north, in Archangelsk, and from there steadily works its way upriver, toward Kotlas. When the lower Dvina is frozen, the upper river often stays ice-free for a longer time."

"How far from the Tsar's lodge to Archangelsk?"

"River miles? A hundred and some, or thereabouts."

"We stay in the lodge until spring—this is your plan?"

"I don't know yet," Zakov said. "We shall see. Possibly."

By spring Bapcat and Jordy would have been gone from Michigan for more than a year, with no contact whatsoever with Jaquelle. It felt even longer than that. Jaquelle would be worried sick. And without an explanation, angry.

37

Early Winter, 1918. Kotlas

"So passeth Second Brain."

"How many souls?" Bapcat asked Jordy for the tenth, or twelfth, time.

"One hundred plus, not counting Zakov's sister Anya and Major Dodge."

"Why would they not be counted?"

"Because Dodge is gone, as is Anya, who abandoned us in Kundar."

"Zakov's wife?" Bapcat asked.

"Gone *long* ago. I think Zakov knew."

Bapcat had pretty much forgotten both women. "Gone where?"

"Neither woman left a farewell note or forwarding address," Jordy said. "Who knows how women think.?"

"I would suggest you not share that opinion in Jaquelle's presence. Or mine."

"When did you become a suffragette?" his son asked.

"The country can't keep half its citizens from voting. It will happen in our lifetime, maybe even in the not-too-distant future."

"Why are you so certain?"

"Jaquelle says so."

Zakov and Crazy Ivan interrupted father and son.

Zakov said, "We have eighty soldiers in Ivan's group, twenty-two civilians, and you, Jordy, Anton, Bezmunyi, his sons, and Elpy."

Bapcat said, "Dodge is gone? Damn him."

Zakov blinked. "Even broken men like that are difficult to hold back. The smell of treasure . . ."

"Gone, too, are Anya and your wife," Bapcat said.

Zakov shook his head, betraying no other emotion.

"All of our company will be fully armed. Supplies are loaded in packs. There is a track through the forest. From this siding, we are ten miles from a river village called Ship."

"It means, 'thorn,'" Jordy inserted, as Zakov continued.

"The path through the forest was once called Alexander's Road, but everyone thought it referred to the Macedonian, not the Tsar."

Macedonian? Sometimes the people around Bapcat talked like foreigners. Had they learned so much of these things in school, which he had seen only a minimal amount of? Probably. He'd learned long ago to keep his mouth shut when such furry topics came up.

Zakov went on. "The road is something between a logging tote road and a two-track, or at least, this was its condition when I was here last year. The upper Dvina runs by Ship, and our crafts are located near there."

"Do we have enough to handle our entire company?" Bapcat asked.

"We have three—two larger craft, which should handle our numbers, and a smaller boat for scouting and reconnaissance purposes. Ivan is sorting us into groups of ten. I will be in the lead group on this march," Zakov said. "Ivan will lead the front ten, and Jordy and you will come last, to pick up stragglers and provide rear security."

"Trotsky is closing in on us?"

"The interval remains, so we shall have a day or more. It will take time for him to sort out what we leave behind. Ivan's demolition squad will be last to leave the train, and will leapfrog forward to get in behind Ivan's lead element. The civilians, including the Chief Engineer and Elpy, will be with the other civilians, in the middle."

Bapcat felt the need to be moving. "The village is ten miles from here? Is the ground firm?"

"A path, once a road. It will not be like blazing a new trail. We can expect some sphagnum and some small sinkholes."

"Quicksand?" Jordy asked, alarm in his voice.

Ivan said, "Black Russian silt can be even worse, but as with quicksand, if you lose your nerve and panic, you could die. Extraction from this black glue can be hard and physically demanding, but it is possible. Everyone must carry a rod or stick to test every step in front of them."

"We have slightly more hours of darkness right now," said Bapcat, "and this should see us to the river." Roosevelt had been a stickler for rules of engagement between armed forces, and because of this, so was the old Rough Rider Bapcat.

"If we are challenged?" he asked Zakov.

"If it's villagers or curious citizens, brush them off, and ignore them. If you have to, threaten them and move on. If it's soldiers confronting us, engage, hold, and send a messenger for reinforcements. Each element in our column provides front and rear security for the next element ahead and behind."

"Do your men understand the principles of cover fire?" Bapcat asked.

Ivan nodded, and said quietly, "You can rely on them."

"Explosives?" Zakov asked Crazy Ivan.

"All set. I decided it was best to use fuel, fire, and dynamite in the ammunition and arms piles. It will be loud and sustained, rolling on for more than ten minutes, I should think."

"You think?" Bapcat challenged.

"Explosives are as much an art as science and engineering," the Russian came back, grinning. "The ammunition will cook off, and the artillery rounds should make quite a spectacular show."

Bapcat asked Zakov, "Once into the boats, how long, and how far, to our landing?" He did not talk about the Tsar's camp. He and Zakov had agreed this should be kept secret until the last possible moment.

"Let us get to the boats before we make that calculation," Zakov said. "Ours will not be a dash downriver. Two boats, each with fifty heads, will not attract attention if we act like we belong. There are logging crews on the river year-round, especially in winter, and they are just now going to interior timber stands to establish their winter camps. The Reds expect this. We will carry axes and saws."

"Guys headed for logging camps with the snow. It's just like the Upper Peninsula," Jordy observed.

Trotsky's special unit badges for the train cars were removed, doused with kerosene, and burned before the big show. Only rail experts would be able to decipher the train's true identity.

Their ten elements assembled, the group began their march. Bapcat and Jordy waited for Crazy Ivan, who showed up running with his bomb team.

"How long?" Bapcat asked.

"Minutes now," Ivan said. "The fires and fuses were hot and going good."

"What if this doesn't work?" Bapcat asked.

"Does the man always worry so?" Ivan asked Jordy.

"He worships small devils and details," the sergeant said.

The explosion was far more than Bapcat had expected. It nearly took his breath away when a massive thunderclap shook the ground, rolling it violently under his boots.

Moments later they were showered with dirt clods, snow scabs, and bark shards.

"What a waste," Ivan lamented.

"So passeth Second Brain," Jordy quipped. "We are Cortez, burning our ships."

Bapcat closed his eyes as a second round of explosions shook the area and secondary fires began to glow.

"Is that siding unusable?" Bapcat asked nervously.

"As is most of one full *verst* of main track," Ivan reported. "There will be no train traffic this way for some time to come."

Bapcat exhaled. The die was cast; they were committed.

"Take you men and go, Ivan. Good work."

"Yessir. Good luck in the rear. Remember, northern Russians fight the Red way—hit and hide, hit again, peck away, but nothing head to head unless they are given no choice."

"I think he means like Indians," Jordy added. "They'll hit from a hiding position and then run. Minimizes the attacker's casualties."

"Sounds very military," Bapcat said.

"Learned it in history class," Jordy said.

38

Early Winter, 1918. Ship

"I see a shadow within a shadow."

Zakov swung back to the rear echelon of the loose formation. He told Bapcat, "Our groups are spread out over a half-mile, and Anton has noticed something. Ivan has taken a look and wants your opinion."

Bapcat looked at his son. "Keep this group moving."

The two men hurried forward, and Zakov pointed out some larches with branches stripped off. He held up a compass.

"The track, if it is one, runs eastward. The markers aren't just larches." Zakov showed him a black spruce, similarly nicked, also seeming to point east.

"A trail blaze," Bapcat observed.

Zakov nodded. "More to the point, it appears to be American-style. Russian loggers and woodsmen mark trails differently.

Bapcat drew a deep breath. "Coincidence?"

Zakov said, "Against my religion, if I had one, and our game warden experience as well. The blazed trail parallels the river."

"The Dvina?"

"No, the Vychegda, which means 'clean.' It flows into the Dvina at Kotlas."

Bapcat studied the marks, closed his eyes to picture the last blaze.

"This trail seems to veer back to the river."

They were thinking out loud now, the way they often worked together, playing off each other's instinctive riffs.

"These markings skirt the nearest village," Zakov noted.

"Your group is secure?" Bapcat asked.

"Yes, fine. Follow the blazes, yes?"

Crazy Ivan showed up, wanting to know what Bapcat thought.

Bapcat said, "I think we ought to know what these marks are and why they are here. What if there are other Americans here?"

Zakov nodded.

Ivan said, "*Da*, I am going with you."

"How far from the boats are we?" Bapcat asked his partner.

Zakov said, "They are just downriver of Ship. I will get our people boarded and hold them until you catch up. You will easily follow our trail, yes?"

Bapcat nodded. It would be as easy as tracking a migrating buffalo herd over the Great Plains.

Zakov said, "Good luck," and left the two men.

Bapcat stood, staring, and said finally, "I see dark in dark on the trail here. Someone has moved through recently, two or three. I see a shadow within a shadow."

Crazy Ivan squinted and said, "I see nothing."

The game warden, offset above the faint sign, put Ivan on the other side, and began tracking. They hit a third small blaze two hundred yards beyond the second, but now branches were stripped on the tree's north side. Maybe this wasn't a trail and all a waste of time?

Morning twilight, faintly hinting, gently lit the smoke-gray sky. The scent of pines and rotten plants was putrid and strange.

Still-hunting now, a few steps, wait, listen, let only the eyes move, sniff the air. Bapcat was first to see movement and froze. He issued a small peeping sound to halt Ivan and crept forward cautiously to see what was moving. An animal? Then came more sound. He stopped and closed his eyes.

A sharp, stark thump, and another. An ax or hatchet, no question. Human, not animal. Ax on soft wood, green, not hard. Every human action created its own sound, if you knew how to hear it. Were the blazers this close?

Circling to his left to the northwest, around the sound, to the other side of it, and into dense, thick underbrush, some kind of shoulder-high perfumed juniper. He pushed slowly into the brushy tangle, and when he got close to the edge, he stopped and peeked out toward the hacking sound and heard a voice.

"I told that cap'n I should be doing this shit alone. You city boys got no business in the woods."

"Potterville ain't no city," a second voiced argued.

Americans for sure.

"It's a damn spitball from Lansing, which makes it a city. The Upper Peninsula, where I'm from, it's country and bush, and a spitball from Lansing sure as hell ain't that."

That voice? Familiar, or was this a foolish thought?

The second voice now, clearly nervous. "You think it's broke?"

"I already told you, I ain't no damn medic, city boy, but we'll splint 'er, just in case. I was smart, I'd leave your city ass here and move on and do my job, let you get yourself out."

"You *can't* leave me. You wouldn't. The captain sent me with you."

"Says you," the first voice said. "All I know is, I found you skulking behind me with all the stealth of a drunk mule. I said I *should* leave you, so stop your damn whining and ee-yawing. You ever splint a broke leg?"

Second voice: "No; you?"

"No, but I had to chop one off once. It was damn messy, and that sonuvabitch wouldn't stop crying and screaming. Should've shot him like a broke-leg horse. Splinting can't be all that hard, but remember, splinting this damn thing ain't the same as fixing it. All we're trying to do is keep from making it worse. This splinting deal is gonna hurt like hell when we get it on, and it will keep hurting like hell and slow us down. Like I said, I ought to splint you and leave you."

"Please don't do that. I'm sorry this happened."

"I'm sorry you ever showed up."

"I was ordered."

"Claims you, City Boy, and shut your damn mouth. If you'd been more careful, there'd be no need for sorry. Intentions ain't no part of this. You've screwed up our job, and now I've got to do something with you, when I should be moving east as fast as I can go."

"Don't take me back . . . it's too far," City Boy whined.

"You don't want to go back?" First Voice asked.

"It would mess up your mission."

"You mean *our* mission, knucklehead. I think I'll give you to the damn Russkies and let them take care of you."

"The Bolos will shoot me."

"They might. Or maybe I should shoot you myself and keep moving."

"You're a nasty man. How'd you make corporal?"

" 'Cause I know not to break my damn leg in the damn bush is how, and you're right, I *am* mean. All this time wasted, making a splint. Wish I could shoot you, but it would make too much noise, attract attention."

"You ain't splinted nothing yet," City Boy. "You got a cigarette?"

"I'm considering cutting your throat and getting out of here. And no, I don't got no cigarette. You can smell them damn things in the woods, especially that shit the Russians call tobacco. Now shut up, City Boy."

"Okay, Corporal Vuke."

"Goddammit, don't be calling me by my rank, dumb-ass. These Russian boys shoot rank first. And don't call me Vuke, neither; you ain't earned no right to that."

Corporal? Vuke? The Upper Peninsula? What were the odds? Corporal Vukevich? Wishful thinking?

He knew a Vukevich from Red Jacket, a bit older than Jordy, face of an angel, stone heart of a violator. People called him Vuke, sometimes Stone Man, habitual violator, and damn good in the woods. He'd arrested him several times for various violations over the years. But here? Was this even possible?

Tracks might show three men, but just two here. Trail sign was hard to read, and maybe the scuffing he'd seen was the one man dragging a bad leg.

He took a deep breath and said, "Stone?"

A rifle rattled and the hurt one's voice yelped, "Bolos!"

The other voice was a while in coming, but calm when it did.

"Who the hell? Identify yourself or I'll shoot."

"Deputy Bapcat."

"*Lute* Bapcat?"

"Point your rifle elsewhere, Stone Man."

"Jesus, what the hell is this?" said Vukevich. "Halfway around the world, and the same goddamn game warden pops out on me in the goddamn woods."

City Boy stuttered nervously, "Y-y-you know this g-g-guy?"

"He's the game warden back home. We know each other all right, don't we, Deputy?"

"We do," Bapcat said. "Tell your man to keep his voice down, Vuke."

Vukevich had curly blond hair and a spiky beard. He was short, like most Russians Bapcat had met, and built like a wrestler.

"He ain't *my* man," said Vuke. "Keep your yap shut, City Boy."

"What the hell are you doing here, Lute?"

"Why ain't you in no uniform?"

"We were supposed to fight Krauts in France but they shipped us to Russia. Where's your unit?" Bapcat asked.

"Way downriver. Which unit is yours, and how come we ain't seen each other before this?"

"My unit is elsewhere, and we've been here almost a year."

"Jesus jampots, Lute."

"How far to our lines?"

"Downriver two hundred miles, give or take. Have you run into the Czechs anywhere?" Vuke asked.

"Way south and east of here, maybe eight hundred miles."

"Goddamn. My captain told me to find the Czechs and bring them back."

"Not likely," Bapcat said. "We're headed back to our lines. The Czechs are led by Kolchak, and he's a long way from here, probably got his hands full where he is. What're your orders?"

"Make contact with Kolchak—he's some kind of admiral? Supposed to link with him near someplace called Vyatka, or Vologda."

"One of those is more than three hundred miles south, and the other, four hundred miles southwest, with nothing but trees and swamps in between. You have maps?"

"What my captain had was pretty rough, and he wouldn't let me take none. I had to memorize them, but I don't think I done so good at that. Where is this admiral fella right now?"

"Pushing into Yekaterinburg, last I knew, which was two weeks ago."

"Eight hundred miles?"

"Give or take."

"Goddamn fool officers."

"Might as well throw in with us and I'll explain everything to your captain."

"Us? All I see is you."

Bapcat said, "Ivan," and the Russian stepped out.

The injured man whimpered.

Bapcat added, "Let's get your comrade splinted properly. We have people waiting."

"I ain't no comrade, pal," the injured man simpered. "I ain't no pinky Red bastard."

"It's Captain Bapcat to you, soldier."

"Oh shit," the man muttered.

Bapcat asked, "You got a name, Broke Leg?"

"Private Hanscomb Dixon, from Gross Pointe."

"I can see bone sticking out, Private."

"It can be fixed, though, right?"

"One way or another."

"I don't want no sawbones striking off my leg, or such."

"No worry; it's not likely to be a doc if it comes down to it."

Bapcat looked over at Vuke. "That leg you took off that time—how'd the patient do?"

"Infection killed him."

Private Dixon said, "Why'd they pick me to go with the corporal? I told 'em I don't know shit about the woods."

"You raised your damn hand, is what you told me," Vukevich said.

"Oh yeah. Well, I thought it would be just the two of us creeping around out here alone, not looking for a fight, while our outfit wants a fight. I never will understand that kind of stupid."

Vukevich said, "Damn draft brung this worthless piece into uniform. He ain't worth nothing in the woods. All he does is whine."

"He won't whine where we're going," Bapcat said.

"Where's that?" Dixon asked.

"You'll see," Bapcat said, leaving it at that.

They secured the man's leg and made a travois. Crazy Ivan hefted the device and they turned north and west to make their way to the river.

—

Anton was waiting for them outside the village of Ship, which was low along the riverbank, all made of dark logs. The roofs were all moss, and the Russian-style vertical logs had turf chinking between them. The place was damp, and dark, and reeked.

Full light now, and Bapcat wanted to hurry.

The boats were below the lip of a steep, fifty-foot embankment and unseeable until you were on the river, or at least most of the way down, on the goat trail to the river's edge.

Zakov greeted them. "Where have you been?"

Bapcat said, "Corporal Vukevich of Red Jacket and Private Dixon of Gross Pointe."

Zakov stared. "*Our* Vuke?"

"It's me, Deputy Zakov. Sam-damn, you're here *too*?"

Zakov looked at Bapcat and rolled his eyes. He answered, "Probably, or perhaps you had too much to drink and I am merely a hallucination."

"We ain't had much alcohol since we left England."

Jordy came over, said casually, "Hey, Vuke."

"I'll be damned," Vukevich said. "Four of us from the same damn place." Vuke looked at Jordy and said officiously, "I'm a corporal, Jordy; use my rank."

"I'm *Sergeant* Klubishar," Jordy said, "Corporal."

"Damn," Vuke said. "I don't see me no stripes."

"Use your imagination," Bapcat said with a growl.

"Get on the bloody boats," Zakov said, pointing. "These two say precisely what they were doing here?" he asked his partner.

"Trying to make contact with Kolchak so the Americans can link up with him."

"Just the two of them—no officers?"

"They're messengers," Bapcat said, and his partner shook his head.

"They say how far the American lines are?"

"Couple hundred miles."

"How big a force?"

"We didn't get that far."

Bapcat was nerved up. They were still two hundred miles from other Americans? Might as well be two million, he told himself as he looked at the first boat.

Elpy was at the tiller of the first boat and announced he was ready to cast off.

Bezmunyi, who was commanding the second large boat, waved Bapcat, Zakov, Jordy, Ivan, and Vukevich into a small craft tied up between the two larger craft. The injured American was loaded into Bezmunyi's boat and Bapcat heard no whining.

The two main boats were fifty or more feet long, with decks three feet below the gunwales and planked sides. They were old and odd and smelled awful, but seemed seaworthy.

A smaller third boat was moored just beyond the first, this one a twenty-footer, planked and low-slung, sleeker than the other two. "Our steed," Zakov said, pointing.

"What day is this?" Jordy asked.

"Day?" Bapcat said, and smiled. He had only a vague idea what month it was, much less the day.

Zakov said, "Once we are moving, any threat will come on us from the water, not the land. The Bolsheviks have some boats, some with guns. A long time ago the Imperial Navy patrolled Russia's rivers, but rarely with much enthusiasm. Expect the Bolsheviks to be far more attentive."

39

Winter, 1919. Green Ground

"I hate how random shit happens in this country."

The three-boat flotilla stopped periodically as they rode downriver. At one stop Bapcat and Zakov got Vukevich off to the side. The two game wardens had discussed this briefly, were veterans of two-on-one interviews, and both knew they needed information to verify Vuke's story. Might be that he and Dixon were deserters or even Red sympathizers. There had been plenty of the latter in Red Jacket and Houghton.

Bapcat gave the corporal a cigarette and lit it with a wooden match.

The corporal took a deep draw, coughed, gagged, said, "Tastes like bear shit," took an even deeper and longer pull, and scowled.

"Who gave you the orders to connect with the Czechs?" Bapcat asked.

"A Brit major, who until recently was a British sergeant-major. Name's McNulty. He has a face that's fat, flat, and angled, like a horse sat on him. Lots of scars, like a peanut shell. He's been around."

"Tell us exactly what he said," Zakov inserted, forcing Vuke to turn his head to look at him.

"He told me to go south to Glazov, then east along the tracks to Siberia until I met the Czechs, and guide them back to our guys. He said the grand plan, from far above the fighting, was to link with the Czechs so we could methodically crush the Sixth Red Army, and from there, go after Russian centers in Petrograd and Moscow."

"He gave you maps and written orders?"

Vuke said, "Hell no. He figured if I got captured they'd maybe think I was just some poor dope who got lost and separated. If they thought I had an actual mission, they'd torture me, or treat me like a spy and shoot me."

"What about your partner, Dixon?" This, from Bapcat.

"Not no damn partner. He was a weird, last-minute thing. Just as I got ready to shove off he ran over to me, said Major McNulty wanted him on the mission."

"Did you question the major?" Zakov asked.

"Had no damn time. I could see McNulty, but he wasn't close to where we were going out, and I pointed at Dixon and held out my hands to say, 'Really? You want me to take this jerk?' McNulty just waved me out of the lines and I went. Maybe he wanted Dixon to disappear. He's a shitty soldier."

"Did the major's instructions and military talk make sense to you?"

Vuke laughed. "No offense, Lute, but I stopped paying attention after he told me to link up with the Czechs and lead them back here. I figured then it might could be a suicide mission."

"Link with Kolchak?" Zakov asked.

Vukevich said, "McNulty told me this Kolchak's an admiral in charge on land, and I wondered what the hell an admiral was doing so damn far from the ocean. I also happen to know there ain't no ocean shorelines for Czechs or Slovaks, so how come the so-called Czech Legion is led by an admiral?"

Zakov said quietly. "Admiral Kolchak's served in the Russian Imperial Navy and earned his rank there. Tell us more about Major McNulty."

Vuke shrugged. "What's to tell? He's a hardheaded Scot leading Royal Scots troops. They're good soldiers, and we've got some worthless White Russians. Most of the Whites run at the sound of a rifle. The White Russians call McNulty *Lyagushka*."

"The Frog," Zakov translated.

Vuke corrected him. "Not *the* frog, just frog. McNulty don't speak no Russian and has no idea what gets said around him."

"But you do?" Zakov said, questioning.

"I get by just fine in Russian," Vuke said. "Have since I was a tyke."

Bapcat was perplexed. A foreign officer commanding American troops? Roosevelt wouldn't have tolerated this. Did President Wilson know—or General Pershing—and did they care?

Vukevich said, "Aw, McNulty's a good-enough egg. Not his damn fault, the crap that goes on above. Word is that when the Brits realized the Yanks were coming to Russia, they quickly bumped all their officers and senior NCOs in rank so that they would be likely to be senior to the Americans, and therefore command. McNulty's better than most of the others, Yanks included. Our boys like him and trust him, and he trusts us. If there's a fight, you can count on the major being in the middle of it, always calm, always joking, always leading. He don't run, never."

Bapcat looked at his partner. "This mass promotion thing, that sound like a British trick?" Zakov had far more experience with such things, and at very senior levels.

"The English and their Empire colleagues are ultimate political animals," Zakov said. "Perhaps this comes from being an island nation, everybody into everybody else's business. The British are born certain that they know better than anyone else about everything, and especially all things military. Since Trafalgar and Waterloo, they're certain that they possess the most gifted military minds on Earth."

"The major didn't give you a map?" Zakov asked Vuke.

"Like I told Lute, he didn't want me carrying no evidence, but he drew one in the mud and I thought I memorized it pretty good, but now I'm thinking, maybe not. I'd already figured I could blend right in with the Russians if I had to, but then Dixon got dumped on me. Without that fool, I'da been long past where you found us and on my way to finding the Czechs."

"Who are still eight hundred or more miles away," Bapcat reminded him.

Vuke said, "I'm in the army and I follow my orders. If I'da known the distances and all, I might have had serious doubts, but I still would have made the effort."

Bapcat knew the corporal had been a crafty, mobile violator, good in the woods, and very good most of the time at evading detection.

"The mud map was pretty general, was it?" Bapcat asked.

"It was general and specific and vague from Glazov eastward. From our lines to Kotlas it was pretty detailed, but less so to the south."

"You were on the east bank of the Dvina when we met you," Zakov said.

"We tried to keep east. The major said most Russian forces were deployed west of the Dvina, so we were less likely to bump trouble by moving down the less-populated side."

"How far downriver are the Russians?" Zakov asked.

"They're strung out all along the Vaga River, which dumps into the Dvina, just above the town of Bereznik. Been all kinds of fights down the Vaga to Shenkursk and Spasskoe, and we had troops as far south on the Dvina as Toulgas and Seltso, but the Reds and crap weather forced us to pull back."

"Where exactly did you cross the Red lines?" Bapcat asked.

"Place called Shegovari, south bank of the Vaga, and we worked our way through some really nasty swamp country with the Russians hugging the high ground, what little there is, and I didn't like the look of the land. The Russians seem to think just being in Russia is enough to guarantee a win. But their security is so much cheap cheese. We slid through holes and around them with no trouble, until Dixon went and broke his stupid leg."

"The hardness of the country worked when Napoleon tried to swallow Russia," Zakov said.

Bapcat had heard of Napoleon, but knew only that he was some sort of French general. He didn't want a history lesson, needed to keep focused on intelligence and security matters.

"Shegovari to where, exactly?"

"We crossed the Dvina below Seltso, and maybe twenty miles south of there we found a boat somebody had stashed along the river. Probably some trapper's. We borrowed it to cross the river."

"How big?" Bapcat asked.

"Big enough, and steady enough for three, but hardly more than a dugout."

"Where exactly did McNulty want you to bring the Czechs?" Bapcat pressed.

Vuke frowned, then laughed.

"He wasn't all that specific. What he said was to get them on boats and float them down the Dvina to link up. I asked him how the hell I was supposed to get boats, and he laughed and said, "You don't. At that point you can let the bloody admiral *earn his pay, laddie*.""

Bapcat lit a cigarette for himself.

"You think we should cross the Dvina again, and follow your route back?"

"Further downstream we get, the worse the winter will be. We heard stories that would curl your toes. Truth is, we were damn lucky to find open water and that dugout. It may already be iced over by now, and if not, it will be soon. What McNulty told me is that the Dvina is always open earlier upstream of Seltso. Downriver ices in first and unthaws last in spring."

Bapcat fought a smile. *Unthaw* was a common term straight out of Red Jacket, back home.

He looked at Zakov. "We can make for Seltso on the east bank and decide what to do next when we get there."

Neither Zakov nor Vuke responded, and Bapcat asked something that had been weighing on him for months. "Are Americans actually *fighting* Russians?"

"Like, almost every damn day," Vuke said.

"Did America actually declare war?"

Vuke looked at the game warden.

"I don't know the answer, Lute, but when Red Ivans are shelling your asses and trying to stick bayonets in your guts, not too many fools're gonna worry much about what is or ain't on paper. We got us a war in our faces, declared or not. We've got dead and wounded and missing, and we think the Reds are holding some of our fellows to trade for theirs later."

Zakov still said nothing, but Vukevich wasn't done.

"What it boils down to is fight or not go home."

Bapcat wondered why the man was even thinking about getting home. The thing about war was that you went and stayed until you were dead, wounded, or it was over and won.

"Why are you talking about going home?" he asked Vukevich.

"Rumor has it the new White Army is going to replace all Yanks, Frogs, Limeys, and Canucks, and we're all getting shipped home. It's the damn Russians' war, ain't it?"

———

The subtle bouncing and surging of the boat beat the hell out of bouncing along on unsteady spongy ground under your boots. The river, at least, provided some push, and they glided downriver, using paddles on the lead craft and rudders on the larger boats. When the river grew shallow and broke into spreads, the passengers used long aspen poles to help push. Bapcat sat aft watching his son up front, with Ivan between them. Jordy was an expert paddler, smooth and instinctive, reading water as effortlessly as he read books.

There were other craft on the river in the immediate area of Kotlas, where there was wider water, but traffic bled off downriver when the Dvina narrowed, and for a while they passed below tall, high banks, good ground for ambushes. Bapcat guessed that the Bolos either lacked troops or their troops and their leaders were lackadaisical in not recognizing and manning such a strategic point. Overconfidence, perhaps?

The old Tsarist hunting camp, Zakov claimed, was ninety miles downstream from Kotlas, and it became apparent immediately downstream of the town that the land was ideal bear country, with all sorts of streams dumping into the river, the banks of which were kitchens and highways for bears. Rivers meant food and cover. Heavy red willows and tag alders lined the shores, and there were dwarf cedars, larch, black spruce, and some conifers he didn't recognize. Now and then they passed under higher ground, with hardwoods that looked a lot like smooth-bark beech, another hint of a bear population. Bears loved beechnuts above all other foods, at least back home. Why would it be any different here?

Bapcat wondered if Zakov meant brown or black bears. This far upriver from the arctic coast, he assumed there would be black bears, same as back home, but he couldn't say for certain.

———

Late in the day, no sign of pursuit or landside recon, but Bapcat saw a heavily traveled area of bankside grass ahead on the far bank and decided to move back upriver to talk to Zakov.

Jordy nosed the lead craft into a low embankment, and Bapcat stepped ashore and waved the two larger boats over to shore. They were on a shelf, fifty or so feet below a hill crest, where a small creek came out into the larger river, opposite the trampled path on the other side of the river. Here there was also a trail, also recently and heavily traveled. It led steeply to the crest.

Bapcat told Ivan and Jordy to stay put while he scouted, and to keep the other two boats near shore until he returned.

The tracks were heavy, not all that old, and led upward from the river, not down to the river. Once on top, the tracks stopped abruptly. What in the world? Why did the tracks stop here? Where did they go? He looked into the sky and smiled at his own stupidity.

A rifle shot froze him and gave him goose bumps, which turned quickly to anger. A fight here, after all this time trying to avoid fights? Would Jordy, despite orders, hear the shot and follow? Good possibility.

Keep your mind on the here and now.

He eased past where the tracks stopped and found a weedy, grassy space, felt the stiff weeds claw at his legs as the trail continued to climb gradually and shift from north to south until he was on top and saw a sandbagged emplacement, the bags stacked around cut logs in a sort of V shape.

He eased over to the structure and examined it. Machine-gun mounts, no gun and no brass on the ground. Abandoned post or never used? Poorly sited. You could see only from the middle to the far shore of the Dvina. High ground was worthless if it didn't let you cover all approaches to your advantageous location. Here only the middle to far side were killing zones, the close bank invisible and far too low for the mount, even if the near shore could be seen. Had someone been here when they'd slid ashore below? Or was this place unmanned? What was the one shot?

Then it dawned on him. A warning to others?

A whisper broke his concentration. "What's taking so long?" Jordy asked. "I heard something."

"Is Ivan secure, the other boats?"

"They're all good; don't fuss. Are there Bolos here?"

"You heard the shot?"

"Was that what that was? I heard what might have been a shot, but this ground eats sound. Are we going to check?"

"No choice." Bapcat knew a shot when he heard one.

"I hate how random shit happens in this country," Jordy complained.

They moved back to the trail, which led past the emplacement, mostly paralleling the river.

"You're sure it was a shot?" Jordy asked as they crept along.

"It was a shot. C'mon."

The trail began to angle down and turn east, away from the river and the high ground, and this led them to a lower plateau. Bapcat thought he heard muffled voices a moment later, and saw all kinds of tracks, and on another trail coming up from the river, a horde of tracks.

"You check the big boats?" he whispered to Jordy, "after the shot?"

"I did. No fresh blood in either, unless you count blood from Dixon's broken leg."

Jordy poked his arm. Clear voices now, talking what sounded to Bapcat like Russian.

"You hearing that?" he asked his son.

"Something about enemies of the people, *narodny*."

Red or White or what? Bapcat wondered. Was this what it had been like in the American Revolution and the Civil War—sometimes not knowing if someone was enemy or friend? The thought left him shuddering. Everyone against everyone; how did you ever get whole after that?

Jordy slid down the trail around him and they moved until the voices were clearer, Jordy whispering translation. "We're neither Red nor White. We're just factory workers without silver spoons. We weren't born shitting gold rubles and now they expect us to fight? Who? Over what?"

Suddenly more new voices, and although still in Russian, Bapcat knew who was speaking.

Bezmunyi and Elpy.

What the heck were *they* doing up here? They were supposed to be with the boats.

Jordy translating again. "Neither Red nor White—so why is Trotsky here?"

"This is not Trotsky," Bezmunyi said.

"We have seen his picture in the newspapers. It is Trotsky, all right. He is the enemy, first soldier of the Reds."

"You are mistaken, comrades. He is a railroad signalman, not Trotsky. He is an actor. We wish no trouble with you and your people."

"You give orders like a general," one of the Russians said.

A succession of nearby quick shots made Bapcat jump, and then Bezmunyi was in front of them, motioning them forward.

Bapcat asked, "Who shot?"

"Our little Trotsky. I had no idea he was armed. Shot them both."

"Why?" Bapcat demanded.

"Local partisans, brigands, who sell to the highest bidder. Can't trust them. They would sell us to the Reds."

"You left the boats," Bapcat scolded.

"We heard the shot and knew you'd heard it. This is Green territory."

"Just two men?"

"Five in all. Elpy shot two, and together we took care of the remaining three."

"Greens?"

"Local peasants, stealing to arm themselves. They welcome nobody, no political party or philosophy, no strangers. They saw our boats upriver and have been scrambling along with us."

"Tracks show a lot more than five men," Bapcat said.

Bezmunyi nodded. "There are more, but this is their advance guard. They sent the others farther inland. They thought we would have a load of weapons and ammunition."

Jordy disappeared and was replaced by Elpy.

Bapcat looked at the trainmen.

"You sounded like you were just going to 'go along' with these thieves."

"Just talking to put them at ease," Bezmunyi explained. "If we can avoid bloodshed, why not? There's been enough spilt."

Jordy came back.

"The dead are in the grass just above where our big boats landed. We might have walked by them. They could have—"

"In the grass, trying to work up their courage," Bezmunyi explained. "We should go."

Zakov waited by the boats and Bapcat told his son, "See how easy it is to hide here? Invisibility is almost simple."

Zakov said, "These people live their whole lives in this, the same as we live in the woods; they have all of our woods skills, and some of their own."

"But they are not very good soldiers," Bapcat observed.

Zakov nodded.

"How far downriver have we come?" Bapcat asked.

"Thirty miles, give or take, a third of the way."

"Camp and rest here?"

"No, let us eat quickly and keep moving," Zakov said. "Let's use night to our advantage and get down to the narrows, where we'll pull over before we move on."

"How far to these narrows?"

"In darkness, a few hours."

"And to the destination from there?"

"At this pace, maybe three days. There will be fewer boats and partisan groups after we get into the narrows."

Bapcat felt the night air chilling fast, and as they finished eating and prepared to shove off, it began to spit snow.

"Snow?" Jordy asked Zakov.

"Practice only. Too warm yet. When the days and nights turn frigid, then we'll be in for the real thing."

40

Winter, 1919. Danse Macabre *on the River Dvina*

"De haut en bas, dies irae."

Immediately before their small force headed downriver again, Bapcat had more questions for Corporal Vukevich.

"Have American troops really been fighting Russian troops since they got to Russia?"

Vuke said, "Almost since the day we landed. The Bolos don't got the stomach for slugfests, however; they're quick to pull out of fights, but instead of pushing them south, the British officers in command ordered all Allied troops to dig in for the winter."

"Brits in command? Of Americans?" Did Roosevelt know?

"Of everyone—French, Canucks, whatever. There are three or four main fronts: the Archangelsk-Vologda Railway; the Dvina River; the Vaga, which dumps into the Dvina and is higher-banked, narrower, and wilder than the big river it dumps into; and we've also heard that Americans and Canadians are digging in along the Pinega River way up north, to protect the eastern flanks of Archangelsk, but we were never sure on this one. Our officers didn't know much more than us."

"You didn't really answer me earlier when I asked—have Britain and the United States actually declared war on Russia?" Bapcat asked.

Vuke shrugged. " I don't know, Lute. I can tell you that both sides are firing at each other with rifles, machine guns, artillery—even planes dropping small bombs. Ain't an enemy firing on you enough to do away with formalities and paperwork?"

A question Bapcat couldn't answer. Maybe this was so, but the legality of the operation wasn't one he could discuss with Vuke, who had more education than did Bapcat, who could read only at a barely functional level.

His quandary persisted. Was this a legal war, or not? And if not, what did that mean for the men who were fighting it? And why were Brits directing American troops? Roosevelt never would have allowed that.

They headed downstream, unanswered questions lingering. Bapcat tried to keep his mind in the boat.

After more than two hours, Jordy turned to look at Bapcat, whispered "Blue," and immediately began back-paddling, pointing the small craft toward the bank they had been closely paralleling. *Blue* was their personal code word for immediate trouble at hand.

The boat bumped to a stop and Jordy stepped back to his father.

"I saw a cigarette ember, low to the ground, our bank, dead ahead, maybe five feet inland."

Bapcat sniffed, faintly smelled it, whispered back, "Secure here."

Bapcat tapped Crazy Ivan's shoulder. "You have the boat."

"*Da*," Ivan said, "I have the boat."

The shore was littered with snags and downed trees and sharp, coarse grasses.

Zakov appeared onshore beside them. "We're going to inspect something," Bapcat said.

"As am I," his partner said. "What do we have?"

"Jordy?" Bapcat prompted.

The boy said, "Fifteen yards ahead, two feet off the ground, think ten after the hour on the clock."

This method of direction had been taught to the boy by Zakov.

"Can we get at it from nine o'clock?"

"I'll look," Bapcat said, but the Russian's hand held him back.

"*Vye nemtsky*—you are dumb to Russian. Because you do not speak the people's language, you earn the label of 'dumb.'"

"I'm coming too," Bapcat said.

"Stay mute," Jordy advised his father, who grimaced. "For a while."

335

The three men slid through tangles of dense ground cover, still too dark to make out any detail. Bapcat's night vision exceeded Zakov's, and virtually anyone the partners knew. Their fellow game wardens called it his creepy gift.

Bapcat knew the smoke source at the edge of a small clearing just ahead and on the riverbank. They would have floated right by it in the dark. He could hear a voice whispering and muttering, in a tone somewhere between happy and burdened. Bizarre.

He tapped Zakov's shoulder. Snowing again.

"*Arrière-pensée*," a voice mumbled to their left.

Zakov whispered, "French for hidden intentions; English accent to the French."

The voice rambled on in mushy, garbled British English, the sort of language and accent the man called Churchill had used—a bit difficult to make out through its slobberiness.

"Dogs remain dogs, the rule and barrier equally unbendable; breed a mix to a purebred and you get a mix, one of God's rules, or the devil's—one cannot be certain which figment of man's imagination rules. Your own fault, Comrade Martin Dudley O'Dea, a fine fix this, old sod."

Zakov glided across the clearing rattling his rifle. Intentionally, Bapcat guessed. No woodsman of his skill would make such a mistake, which suggested he was trying to act like someone less than he was. Why?

The voice came, "*Dobit menya? Delative rasto chatpulya.*"

Zakov answered in English, "We've not come to finish you off, comrade. Why should you think that?"

The man was half sitting and leaned against a rock, tilted to his right and using his left hand to help prop him up. Bapcat had seen many men die. This one was definitely on his way out.

"Me erstwhile comrades shot me in the guts and broke me knobby knees with their rifle butts, left me here to contemplate what time I have remaining before the wolves smell my blood and come to feast on me." The man continued, "I must say, one comrade left me a generous plug of tobacco, no doubt stolen from another comrade, and a second comrade left me a syringe and six vials of morphine, tokens of parting friendship.

Should count meself rather lucky, I suppose. Usually it's one pop in the back of one's hat, and administered whilst walking, with no forewarning. Who're you lads—fellow travelers from afar?"

Back in Red Jacket, some budding Communists, Reds, and anarchists called themselves Travelers; Bapcat had no idea why, but they tended to be strange folk. Most of them at home were all talk.

"Does it matter who we are?" Zakov asked in English.

"Believe Sir Morphine's magic is wearing off," the man said. "Got any to spare, old boy? Hated to use all mine, but then, why conserve, eh? The lads left me a rifle with no bullets. Shouldn't complain. Plenty of tobacco, and so far, St. Morph and me, we've managed. Have to say, the pain's not horrible."

"You a soldier?" Zakov asked the man.

"Difficult question, old salt. Spiritually, certainly not. Technically I'm conscripted, untrained and unmotivated, hardly a soldier by any proper English definition. Or Irish, for that matter."

"You were traveling with soldiers?"

"No doubt some of them are that, but most . . . *les canailles, en fran-çais—oui*, the mob, the mass—energized, with no direction."

"How many in this mob, and what do they call themselves?"

"Sixth Red Army, Sixth Vologda Shock Troops, Vologda Regiment."

"You volunteered?" Bapcat asked, discarding the mute role, wanting the man to know he was outnumbered.

"I reckon that's true in a loosely relative sense, old duff. Easy choice, that: step up, or spend eternity swinging in the breezes from a lamppost. Do I hear Yank in that last voice?"

Zakov ignored the question and asked, "How many in your troop and regiment?"

"Not at all certain, old crock, never been the eyeshade type. All sorts of numbers bandied about by the Bolos, but these Red buggers will lie to your face about the color of green grass, won't they now? Heard several times we would be three thousand under Colonel Syurpriz, which is no doubt a nom de guerre."

"Indeed," Zakov retorted. "Colonel Surprise. Are we to understand that you are part of a deploying force?"

"Of late; *was*, old chap, not *am*. Tense counts, *da*? The new Red Army does not willingly share information downward, despite all the posters and slogans of equality and such bunkum. Word among my comrades was that we were marching east to eventually turn north toward the Pinega River country, where we would move past a large foreign troop concentration and come back down behind them from the north, like starving birds of prey. A surprise attack, *da*?"

"Which foreign forces?" Zakov asked.

"British occupiers, including Yanks, have been moved to Pinega from Archangelsk, but the foreign force's eastern flank is nothing but bloody wilderness, you know, *versts* and *versts* of *versts* and *versts*, stretching all the way north to the bloody White Sea."

"Pinega is a long march from here," Zakov said.

The injured man groaned. "No hurry, no worry. Winter will come soon, in full muscle, and me lovely British brothers will be gobsmacked by the realities of Northern Russia. Fighting in the snow and cold pits one against multiple enemies, most all of them not human."

"Your unit trained together?" Zakov asked the man.

"S'far as I know, there was no training whatsoever. Most of us were conscripted and handed empty rifles with a rather drunken, cloying stench wafting off the so-called political officers. Assured us we'd be given bullets when it was time to fight."

Bapcat spoke. "You were told you'd be fighting the British?"

"Bloody hell, Yank." The man laughed. "An American gent behind Red Lines? The commissars were quite emphatic that the Allies could not possibly penetrate the People's Lines, yet here you are, in the flesh. Quite astonishing."

"Were you or were you not going to fight British soldiers?" Bapcat asked again.

The prone man chuckled. "Last I knew, sport, and not officially, mind you, we had a colonel by rank, a former Tsarist officer, there at Trotsky's insistence. The rest of our officer mob were political swine and rank military amateurs; how's that for the people's swill, the ignorant led by the equally ignorant? We had a few former small-unit officers suddenly elected to run operations they admitted were too large for them. The whole thing is a fool's errand, Forlorn Hope and all that stupidly heroic noise to make war without a chain of command or rules of engagement, and to attack head-on, all-out, but me Bolshevik brothers tend toward a sort of airy-fairy, temporary, ad hoc approach to most things, effectiveness be damned."

"Your own comrades shot you," Zakov said.

"Was like this, see. Word went through the ranks, we couldn't sort it from rumor, and one of the comrades felt compelled to put forward that I was English-born, -bred, and -educated, the whole lot, yes?" The man took a shallow breath. "I laughed at the blighters—a severe mistake, in retrospect."

"And here you are," Zakov said.

"I tried to defend myself, of course, pointed out passionately and eloquently how I had come to teach Latin and mathematics. I tried to dodge the fact that I came to tutor brats of aristocrats and landed in a classroom with unwashed urchins in Vologda. They were *not* swayed. I then explained to them rather patiently that mathematically, one cannot prove a negative, but they remained unmoved. 'We have accused you of spying, which makes you a spy.' There was a show of hands in support of the secret court's verdict, and there were no objections or abstentions. Our elected captain stuffed me guts with a bayonet here, where I lay, and marched the men eastward. Two of me lovely comrades circled back with tobacco and morphine, as I previously explained. Might I borrow a bullet from you lads? I promise not to waste it."

"How many men with you?" Bapcat asked.

"Hundreds, I suppose," the Englishman said. "Couldn't give you a specific head count."

Jordy came into the clearing. "Ivan just found two Russians killed by bears. Right by our boat. He sent me to fetch you."

"Any sign of the animal?" Bapcat asked.

Before Jordy could respond, a huge bear burst out of the river, shaking itself mightily, and ran inland, crashing its way loudly through the underbrush.

"Bears?" the dying Enlishman exclaimed. "Astonishing. This new snow will finally drive the beggars to hibernation."

"What Russians?" Zakov asked Jordy.

"Close to the boat, no rifles, no bayonets, no bullets. The bears dragged the bodies, but abandoned them. They may come back."

They left the Englishman and went to see the dead men.

Uniforms identical to the injured Brit. Zakov knelt and examined the dead.

"Throats cut; not usually how a bear works. Men killed these soldiers."

Bapcat looked back toward where the dying Brit reclined.

Zakov said, "Grandfather Wolf."

After a minute or so, two men stepped out, both covered in bear robes, the huge animal heads intact as hoods.

Bapcat was speechless. Black Wolves, in the flesh.

"Colonel," the larger of the two men said. "We knew you would eventually come this way. The Bolsheviks have announced the Tsar's death—'while attempting to escape.' You have the royal family with you, Colonel?"

"They are dead," Zakov said. "All of them murdered in a small room in Yekaterinburg. Their retainers and staff, too."

One of the Wolfmen hissed and blessed himself in the Eastern style, right to left rather than left to right, as Catholics did. There were some Eastern Orthodox believers in Red Jacket. The difference in blessings had never been explained to Bapcat.

"You're certain they're all dead?" a Wolfman asked.

"One of us saw the executions," Zakov told them.

"How many are you here, just three?"

Zakov said, "A hundred, most behind us."

"Winter is showing some early muscle," the larger man said. "But a hundred are welcome. We were prepared for more."

"I expected the rendezvous farther downriver."

"As did we, but the Elder has men everywhere, watching, and there are forces of varying sizes everywhere along the rivers, Red, White, Green, Nothings."

"The place is safe?" Zakov asked.

"We are secure and shall remain so. The Elder has seen to it, as he always does. When the Elder heard news of the Tsar, he stationed men all the way upriver, to just below Kotlas. Probably you've been watched. The river is clear from here down. Start going again when the light is good. You will be met midday."

"We just saw a bear coming out of the river," Zakov told the men.

"Making its way to its denning area. You may see more."

Zakov told them, "A Bolshevik force, possibly several hundred, went east from here, angling toward Pinega."

"We have followers on them. If they move where we don't want them to be, we will deal with them. Otherwise, their ignorance is our bliss. Do you wish us to deal with the injured Englishman?"

"Were the two dead men with him?"

"No, they are deserters from the force, their presence here a coincidence—God's will."

Zakov nudged his partner. "Let's go."

Jordy was standing by the Englishman and Bapcat asked his son to bring the little boat downriver to them.

"You fellows are on your way, I take it?" the dying man said. "Parting is such sweet sorrow."

Zakov handed the man one bullet.

Said the Englishman, "*De haut en bas, dies irae.* Thank you, comrade. I shall use it in good faith."

The boat bumped to shore, Bapcat got into the stern, Zakov into the middle, and Ivan used a paddle to push them off the bank into the current.

"What did the Englishman say at the end?" Bapcat asked.

"The French part means 'from top to bottom,' and the Latin bit, 'days of wrath.'"

A minute later they heard the hushed cough of a single muffled rifle shot.

41

Winter, 1919. Tsar Alexander's Camp

"On such irony spin the spokes of history."

A half-dozen Wolfmen met the lead boat at midday, the two larger craft trailing somewhere behind them. Bapcat and Zakov left Jordy and Ivan to meet Bezmunyi, to help them get ashore, where they would follow their guides inland.

Bapcat and Zakov had their own guide, who led them into an immense black spruce swamp. There was no discernible trail that Bapcat could see, only spots of snow here and there. Their guide somehow managed to keep them on a sinewy line of firmer ground.

"There," Zakov said after a slow three-hour hike.

Bapcat saw nothing but swamp and a slight rise of elevation that stretched roughly north and south. Beyond this one feature, nothing.

He looked at his partner and shook his head. "Nope."

Zakov said quickly, "A clue: No straight lines, vertical or horizontal, and no hints, which is a hint itself." The Russian was grinning.

Bapcat said, "All I see is swamp and a low berm, not a ridge, though some might be tempted to call it that. It runs north to south and can't be ten feet at its highest point."

Zakov said, "Think hummingbird's nest."

Bapcat hated games and puzzles. He closed his eyes. Hummingbird nests tended to be invisible in the wild, even to experienced eyes. Hummingbirds knew how to hide things in plain sight.

"Natural skin of lichen spun with spider threads," he said.

"Exactly," Zakov said. "*Bricolage* is a French word, meaning to build with whatever materials are available, and native, nothing brought in from elsewhere."

"I still don't see anything," Bapcat admitted.

Zakov waved a hand at their guide, who pulled on the peak of a six-foot-high black spruce, which, when flipped on its side, revealed a dark, obviously man-made opening into the slight rise Bapcat already had identified.

Bapcat looked into the hole, which seemed to descend at a 45-degree angle.

"The Tsar's camp? Not exactly grand."

Zakov smiled. "The Tsar had many qualities, and simplicity was a significant one. He liked his hunting camps on the primitive side, not some remote Hermitage."

Hermitage? Bapcat had no idea what Zakov meant.

"This is the way in?"

"One of many," the Russian said.

"I couldn't see it at all."

Zakov said, "Confession, my friend: Neither could I—now, or when I first saw it so long ago. But the guides know, and if we lived here, we'd know too. No stranger can see what's here. It's ingenious, even a work of art. The French claim to have invented camouflage, but we Russians have taken the practice far beyond the discoverer's vaunted imaginations or abilities.

"Alexander had a passion for natural things, his camps included. He wanted them unobtrusive and invisible, and he always talked about hosting his guests in the natural world, this, a side of the man few were privileged to see, and most could not even imagine in someone known to be so brutally direct and blunt. This place was a state secret and remains so. I suspect that even if the Bolsheviks mine Imperial records, there will be nothing of this anywhere. The secret is passed person to person, by voice."

"This Tsar was a good man?"

Zakov squinted. "Good? He was complicated: simple in some ways, stubborn, opinionated, direct, and raw, like the Russian people, and unlike his kin, the man loathed the waste and pomposity of the Romanov royal lifestyle. He liked to summer with his family on the Finnish coast, living simply. He was an unbelievably strong man, physically and mentally, shrewd without telegraphing it. Alexander feared no man and threatened no one. But it was under him that a plot against his life was discovered. Five men were arrested, tried, and executed, including one Alexander Ulyanov," Zakov said.

Bapcat said, "And?" Was there a point in this history lesson?

"Ulyanov was Lenin's brother."

Now he understood. "Surviving brother does what dead brother failed at."

"Russians elevate vengeance and payback to high performance art," Zakov said.

"Five men executed for trying to kill the Tsar, and this leads to the killing of thousands?"

"Or millions," Zakov said. "It's not yet decided who will rule here or how."

"Crazy," Bapcat said.

"On such irony spin the spokes of history."

His partner's words often baffled. Spokes of history?

"You're saying Alexander was not a good man?"

Zakov blinked. "Not especially good, but he had wide interests and deep, often unbendable, and for many, unbearable principles."

———

After two hours underground they settled into an area called the Map Room, with dozens of shelves lined with leather-bound books and racks of paper and rolled vellum maps mounted on wooden dowels. The inner workings of the camp were neither ornate nor exotic. Everything was simple, plain, and sturdy, built to last. Bapcat had seen twenty-plus rooms, none of them expansive.

"How many Wolfmen here?"

"You're concerned about space?"

"We have a hundred heads."

"There is more than ample space, my friend. You haven't seen even a fraction of what's down here. This camp is huge and sprawling."

"*Why* haven't I seen everything?" Bapcat asked.

Zakov studied his partner. "You doubt my judgment?"

"That's not it. You know I have a poor imagination and need to see things for myself."

"Don't undersell yourself," Zakov said. "Very well; follow me, comrade."

Three hours later, Bapcat declared he had seen more than enough of what had soon begun to look all the same to him.

They returned to the Map Room, where the Wolfmen had installed a samovar. The camp, Bapcat now saw, was cut into a spider of limestone that seemed to twist and wind all through the area, all of which, as he had experienced, was invisible from the surface, the only possible clue, the one inconsequential upfold of ground he had seen. Most of the underground was divided into segments and rooms by simple wood panels or heavy wooden doors. The only steel door was in the Map Room.

"The crown jewels?" Bapcat joked, pointing at the door.

"Yes, in fact," Zakov said, playfully or mysteriously. Bapcat wasn't quite sure which, and before his partner could explain, a Wolfman came in and babbled in Russian at Zakov, who turned to him and said calmly, "A Bolshevik column has been seen, moving this way. Four hours out, perhaps five."

"Bound for here?" Bapcat asked.

"Moving west in this general direction, its intent to be determined. We will decide whether or not to intervene once we gauge their intent. We shall deploy accordingly and keep a close watch."

"Can you use Ivan's men?"

"Not yet. This ground is too complicated. It's too soon for them. Perhaps later. The Wolfmen can handle this."

"Would it be better for us to keep moving north to find American troops?"

"The Wolfmen report Bolo forces all along the river right now, between here and Allied lines. We'd never get our boats through, and there's no good trail on either side of the river. Our best choice is the original plan: Remain here and wait for spring. When we move again, we will have early open water and only some snow, which should make for easier going. There are good maps and charts here to help us prepare."

"If the Bolos aren't making a drive toward this place," Bapcat reminded his friend.

"Relax," Zakov said, and used a huge old key to open the great steel door.

Bapcat walked in and looked around as Zakov lit a lantern. They were standing in a long corridor with a snug, wooden floor. Along the walls were eight four-foot-in-diameter portholes about twenty feet apart, which immediately reminded him he was underground. He broke into a sweat.

Zakov said, "Secret of the room," and held his lamp close to one of the portholes.

Bapcat thought he saw something move in one of the portholes and took a step backward.

"What the—?"

"Bear," Zakov said. "Not just any bear, but a survivor bear, a monster of unreal proportions, a species that lived in the times of cavemen. Some scientists now refer to them as cave bears. There are eight of them in hibernation here every season. This is the only place in Russia, and probably, in the world, where these ancient creatures survive."

Bapcat squinted. "It looks like a brown bear."

"Cave bear, my friend—a true treasure. This population has been under observation since 1870. The Tsar's experts are the ones who decided these were cave bears. More irony. This limestone cave formation was theirs long before it was the Tsar Alexander's."

Bapcat had never heard of cave bears.

"The experts think there are brown bears in this region who share cave bear blood, though this remains entirely speculative. These things look like meat-eating, killing machines, but they prefer vegetables almost exclusively. The Black Wolves understand this and leave the animals in peace. There are, of course, rumors circulating in neighboring regions, and some hunters are anxious to kill one of these creatures, but the Wolfmen have been able to prevent this from happening—so far. These creatures are an unknown part of Russia's natural prehistory."

Bapcat had heard enough of vegetable-eating bears. "If the Bolos are headed *here?*" he asked.

"We will have to kill them," Zakov said. "The Wolfmen have been preparing for this for a long, long time."

Bapcat took a final look at the enormous bear on the other side of the thick glass.

"How can we fight if no war has been declared?" This still nagged at him.

"While we are here, we shall fight as Wolfmen, not as American soldiers. Think self-defense *in extremis*. Protect ourselves, the Wolfmen, and these special animals. Is this not our sworn charge back home as deputy game wardens?"

"We are not back home," Bapcat pointed out.

He needed to see Jordy and have him close. If there was to be a fight, he wanted his son beside him.

Six hours later the Wolfmen announced that the Red column had changed directions and the camp was secure, with all of the people from the flotilla now safely underground and settling in.

Zakov looked at Bapcat and yawned.

"You need a shave. You look like a winter yak."

Bapcat had never heard of anything called a yak, but it didn't sound good. He answered, "And you smell like one."

42

Winter, 1919. Map Room Drop-In

"*Zlad*," Zakov said solemnly. "Treasure."

Vukevich got on with the Wolfmen's headman as if he'd always known him, but Zakov assured Bapcat the apparent closeness was no more than simple Russian hospitality, and that by custom, even enemies would be treated in similar fashion. Russia might be lawless and in free fall elsewhere, but here, there were customs and rules that abided.

It seemed obvious to Bapcat that despite Vuke's claims, the man's map-reading skills were suspect. It had taken quite a number of days with him to wrest out the longtime violator's travels south from what Vuke called Allied lines. Bapcat eventually got the route on paper and compared it to maps the Wolfmen had. Bapcat use wooden pins to mark the stopping points of Vuke's journey, connecting them with thread to show the route.

The deputy game warden sensed that the map and markers were drawing a blank in Vuke's mind, and when he asked if this was the route he and Dixon had traveled, Vuke nodded, said, "Ya sure, she look pretty good, dat map dere. We move north soon?"

"We've got a hundred people, Vuke. Takes time to plan moves."

"Yah, she's real mob, dis; be impossible sneak whole bunch north downriver."

"Zakov wants to winter here, wait for open water in spring."

"Makes sense, eh. Other side dis river got few roads or trails, and she's bloody damn hard going, mostly dat pesky, bouncy muskeg. Best bet is cross ice, go over snow wit' *les raquets*, or da skis, eh?"

"We're looking at all options," Bapcat told the man. "How's your partner?"

"City Boy? He's not my partner, and you can't fix what's broke in a fool's head. Anybody gets stuck with him is in for it. Besides, he seems pretty happy right here. An *inside* boy, that one. Seems to like these Wolfmen and makes out like he's the assistant head Wolf-in-charge or something. The Wolfmen, they seem real polite, but pay no attention to him. Dixon told me he might just stay here when we leave, and I didn't say nothin'. The man's a fool, figures there's better odds here underground then risking taking a bullet outside trying to make it back to our own lines. Major McNulty seemed he wanted me to take the guy, but I always had in mind the guy would desert and maybe the major sent him just so he wouldn't have to deal with him, you know—one less problem wit' all the stuff the major was dealing with. Ask me, we should leave him behind, save us, and the Army some trouble."

"Not our job to make a decision like that. If he's army, he goes with us."

Vukevich made a sour face. "What the heck *is* our job, Lute?"

"Get to our lines, follow orders from there."

Vuke shook his head. "You fellas being here, I find all this real hard to figure. You fellows ain't yet said why you're so far outside our lines, eh?"

"Orders, Vuke, which is all you need to know."

"No sweat off my back," the former violator said.

— ᵔ —

Bapcat spent most of his days looking in on the rest of their company, trying to assess their mental and physical condition. Bezmunyi seemed overwhelmed to be reunited with his sons.

Elpy kept company with Jordy and Anton. Ivan hung around his men, who clearly trusted his leadership and seemed ready to follow him without question. He'd seen similar trust in leadership in Colonel Roosevelt in Cuba. It was rare and an astonishing thing to be a part of.

Nights Lute spent in the Map Room, where Zakov usually joined him. It had been some time since the Russian had talked about the mystery intruder from a week or so after their arrival, right after the Bolo threat had dissipated.

—

Lute remembered they had been in the Map Room that night when the chief of the Wolfmen rushed in and whispered to Zakov, who looked at Bapcat and said, "Security reports a stranger."

"A stranger?"

"Unidentified."

"Will they challenge him?"

"Only if he poses a direct threat."

"Strangers are rare here?"

"Rare enough, and from the descriptions I'm getting, I think there's some possibility this is your major."

Bapcat said to Zakov, "Could Dodge know about this place?"

"We can't rule it out. He seems to get around Russia rather efficiently. He looks and acts the brash American, but he was born here and has a Russian soul."

"And if it is Dodge and he's trying to get here?"

"I should wonder why; is it simply to rendezvous with us or for more nefarious purposes?"

Bapcat grunted. "Nefarious?"

"Russians would suspect he is *zloi, likhol okhotnik*; in English, the wicked, evil hunter."

"Hunter of what—us?"

"*Zlad*," Zakov said solemnly. "Treasure."

Bapcat had entertained similar thoughts earlier.

"What the hell would he be after here?"

Zakov said, "*Bubny* . . . the Tsar's."

"The Tsar's booby?"

His partner rolled his eyes. "*Bubny*. Diamonds."

"The Tsar's diamonds are here?"

"Certainly not all of them, but there is a substantial cache."

"Is this widely known?"

"Among the Wolfmen. Remember, this place is a state secret."

"Wolfmen aren't tempted to help themselves?"

"The price would be too high," Zakov said. "These people are about honor and duty, not wealth. I'm done talking now. I need sleep."

Bapcat wasn't ready to let it go. "You think Dodge is on government business or his own?"

The Russian raised his jaw as he sometimes did when he was trying to think deeply.

"I should think a blend of the two. Why?"

"Not sure, but something about that man has grated from the start. Did he come into Russia with you?"

"Why do you ask?" Zakov said.

"He makes decisions, and he has some grit and some abilities and skills, yet the whole package doesn't seem to equal the parts. You met him before you got here?"

"I never met him, but I observed him at a distance. The original plan was for him to guide me in under an embassy umbrella, but I convinced Mr. Churchill that I could work more effectively alone. Churchill ordered a submarine, remarkable gadgets, those, and I came ashore alone. The Royal Navy men were quite thorny about carrying me—drop-offs, I gather, are something rather new and nerve-wracking for them—but it was Churchill's idea, you see, and they dared not sail their tempers too close to his winds. I came ashore just above Murmansk. You came in the same way, yes?"

"It was not a pleasure voyage," Bapcat told his friend, shuddering at the memory of tight quarters and confined darkness. "Dodge was with us, acted like such landings were old hat."

"After me, perhaps, it is becoming so, but clearly not before."

"Dodge was a Churchill pick for this duty?"

"America's choice, I believe, but precisely who selected him or why, we shall never know. Now I'm really done talking. May I please go to sleep now?"

Bapcat considered making a joke about it being a free country, but this was not a joking matter, and he wasn't at all sure Russia was a country anymore. Nobody seemed in charge and no rules seemed to apply to anyone, except in the sprawling, limestone cave royal hunting camp.

———

At what Lute thought was the end of the night's intruder another Wolf-man came in, spoke to Zakov, and left.

Zakov said, "The Wolfmen lost the intruder, whoever it was."

Bapcat asked, "When?"

"A week ago."

"I thought all this stuff was happening now?"

Zakov shook his head, said, "No."

"They lost him?"

"It happens. They've been keeping me apprised. These men are experienced at cat-and-mouse, but they are not sure what happened. One minute he was there and the next he was gone."

"Is this normal—for them to lose those they are tracking?"

"It's rare for them to lose anything, but it happens."

"Will they try to figure out what went wrong?"

"They think he veered north and was never headed this direction at all."

"Their reasoning?"

"There are two old Tsarist trails that run north. If one knows where they are, they're easy enough to read and follow."

"North to where?"

"Seltso . . . eventually."

"Americans there?"

"According to the Wolfmen, possibly some, but most believe the Americans are somewhere north of there—certainly in Bereznik, which is the main river port for Archangelsk."

Bapcat said, "Currently iced in."

"No doubt." Zakov raised an eyebrow. "The Wolfmen say come spring, the ice will go out upstream before it goes out below Bereznik."

"How long before?"

"Two weeks; a month. It varies each year, and we will have all winter to ponder it."

Each winter was its own, just like in the Upper Peninsula, Bapcat thought.

"Something's not right."

Now Zakov was sitting up. "Your word *something* is pathetically less than precise."

Bapcat said, "I feel what I feel."

"Feel it *now?*"

"Still, yes, now."

"Let us have light," Zakov said, grabbing a lantern and a wooden match.

Bapcat lit two tapers and gave one to his partner. Bapcat slowly walked the perimeter of the Map Room, pausing often, holding out the candle, listening, sniffing the air. He eventually stopped at the wooden shutters which the Wolfmen had pulled closed over the portholes to the bear dens.

"Thought I heard a sound somewhere over here," he told Zakov, who opened the shutters, but the den was dark and it was hard to see.

Zakov brought his lantern to the glass port and held it up, moved it around, looking for an angle to see through to the other side.

Bears had always fascinated Bapcat. The magnificent creature in this den had a huge head and body; how an animal that size could subsist solely on greenery was beyond him, but so too did elk and moose, while certain chipmunks cannibalized their own and deer sometimes ate minnows out of streams. Mother Nature surely had her reasons, and who was he to question her wisdom or her handiwork.

They left the shutters open and went to sleep.

❧

First thing next morning, Bapcat went to eat breakfast with the Chief Engineer and Crazy Ivan, to talk about supplies and other issues involved in the eventual trek north to the American lines.

When he got back to the Map Room, he found the Wolfman chief and Zakov in front of the porthole.

"We should have closed that last night," Bapcat apologized.

"You should look, comrade," Zakov said.

Bapcat stood close and tried to see. Something inside had changed, but it took time to figure it out. The animal had shifted position and now lay on its side, its great hairy belly facing the Map Room. It looked like it was curled around something.

"Is there a cub?" It was too early for cubs, but this bear was not like those he knew.

"Bears are bears," Zakov said.

He then said something to the Russian leader, who laughed.

Zakov said, "Look closer, wife."

It took some seconds of concentration before he saw.

"Good grief, that's *Dodge's* pack! Is Dodge in there?"

Zakov said, "How do you know it's the major's pack?"

"It's wrapped in woven red cords. Only one I've ever seen like it."

Zakov said, "Neither exclusive nor convincing evidence."

"Braided from dyed horsehair or elk sinew or something. Dodge had this cord on his pack when we landed at Murmansk, and later, when we saw him at the burial site. Is he in the den too? Can we get him out?"

Zakov sighed. "If he *is* in there, he is now in pieces, inside the bear."

"What happened to eating greens and such?"

"In their dens they will kill anything they find. Life gets reduced down to fat, and anything that will make fat is consumed."

"Good grief," Bapcat said. "Why would Dodge go into a bear's den?"

"Perhaps that was not his intention."

"Are you sure there's a person in there?"

"Look on the lower right of the porthole."

Bapcat looked, saw the reddish-brown smear. "Blood?"

"Presumably."

Bapcat sighed. "An awful way to die."

"The irony is overwhelming," Zakov said.

"Irony?"

"There were diamonds in his pack, remember?"

Bapcat remembered.

"Somewhere inside that den is a vault filled with more diamonds."

"The Tsar's vault is in there?"

"There is a small vault in each den," Zakov said.

"I thought the Tsar wanted to protect these bears."

"Why should they not earn their keep in the hotel their Tsar built for them?"

"The dens are empty in summer."

"Other measures are taken then," Zakov said, closing the shutters.

43

Breaking Spring, 1919. Crossing the Icy Dvina, from Hell to Hell

"I told him you are Nostradamus when it comes to reading ice."

Many cold and snowy months had passed since they'd gone underground.

Bapcat was listening to the Wolfmen's Elder as he delivered the latest scouting report, Zakov translating. The upper river was ice-free down to its confluence with the Vaga. From there north to Archangelsk, the big river was one solid ice jam, shifting and moving on God's whim, temperature shifts, and the winds every day. Most crossings by enemy troops were being made westward by small boats, above the ice jams. The Reds had snipers arranged along high ground at several locations, the snipers not always alert and dutiful, and never many of them in any given location, but enough to inflict some casualties on any unsuspecting landing party.

"Will the boats be out of sniper range if we float down the eastern shoreline?" Zakov asked the Elder in Russian, and the man nodded.

Zakov looked at Bapcat. "We can get our boats by the shooters down this side."

The headman immediately wanted to know why they would do this; why not attack and kill the Bolsheviki snipers?

Bapcat was having his own thoughts.

"Have him tell us about the ice jams," Bapcat told his partner.

Zakov translated after the Elder finished.

"He says the ice was put there by the Devil to crush his enemies."

"Ask him if the Tsar's men are the Devil's enemies."

The headman seemed flummoxed by this, and Bapcat immediately amended the question.

"Alexander's men, not those of Nicholas."

This, when translated, brought a relieved nod.

Zakov said, "He says God was always with Alexander, but flung his arrows at Nicholas the Bloody."

Bapcat smiled. "These ice jams; what colors are they?"

A confused headman listened to Zakov, said, "*Sin'ka, zelen, prosed.*"

And Zakov translated to English, "Blue, green, gray."

"No purples or lavenders?" Bapcat asked.

The headman conferred with his scout, and Zakov translated.

"Such color is found in only one place, there every year, always in the same place, and it is the most dangerous place on the river this time of year."

"They know it to be dangerous, or they have heard this from others?"

"It has always been so," the headman told Zakov in Russian.

Purplish and always there. Bapcat had seen such formations in the Upper Peninsula. Purple meant temporary ice bridges formed by massive pressure ridges.

"We'll cross at the purple," Bapcat announced.

The headman's eyes bugged out when he heard this, and he yelled at Zakov, who said to Bapcat, "The Elder says you have a death wish and no brain, but I told him you are Nostradamus when it comes to reading ice."

"The notredamus where George plays football?" Bapcat said.

George was their young friend George Gipp of Laurium, who had worked various jobs for them and whom they considered family.

Zakov sighed. "That is Notre Dame, his college. Nostradamus is a long-dead Frenchman some fools think could read the future—even ours."

"What's that got to do with ice?"

"I was trying to pay you a compliment."

"What's the headman say now?"

The Elder shook his head and walked away with no further comment.

The ice report was as Bapcat hoped, but it would take time to move so many across in broad daylight.

Crazy Ivan wanted to take one boat with twenty men, cross at night above the western-bank snipers, and kill them. Bapcat reminded the Russian that with increasing snowmelt, the river was high, and there would be no way to maneuver the boat back upstream against the current, and across to the others, who needed it.

Ivan grumbled, "But to cross ice we've not even seen?"

"The color tells me what I need to know," Bapcat said, hoping river ice here behaved as it did back home.

Ivan said, "I met a beauty with purple hair one time in Manchuria. I was sure she was what I wanted. What I got was Chinese black clap. You have a hundred souls in your care. You have to be certain about this ice thing."

⌐ ⌐

As soon as he saw the ice color he knew he was right. He quickly devised a plan. He and Jordy would cross first, marking the way with fresh black spruce boughs. Ivan and twenty of his best fighters would cross right behind them. From there Ivan would take his ten best and go clean out any snipers, while Jordy and Vuke would greet and guide the rest of the group across. Zakov and Bapcat would remain with some of Ivan's men as a rear guard.

From his memory of the old Tsarist maps, Bapcat guessed the crossing would be about a quarter-mile, bank to bank, even with the shorelines stacked with ice mounds.

Bapcat explained to Ivan where he wanted explosive charges placed. Once they were all safely across, Ivan would blow apart the ice bridge and make pursuit impossible.

⌐ ⌐

In the end Bezmunyi took over the reception role on the far bank and Jordy went with Ivan's hunting party to find Russian snipers. Bapcat heard

358

distant shooting, but the move was committed, and now he needed to focus on his new role keeping everyone crossing the ice bridge in Jordy's absence.

The route had been marked by small spruce boughs and ten of Ivan's men. The Chief Engineer went in the front rank to ward off any unexpected Bolo reception. Bapcat scampered back across the river ice to start moving the others, and at the end of the line on the far bank he found Zakov and ten of Ivan's soldiers, tense and deployed in a fan behind the others.

"What's going on?"

"We seem to have a follower," Zakov said.

"Sighted?"

"He'd better be to cross this ice," Zakov quipped.

"This is no time for jokes, Pinkhus Sergeyevich."

"It is so like a wife to step on her dear husband's fun."

"You get the rear security detail across, and I will go see who finds us so interesting."

After months under the ground and snow, Bapcat felt good to be outside and moving again, to have a purpose beyond waiting and stewing over the past and future.

"You go alone?" Zakov said.

"So we are born, so we shall die," Bapcat said.

"Your words are proof that homespun philosophers have little common sense. We shall see what is there together, comrade."

Since joining the Michigan Conservation Department they had operated like twin shadows, able to move in dicey moments with few words and only the occasional look or sleight-of-hand gesture to communicate.

Zakov wagged an ungloved hand at a pile of snow on some lowbush cranberry plants ahead of them. Bapcat saw a blurred scrape or print, no sole; a mukluk? Bolos? he wondered. If so, was this a scout?

With their rear guard making their way across, there were only two of them to block any pursuing force. How much time would Jordy and Ivan allow before blowing the explosives strung across the river?

Zakov was holding the palm of his hand parallel to the ground and pressing it slowly downward. Bapcat looked at his partner's eyes and followed their line to more imprints in the snow. The follower was either inexperienced or inept, or both. No scout could be so sloppy and stay alive for long.

His Russian partner's hand turned on its side and made a slow, arcing turn that started left and then veered gradually right. Bapcat nodded and made the opposite sign with his hand and started advancing, expecting that they would rejoin somewhere ahead in the dense black spruces.

The temperature was hovering around freezing, with a dull sun lighting the gray skies. Snow and ice gaudily dripped from tree branches, making it noisy and easy for their purposes. Bapcat saw some dark blemishes on scabs of porous ice. Blood? Still-hunting now, bent low, immobile, letting his eyes do the moving and searching, waiting, then moving slowly ahead a few paces, repeating, and, above all, remaining patient and alert.

Had Zakov seen the blood? There were no tracks right here, only the spots, which he assumed were blood. Two men? Injured animals and men were equally unpredictable. Where were Ivan's men now? Halfway—more? In place on the far bank?

Still-hunting taught you to look for things which didn't belong in order to see what was actually there: shapes, colors, sounds, smells, movement, never a whole animal or person, just a part, a suggestion, which your brain had to learn to assemble into some semblance of a whole. Bapcat knew he preferred wholes over pieces, conclusions and identification over suggestions and maybes.

How far to his left was Zakov? What was he seeing?

Freeze!

A color that didn't fit, a dark and unnatural green in a landscape of gray and pale brown. Light striking whatever it was—wood rot, reindeer lichen? Old fungi exposed or woody growths? His brain whispered: man-made. He froze, not moving, not breathing.

A voice startled his concentration.

"If you've got some manufactured smokes, I would beg one and be forever in your debt. Another puff or whiff of *makhorka* and I shall simply die. I would rather smoke dry cow flops."

Dodge? How?

"You're dead, Major."

"As you can hear, Captain, I am quite convincingly still among the living and not the prodigal son returned home. That is because I see no need to beg forgiveness from anyone, certainly not God, who we have all seen quite clearly has no interest in Russia or Russians. The Bolos need not declare religion dead and gone. It's already been abandoned by most Russians. Do you or do you not have a smoke?"

"Show yourself," Bapcat ordered, pointing his rifle at the voice and patch of dark green.

"You dare use such a tone with your superior officer, your commander?"

"*Please* stand so I can see you, Major. I'm in charge now. Rank means nothing here."

Dodge said, "I prefer to sit; in fact, I insist on it."

Bapcat still couldn't make out the man. He had almost walked right past him, and this did not sit well. Dodge hiding? No, he was talking, which suggested he wanted to be identified and found. Or did he? Dodge was impossible to read.

"You died in the bear's den," Bapcat ventured.

"Was *that* what it was? Sounds like a messy way to check out. Astonishing. I saw it only as a handy hole sent by Providence. All I knew was that my nemesis and foe had no idea there was a hole there. He was there one moment, gone the next. Never made a sound. One step toward me with his rifle leveled and poof, gone.

"Come forward, Captain," Dodge continued. "I hate talking through this damn shrubbery. Was there a bear in the den?"

"A very unhappy one," Bapcat said, easing forward. "The man's dead. We saw your pack, the red cords, thought it was you."

"An understandable conclusion. No tears shed by me for that bastard. He dogged me for weeks, already got some of my diamond stash, and wanted to finish me to close the job."

"You've been following us," Bapcat said, trying to refocus.

"I can't say I knew it was you, chum, but I saw what I took for White soldiers, and they looked organized. They had obviously found a way across the river. I was simply waiting my turn, you might say, but as it turns out, I'm glad it *is* you, Captain."

"Do you know where our lines are?" Bapcat asked.

"Educated surmise and some familiarity with geography helps me guess where they might be, but listening to chatter among Bolo troops helps even more."

"You talk to the Reds?"

"Only when I have to. Mostly I listen from hiding, or did. Russians and secrets are soon separated."

"Seems to me the Reds did a pretty good job keeping the hiding place of the Tsar and his family secret."

"To outsiders, perhaps, but inside it could hardly be called a secret. To effectively spy here, you need someone who is *here*."

"You were in the grips of gewgaw fever when last we saw you," Bapcat told the marine.

"Appearances deceive, books and covers, all that, Captain. I was simply following orders, as are you."

"Is that what you're doing here?" Zakov asked, his rifle at the ready.

"Ah, the elusive Russian," Dodge said. "I was certain you would by now be holding a White generalship and be busy sorting out toy soldiers, fools, and the inept from the true warriors. God knows, they have plenty of fools and inepts. The Bolos were amateurs to start out, but thanks to Trotsky and the professional White soldiers he's hired for leadership jobs, the Bolos are steadily learning and growing. The Whites, meanwhile, wallow in self-pity and petty aristocratic politics. With a real leader, the Whites could crush the Reds as easily as swatting a fly."

"A role you might relish?" Zakov asked.

Dodge smiled grimly. "I was born here, but I am now American through and through, my friend. I am no longer of this place, nor it of me."

"We're not Whites," Bapcat told the major. "We're US Army, and we are headed home."

"A noble and shared goal," Dodge said. "But I have clearly seen that your fighting force is Russian."

"We have what we need," Zakov told the man. "You went your own way."

"And I have returned."

Bapcat had the sudden thought: How had Dodge gotten this far on his broken leg?

Zakov said gruffly, "You won't find God's boundless mercy here, Dodge. You may have come back from the dead, but to us, you are lost and gone. Where's your treasure?"

Audible sigh, followed by, "Ah, the treasure. Of course, you wish to secure a share of the spoils."

"What magnitude of spoils?" Zakov asked. "And where?"

"Three boxcars of Tsarist bullion, a miscellany of jewels—some of which you've seen. The Reds are, despite Lenin's claim to human and political purity and parity, nothing but cheap buccaneers." Dodge chuckled. "I suspect they fear being caught and found clinging to their little spoils and joys. By the way, there are, by my count, twenty-eight additional boxcars unaccounted for. Thirty-one in all."

Zakov asked, "In whose possession?"

"Alas, details elude public knowledge. Some rumors allege Admiral Kolchak's Legionnaires have them, but rumor without substantiation is just so much hot air."

"Where are your three boxcars?"

"Quite safe and secure, thank you," Dodge said, "their whereabouts known solely to me."

"What happened to the Allied effort to recover their assets from Russia?" Zakov said.

"On hold, I should think, in abeyance, if you will, in absentia and so forth. These things may someday be recovered—perhaps. Time and history will tell."

"Recovered by the Allies, or you?" Bapcat asked quietly.

Dodge grinned and shrugged. "That's your distinction, comrade, not mine."

So many worthless words from the man.

"We want to see your orders, the ones that deal with gold and such."

"One does not carry explicit papers, or any papers, for that matter, except those few needed to make one's way."

"Which leaves us only with your word."

"You know me as a brother officer, dispatched by Roosevelt and Churchill. I am legitimate and credentialed, beyond reproach, and I have decided in my role as senior officer present to accompany your ragtag expedition."

Bapcat reacted quickly and calmly. "Your rank doesn't amount to snake spit. I command these ragtags, who, if I decide they ought, will escort you from here to the provost marshal. You may be legit, but if something looks, smells, or sounds like it came out of a bull's back end, well . . . that's what it is. No more talk, Dodge. We're moving, and you can come along or stay; it's your choice."

Dodge said, "The word from Roosevelt was that you were a man of hard heart. I can see that now, but not when we started out. It remains to be seen if you have it in you to give the ultimate order."

Bapcat stared at the man, who seemed too still, strangely so, like a statue.

"Ultimate order?"

"To leave men behind."

"Why would I do that?"

"Come closer. Let me whisper a secret to you."

Bapcat glanced at Zakov, who was scanning east into a rolling cold mist.

Bapcat stepped closer, and Dodge whispered, "Closer . . . this needs to be just between us."

Bapcat bent over and Dodge said, "I'm bait, Captain. There are twenty enemy troops poised in the swamp to the east. Don't look."

"Waiting for what?"

"They're Russian," Dodge said. "Whim, God's hand, a wind, who knows. I want you to withdraw now, while you can."

Bapcat looked into the man's eyes, dull and glazed. Pain?

"Your leg?"

"No, it's a bloody bullet near the spine, and I've no legs, just arms. Leave me and I'll give the Reds something to think about. Got a grenade?"

He didn't, but Zakov stepped over and handed one to the major, along with his rifle and three clips.

Bapcat whispered to his Russian partner, "Head for the other side. Tell Ivan and Jordy to blow the bridge when they see and hear me."

"You?"

"Right on your heels."

Zakov turned nonchalantly and strolled into the river mist.

Dodge juggled the grenade in one hand.

"Your turn, Captain. Nice knowing you."

"I don't like this," Bapcat said.

"Git," Dodge said, turned slightly, put his rifle to his shoulder, and fired a round into the mist to the east. "Your cue, Captain. Exit stage rear."

At that moment several shots cracked and a huge dark bear charged between the ambush and them, swerving toward the Bolos, which brought more shots and a laughing Dodge, yelling, "Exit stage left, pursued by bear, the ultimate stage direction!" He fired another round, which this time was answered by a fusillade, and Dodge laughed even harder. "Poor bastards have no discipline. They are shooting at our ursine ally. Run, Captain, run!"

Bapcat scrambled into the fog and mist as more shots popped behind him.

Dodge. How could you figure such a man?

He ran, bent low, watching for spruce ice bridge markers, and as shots grew fewer and fainter, he heard the muted thump of a grenade. As he ran through the soupy air he saw a figure ahead and heard Zakov yelling, "To me, Lute, to me! *Now*, Jordy, *now* Ivan!"

Bapcat jumped over the last ice pile to the far bank and saw only a few men.

"Where is everyone?"

"Moving toward our lines. Vuke's leading. We remain here to make sure nobody gets through."

Jordy was beside his father and said, "Follow me," and Bapcat, too winded to protest, stumbled north, clinging to his son.

He saw blood on the boy's sleeve. "Your arm?"

"It went through clean."

Shot? "Has it been cleaned?"

"No time yet. And cleaned? Out *here*?" His son grimaced.

When the dynamite tore through the ice jam, the earth seemed to shake, and then it was showering ice clods and needles and both men dropped facedown and put their arms over their heads. Were Zakov and Ivan all right?

44

Breaking Spring, 1919. Firefight at Mezhdu Bridge

"People back home, we hear, are not happy about their
boys having their arses bared in Bolshevik Russia six
months after the war with Germany has ended."

The new sound hatched gradually rather than all at once. One moment
they were moving quietly to join the rest of the group, and then heavy
machine-gun fire began to the northwest. The snowy spruce forest
absorbed much of the sound, and Bapcat could pinpoint neither the distance nor the specific direction of the gunfire. He stopped Jordy with his
hand, saying, "That's a fight."

They kept moving forward, and not long thereafter they came across
Bezmunyi, his sons, and Elpy and Anton, who had also heard the fight
start.

Bezmunyi said, "It started west of here."

Anton stared at Jordy's arm and touched it gently. "You're hurt."

"I suppose you're a *doctor* now?" Jordy said sarcastically.

"I could be if I chose," Anton shot back.

They sounded like brothers, or what he imagined bickering brothers
sounded like.

Vuke came out of the spruces, and even with the clammy cold he was
soaked by sweat and melting snow.

"The Mezhdu Bridge is still in place," he told them. "The Allies have
two machine guns on high knobs on the other side and just beyond the

bridge. They've got a full field of fire south against anyone trying to get across or even to converge on the bridge."

"How far?" Bapcat asked.

"A mile, maybe a little more," Vukevich said. "There are a lot of Bolo troops west of us. We're on their east flank, but they don't seem to be paying any attention to us or this flank—at least, not yet."

"Are they after the bridge?"

"Seems that way," Vuke said.

Bapcat said, "Show me," and they were gone.

An hour later they were back, and by then Zakov and Crazy Ivan had joined the group, after making sure the ice bridge was down.

Bapcat told them to smoke as he laid out his thoughts.

"The Red flank is exposed. If Ivan launches an attack westward from here, our civilians can slip along the river to the bridge under a white flag."

"I will carry the flag," Anton said. "I am small but strong."

Bapcat patted the boy's shoulder. The kid had grit, no fear.

Ivan said. "They might turn their guns on our people."

Bapcat nodded. "They could, but I don't think they will. If there's a fight in front of them, and no bullets coming their way from that fight, they're likely to be curious—on guard and alert, but curious. Once they see the white flag and know our intent, which the Chief Engineer will deliver to them, they will cover Ivan's fighting withdrawal."

There was almost no discussion, just nodding heads.

Bezmunyi, Anton, and Bezmunyi's sons would each carry a white flag and walk together. The sight of children might buy the group more time, make Allied soldiers delay shooting.

"Where will you be?" Ivan asked Bapcat.

"Jordy, Zakov, Vuke, me, we're all with you, but this assault is yours, and we follow *your* orders."

Ivan nodded, smiled, and laid out a simple assault plan in few words. When they all understood their roles and agreed, he went to assemble and organize his men. So far the group had survived. There were two or three wounded and sick on makeshift litters and some walking, fighting-wounded like Jordy, but no deaths so far. The fighting force was largely intact and almost eager for what came next.

The Bolos had fought hard for ten minutes, then fled, leaving weapons and wounded behind.

Bapcat and Ivan were last to cross the Mezhdu Bridge over *Polumertvyi Rechka*—Half Dead River. The bridge spanned a narrow deep chasm, and Bapcat glanced down only once. As his foot hit the bridge decking he felt something white hot bite into him, and he was immediately disgusted. After the fight they had just come through, *now* he gets hit—and in the ass? The bullet failed to knock him off balance, and it didn't hurt yet, but he wondered what medical troubles lay ahead. He put it out of his mind for the moment and got on with getting over to the Allied troops on the other side of the narrow wooden span.

A short Canadian officer stood waiting with a riding crop tucked under his left arm.

"Captain Bernardski, Third Sudbury Wolves. Who and what might you lads be?"

Bapcat looked the Canadian in the eye. "Captain Lute Bapcat, US Army. Your Mr. Churchill sent us here a year ago to find the Tsar and his family. We came ashore north of Murmansk, delivered by a British submarine. We need to report to Mr. Churchill."

Bernardski grinned. "Winston's neither a brother Canadian nor is he readily available, old scoop. I'd wager there's to be a fair delay before your parley finds fruition."

"Your fellas on the machine guns?" Bapcat asked.

The captain nodded.

"Great shooting."

"All for bloody naught," the Canadian said. "Your lot has arrived just in time for a mass pullback. General Ironside calls it a strategic withdrawal, which is patent bullshit. Where in the States you fellas from?"

"Keweenaw County, western Upper Peninsula of Michigan."

"We're virtual neighbors," the captain said. "Mining's Sudbury's game, too."

The Canadian looked at the ground and said quietly, "Believe you've sprung a leak, old man. Let's get you to hospital and let our medicos have a look."

"Hospital? *Here?*"

"Log cabin in its former life, but having our docs at the Front has saved some of our boys. This way we can evaluate, treat, and manage right here. We get the seriously wounded stabilized and then the natives run them north to Bereznik with sledges pulled by reindeer teams. From there it will be by boats to Archangelsk. Whole system's rather clever and brutally efficient."

"The river's clear of ice?" Bapcat asked.

"Clearing fast is the word we're getting. Some sort of ice break upriver seems to have broken loose and rammed its way down. This surge is wreaking hell on the lower river ice. We already have one large boat in the water and working. Bloody good thing, whatever caused the ice breakup. We've literally been frozen in place for months. People back home, we hear, are not happy about their boys having their arses bared in Bolshevik Russia six months after the war with Germany has ended. An armistice was signed last November."

Armistice? Bapcat grabbed the Canadian's arm. "The war's *over?*"

"Not for us, mate."

"Everyone's pulling out?" Bapcat asked.

"Every country, with Yanks going first. But since you came in with the English, Captain, I'm guessing you'll go out with them, too."

Bapcat was beginning to feel some discomfort.

"Three of us came in. One gave his life for the others. We came to connect with Zakov, who will go out with us. We also have a hundred Russians we want to take with us."

The captain smiled. "The way your boys just fought the Bolos coming out, we'll be happy to have you and your lads. Been a steady stream of Russians begging to get out since we got here last year."

45

Breaking Spring, 1919. Lady Anya and Her Giant

"Nobody kills wounded prisoners!"

Jordy announced that his captain needed medical attention.

"Get his trousers off," a cadaverous man in a blood-covered smock ordered as he limped into the room. The man had white hair, pinked by what Bapcat took to be blood.

"It's not that bad," Bapcat protested as two soldier orderlies grabbed and pressed him facedown on a table made of a door balanced on sawhorses.

"You're lucky it didn't core you like an apple," the snow-haired man said, poking at Bapcat with something sharp. "Not bad," the man said, "not bad at all. Just sort of burrowed a canal through the red meat and flew off to eternity. Some well-placed stitches and you should be good to join the retreat. What's your rank, soldier? You are a soldier, yes? Pointed fur hat, felt boots. You look like a bloody Bolo serf. What bloody army don't wear proper unis?"

"Captain Bapcat, United States Army. The Bolos all have a piece of red ribbon on them."

"Don't get many live Reds here," the man said. "Our boys keep shooting them, and if they lay out in the snow overnight with a superficial wound, they freeze to death. Yank, yes? Come through the whole Bolshie army, one of your lads told me."

"Not as dramatic as that," Bapcat answered, adding, "It burned."

"What burned?"

"The bullet," Bapcat said.

"Neither here nor there," Snow-Hair said, poking again at his wound. "Let's get you stitched and on your way."

"You're leaving too?" Bapcat asked, assuming the man was a doctor.

"The room's full of wounded who can't be moved. G-2 reports the Reds are so far treating prisoners rather decently. My job's to get men home alive, which doesn't include or impose a time schedule."

The man poured something on the wound that sizzled and bubbled and Bapcat said, "Jordy?"

"Right here," the boy said.

"They should take a look at your arm."

"Already have. Another doc stitched me up, and I'm ready to go soon as you're done."

"Doc?"

"He's got the needle in your behind," Jordy said.

"Name's Henriksen," Snow-Hair said. "Can't get over your exotic costumes. Sure you're not one of those Red whores who fled home to Mother Russia and now seeks salvation, from St. George and Uncle Sam. Seen a few of that kind, we have."

Before Bapcat could answer the man's obnoxious question, the cabin door flew open, slammed against the wall, and a half-dozen men in black fur shapkas poured into the room, followed by the biggest man Bapcat had ever seen, taller and more massive than his late friend Louie Moilanen from Hancock, who had been officially measured at seven-foot-three.

The giant was growling in Russian and spitting as he yammered, and Bapcat heard his son translating quietly and calmly. "He orders his men to shoot all prisoners and patients. We are a drain on his resources. We are to be shot now, here."

A woman's angry scream raked the room, smothering the ranting giant.

Bapcat turned his head sideways to get a look and he felt the doctor still working, not missing a stitch, despite the tumult. Jordy again, translating. "Nobody kills wounded prisoners! I will not allow this!"

She punched the giant's chest and pointed a revolver at his enormous head. "You will die first."

"Bah, Milochovsky has a war to fight," the giant said with a snarl, pivoted, and left, his men in tow.

Bapcat looked at the woman, buried in furs. Zakov's sister!

"Sister," Zakov said, sliding in through the open door.

"You shall address me as Lady Anya."

"Where is my wife?"

"Dead. She lacks our constitution, brother."

Jordy surged from Bapcat's side to the door and went outside, shouting, "Nobody threatens my comrades, my allies, wounded men, or my father!"

Bapcat rolled off the table and stumbled after his son, reaching the door in time to see the giant turn and grin and say something, just as Jordy raised his Mosin–Nagant and fired, hitting the man high in his massive forehead, which caused the man's legs to start to buckle. The Russian giant began to spin in slow circles, like a large wolf matting grass for a nest, with each revolution dropping lower, until on his final turn he pitched facedown in black muck and snow.

Jordy immediately began shooting the giant's soldiers, who tried to fight, but were taken by surprise and all fell before they could react.

Jordy looked back at his father and saw Zakov with a rifle, ready to fight.

Bapcat asked, "What did he say before you executed him?"

"He said, 'Finally one who will fight face-to-face, like a man.'"

Bapcat felt dizzy, but Zakov had a grip on his elbow and steadied him.

"I don't need your help," Bapcat grumbled.

"I agree," Zakov said. "What you need is to let the doctor finish sewing that canal in your arse, and more importantly, you need your pants."

Zakov looked at the dead giant and said to his sister, who showed no emotion, "The great giant Red commander Milochovsky, I presume. Your lover."

"He is nothing, brother, but because of him, I have found my calling. Nursing."

"Lady Anya," Snow-Hair called out, "get that man back on the table so I can finish."

Anya took Bapcat's arm and took him inside.

"The Reds will shoot you if you are captured, sister," Zakov said.

"They wouldn't dare," she said.

When the stitching was done, Zakov handed his partner his trousers.

"Milochovsky came across the river west of here and has flanked the retreat. We need to get moving."

The doctor called out, "I'm not quite done with you, Captain," but Lute Bapcat was already dressed, had a rifle in hand, and was moving northeast after the main body of retreating soldiers.

"Yanks," the English doctor said to Lady Anya. "As impetuous as you bloody Russians."

46

Late Summer, 1919. England Again, Briefly

"Bastards," Churchill said with a spitty snarl.

The American troops left in late spring, and Bapcat's company remained with the British throughout the rest of the summer. There was no submarine this time. The light cruiser HMS *Crusader* docked in Southampton after a seven-day voyage from Russia, over almost placid water. A Royal Army lieutenant colonel met them at the top of the gangplank and led them down to a black Bentley, parked in an alley between large soot-covered warehouses. The motorcar was polished brighter than any army dress boots Bapcat had ever seen.

Churchill sat in the back, his thinning red hair plastered to his sweaty skull.

"We were rather afraid we'd lost you gentlemen after the Reds announced the Tsar was shot whilst attempting escape," the Englishman said.

Bapcat said, "Sir, Major Dodge died to help us get out of Russia, and the Tsar, his family, their servants, and friends were shot by the Reds in Yekaterinburg."

"Dodge is dead? Was he empty-handed?"

It was true then, the Allied interest in assets.

"He found thirty-one boxcars filled with Imperial gold bullion and jewels. He managed to recover some jewels, but lost them along the way."

"You have them?"

Bapcat said, "No. A bear has them."

Churchill's eyebrow arched, and he asked, "Liquidated the royal family, is that your claim?"

"Yessir, the Reds murdered them all."

"Evidence or hearsay?"

"Evidence from the guards involved and one of our men, who witnessed it."

"Which of you?" Churchill demanded.

Jordy sheepishly raised his hand. "Me, sir."

"Crown prince, Tsarina, princesses, all of them?" Churchill asked.

"Yessir. It was brutal."

"Bastards," Churchill said with a spitty snarl. "Well, lads, you've certainly done everything asked of you."

He took three blue boxes from a leather bag on the seat beside him. Each box contained a gaudy medal and matching ribbon, and Churchill named the honor, which meant nothing to Bapcat.

"Well earned. Your courage and fortitude are now officially noted. Too bloody bad about Dodge. Did he die bravely?"

"None have died braver," Bapcat told the Englishman. "We're told we need to get medical clearance from your doctors before we can make our way home."

Churchill sputtered. "Doctors' clearance? Bosh and pish! That rule was intended only to screen for Spanish influenza. Any of you lads have that bloody flu?"

They all shook their heads and Churchill said, "Thank you for your service and your courage, gentlemen. The *Crusader* shall deliver you to Halifax, and a train will carry you from there. You should be there in a week, weather permitting."

Ship refueled, eight hours later they were steaming west into the gray Atlantic Ocean. All of them repaired to their bunks and slept until awakened by the skipper's orderly.

"Captain's compliments," the man said. "You are invited to join him and the ship's officers for a celebratory dinner."

Bapcat looked thick-eyed at the emissary.

"Our respects and thanks to your captain, but these bunks won't let us go yet."

The sailor laughed and said, "Skipper guessed this, says the mess will take care of you when you are ready."

The man lingered in the hatch. "What was it like in Russia?" he said.

Zakov said, "How would we know?"

The man said, "But . . . scuttlebutt says that—"

"Never believe scuttlebutt, young man," the Russian scolded gently.

Before sleep took them again, Jordy said, "Doesn't feel like we did much over there, does it?"

"Glories of war," Zakov, said, yawning. "This is how it ends most of the time, weary men headed home, wondering if they made even a small difference."

"Did we?" Jordy asked.

"You have a shiny medal from the English that says so."

"That doesn't meana damn thing," the boy said quietly.

Bapcat grinned. His son had learned something important.

47

Fall, 1919. Gang of Nine, Halifax, Nova Scotia

"Good morning, Captain Bapcat. I'm sorry to report there's a bit of a problem with your lot's paperwork."

Rain falling, not of arkish dimensions, but more the wash-away-everything-but-sin kind, steady, gentle, relentless. Bapcat cinched his black rubber slicker hood tighter. Halifax was not far off now, and after that, Fort Custer, and who knew how long the army would take to muster them out and send them home?

The voyage from England had been easy and relaxed. The Gang of Nine, as Elpy had named them, spent most of the voyage sleeping and eating Royal Navy chow, trying to put on the weight lost from over a year in Russia. The gang consisted of Bezmunyi, his two boys, Elpy, Jordy, Zakov, Anton, Vukevich, and himself. Ivan and all his men had asked in England to go to France to join Russian expatriate forces there. What sort of immigration problems might lie ahead for him, with the Russians, he couldn't imagine, and decided not to try. They would deal with it as they had to.

The rain and low scudding clouds rendered the Halifax waterfront a miserable, slaggy gray, but the ship's sailors were in high spirits, in anticipation of what lay ahead. Having delivered their human cargo to Canada they were being granted a week's shore leave in the city, which, according to the Crusaders (they called themselves after their ship), was overrun by randy Canadian "bush bunnies eager for dance, a drink, and a one-bob rogering." Expectations were running high.

Gangplank finally in place, the ship's captain appeared next to Bapcat.

"Good morning, Captain Bapcat. I'm sorry to report there's a bit of a problem with your lot's paperwork. You and your men are directed to meet the customs superintendent at the harbormaster's office at half-nine this morning."

A statement, not a request. Half-nine meant nine-thirty. How could Englishmen and Americans speak the same language so differently? He shook his head.

The ship's captain added, "Harbormaster here's a fine fellow, retired Royal Navy, name of Lemieux, Please convey Captain Redrocks' regards and tell him I'll be in touch about lifting a mug of grog while we are in port."

"Yessir. Where is this harbormaster's office?"

"No need for a map," the captain said. "I'm detailing some of my lads to deliver you."

Bapcat's legs felt rubbery from almost two straight weeks at sea. Solid ground didn't feel so solid, but the crutch the ship's doctor had insisted he use helped his stability. He had been shedding it at every opportunity on their way across the North Atlantic, but Jordy or Anton always retrieved the damn thing like a dog's favorite stick. The crutch did not alleviate the discomfort in his butt and seemed always to be in his way.

The harbormaster's office was in a low tower, which puzzled Bapcat. Wouldn't a higher tower in a more-open setting afford a better view of his kingdom? There were no orderlies at the door and no guards. Inside there was a large man with a beard the color of white icing, flashing blue eyes, and a deep voice that rattled walls. The man's forehead was scarred by what Bapcat guessed was fire.

"Captain Bapcat, US Army, party of nine, reporting to the harbormaster's office, as ordered, sir."

He didn't know if the bearded man outranked him or not, but when in doubt, he always assumed higher rank than his and acted accordingly.

The man had a twinkle in his eye. "Ah yes, my Yanks."

"Captain Redrocks sends his compliments and says he will be in touch about a pint of grog this week."

Harbormaster Lemieux grinned and nodded. "Reggie loves his grog—in shorebound moderation."

"You wanted to see us, sir?"

"Me?" Lemieux thundered. "Not me, Captain. There's a lorry standing by to take your crew to the city rail station."

Rail station? What the—?

"Sir, I thought we'd meet immigration here and undergo the medical evaluations they didn't do in England."

What the heck was going on?

"The *Crusader* escort will take you lads in the lorry to the station."

"May I ask who we are to see?" Or was it *whom*? He could never keep this distinction straight.

He got no answer.

—◦—

It was a twenty-five-minute ride through the city's streets to the station. The city was already into its day, with trucks and some black Fords, various carts, and men in dark coats, a few sailors stumbling around the sidewalks outside certain establishments with gaudily dressed women. A few horses here and there, and Bapcat found himself scanning upper-story windows and rooftops for snipers, but saw none and felt none. Sometimes a sixth sense was better at keeping you alive than the five senses you were born with.

They were met by a short old policeman with a nicotine-stained walrus mustache of impressive proportions.

The man snapped together his black brogan heels. "Captain Bapcat?"

"Sir," Bapcat answered.

"You and your men, please follow me," the man said, pivoting and starting to march into the rail station.

Bapcat hesitated. "Whoa there. Excuse me, officer, but follow you *where*?"

The man grinned. "Orders from above, sir. I just follow orders, eh?"

They filed into the station, the cop briskly leading them through a corridor that took them to the platforms and trains, a great green birdcage of metal over their heads, fancy art that did nothing to keep out the salty mist.

"Deputy Bapcat," a female voice called from his right, and he looked over.

Jaquelle? How?

As stunningly beautiful as ever, and in charge, as usual.

"Good God, Deputy, where's our son?"

Jordy came up from behind and embraced his mother, who eyed his arm sling, but addressed her husband.

"Not a bloody word from you scamps in over a year, sir, until a bumbling general calls to inform me some months ago that you were possibly missing, but they weren't giving up on you—yet. Good God, Deputy Bapcat. And then finally a wire from you from England, and what do I read? You were in *Russia*? What in blazes is in *Russia*? My boys, I thought, were headed to France to fight the Bosch, and here came this telegram from England. *Russia*, sir? *Russia!*"

"They came to find and rescue me," Zakov said, stepping forward.

Jaquelle Frei clucked indignantly. "Did they now?"

"Successfully, I'm quite pleased to report," the Russian added.

Jaquelle snorted. "As you well know, Deputy Zakov, Deputy Bapcat *always* finds what he is looking for, even an individual who disappears without so much as a howdy-damn-do. Personally I can't see that his finding you is a plus for the likes of us."

She turned to Jordy. "Was your war all you had hoped for? Did you win your gaudy gewgaws?"

"I'm glad it's over, and we're back with you." He hugged her again.

Anton stepped over to her and looked up. "He is a very brave soldier, our Sergeant Jordy," the boy said. "I'm Anton."

Jaquelle made eye contact with her husband and raised an eyebrow.

Bapcat said, "Anton, this is my wife, and Jordy's mother."

"She is very beautiful," Anton said.

To Jaquelle, Bapcat said, "This is Anton. He is very confident and direct."

Bapcat then introduced Chief Engineer Bezmunyi and his sons, and Elpy the Actor, and Vukevich.

"Vukevich?" she said to Bapcat. "I seem to recall one of your occasional clients before Russia was a Vukevich."

"One and the same," Bapcat said. "I doubt we'll have any more violating from him."

"A brash prediction. Predicated on what, Deputy?"

"I'm hiring him as a deputy warden."

Jaquelle smiled. "Mr. Take-Charge."

Bapcat briefly explained the history of the others and concluded, "They want to become Americans."

"Do they speak English?" Jaquelle asked.

"Better than you and me talk Russian," he told his wife.

Jaquelle joined her hands together. "This chitchat is all quite lovely and exciting, but our train awaits us so we can depart. Let us delay no longer! Climb aboard, fellas, and let's head for home."

"We *can't* get on that train," Bapcat told her. "We have official things to do here and at Camp Custer at Battle Creek."

"Nonsense," Jaquelle said. "You'll muster out in the Soo. It's all been arranged. Fresh uniforms are waiting for you on the train, decorations included. The government took you away from me for more than a bloody year, but now *I* have you back and I damn well intend to keep you."

"Also me?" Anton asked.

She eyed the boy. "Can you read and write?"

"Elegantly," the boy said, and Jaquelle let loose her braying laugh.

"Muster out in the Soo, bypass Canadian and British red tape? Who arranged this," Bapcat asked. "Colonel Roosevelt?"

Jaquelle's smile dissipated.

"Oh my God, Lute. You've not heard? The president passed away in early January. It's said that he succumbed to some disorder contracted in his jungle wanderings. I am so sorry, husband."

Bapcat felt the air go out of him, but steeled himself. Roosevelt dead? It had always felt like the man was bulletproof, immortal.

Jaquelle said, "Before we board, let's get all of you for a group picture." She pointed. "Mr. Nara has come all the way from Houghton to do the honors for me and for history."

They all shuffled into position with the photographer arranging them. Nara then backed to his camera, hid his head under a purple fabric drape, and told them all to stay still and smile.

Jaquelle looked at her husband with a crutch, Jordy in a sling, and Zakov. She shook her head and said, "All you three need now is a flute, a snare drum, and a flag to look like poster children for pacifism. Here stands what the government gives back when war is done."

She paused, stepped over to Bapcat, and took hold of his arm. She whispered, "I trust you didn't hurt anything of recreational value?"

Bapcat said, "Not that I know of."

She squeezed his arm. "Good—because you and I have a railcar to ourselves for the duration."

Author's Note

The obscure, highly secret nature of Lute Bapcat's mission to Russia has been held deep under the highest security classification for one hundred years. It was earmarked for possible public release in 2019, but after careful consideration, the reviewers decided—for reasons they did not share with the public—to put the records under another one-hundred-year embargo—perhaps because of current Russian–American conflicts and issues. Bottom line: We shall not know in our lifetimes what exactly happened to Lute et al. over there in 1918–1919, except for what I've been able to glean from available sources, including family letters and journals, newspapers, and surviving relatives of the principal actors herein.

The American, British, French, and Canadian occupation of Northern Russia and the Far East (Murmansk, Archangelsk, and Vladivostok) was quite real and involved a lot of soldiers from all across Michigan and upper Wisconsin. Our men, in fact, fought the Reds almost the entire time they were in Russia, from their landing in the fall of 1918 to their withdrawal the following summer, more than six months *after* the Germans and Allies inked the Armistice, November 11, 1918.

—Joseph Heywood
Alberta, Michigan